INTO
OTHERNESS

VOLUME III OF THE DRAGON LORD CHRONICLES

MILES O'NEAL

INTO
OTHERNESS

VOLUME III OF THE DRAGON LORD CHRONICLES

nine realms
press

First Edition, 2017
Printed in the USA
ISBN: 978-0-9971129-7-9
Publisher: Nine Realms Press, Round Rock, TX

Illustrations: Alli W. Ritchie
Cover and interior design: Allison Metcalfe Design
Editing: Inksnatcher and Sharon O'Neal
Library of Congress Control Number 2017916207
04 04 06 13 14 98 98

Dedicated to all the people who loved me and believed in me even when I didn't, especially:

☉ in memory of Nicholas Pomponio, Jr, and in honor of Alice Pomponio—surrogate parents in my desperate college years,

☉ in honor of Bill Vanderbush, who reminded me who I was, and that it was good to be me.

TABLE OF CONTENTS

SYNOPSIS

Despite the truce between dragons and humans brokered by the Lord of the Western Isles—the eldest and chief of dragons—a few rebel dragons still wreak havoc among both dragons and humans. Their leader is the mad dragon Argyll, nemesis to Gerald the youngest dragon lord.

While Gerald was about the high king's business addressing old grievances against dragons and dealing with a rogue inquisitor, Argyll was busy plotting against Gerald and his home village of Kiergenwald.

At the end of book II, *Nemeses Unexpected,* Gerald learns that Lord Scythia—the dragon lord training Gerald's fiancée Sally—has disappeared along with several others from Kiergenwald. Part of the forest was destroyed, and Scythia's sword was found under mysterious circumstances, along with a scale that might have come from Argyll.

King Donald sent Gerald and Captain Murdoch (graciously carried by the great dragon Nain) ahead to Kiergenwald, with dragon lore master Cuthbert and Kenna of the faerie close behind. A dozen warriors will follow on horseback. At least one other dragon watches out for the village. Sally is safe . . . so far.

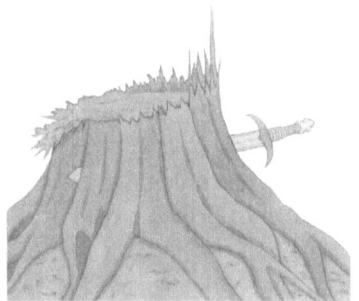

CHAPTER ONE

THE SWORD
& THE STONE

"Here is Kiergenwald," the large gray dragon carrying the warriors cried over the noise of the wind, "but I see no trace of Argyll." As Gerald struggled with the blanket wrapped around him for the flight, Nain began to drop toward a large clearing. Gerald smiled as he realized the sun was behind them; dragons preferred to fly out of the sun.

The clearing was new and still full of downed trees, many in pieces. Nearing the ground, Gerald saw the trees had been broken rather than cut. Some were large. Many were blackened. So much of the ground was scorched that Gerald wondered why the forest had not burned. It certainly looked as if a dragon had fought something or someone here.

As they flew over the center of the clearing, Nain again flew skyward. Murdoch, wrapped in a blanket and held safely in one of Nain's front claws like Gerald, hollered something Gerald could not quite understand.

As Nain banked to circle the clearing, he replied, "I am checking to make sure no one is hiding nearby." They saw nothing but trees, rocks, brush, and a handful of people staring up, some with swords drawn.

Perhaps, Gerald thought, *those below have not heard that good dragons would be arriving bearing friends.* A few seconds later it hit him. *They've no way of telling good dragons from bad! We'll have to find a way to solve that problem.*

Nain landed on his back claws, letting Murdoch and Gerald drop a few feet to the cleared forest floor. Then he flapped his wings hard to ascend. Before either man could ask, Nain bellowed, "The dragons will watch from the heights. If Argyll or his cohorts return, we will engage them in the air."

He was well out of bow shot before more men came out of the forest.

One waved as he sheathed his sword. "Ho, Gerald!"

"Cle!"

As the village's warriors drew near, a slender young man ran from behind a nearby felled treetop, waving a sword. "Stay back! I'm mad! I'll kill you all!"

Murdoch reached for his sword, but Gerald stayed his hand. "It's my brother, Neakal."

"What's he playing at?"

"I have no idea."

Neakal leaped to the top of a large, rough stump. It looked as if the tree had been torn from it the way a child snaps a branch from a small bush. Something gleamed at its base.

"Neakal!" Gerald cried. "What are you going on about?"

"I'm mad! Mad, I tell you! I touched the sword and I'm cursed!"

"What sword, brother? The one you hold?"

"Of course not! The one at my feet, left by some evil spirit in this stump! As I tried to pull it out, a woman appeared. She said it was cursed and she wished I had not touched it. She said I was now cursed and mad and doomed to kill those I love, but I am fighting the curse, Gerald. Leave me to die! And touch not the cursed sword in the stump!"

Neakal leapt from the stump and ran to the south of the clearing. Before any could give chase, Selene landed before Neakal.

"Stop, child," she said kindly.

Stunned at having a dragon land in his path and speak to him, Neakal did just that. His sword hung limply at his side as he stared at the deep purple creature before him.

Gerald and Murdoch ran up but stopped ten paces from Neakal. The dragon ignored them, looking intently at the wild-eyed young man.

"You are Neakal?"

Neakal nodded dumbly.

"I heard you." She looked around. "We all did. Who is this woman of which you speak?"

"I, I don't know," Neakal stammered. "She just appeared when I touched the sword. She spoke and I knew it to be true."

"And where did she go? How did she go? Where did she come from?"

Neakal looked distraught. "I don't know! But I felt her power!"

Selene moved closer, sniffing. Neakal tensed and gripped his sword more tightly.

"You need not fear me," Selene said. The surface of her eyes seemed to spin slowly and Gerald thought Neakal was staring at them. That was good; it should calm him down.

Selene sniffed again. "What are you wearing beneath your tunic, on that chain around your neck?"

Neakal had to think a moment. Then he reached into his tunic and pulled out a large, yellow gem that glowed in the sunlight.

"This. I found it. Or rather, one of the pigs unearthed it, rooting around. It glowed faintly, even though it was a cloudy day. I cleaned it up and planned to give it to Sally, but somehow I ended up wearing it."

"And what did this woman look like?"

"Tall. Dark. Beautiful. Like a queen above all queens. I was amazed she would speak to me, much less care about me."

"What of her eyes, Neakal?"

Neakal looked into the distance, as if Selene were not there. He smiled. "They were unlike any eyes I have ever seen. Instead of white, hers were a bright yellow. Her irises were a delicious golden brown. And the centers . . . deep wells of wisdom and history."

Selene said nothing for a moment, waiting for Neakal to fully return to the present. He jumped when he did, as if startled to find a dragon before him rather than a yellow-eyed queen. Selene continued, "You think she cared for you?"

"She would have spared me the curse!"

"I think rather she wished you had not found that jewel."

Gerald interrupted. "Selene, was it Morgan le Fay?"

"It could be no other. I would know her stench anywhere."

Gerald's eyes grew bigger. "You knew Morgan le Fay?"

"Not well, but yes. We all knew her and Merlin."

Neakal interrupted. "But what do you mean about finding the jewel?"

Selene snorted, blackening what little grass had survived. "Morgan, like any human, like any faerie—for she was both— began as good, but she grew in her lust for power, her vanity, her jealousy. There was a mysterious figure influencing her. Merlin nearly died trying to find who it was. She turned to evil and her power grew. There were three stones, gems she wore— one of which is now worn by Neakal—that we believe were given to her by this unknown power. There were a dozen gems of power. Most were used for good. Merlin's mother, Adhan, wore such."

Gerald interrupted. "That stone has been found! It is . . ."

"Hush, Lord Gerald. We trust the one who has that, but it should not be spoken of.

"At any rate, the gem Neakal wears was the source of much of Morgan's power, and into it she poured the parts of herself she no longer wanted—things such as compassion. The stone devoured them and grew more powerful.

"When the sorceress was defeated, her gem was lost—probably near Camelot, but certainly not here in Argyll. There has not been even a rumor of it since. I would very much like to know how it came this far north—much less here—to be unearthed by a pig."

Neakal was fidgeting now. "But what of the curse? What of me?"

Selene stared at the gem for a long moment. Then she looked at Gerald. "Will you lay your blanket upon the ground?"

He did so.

"Good. Neakal, would you please take the necklace off—do not touch the gem if you can help it—and lay it on the blanket?"

Neakal did so, surprised at the reluctance he felt.

As he stepped away from the stone and the blanket, Neakal straightened up. "I feel like myself. Uncursed. Normal." He stared in awe at Selene. "Thank you, dragon. What is your name?"

"Selene."

Neakal bowed and Selene bowed her head back.

"Selene, Gerald has told us of you. Thank you for all you have done, and especially today for freeing me from that curse. That vile witch!"

"You are welcome." She looked at him a bit more. "You have served your family well. You survived the curse and an encounter with what remains in the gem of a powerful sorceress. Well done." She breathed gently on Neakal. Gerald caught hints of flowers he could not name. "Blessings, Neakal, in all you do."

Gerald noted Neakal's skin shone with a faint reddish tint. Now he knew what he must have looked like for a moment upon the Hill of Secrets.

Neakal stared at his hands while Selene continued. "Nain is

here and Younger comes. Others will be here shortly. Wrap the gem up, Lord Gerald, and I will take it to Nain, who will see it goes elsewhere."

Gerald folded the gem in the blanket, trying not to touch even the blanket where it met the stone. It might have been his imagination, but the stone felt malevolent. *Then again, it is,* he thought. *It convinced Neakal he was cursed.*

Promising to return quickly, Selene snatched the blanket up with her left front claw and flew away toward the east. Gerald realized Cle and the others now stood with him and Murdoch.

Neakal turned around. "Gerald, I . . ."

Gerald enveloped him in a hug. "Brother, it's good to see you!"

Neakal hugged him back and gave up trying to apologize.

"Are we still brothers, Gerald? Cynthia adopted me this week. Formally!"

"She can't take that away. I guess that makes her my aunt now."

Neakal laughed, clearly relieved.

Murdoch moved up and introduced himself. "Now what's this about a sword?"

"Ah. The sword in the stump. Come see!"

The jagged stump was nearly three feet across and two feet high at the highest spot. It was oddly colored—various ugly shades of yellow glared between blackened streaks. Oddly parallel lines on reflective surfaces made it look more like a giant crystal than wood. A sword was buried up to the hilt against one side of the tree. The tip poked out the other side.

"That's the sword. No one knows how it got into the tree. We've all tried to get it out, but it won't budge. It's like the stump has a death grip on it."

"Or it's waiting for King Arthur," Murdoch quipped.

Curious, Gerald reached down and grabbed the sword. It moved easily in his hand, but just then others shouted.

Looking up, Gerald stared into the eyes of Younger flying a mere ten feet above their heads. The white dragon shook his head gently at Gerald.

Gerald froze and made himself let go of the sword. He wasn't sure what Younger had meant, but given Murdoch's joke, Gerald didn't feel like trying the sword at the moment.

After staring at the sword for the space of two heartbeats, Gerald looked for Younger, but he looked in vain. The Eldest's younger brother had disappeared against the backdrop of sun-drenched clouds.

CHAPTER TWO

REUNION

"Gerald!"

Gerald turned toward the east. Shading his eyes against the sun peeking through the trees, he saw three women striding out of the woods. All three carried targes and swords, clearly ready for battle.

Gerald's fiancée, Sally, led the way, walking rapidly but glancing constantly around. She relaxed when she realized the men's swords were sheathed despite the dragons overhead. More people came from the trees to his left. Cuthbert and Kenna strode rapidly toward them as well.

As the three women drew nearer, Gerald recognized Cynthia, the healer, and Cle's wife, Myrna. Cynthia and Myrna sheathed their swords and slung their targes over their backs. Sally followed suit once she neared Gerald.

Cuthbert and Kenna arrived first. Kenna moved ahead and embraced Gerald for a moment before he and Cuthbert gripped forearms. Cynthia ran to hug Neakal as Myrna and Cle embraced.

Murdoch smirked. "Does Lord Gerald need a hug from me?"

"I'd as soon hug Younger, thanks."

Sally ran the remaining few feet and hugged Gerald tightly. "It's good to see you!"

They kissed briefly before Gerald replied, "It's good to see you, my love."

Kenna and Cuthbert squatted and spoke quietly as they examined the sword and stump while the rest watched. Cuthbert stood and smote the trunk with the flat of his sword. It rang out as if he had struck stone.

Kenna's hair, always moving slightly as if in some otherworldly breeze, seemed drawn to the stump. She pulled her hair back and tucked the ends into her belt. She grabbed the sword and pulled, but it refused to budge.

Kenna and Cuthbert stood. She spoke to all nearby. "We do not understand how the stump became crystal. Dragon fire was involved, but more than that. We suspect that somehow the magic of Morgan le Fay was involved." She glanced down. "Whose sword is this?"

Sally moved closer, staring at the hilt. "It's Lord Scythia's."

Cuthbert glared at the sword. Gerald involuntarily backed up a step. He had never seen Cuthbert look this angry. The dragon lore master resembled a thunderstorm about to hit.

Cuthbert stared about the clearing, thinking hard. "There are few dragons alive who could conquer Scythia. Most would have to take her while she slept." His eyes swept the destroyed section of forest. "Clearly she was not asleep."

Sally also glared, but her eyes were focused on a dull green scale she was holding. It was twice the size of her hand. "Is this not Argyll's?"

"Yes!" Gerald replied.

Cuthbert held out his hand and Sally handed the scale to him. "Almost certainly," he said before handing it back.

Murdoch spoke. "Kenna, Morgan le Fay was discussed here but moments before you arrived. Why do you invoke that name?"

Kenna glanced at the trunk with the stone, then at Cuthbert. "This spot reeks of her. And the trunk has turned to stone, with ugly yellow streaks in it. Did I not know for a fact she were dead, I would suspect her hand had been involved. And yet something of her was."

Neakal turned beet red but spoke up. "I was wearing a necklace with a gem that had her power. That's why I thought I was cursed. The purple dragon, Selene, saw it and helped me get free." As he spoke, Selene landed quietly nearby.

Kenna looked closely at Neakal. "And then she blessed you." She looked at Selene, smiled, and bowed her head. "Ever your fate and Morgan's intertwine, even with her dead these many years."

Selene smiled in return, causing Neakal to retreat a step—a dragon's smile was a fearsome sight. "Just so she does not bother me once I go beyond as well. If she does, we shall see whether dragon fire works in that realm also."

Kenna's laugh was so fey, she might have been related to Morgan. She spoke confidently. "No evil will touch us once we pass the veil. And no mortal holds the power to change that, even one so powerful as le Fay."

Gerald and his friends stared in awe. Kenna radiated an eerie white light as she spoke. Her hair freed itself from her belt and spread out like a giant halo. A spring meadow's scents filled his nostrils. He gaped about looking for flowers but found none.

Then he noticed that white bluebells bloomed where Kenna had squatted, despite it being nearly October. He smiled but said nothing.

Neakal sidled over, still visibly glowing. He spoke in a very low voice. "Gerald, where Kenna sat by the stump. Those are white bluebells, right?"

Gerald squinted as if he couldn't see them well. "If you say so."

"But that would mean Kenna was a faerie! It's too late in the year for bluebells, and white ones grow where a faerie sat! Did you see her shine, and her hair?"

"Maybe she's more dragon blessed than any of us."

"That doesn't explain the white bluebells. I've heard of them, but I've never seen them before."

Gerald nodded thoughtfully. "Perhaps you should ask her."

Neakal gave Gerald an odd look. "You don't seem very interested."

Gerald smiled. "Perhaps. I've had to learn to act the same whether I know things or not. It's part of being an envoy."

"Envoy?"

It was Gerald's turn to look oddly at Neakal. "You haven't heard?"

Neakal watched Cuthbert and Kenna start toward them. "Perhaps."

Gerald snorted and moved back to the stump to meet the others. Before he got there, Selene called.

"Dragon lords, please come here. Sally, Cynthia, please join us as well."

They all walked toward Selene.

Neakal spoke up determinedly. "What about me?"

A wisp of flame—dragon laughter—escaped Selene's mouth. "You should come as well, Neakal. This may concern you."

Neakal regretted speaking but hid it well as he strode to join the rest.

Selene spoke so softly that Gerald almost missed the first words. "The stump has turned to a kind of stone by a combination of dragon fire and sorcery. Do any of you know how?"

Cuthbert sighed. "The sword, of course."

"You said it was Scythia's."

"And, indeed, it was hers as well. She inherited it, and is the last of that lineage."

"How could she wield such a thing unchanged?"

"I would not say unchanged, but she was able to bend it to good. She was—I hope is—an amazing woman."

Selene stared at Cuthbert. "Is she of the faerie?"

Cuthbert smiled. "Was Morgan?"

Kenna replied. "According to our legends, she was part faerie."

It was Murdoch's turn to stare. "Legends? I thought the faerie knew such things beyond doubt!"

"Morgan le Fay was perhaps the most powerful sorceress in history. She had gone further along the road to evil than any other sorcerer. She distorted the minds of all who drew near. An elite cadre of my father's kin died in battle with her. She came through nearly unscathed. Had not dragons intervened, we do not know what would have happened. As it is, even the dragons who took her unawares were dazed after the battle. We know little of who she was otherwise, but there is no doubt she is dead."

Gerald spoke in the silence that followed. "What does this have to do with the sword?"

Cuthbert sighed again. "The sword was taken from Morgan's remains. It was hers."

"How can that be? Everything she touched is cursed!"

"First off, that is not true, or even the ground she walked on, the air she breathed, would be cursed. Beyond that, curses can be broken. Beyond that, some people are immune to such things, or at least to some of them."

Sally finally spoke. "So Scythia was immune to curses? Even Morgan's?"

Cuthbert looked around and waved everyone closer. They all leaned in, Selene's head nestled between Sally's and Cynthia's, her breath warm on their faces. Cuthbert spoke in a whisper. "Scythia is a direct descendent of Morgan le Fay and, as I mentioned, the last of that line. They have been few and quite secretive, lest others try to kill them out of hand. They guarded the relics Morgan left behind, over time removing many of the curses by sheer will of using them for good despite their influences.

"Long have they sought the three gems from her necklace, of which the most powerful was the one Neakal found. One was destroyed. Another was recently bartered away from a druid one of Gerald's classmates met."

Gerald interrupted. "It was Eoin."

Cuthbert nodded. "Selene now has the third. It and the druid's stone will be destroyed by the dragons very soon. These are the last known relics radiating le Fay's evil." He grimaced. "And the stump, of course."

Cynthia spoke. "Scythia was here. The gem was here. Is there a connection?"

"Not that I am aware of. Scythia came to me a year ago to discuss a dream. In it she was battling alongside a young woman, a dragon lord. In this dream, I appeared at odd times to hand things to the other dragon lord. Scythia sought me out to ask if I knew what the dream might mean. Sally had already been on my mind, so I sent Scythia to train her. As of yet we have no idea what the stone was doing here."

Cynthia turned to Neakal. "When did you find it?"

"I don't know when the pigs dug it up. I found it the same day all this happened." He spread his arms and gazed around the scorched earth and felled trees.

"I think that's all of that," Cuthbert said. Everyone moved apart a little. "Sally, how far have you and Scythia gotten?"

"We were up to two hours a day of swordplay."

Gerald frowned. "All at once?"

"No, we would go for an hour at a time."

Gerald was impressed. Apparently it showed on his face.

Sally smirked. "I'm tired and still a bit sore after an hour, but I'm getting better. And she's been teaching me dragon lore, politics, and history as it relates to Argyll and the surrounding kingdoms. She was also keeping me up on Gerald's adventures—or at least whatever word Cuthbert sent her—but then Gerald's Voices arrived with such news on a regular basis, so we used the time otherwise. She hadn't mentioned le Fay."

Cuthbert spoke. "I believe Scythia is the equal of any man in Argyll in terms of swordplay and tracking."

"Oy!" Murdoch said.

Cynthia snickered. "Wounded over the idea a woman could best you, Lord Murdoch?"

Murdoch snorted. "I got over that a dozen years ago, when Scythia taught me things years of practice and battle had not. I was remembering those lessons. One left me limping for three days."

The others laughed.

Murdoch continued. "But the question now is what has happened to her. Does no one know what happened here?"

Cynthia gazed quickly around. "Termites?"

"Clearly, but I was thinking in terms of details."

"One huge, green termite. Breathing fire."

Kenna spoke. "Did none of you hear anything?"

Cynthia and Sally shook their heads. Sally added, "There was a brief thunderstorm. It must have happened then."

"Even so, there is a great deal of damage," Cuthbert said. "Murdoch and I together would be hard-pressed to fight Argyll long enough for this to happen."

Murdoch scratched his chin. "Unless Argyll was just clearing space, or leading her on."

They all looked around. The idea had merit.

Selene called out, "Nain is coming."

A moment later Nain had joined them. "Three dragons watch over us from above. I bring news after talking with Voices. Argyll was lying in wait here; we do not know for whom. Scythia came during the storm, holding light in her palm as the faerie might. Argyll began destroying trees to make room to fight, or perhaps to spread his wings and fly, but either way they fought. Scythia wielded both sword and light. Argyll's fire could not touch her, but neither could she get close enough to do damage with her sword. In the end he slapped her with his tail. She flew at least the length of that tail into the trees. Argyll stuck his head in after her. After a moment he retreated and did something with the stump. Whatever he did, he breathed fire upon the stump more than once. The woman who spoke to Neakal appeared and watched as he did this. She dropped something onto the stump before disappearing. Argyll flew away after killing the watching Voices. One Voice was knocked into a bush—stunned and unseen by Argyll. This Voice has just come to his senses and seeks Scythia."

Everyone spoke at once, but Kenna's voice overrode the others. "Where was she thrown?"

A Voice circled Nain's head, said "Follow me!" and flew to the western side of the devastation. It stopped at the upright trees and waited. The others hurried to the trees. The people spread out to comb the area.

Nain's roar froze them all: "Come back! She is found!"

As they neared the edge of the trees, they heard a Voice calling, "Here! Here!" They congregated around the largest tree in the area, a sessile oak at least fifty feet tall, but with many low branches. Where the Voice hovered, they could see hints of color through some broken tree limbs. The Voice continued, "She breathes, but barely."

CHAPTER THREE

A TALE OF TWO
WARRIORS

Several of the men and women approached the trunk to climb up to Scythia, but Nain darted in and tore out entire branches. Gerald and the rest had to dodge and fend off falling limbs. They all soon wore twigs, leaves, and acorns. Nain gently wrapped his lips around Scythia's legs and pulled her from the tree, lowering her to Murdoch's and Cuthbert's arms. They in turn laid her on the ground. Cynthia pushed through the crowd and everyone else moved back.

Scythia's left arm bent where it shouldn't. Bloody spots indicated at least two chest wounds beyond the one a small piece of oak protruded from. Cynthia checked her quickly and spoke.

"Her breath is weak and ragged, as is her pulse. We must get her to my house immediately." She looked up at Murdoch. "Can some of you carry her?"

Nain answered before Murdoch could. "I will." He opened his mouth and extended his tongue to his lips. Murdoch and Cuthbert hoisted the unconscious warrior quickly but carefully into Nain's mouth. Nain knocked two more trees down with his tail before glancing at Cynthia, who took off at a run that belied her sixty years. Nain followed Cynthia while the others followed close behind him, staying well clear of his tail.

Neakal caught up with Gerald. "I thought dragons had spikes on their tails."

"I've not seen many that do."

"How many have you seen?"

Gerald shrugged. "Around two hundred."

"Two hundred!"

"Well, most of those were at the dragons' moot. I didn't deal with many, but I saw them."

They walked on in silence. Nain stopped at the edge of the village while Murdoch, Cuthbert, and Kenna hastened ahead to reassure the villagers. Nain's head followed Cynthia as far as his neck would allow before lowering Scythia again into Murdoch's and Cuthbert's arms. They carried her another fifty paces to Cynthia's home.

Kenna followed them inside. The men reemerged almost immediately. Murdoch beckoned Sally and Neakal. "Cynthia would speak with you, Sally. And Neakal, she will need you to run errands. Druze is here and will help as needed, as will Kenna. If Cynthia needs anyone else, she will send Neakal."

Cuthbert spoke. "We should wait here for now, Gerald. Nain, thank you for your help."

Nain bowed his head, terrifying some of the villagers watching several houses away. "It is an honor, and the least I can do to amend what Argyll has done here."

Gerald frowned. "No dragon owes us for Argyll's actions but Argyll!"

Nain mimicked Gerald's expression as much as a dragon can. "But not all humans see it that way. We do what we can to help them understand dragonkind is not their enemy. For too long we saw each other only that way."

Gerald blinked. He had spent so much time among dragons lately that he had forgotten how much men and dragons had hated each other—indeed, how he had for several years wanted nothing but to kill dragons. Gerald turned to face the growing crowd.

"Remember that other than a few rebels, we are at peace with the dragons. This dragon and those circling above are our friends, here to protect us from the one who hurt Scythia and tore up the woods."

There was quiet muttering but no open dispute. A woman tentatively smiled at Nain and spoke.

"Thank you." She paused, at a loss for what to call the dragon. "We appreciate your help."

Nain bowed his head again. "You are most welcome, gracious lady."

She blushed. "I am no lady."

"You have the bearing of one. Dragons care far more for character than for titles."

"Who is that?" Gerald asked quietly.

Myrna, who had just appeared beside Gerald, hugged him before answering. "That is my cousin Morag. She arrived recently. She is bolder than I."

Cle interrupted. "She may speak boldly, but you are every bit as bold, love. Just a touch quieter."

Myrna snorted, but a smile played across her lips.

Gerald stared. "I should have seen the resemblance. She's beautiful in the same ways as you. Her hair reminds me of Kenna's, except it stays where she wants it to. How much time does she spend on it?"

Morag's hair was a complex set of braids and loose strands, with flowers woven into it. Myrna replied, "Far less than you might think. Never have I seen a woman with a gift for hair like hers. When she arrived, she wondered how she would live. Of course we put her up, for now, but already women barter with her to have their hair done."

"She came unexpected?"

"She did. Her husband was killed in Urquhart."

Gerald and Murdoch froze. "In Urquhart? What happened?"

"Her story is jumbled. There was a rebellion. Somehow dragons were involved, and the high king's men. She doesn't know everything, but Urquhart's king was an evil ruler. Morag's husband Rory helped lead a rebellion to cast off King Urquhart's yoke. During the fight, dragons intervened and destroyed much of the castle. The dragons ended the fighting and held everyone until the high king arrived. The old king and his men who lived were exiled. The rest of the people were freed under a new ruler, but Rory died fighting when a piece of wall fell on him. I am surprised Morag is not bitter toward dragons."

Gerald took his aunt's hand. "The dragons were ambushed by some of the king's men. That is why dragons assaulted the castle. The dragons took no life unnecessarily. And it was they who exiled King Urquhart and his men. Had High King Dugald not given their fate to the dragons, their heads would have adorned poles around the remains of the castle."

Myrna stared at Gerald. "You already knew? Why then did you ask?"

"Murdoch and I were there as the high king's envoys." He ignored Myrna's gasp. "We left with the dragons just as the rebels attacked. We heard the aftermath later from the high king and others. I had no idea you had a cousin there. I suppose there is much we need to catch up on."

A bemused expression on his face, Cle put his arm around Myrna's shoulders and spoke. "I reckon there is, Lord Gerald. You and Murdoch envoys!"

Murdoch cleared his throat. "Technically Gerald was the envoy. I was just along for moral support. With my sword at his service, of course."

Gerald hung his head. "Even now Captain Lord Murdoch baits me."

Myrna spoke again. "You shall tell us over lunch, but now you should speak with Morag."

Gerald turned to Murdoch. "Will you come?"

"Do you ask as high king's envoy, or as my warrior?"

"Whichever has the better claim upon your attendance."

Myrna laughed and tugged Gerald's hand. "My lord cousin, you should go alone, lest you overwhelm her. Here, I will introduce you. We have told her of you already."

Gerald refused to budge. "What did you tell her?"

"That you are our cousin and hand-fasted to Sally, of course."

Gerald gave in and went with her, shooting a look at Murdoch, who merely smiled.

"Morag, this is our cousin Gerald we spoke of."

Her eyes lit up. "The youngest dragon lord!"

Gerald eyed Myrna reproachfully.

Myrna raised an eyebrow. "Oh, yes. We did mention that."

Morag embraced Gerald. "Thank you, cousin! We heard the high king's envoy and his captain had encouraged Derek, and your dragons helped end the fighting when it started to go badly for us."

Gerald gulped. He desperately wished Murdoch were at his side. "It was rather more complicated than that."

She let go of Gerald and smiled sadly. "It always is. People speak of Rory and the rebellion as if it were an easy thing one way or another. It was not."

"I am sorry Rory died," Gerald began.

"He died fighting for what we believed in. I nearly died. Part of me wishes I had, to be with Rory, but Father MacPherson . . ."

"How did you meet him?"

"He came with the high king and his party. He somehow heard of my story, sought me out, and talked long with me to convince me my life had purpose. I am still of two minds, but am content to live now."

"How did you almost die?"

"Fighting," she smiled triumphantly. "I came upon a guard sneaking up on one of our friends, a groom named Owen. The guard had raped a woman I knew. I slew him from behind as he prepared to kill Owen. Two others saw and came after me. Outnumbered, I ran. I tripped at the bottom of the stairs and fell through a door onto the ground. As the guards came through the door, a dragon appeared and batted them away with her claw. The dragons stopped all the fighting and held king's men and rebels alike for the high king, but I managed to escape. I hid in the woods. It was there Father MacPherson somehow found me. I eventually fled here where I knew Myrna lived."

Gerald looked at her a moment. "You did not stay to hear what happened?"

She sighed. "We had lived there only three months. I had no close friends; I know not why. I never had such a problem elsewhere. I had no reason to stay there with Rory dead. My parents and brother live far to the north. It is much too cold there, so I came here. Myrna and I had been close as children, and I had heard she was here."

"Gerald!"

He looked back. Cuthbert and Myrna were both beckoning him. Cynthia and Kenna stood with them. "I must go. Farewell, Morag."

She embraced him again. "Farewell, Lord Gerald. And thank you again."

As he hastened back to meet the others, he realized how little he had actually told her. Later he would make amends.

Everyone looked grave. Sally stood between Myrna and Cle, looking stricken. He went to her and held her. "What happened?"

Cynthia shook her head angrily. Kenna spoke softly. "Scythia appears bewitched. Her breathing and pulse are stable now, but too slow and weak to sustain life. Yet she lives, or seems to."

"Seems to?" Gerald demanded as Sally grew more rigid.

"Gerald, none of us have seen anything like this." Kenna swept her arm around to indicate the group, including Cynthia and Cuthbert. "She breathes. Her heart beats. She is warm. So she appears alive but she reacts to nothing. We had to fight to open her eyelids."

She paused, glanced at Cynthia, and continued. "The whites of her eyes are yellow—the same putrid yellow of Morgan le Fay's gem and that stump. And they glow faintly in the dark, as if in twisted mockery of a dragon's blessing.

"There is far more here than a mere fight with Argyll."

CHAPTER FOUR

WHERE THE SPIRIT
WALKS ALONE

Myrna called a few people over and gave a summary of the facts. She then sent them throughout the village to explain the situation and ask people to stay away from Cynthia's. They could go instead to see Aaron, who had spent a decade learning from Cynthia. Eilidh, as versed as Aaron in the healing arts, volunteered to guard Cynthia's door and redirect inquiries to Aaron, or take care of small matters herself.

Cle promised to send food and drink. Myrna offered to have someone else spell Eilidh after suppertime, but the young healer assured Myrna other healers would soon arrive from neighboring villages to help.

"How did you arrange that?"

Eilidh shook her head. "I didn't. Dragons did and sent a Voice to let me know. Apparently Cynthia got word to one of them."

"Oh." Myrna looked around.

Cuthbert nodded. "I passed along her request via Voice to Nain. He and other dragons sent Voices to villages nearby. Cynthia told us what to say to convince them the messages came from her. Presumably it worked. Three villages are each sending a healer." He paused with an amused expression. "May we eat now? Lord Gerald's stomach is rumbling."

"As if yours isn't?" Murdoch scoffed. He looked at Eilidh. "You have many healers for a small village."

She smiled. "Druze is Cynthia's granddaughter. Aaron and I came to learn from her. She is well known. I will soon return to my village. Our healer is quite old. Aaron is staying until Cynthia no longer needs him."

Myrna invited the visitors to lunch. "Sally sent word last night that you would all be here, so I've a cauldron of stew and plenty of bread and cheese. I hope you don't mind goat." She glanced sideways at Gerald and added, "We might have a bit of bacon somewhere, too."

"Good," Gerald retorted. "That way I can save the ten pounds in my sack for later."

Myrna's head whipped around. "What?"

"King Donald sent it as down payment in case you were willing to house these vagabonds."

She looked at Cle, who shook his head and lamented, "I suppose it beats having our heads on pikes."

"I can't argue with that, oh wisest of husbands. Lord Gerald, we accept the payment for these poor waifs. And lucky for them or I'd have had them slopping the pigs instead of eating them."

Gerald spoke quietly to Murdoch, Cuthbert, and Kenna. "Wait until you taste her bacon. She claims it's an old Roman recipe. All I know is it's amazing."

Kenna looked impressed. "Is it made with figs and pepper?"

"Yes. How did you know?"

She smiled. "It's an old Roman recipe." Kenna cut off Gerald's response. "Yes, I ate it with the Romans. I was but a child, though."

Murdoch clapped Gerald's back. "One day you will learn not to ask."

"I didn't ask!"

"But you were going to," Kenna replied.

"Was I?"

"Ah. The clever envoy returns."

"Perhaps."

They had arrived. Cle opened the door and waved them in.

Myrna pointed down. "Please sit while Cle and I bring the food. It's crowded enough; we don't need everyone up and moving."

They sat. Myrna handed out wooden plates as Cle headed outside. By the time he returned with two pots of stew, Myrna had placed two loaves of bread and a wheel of cheese on the floor in the middle. Cle placed the pots on stones atop the woven mats that covered the floor. Each pot sported a ladle.

Cle and Myrna then passed around pewter mugs of wine, mead, or water as requested. Just as they sat, the door opened. Sally entered. She frowned at something and hesitated. Gerald moved to make room between himself and Kenna as Cle jumped up to get Sally food and Myrna went for another mug. Sally sat slowly between Gerald and Kenna.

Myrna asked Sally, "Is Neakal coming as well?"

"No. Cynthia wants him there."

Kenna spoke slowly, choosing her words carefully. "I doubt there is anything they can do for Scythia besides sit her up and give her sips of water or broth."

"I know. Cynthia said as much, but she wants to stay with Scythia."

Cle spoke up. "I sent Argus over with some of the stew. Cynthia already has more bread and cheese than half of Kiergenwald."

Murdoch swallowed and spoke. "Thank you for feeding us. This is good, better than lunch many days at the castle. Do you always eat like this, Cle?"

"Only when we have a faerie princess visit."

Gerald looked guiltily at Kenna. "I didn't tell them!"

Sally smiled. "Nor I. But I warned Gerald that Cle would likely know."

Kenna arched an eyebrow at Cle, who had the grace to blush.

"I was but guessing. Thank you all for the confirmation!"

Kenna looked at Cuthbert. "Shall I remove their memories?"

"I think not. You might remove something else by accident."

Myrna looked shocked. Cle's hand went to his belt knife. Gerald caught his cousin's eye and grinned. Cle relaxed.

Kenna slumped. "My apologies. I was joking. We cannot do such things, nor would we."

Myrna reddened. "My apologies as well. When worlds meet unexpectedly, there is oft no time to sort out truth from old wives' tales."

Cuthbert spoke, wiping his beard with his sleeve before he did so. "We should discuss what has happened."

"Do we really know what has happened?" Cle asked. Everyone but Kenna nodded in agreement and looked at Cuthbert.

Cuthbert replied slowly and carefully, as was his wont when teaching. "We know some things. We know from Voices that Argyll hid in the trees. We know that Scythia approached Argyll during the storm 'holding light in her palm.' We know that Argyll began knocking down trees, either to escape or attack. We know that Scythia fought Argyll with both sword and light, and that she was thrown into a tree. We know that Argyll lost at least one scale to Scythia's sword and that he flew away after vanquishing her.

"We also know that Neakal found a powerful relic of Morgan le Fay's and that something of le Fay appeared and spoke with him. We know that Scythia's sword is embedded in a tree trunk enchanted in a fashion reminiscent of le Fay's magic. This tree trunk has been turned into what appears to be stone, again reeking of le Fay, and that Scythia seems to be under the influence of the long dead le Fay—as if Scythia herself were a relic."

Cuthbert sighed. "The dragons have agreed to destroy both Neakal's gem and the one obtained from the druid priest down south of us, near the eastern coast, but Kenna disagrees with that decision."

"I do," Kenna agreed. "I know le Fay was evil and her relics are still powerful, but there are things we can learn from them. There are those among my people who study such and who are not influenced by them, at least unduly. I believe we should hold off destroying anything of le Fay's until the faerie have examined it."

Gerald looked at Myrna and Cle, who were looking at each other inscrutably. After a moment, Cle nodded. Myrna turned to face Kenna and spoke.

"This is all new to us, but we have heard of le Fay our whole lives. We have heard nothing that suggests any good can come from this. Nothing. What could you hope to learn?"

"I do not know," Kenna replied calmly. Gerald began to relax until he realized Kenna was radiating calm as only the faerie could, like an elemental force.

Despite the faerie magic, he managed to glare at Kenna. *It's probably a good idea, but I still resent it,* he thought.

Kenna continued. "My people are interested in all knowledge. We never know how things might connect. It may be—may, I say—that something gleaned from studying these relics will work together, with older knowledge of le Fay and her magic, to show us a way to help Scythia's spirit find its way back."

"Back from where?" Sally demanded.

Kenna turned to her right and smiled sadly. "Wherever she wanders, Sally. I don't know where she is, but . . ." She paused, appearing to look right through Sally. Her eyes focused on an extreme distance and her voice dropped in both volume and pitch. "Her body and soul are here, held captive by dark magic. Her spirit wanders elsewhere, doing I know not what. If I had to guess, that stump in the broken woods might be—among other things—a portal to some place we cannot reach or imagine, a form of otherness. I cannot say whether it is safe where she goes; I know only that we must keep what remains here safe or she dies.

"The faerie have brought people's spirits back from strange lands before, though I have never heard of one affected quite like this."

Her voice trailed off. Her long hair wrapped itself like comforting arms around her body. Kenna focused on Sally's face again and her voice returned to normal. "Sally, I will be honest. Very little scares me, but Scythia's glowing yellow eyes are terrifying."

Sally turned to Gerald as angry tears formed in her eyes. "How can we save Scythia?"

Gerald looked from Kenna to Cuthbert. "What say you, Cuthbert?"

Cuthbert almost growled. "I am far more familiar with dragons than with wizardry! The dragons hate le Fay and everything to do with her. They suggested in the first place that the gems be destroyed. Perhaps we should have invited a Voice to lunch; they could then send word to the dragons of all we have said."

"And yet we did not. Murdoch?"

Murdoch looked around the room, his eyes coming to rest on Kenna. "I am inclined to follow Kenna's advice. Cuthbert, have you no opinion at all on this matter?"

Cuthbert stared into his empty plate on the floor in front of him for at least two dozen heartbeats, as still as stone. Finally he looked up. "The dragons have yet to lead me astray." He looked at Kenna. "But neither have you. We will need safeguards, you know."

The faerie laughed—a long, low, musical sound. Gerald

thought, *If a dragon laughed aloud, it might sound similar, if deeper and louder.*

Kenna composed herself, her hair falling back behind her. "We always have safeguards, my lord. My father and two others consider such things in a cave near a volcano. Should anything go wrong, they are prepared to throw the cursed things into the fire. Selene has sent Neakal's necklace there. When it arrives they will begin preparing for whatever may come. If something evil appears, these three—along with their guards—will work together to force it into the fire as well. Normally there are three guards, but for le Fay's relics there will surely be a dozen. And they will welcome dragons as additional guards."

"What do you mean, 'if something evil appears?'" Sally asked. Gerald nodded.

Kenna's mind again seemed to go afar for a moment before answering. She shuddered. "Morgan le Fay fought like an army of demons. No one is quite sure who killed her, or exactly how. The remains looked to have her face and clothes. The sword was hers and proved itself so over time. She has not been seen again since, but there are those who wonder if somehow she hid her true self somewhere, awaiting a chance to revive."

Sally gasped. "Could she come back in another's body?"

Kenna looked at the floor. "I do not know. None of us know. We can only speculate. We do not believe it is possible, but we do not *know*. And since you clearly speak of Scythia, I will admit that given her state—especially her eyes—the thought has crossed my mind."

Cuthbert nearly choked on a piece of bread. "Then she should not be here! We must ask the dragons to take her elsewhere at once."

"Where?" Cle asked, happy Cuthbert had broached the subject.

"An excellent question." Cuthbert turned back to Kenna. "Where is this cave in a volcano? And who would investigate the relics?"

A wan smile flickered across Kenna's face. "The who is easy: my father and two women of my kind. All of us share knowledge of such things, but these three are the best at delving into secrets. We call them the triad.

"As to the where, the dragons know. Or a few of them do. Selene's mother knew, but she is gone. If a dragon—I would recommend Selene—were to carry Scythia to a certain place in Albania, the faerie would have a dragon who knows the volcano meet Selene, take Scythia, and get her to the volcano. As it took dragons to defeat le Fay before, I would certainly want them there just in case."

"But . . ." Sally looked horror-struck, "what if le Fay came back in Scythia?"

"Then if the faerie could not cast her out, I am afraid she would have to burn."

Sally buried her face in Gerald's shoulder, fighting tears.

Gerald asked Kenna, "What and where is this Albania?"

"It is a country far from here, well across Europe."

Myrna spoke up. "And you would risk this? Le Fay coming back, Scythia dying?"

"There is no more risk than now, Myrna. I do not believe le Fay can come back, but I can make no promise."

"You could destroy all the relics! Would she not be free then?"

"I have no idea. None of us do. She might be free. Or perhaps all the power of the relics would enter her. Or perhaps she would die. We need to learn."

"So we should send her to the triad!" Myrna insisted.

"We cannot send her unless they ask for her, and they have not. They will want to divine the nature and power of the relics first. Is there a cave hereabouts?"

Those of Kiergenwald looked at each other and shook their heads. Cuthbert spoke slowly. "I could ask the dragons to make one, if there is a solid mountain nearby."

Cle's eyes lit up. "Northwest, just across the river. We call it Craneshead, though none know why. You need not go far up?"

"So long as dragons can dig a tunnel at least fifty yards in, well below the summit, it will work."

"Then look at Craneshead."

Cuthbert nodded. "I will speak with the dragons. Kenna, can the faerie send guards and healers to watch over her?"

Cynthia interrupted. "None will argue if the faerie send healers, but we will be there as well."

Kenna smiled briefly. "Good. There is only one I would ask. And we can post guards. I would have a dragon nearby though, just in case."

Everyone but Kenna and Cuthbert now wore some semblance of Sally's horror.

"Cuthbert," Gerald asked, "do you still agree with Kenna?"

"I must."

Gerald set his chin atop Sally's head and closed his eyes. Eventually he spoke. "Then I fear we have no real choice but to do this."

Cle and Myrna nodded assent. Murdoch spread his hands as if to say he could not argue.

Myrna stood. "Gerald, let's get Sally home. She did not sleep last night."

He agreed and helped Sally to her feet. The others stood, nodding to one another as they moved silently into the early afternoon.

Once outside, Kenna pulled Cuthbert aside and asked quietly, "Has any dragon ever mentioned where in Albania this is?"

"Only two have ever referenced it as far as I know: Selene's mother, Andromeda, and a dragon named Glorious."

"You knew Glorious?"

"We met. Andromeda told me there was such a place. Glorious

told me it was in Albania, somewhere in or near the Accursed Mountains."

Kenna stared off to the east. "They spoke truly. Let us hope the mountains do not live up to their name."

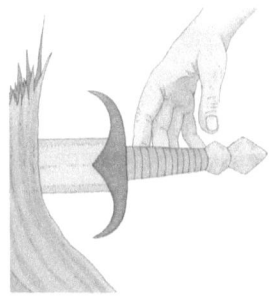

CHAPTER FIVE

MORTICUM'S DRAW

Myrna and Gerald got Sally to her bed. Sally removed her sword belt, lay down, and at once fell asleep, though her eyes still leaked slow tears. Myrna closed Sally's door behind them as they left.

They moved away from her door before speaking in low voices. "Myrna, Scythia was staying here, right?"

"She was, Gerald. Are you wondering who will stay here now?"

"Yes. Even were I not here, I would not leave her alone."

"I cannot stay; Cle and I have a houseful. And there is not enough room for many here. We might ask Kenna."

"I would rather not. People inevitably wonder about the two of us."

"Ah, true. They have no idea she is, what, a thousand years old?"

Gerald laughed. "I have no idea. She won't say."

"I don't blame her." Myrna did not immediately offer another name.

"What of Morag?"

"She has nightmares and sometimes cries out in her sleep,

but it might work if no one else can help."

"Let us think on it. If we come up with nothing else by supper, you can ask Morag."

Sally's door opened and she leaned against the post. "In my dreams, Scythia wakes up with those yellow eyes, goes to the Broken Woods, returns with her sword, and starts to kill us all. None can stand before her, dragon or human." She burst into tears.

Gerald got to her and caught her as she started to fall. He took her to the cushions near the fireplace and sat down, pulling her to his shoulder. She sighed, shuddered, and relaxed almost instantly into sleep.

"Perhaps, Myrna, you could ask Morag sooner," Gerald pled.

Myrna nodded and left. A few minutes later she returned with Morag, who carried a small bag over her shoulder.

"Lord Gerald, I shall be happy to stay here, but I hope I do not cause problems if I cry out in my sleep."

"We'll chance it. Thank you so much."

Someone knocked at the door.

"Come," Gerald said in the softest voice he thought could be heard.

Cuthbert entered, came straight to Gerald, and squatted. "How is Sally?"

"She was having nightmares about Scythia being possessed and killing us all."

Cuthbert looked at Morag. "Cynthia, or for that matter Eilidh, should have something that will help her sleep more peacefully." Morag nodded and hastened through the door.

Cuthbert looked at Sally. "Sally. Sally!" He spoke quietly but firmly. She did not respond. Gently he pulled up an eyelid. Satisfied with what he saw, he released it. "She is deep in sleep. I suspect she will remain at peace while you hold her. Once Morag returns with something peaceful to drink, we need to go talk." Cuthbert lay down, closed his eyes, and appeared to fall asleep as quickly as Sally had.

Gerald looked back and forth between Sally and Cuthbert, fighting not to laugh.

Morag was back within five minutes. She held a small, sapphire blue bottle and an ivory-colored cup. Removing the stopper, she poured a few drops into the cup. She added a bit of wine from the table nearby, swirled them around, and woke Sally. Sally drank it, made a slight face, kissed Gerald's arm, and fell back asleep.

"Eilidh says she will sleep much better now."

Cuthbert opened one eye.

As Morag went to rinse the cup, Gerald asked, "Why the dragon bone cup?"

Morag froze and stared at the cup. "Is that what it is?"

"It certainly looks it from here. Is it far lighter than you had expected?"

"Yes."

"Drop it."

"What?"

"Drop it."

"No!"

"It won't break if it's dragon bone."

"But if it's not, I'll have a mess to clean up. Anyway, Eilidh insisted I use it, and she expects it back."

Cuthbert spoke quietly. "It will be dragon bone. Some strong potions can react with lesser materials. Using dragon bone assures they are full strength and have no unexpected effects."

The cup made oddly musical sounds as it bounced lightly on the floor. Morag smiled as she picked it up and examined it. "You were right. Not a scratch or chip."

Gerald laughed and turned to Cuthbert. "I thought you had fallen asleep."

"I was merely resting and meditating on recent events."

Morag rinsed the cup in the dish pail, dried it on her shawl, and placed cup and bottle on the mantle. "Three drops and a large sip of wine, mixed by swirling as needed. Now. Lord Gerald, what are your plans?"

As Sally was sleeping peacefully, Gerald slid her gently off his shoulder to the mat. "I need to go somewhere with Cuthbert for a bit. I will return later for my traveling bag and go elsewhere to sleep."

"Very well. Please knock when you return. For weeks I have slept with a knife at my side, and I sleep softly, ready for battle. I have not been able to break the habit."

Cuthbert rolled onto his right side and leaned on his elbow. "I don't know that I would try to break it just yet."

Gerald and Morag stared at Cuthbert. Morag asked, "What do you fear?"

"Nothing in particular, Morag, but I feel the need to be on guard."

"Very well," she said again.

Gerald kissed Sally's forehead and stood. Cuthbert joined him. Gerald gripped Morag's arm. "Thank you, cousin."

She gave him a fierce hug. "Thank you all for taking me in, for being family."

Gerald grinned. "I know the feeling. You're welcome." He pulled away and followed Cuthbert out the door.

"Don't forget to knock!" Morag called softly.

Gerald laughed. "Knocking at my own door so as not to be killed as a thief." He shook his head. "Where are we going, master of dragon lore?"

"Where we can talk without being overheard and where we can ponder the great mysteries lain upon us."

A few minutes later they were back in the Broken Woods, wending their way around, over, and under uprooted, broken, and burned trees. Cuthbert led the way to the bizarre stump with the sword in it. Looking around, he pulled over two broken logs to sit upon.

"Would you like a seat, Gerald?" he asked as he sat on one.

Gerald sat. "For now. I am tired but cannot promise to stay put."

"I understand." Cuthbert looked around, searching the sky and ground as well as looking around them. "Gerald, Younger says you may have a question about something."

"I have many. Which might he have meant, I wonder?"

"The Voice did not say."

"Voice? Why would it not have said?"

"Because there were people around. She waited, but there were always people."

"She? You can tell?"

"Of course. They are as different as you and Sally."

"Of course they are. Which means I must wonder about Sally and myself."

"At any rate, she did mention his shaking his head."

"The Voice?"

"Younger. The Voice is still a she."

"Oh! That." Gerald stared at the sword in the yellow-streaked, stony stump and saw the scene again in his mind. "No one seemed to be watching. I gripped the sword and pulled. It slid easily within the stump, but I noticed Younger watching. He shook his head. I froze. He nodded. I slid the sword back the little it had come out. He nodded again, ever so briefly. I hoped to ask what it meant, but have not seen him again."

Returning to the present, Gerald realized Cuthbert was standing agitatedly a few feet farther away. "You did not dream that the sword moved?" demanded the dragon lore master.

"No," replied Gerald. He stared at Cuthbert, who stared back. "Why? What does it mean?"

Cuthbert looked around again. He peered closely at Gerald's face and relaxed. "I will tell you in just a minute, dragon lord, but first I must ask you to show me." He gestured at the sword.

Slowly, nervously, Gerald reached for the hilt. It was ice-cold when he touched it, but it immediately warmed in his hand. He pulled gently and the sword slid half a foot from the tree trunk. As it moved, it made a singing noise reminiscent of Draebard in the hands of King Dugald's master armorer, Macafee.

"Let go!" Cuthbert commanded.

Gerald let go slowly. "The sword . . . my hand . . . they did not want to let go of one another."

"Ahhhhh . . ." Cuthbert took two quick steps and perched again on the broken log. "Can you push it back in with your boot?"

Gerald tried to nudge it in, then to force it. It did not move. In frustration he drew back his foot to kick it.

"No," said Cuthbert.

Gerald dropped his foot beside the other. "Why?"

"We are almost there. Can you hold the hilt in something and replace it?"

Gerald wrapped his hand in his tunic and tried. The sword would not budge, but grew hot. His tunic began to smoke. "Sorcery!"

"I had heard there might be some about. Try with your bare hand again, if you don't mind."

Gerald did so with trepidation, expecting to get burned, but once more the sword was cold for an instant, then warm. It resisted, but he was able to push it back in. It sang again, but sounded irritated to Gerald. He said as much.

Cuthbert gestured to Gerald's log, so Gerald sat. Sighing, Cuthbert warily reached for the hilt. He slapped it. Nothing happened. He grasped it. When nothing seemed to happen, he pulled. He moved, squatted before the hilt, and pulled with both hands. Nothing happened.

Returning to his log, he inspected his hands carefully. Satisfied, he turned to Gerald.

He spoke slowly and thoughtfully, in the manner Gerald knew from many intriguing lectures and tales. "There are numerous—oft conflicting—stories of the sword of Morgan le Fay, and indeed of everything about her. But there is one tale common among men, faerie, dragons, and others: that Morgan was fascinated by Arthur's sword, Excalibur, drawn from a stone to prove Arthur's right to rule."

"I thought Arthur was given the sword by the lady of the lake."

"There is also more than one tale of how Arthur obtained the sword. But the tales we are concerned with say that at the times Morgan needed to put her sword aside, she would enchant something to hold the sword, turning the object to stone. The tales also say Morgan alone could withdraw the sword."

Silence seemed to envelope the woods until Gerald could hear the blood in his veins, pounding loudly enough to wake Sally off in the village. Or Scythia. He shivered.

"And yet you are clearly not Morgan le Fay. There is nothing of Morgan about you. The druids would have sensed it. The dragons would have known. Kenna would have known. I checked your eyes again a minute ago; they are yours, nothing like the eyes in Scythia's head at the moment."

"Why did Younger tell me not to draw the sword? Oh! If anyone had seen me and known the tale . . ."

"Yes, Gerald. If you think your life has been rough before now, try to imagine a life in which people think you are Morgan le Fay, or at least her heir."

Gerald shook his head. "I will not even think of such a life. That way lies madness.

"But the sword! When I touched it with bare flesh, it was

icy for an instant and then warm—warmer than my hand, but not uncomfortable. And it was as if it were alive, trying to help me remove it. It resisted my replacing it, although it still went. And did you hear the songs? Joy and triumph on removal, unhappiness at being replaced."

"Songs?" Cuthbert's eyes wandered between the sword and Gerald. "What songs?"

"You heard nothing?"

"I heard only a sound similar to a sword moving in a metal scabbard."

"Have you heard a dragon sword sing at the sharpening stone?"

Cuthbert laughed. "I have sung right along with them!"

"It was somewhat similar. Did you not hear it?"

"Alas, or perhaps happily, no. I suspect that ability goes with the ability to possess the sword."

Gerald grimaced. "Let us not use that word."

"Very well. The ability to draw and wield the sword."

"What do you recommend, Cuthbert?"

Cuthbert did not answer. He scanned the sky and eventually waved. Then he smiled at Gerald. "Dragons, of course!"

Soon a shadow grew swiftly about them. Selene landed gently nearby a few heartbeats later.

"Lord Cuthbert, Lord Gerald." She bowed her head.

They bowed in return. Cuthbert spoke. "Selene, do you know what this is?"

Selene laughed small flames. "Do you?"

"I believe it to be the sword of Morgan le Fay."

"Indeed, Lord Cuthbert. It is her sword, Morticum, oft known as Liquid Death."

Gerald blinked. "What can destroy it?"

"Perhaps three strong dragons breathing their hottest flames upon it at once. But only perhaps. And certainly not here. The flames would burn the woods and likely Kiergewald." She eyed the stump distastefully. "The stony base of the tree is deep in sorcery. To try here might kill dragon, faerie, and human alike."

"What can be done?"

"If the sword can be removed, we can wrap it and have it taken to the secret place where the faerie sometimes examine dangerous magic. There is supposed to be a volcano there. The faerie might wish to examine it. I would simply destroy it."

"And yet," Cuthbert interrupted gently, "Lord Scythia has long bent this sword to her will. Until now. All thought it safe in her hands. What changed?"

"I do not know any more than you do. Nor do the faerie. If you would know that, then find one who can remove this sword and send it to the faerie. The dragons see no other way forward. The Eldest agrees. The sword must go with dragons to the faerie, either for examination or for destruction.

"As Scythia cannot currently draw the sword, I fear we must ask Lord Gerald to do it. I can take the sword, with an escort, to Albania to await a dragon who knows where it needs to go."

Gerald glared. "Why me?"

Flames of laughter escaped Selene's lips. "Gerald, I was only a mile above and I am not blind or deaf. Clearly you can remove the sword."

Cuthbert snorted. "I should have thought of some of you being overhead. I am slipping in my dotage."

Selene laughed fire again. "You children."

Cuthbert thought a moment. "Gerald, we will need to return here late at night. The dragons will watch to make sure no one else is around. You can remove the sword under cover of darkness. No one must know! We will tell your friends and family—I am sorry, but I must insist—only that the dragons took it."

Gerald looked rebellious for just a moment; part of him never wanted to touch the sword again. Another part desperately wanted to, which scared him. Suddenly his eyes opened wider. "On one condition."

"Condition? What condition?" Cuthbert demanded.

"That I go to Albania."

CHAPTER SIX

DANGEROUS TOYS

"And why is that?" Gerald stared at Cuthbert. "I don't know." He shook his head and stared around. "I have no idea why I said that."

Cuthbert stood up and stretched. "Let us walk a bit as we talk."

The dragon lords bowed to Selene as she returned to the sky.

They walked in silence for a moment before Gerald said, "I thought we were talking."

"My apologies. We should be. Whatever reasons drove your demand, there are three reasons I cannot grant it. First, you still owe King Donald two years of service. It is not up to me to send you somewhere in the midst of that, or even to recommend it when there is no special reason for you to go."

Gerald blushed and opened his mouth to reply, but Cuthbert kept going. "Second, only a handful of faerie and three dragons know where the triad delve into mysteries from which they wish to shield the rest of the world. And third, few of us have even heard of Albania, much less know anyone there. You would have nowhere to stay, nothing to do, no one to talk to. I have no idea what language they speak, but I seriously doubt it is Scots."

The red had slowly faded from Gerald's face, but he looked a bit stunned. "I'm still not sure why I said that. Forget it."

"Do you still want to go?"

"I care less with every passing moment."

Cuthbert kept walking, leading them soon back to the sword. "What about now?"

"Now what?"

"Do you still want to go?"

"Yes. I mean no! I . . ." He looked helplessly at Cuthbert. "Yes and no all at once."

"Let us return to your home."

"Remember to knock."

"An excellent point."

As they approached the line of unbroken trees, Cuthbert stopped. "And now, I presume, the desire to go to Albania has left."

Gerald watched a dragon's path high above for a moment. "You are correct. What are you doing?"

"Searching for influences, Lord Gerald. You were not yourself back there. When we move away from the sword, or the stump, or perhaps the combination of the two, you are more analytical and less inclined to demand time in Albania. When we approach the sword, the stump, or confluence of the two, your mind leans in strange directions."

"Yes." Gerald looked back toward the sickly yellow tree trunk. "It does seem that way . . . ." He thought a moment and shuddered.

Cuthbert asked, "What is it?"

Gerald hesitated. "My eyes. They weren't yellow or anything, were they?"

"No, Lord Gerald. You showed no signs of possession or

corruption. It seemed more a compulsion or confusion."

"And you still want me to come get the sword?"

"I want you to draw the sword out of the stump, wrap it in dragon hide, and give it to Selene to carry away. We will have Kenna with us as well, to help counter whatever evil spell is assaulting you."

"You felt nothing, Cuthbert?"

"I was on my guard. Whatever was there did not touch me, but I could feel something. I have no idea what. I have never felt it before and I will be content if I never feel it again. At least after tonight—when we return to remove the sword."

"Will Murdoch come?"

"If you like."

"I would feel better with him there."

"Very well."

They had reached Gerald's house. He knocked. There was no answer. Slowly he opened the door, staying behind it. He peered around the door slowly. Sally slept quietly on the cushions, but there was no sign of anyone else.

"Hello," Gerald said softly. Then louder, "Hello!"

"There you are," said a voice behind them. Gerald whirled around to find Morag grinning at them. "Are you expecting trouble?"

"I was making sure you were not going to hurl your knife at me."

"Ah. Not this time. I went to borrow eggs from Myrna." She held up a small basket.

"I was thinking I should get my things . . . ."

"There's no need. After supper I will be gone. Cynthia will stay the night with Sally, so you may stay here as well."

Gerald's eyebrows rose higher. "Cynthia? But what of Scythia?"

"Druze will remain with her, as will Eilidh. I will stay there.

If they need help they will send me for Cynthia."

"In that case, if Lord Cuthbert needs nothing else for now, I will attend to the animals."

Cuthbert shook his head no. Gerald strode off purposefully toward the pasture behind the house. He worked steadily with the animals for several hours, which took his mind off Sally, Scythia, and the loathsome Morticum. When Myrna called his name for dinner, he was not quite through, so it was another fifteen minutes before he arrived to eat.

As he sat down, Myrna placed a platter of food before him. "Lord Murdoch insisted I put aside some bacon for you."

"He always watches out for me." Gerald looked over the food in front of him. "So where is it?"

"He ate it."

Murdoch smirked from across the table. "Just like at the castle, Lord Gerald. It doesn't pay to be late."

"Late? Anyone stealing my bacon risks becoming late!"

Murdoch started to offer to return the eaten bacon, but Myrna's expression stopped him. It did not wipe the smirk off his face.

Around midnight, Cuthbert and Gerald approached the crystallized stump. A faint yellow light came from somewhere ahead. In it Gerald could make out the shapes of Murdoch and Kenna, who he was expecting. The unmistakable shadowy bulk of a dragon was there too, its eyes reflecting the yellow light.

Yellow eyes! Gerald suppressed a shudder. *That's the last thing I want to see around anything of le Fay's!*

On edge, he thought he could feel something as they approached the sword this time—a faint but intense desire he could not identify. Mysterious, fog-ridden mountains loomed in his imagination. Dragons flew above them, approaching out of a full moon several times larger than life.

He was pulled back to reality by the stump's sickly yellow light.

The eyes belonged to Selene, the deep purple of her hide ignoring the sorcerous light even as her lavender eyes reflected it.

Murdoch stared broodingly at the sword. Kenna smiled, radiating peace. Albania laid no spell on Gerald this time.

Cuthbert spoke first. "Have you tried the sword, Murdoch?"

Murdoch looked up. "Kenna insisted I try. It refused to budge. It might be a part of this accursed stump. Kenna said she tried earlier, and so did you."

"Yes. So far no one has moved it but Gerald."

"Then let us see whether he can remove it."

The others moved aside. Gerald squatted down and grasped the sword hilt. Almost before he moved, the sword was sliding out. The next thing Gerald knew, he was holding the sword aloft, pointing it at the moon. A victorious note started as soon as the sword moved. The sound hung in the air as if the sword were still ringing against the stony stump.

"Gerald!" Murdoch cried in a quiet voice. "What are you doing?"

"I'm letting the sword do what it wants to do."

He lowered it, which took far more effort than hoisting it had. "The sword wants to be aloft. It seeks the moon. Why would it do that?"

Kenna hissed and held out a piece of dragon hide. "Wrap the sword first, then we will talk more."

Gerald reluctantly placed the sword on the dragon hide. Kenna wrapped the hide around the sword and knotted a slender rope around it. The mountains receded in Gerald's mind.

After a moment's relieved silence, Gerald asked, "Did anyone else see mountains?"

"Great jagged mountains?" Murdoch asked.

"Many slender, tall peaks?" Kenna added.

"Shrouded in mysterious fog under a giant moon? No," Cuthbert replied.

The others laughed. Each had seen something similar, though none knew why. Even Selene—who was unaffected by le Fay's sword—was at a loss. "I felt nothing," she said. "Although that light is loathsome. I feel as if I need to bathe. Let us move away from it."

Twenty yards away, they stopped. "I feel clean again," Selene said. The others agreed.

"Those mountains," Murdoch said, "were definitely not Scottish."

The others concurred.

After a moment, Selene sighed, nearly blowing Gerald off his feet. "I suspect they are in Albania. Mother spoke once of her trips there. One of her landmarks was a series of peaks she called the Teeth. As in dragons' teeth." She pulled her lips back, baring her long, pointed teeth. "They sound similar to what you all mentioned."

Kenna nodded agreement.

"Do you know the way there?" Gerald asked Selene.

"She described how to get to small mountains on the Albanian coast. From there I cross a lake and fly inland to the Teeth. Beyond that I know nothing; the rest of the route is secret."

"And you know what the Teeth look like?"

"Yes. She not only described them at length, but she drew them on a rock for me."

Kenna hissed again. "She should not have drawn them, especially on a rock!"

"After I looked at them for a minute, she scratched meaninglessness over them, broke the rock, and we melted it with fire."

Kenna laughed. "I should have known. Forgive me."

"It is not for me to forgive and my mother is no longer here, so we shall assume you are forgiven, if such is even necessary."

Murdoch asked, "So you are the courier, Selene?"

"Yes. I volunteered since I know the way; both the Eldest and the faerie agreed. I will carry the sword and other relics to the Teeth. Either dragons or faerie will meet me there and take le Fay's toys with them."

"Toys!" Gerald snorted.

"Dangerous toys."

Kenna spoke. "Selene, if there is nothing else you wish to discuss, you should probably go. And we should return for the night."

"I am ready."

Kenna handed the wrapped sword to Cuthbert, pulled a smaller parcel wrapped in wire and bearing a hook from her sleeve, and unwound a slender rope from her waist. She used the rope to tie the parcel around Selene's front left leg. "My notes for the triad," she explained.

Cuthbert handed Selene the sword as she spoke. "Farewell, friends. I hope to see you within a week."

Before they could reply, Selene was airborne. Two other dragons dropped to flank her and they flew off southeast. Gerald noted the moon's position and smiled. "Do dragons ever *not* fly out of the moon at night?"

Cuthbert laughed. "Assuming there is a moon to be seen, very seldom, Lord Gerald. Very seldom."

CHAPTER SEVEN

FIGHTING UPSTREAM

Gerald watched until Selene and her companions disappeared. He eventually pulled his gaze back from the glorious night sky to look around. Kenna stood nearby. Cuthbert and Murdoch strode past the pale-yellow light of the stump, talking quietly. Gerald opened his mouth to say something as he started to move. It was then he realized his sword arm felt like stone and he stumbled.

Kenna moved like lightning and caught him. He could barely stand again with her help. He groaned.

"Gerald! What is it?"

"My arm! I cannot move it. It weighs a ton. And it leaps between icy and warm as the sword did. That's all I can feel. I can see your hands on me, but not feel them. The arm weighs me down. I will fall if you let go."

She stared at his arm briefly. She started to say something, then swiftly looked around for help. Gerald did as well, but far more slowly.

"Where did they go?" he asked.

"I don't know," Kenna answered hesitantly. "They could not have gone anywhere that fast. Let us head back to your home, but keep your eyes open. Can you stand if I hold you with one arm?" She put her arm under Gerald's and around his back.

"I think so. We can try, but let's steer well clear of that stump."

"I plan to. That accursed witch!"

Holding Gerald upright with her left arm, she extended her right arm palm up and concentrated. A bright white ball—a tiny thing promising a dangerous power—appeared in her hand. Kenna closed her fingers around it to hide the light, but it glowed redly through her skin.

They made their way across the treacherous, wood-littered landscape, the partial moon now high enough to mask the sorcerous yellow of the stump. Gerald felt a little strength return as they moved past and away from the stump, but they moved so slowly.

"It feels," Kenna mused, "as if we are battling our way up a rapidly moving stream, does it not?"

"That's exactly it," Gerald agreed. "But it seems to be getting easier the farther we are from the well."

"The well? What well?"

"The . . . the stump. It's like a well of something sickly, something poisonous, pouring out. Urquhart's well . . ." He laughed shrilly.

Kenna realized his arm was hot. She touched his forehead. He was feverish. He seemed less steady but somehow stayed upright. She managed to move faster.

The light went out in Kenna's hand just before she knocked at Gerald's door. Having knocked, she did not wait. As they crossed the threshold and she prepared to ask for help, Gerald suddenly stood straighter, taking weight off her arm. He shook his head and she could feel his body cooling to its normal temperature.

"Well!"

They looked down. Sally lay on the cushions, wide awake. "Where have you two been?"

Gerald opened his mouth, but Kenna spoke first. "We just returned from sending the sword away."

Sally sat up, glaring. "You look like two lovers back from a walk."

Kenna tentatively let go of Gerald, who seemed fine now, if a bit dazed.

"There is something cursed about the stump and sword, Sally, and Gerald was weak. I had to support him until just now. Gerald, how are you feeling?"

"Fine." He shook his head, trying to clear it. "I'm always fine with you."

"How is your arm?"

He looked first at his right arm, then his left. He arched an eyebrow. "They're both fine. Should they not be?"

"Gerald! You said your sword arm felt made of stone and it went icy and warm. You felt feverish!"

"I don't recall. Where are Murdoch and Cuthbert?"

"They left as we watched Selene fly away. Don't you remember?"

"I remember Selene with the sword and something else you gave her. And then we were here."

"Time. Le Fay's magic tried to freeze us in time, just as it has Scythia."

"Hmmm," was all Sally offered.

Kenna could not read Sally's expression. This bothered her.

"I'll leave you with Sally, then, Gerald." She looked around. "But where is Cynthia?"

Sally shrugged. "She had to go help someone. She woke me and told me and said she would send someone. Whoever it was doesn't seem to have arrived."

"Shall I stay until they do?"

"I doubt it matters. I need to sleep." She picked up the dragon bone cup on the floor beside her, glanced within, drained its meager contents, and lay back down. She was asleep almost immediately.

Kenna moved away from Gerald. Other than having gotten rid of the relics, the night was not going well. There were too many mysteries and Sally seemed jealous.

"Kenna, are you okay?" Gerald was rubbing his sword arm absently.

She thought for a moment. "Let's say yes. I will get there as quickly as possible."

"Whatever you did tonight, thank you. I don't remember any of what you described. I don't remember anything. Was I bewitched?"

"Possibly. You mentioned Urquhart's Well."

Gerald looked completely baffled. "King Urquhart believed some poppycock about a magic well that had its cover removed, and its waters filling up a huge glen to create Loch Ness—the loch in front of his castle. He wanted the dragons to drain the loch, cap the well, and restore the glen to its former verdant glory."

"Was he mad?"

"A bit mad and rather evil. A faint echo of Morgan le Fay, but troublesome enough to drown a hand-fasted woman for refusing his less than subtle advances. He drove his people to overthrow him."

"I heard there was a rebellion. I wondered what happened."

"There's more to it than that, of course, but it gives you some idea of the man."

They spoke softly, glancing from time to time at Sally, who slept on.

The door opened and Cynthia walked in.

"Well, I'm back. Old Matilda fell and broke a bone in her leg. The fool was out looking for ghosts in her pasture." She looked at Sally, then at the cup on its side nearby. "Did she drink that or spill it?"

"She drank it as we watched," Gerald replied.

"Good. She'll sleep another eight hours. Ought to be better after that."

Kenna looked intently at Cynthia. "Is there anything wrong with her beyond exhaustion and nightmares about Scythia?"

Cynthia looked back just as intently. "Shrewd. There is something, but I cannot put my finger on it. If I didn't know better, I'd think she'd been wearing that damnable necklace instead of Neakal."

Kenna nodded her head. "It certainly feels that way."

"And she's not the only one," Cynthia continued.

Gerald finally snapped out of his daze. "Who else?"

Cynthia rubbed her palms against her eyes. "Half the village. Matilda, for instance. She couldn't explain why she thought there were ghosts in her pasture, but she was convinced there were and she had to deal with them tonight. She was going to crawl back out to hunt them until I assured her the youngest dragon lord would take care of them in the morning while they slept. So please drop by at some point and tell her they are taken care of, Gerald.

"And Druze! Tell me, Gerald, when was the last time you heard Druze snap at anyone?"

Gerald thought hard. "Never. In seven years I have never heard her snap at anyone, and she's certainly been provoked."

"Well, she snaps at me almost daily. She has snapped at Scythia twice for not moving. She snapped at me for pouring wine too loudly . . . ."

Kenna interrupted. "But not all? What of you, Cynthia?"

"I think I'm fine, but so do all those people."

"You seem to be acting yourself around us. Doesn't she?"

Gerald nodded assent.

"I need to get back," Kenna said, walking quickly to the door. She turned back for a moment. "I hope you all sleep well. Good night." She was gone almost before Gerald realized the door had moved.

He felt a bit lost. Sally was angry, Cynthia had reverted to silence, and Kenna had left. Murdoch and Cuthbert were probably asleep. Disgustedly, he started toward his room. "Goodnight, Cynthia. Let me know if you need anything." He blew a kiss toward Sally. Not wanting to chance chance waking her, he went straight into his room and closed the door.

Sally woke in the wee hours of the morning, thinking she heard footsteps as she had months ago when nightmares about Argyll had plagued Gerald. She looked around, but the darkened room held no menace. She heard Cynthia breathing nearby. She could just hear Gerald snoring in his room. She hoped desperately he was alone. Sally fell back asleep, feeling worse than she had after the nightmares about Scythia.

CHAPTER EIGHT

A PROPER FLUMMOXING

Gerald awoke at daybreak. He lay for a few minutes listening to the sounds of morning—insects buzzing, birds singing and chirping, goats fussing at something nearby, pigs grunting in the distance. He mulled over the events of the night before, frustrated to realize he still recalled nothing between Selene flying away and standing inside his home with Sally glaring at him.

He felt sad. He felt annoyed. Remembering what Cynthia had said, he tried to shake the feelings off, but they remained. He grunted, rose, changed clothes, and wandered into the main room.

Cynthia sat with eyes unfocused, her left hand on Sally's forehead. Gerald couldn't tell what she was doing. As she did not seem to notice his arrival, he left and walked leisurely to Cle's house. Smelling bacon and hearing voices, he stuck his head in the door. Everyone was up and eating.

"Ho, cousin!" Cle managed to say, despite a mouth full of food. Murdoch and Cuthbert nodded. Myrna pointed toward the food, smiled, and kept eating.

Kenna sat to the side, leaning against a wall, staring at a bit of string she was playing with. "Good morning, Gerald," she said faintly, clearly lost in her thoughts.

Gerald ate his food and was halfway through an enormous mug of coffee when there was a quick, staccato knock on the door. "Come in," Cle called.

The knock repeated. Glancing at the others, Cle slowly got up and headed to the door, where the knocking continued even after he said again to enter. Murdoch jumped up, catlike, and moved silently beside the door, knife in hand. Cle glanced at Murdoch, pushed the door hard, and stepped back.

A Voice squawked and tumbled backward from the door. Upon recovering, it darted into the house and landed on the floor beside Myrna's food. "Good morning. Or it was until you assaulted me for knocking at your door. Next time I will bring a dragon and storm the battlements!"

Cle stood with his mouth open, caught completely off guard. Murdoch grinned and put away his knife.

Cuthbert laughed, bringing Cle to his senses. "Based on its tone, I think this must be Gerald's Voice?" Cuthbert mused.

Gerald bowed to the Voice, who bobbed back at him. "Greetings, Voice. Was your flight pleasant? What news do you bring?"

The great black bird tilted its head. "No one asks a Voice if her flight was pleasant. Not even other Voices."

"Have I broken etiquette? Need I fall on my sword in repentance?"

"No, I have simply never heard of such a thing happening. Perhaps I will ponder this later. Or perhaps I will simply hunt something juicy to eat.

"But I did not come to exchange pleasantries, so I will not ask whether your flight was pleasant. I will simply note that King Donald's party will be here by noon."

Myrna jumped up. "The king is coming?"

"No. His party approaches. The king is not with them, but a queen is."

"A queen!"

Gerald eyed the bird suspiciously. "Would this be a dark-skinned queen?"

The bird bobbed. "Of course—K'Pene the healer."

"She renounced her throne, you know."

"She is nevertheless a queen. It should be quite obvious to anyone with eyes in his head—even a human."

Murdoch cut into the conversation. "Is Folkvar leading the party?"

"He is. He said they will pitch camp in the woods near where the battle took place and asks to be met there."

"How will they know where it is?"

"Voices travel with them, and they know dragons fly above it to keep watch."

Murdoch nodded. "Thank you."

"Is there any message you would have me take them?"

"I can't think of anything," Gerald replied.

Cuthbert spoke. "You should send word back thanking them and saying we will meet them as requested."

"Please do," Gerald said to the Voice.

Myrna asked, "Do you want food or drink? Can you eat this?"

"Thank you. I could, but I really want something alive, preferably something that puts up a fight." She stretched her wings, but hesitated. "My journey was pleasant. I hope all of yours are."

Cle had unshuttered the largest window. The Voice left, her wingtips brushing the window's frame on the way out. Still a bit flummoxed, Cle said, "I have dealt with very few Voices, and none like that."

Cuthbert laughed. "That was one of Gerald's, so of course it is impertinent."

"Gerald's?" Cle and Myrna cried as one.

Sighing, Gerald explained. "The rules have been changing."

Murdoch interrupted. "Can they change the rules? I thought the rules governing such things were immutable."

Cuthbert answered. "The rules of debt and balance are, having been laid down since creation. Voices were bred magically by dragons with Merlin's help. Dragons and Voices agreed on the rules of their society and they are free to modify them as they wish."

Gerald went on. "When a dragon passes from this life, its Voices may now choose a dragon lord instead of another dragon. When Goyim died, some of her Voices chose me. She was known for her wit, and a dragon's Voices take on the dragon's personality." He shrugged. "Life keeps getting more interesting."

Myrna shook her head. "Where I was born, the priests would have called that bird a familiar and used it as evidence you were evil."

"The ex-priest I met in Edinburgh thought that. It was evidence against me for his private inquisition."

Cle's and Myrna's eyes grew wider. "Have you not heard this either?" Gerald asked. "I sent Sally word of these things."

"We've all been busy. You must catch us up on events."

"I will try, but for now I need to get to work. Between Sally's malady and the time Neakal thought himself mad, the animals were somewhat neglected. And I noticed other work that desperately needs doing."

"Myrna and I have chores as well," Cle said.

Murdoch stood. "I can help you or Myrna so the other is free to help Gerald. That way we can share stories and the two of you can share them later."

"That would be excellent, Murdoch. Thank you. Gerald, what do you plan to do today?"

"The fences are in bad shape. I need to replace some posts. I also want to build a stone wall for part of it. Neakal and Sally have collected stones for months."

"Then I'll go with you, if Murdoch doesn't mind helping Myrna muck out the barn."

"It's been a while," Murdoch said, "but I think I can still use a shovel." He mimed flinging manure.

Cuthbert arose. "I'm going to the Broken Woods to speak with the dragons."

Kenna said nothing, still staring at the string she manipulated between her fingers, constantly weaving new patterns. The rest drained their drinks. Myrna asked Murdoch to help her with the dishes before they went to the barn. He began telling her in a low voice of Gerald's and his journey to Edinburgh, and of the journey afterward as the high king's envoys. As they headed outside, Murdoch glanced at Kenna. She nodded goodbye almost imperceptibly, but she seemed less tense. It distracted him and he fell silent for a moment.

"Murdoch, don't you dare lose track. Keep talking!" Myrna demanded. He grinned and complied. While he seldom craved attention, he didn't mind when it came his way.

It was about an hour past noon when a dozen horses and riders rode into the battle site. K'Pene was first off her horse. She darted over and hugged Gerald, kissing his cheeks. Sally looked disconcerted, but was mollified when K'Pene greeted her in the same manner.

Then K'Pene went to Murdoch. Gerald noticed Murdoch's hug lasted much longer than his. He grinned; he would love to see Murdoch and K'Pene together. Folkvar and the men came over and clasped forearms with Gerald, who introduced them to Sally, Myrna, and Neakal. Justin and Eoin both blushed a bit when Sally hugged them; they had known each other for some years but had never been close. When she hugged Folkvar and didn't let go, he picked her up and spun around twice before putting her down. She laughed for the first time in days. Gerald looked away, wondering why her laughter didn't make him happy.

Folkvar looked at Murdoch. "How do you wish us to deploy?"

Murdoch started; he had somehow forgotten that Folkvar had not come just to bring K'Pene. He thought quickly. "There is no threat of that sort. I don't think there's really anywhere in the village to house you." He looked approvingly at the camp they had made. "It's up to you whether you stay together, station pairs of guards around the village, or something else. We should send Voices to King Donald to see what he wants you to do."

"I wish we had known. We made great haste to get here. The horses are exhausted."

Murdoch shrugged. "I'm sorry, Folkvar. It's been crazy here, and none of us are thinking as clearly as we should. I'm actually reconsidering having you this close to yon stump. Morgan le Fay's magic lies heavily here."

Folkvar spat. "I fear no witch, alive or dead."

"This isn't fear. It's caution."

"I will not argue with that."

Murdoch looked around and saw K'Pene with Cuthbert by the bewitched stump. "I should probably join those two. I will check with you again after seeing if K'Pene has any thoughts on le Fay's legacy here. See if Gerald needs anything."

Murdoch walked quickly to the stump. They were just out of hearing range, but Gerald saw K'Pene stand and sniff the air. She slowly turned in a circle, left hand shading her eyes, right hand palm up in front of her. After a third circle, sniffing all the while, she pointed. Cuthbert and Murdoch walked beside her as she headed toward the tree line closest to the village.

Kenna appeared where the path to the village exited the trees. Gerald felt Sally stiffen. Kenna changed course to join K'Pene and her party. They walked into the woods, K'Pene scanning ahead with her eyes shaded, apparently still sniffing.

"You're tense," Gerald observed.

Sally relaxed. "Sorry."

He took her hand. "What's wrong?"

She turned to look at him.

"Since you've been home, you and Kenna are constantly together."

"We're working on the mystery! And you know she's like a sister to me."

"You looked like lovers the way you walked in last night." She let go of his hand. "And you couldn't even think straight around her."

"Sally, it's you I love. It's you I plan to marry."

"I hope so." She took his hand again, but tentatively. "Nothing is right anymore."

"Kenna thinks it's le Fay's influence."

"Le Fay is dead."

"I know she's supposed to be, but something is wrong. I can't remember parts of last night, but Kenna said my arm was like a stone after Selene carried the sword off. I could barely walk. Cynthia says half the village is acting strange. And of course there's Scythia. And don't forget how Neakal was, wearing that necklace."

"How did they get the sword out?"

"I pulled it out."

"You? But I thought . . ."

"Yes. That's why Cuthbert had me do it secretly, because many people thought that." He thought for a few seconds. "I thought that!"

"You looked bewitched, hanging onto Kenna."

"I must have been, but by the sword and the stump, not Kenna. My arm still felt unnaturally heavy, even later."

Sally visibly relaxed. "Have you any idea what K'Pene is doing?"

"None. But Folkvar is waving. I should see what he wants."

They clambered over the two biggest tree trunks to get

to where Folkvar waited by trees that still stood. How odd, thought Gerald, that the unscathed trees look so out of place here.

The men had finished setting up camp, so Gerald led them into the village. Justin and Eoin immediately split off for a brief visit with family and friends. The bulk of Folkvar's party remained with Cle and Myrna, who insisted on feeding them. Gerald and Sally took Folkvar and his cousin Norbert to Cynthia's house to meet the healer and check on Scythia.

Cynthia shook her head. "There's been no change. It's right out of an old tale, a typical sleeping warrior princess. Except that her sword has flown away and her eyes glow yellow." She looked warily at the visiting warriors and asked, "I suppose you two want to see her eyes?"

Folkvar and Norbert looked at each other and shook their heads.

"No, thank you," said Folkvar.

"Not in the least," agreed Norbert vehemently.

Cynthia looked pleasantly surprised. "Oh." She led them outside. "I want some sunlight. It's a beautiful day."

"Yes, it is!" cried Druze as she came out to join them.

Cynthia arched an eyebrow. "Are you well?"

Druze looked perplexed. "I'm fine, Grandmother. Should I not be?" She smiled. "And look! You brought me suitors! Or are they yours?"

Everyone stared at Druze, albeit for different reasons.

"You're back to your old self," Gerald observed.

Druze stared back and forth between him and Cynthia. "What's wrong with you two?"

Cynthia answered. "You haven't been yourself the past two days."

"Haven't I?" She looked confused. "Who have I been?"

"Someone grumpy."

Druze looked horrified. "Me?"

"You."

Druze was speechless. Gerald and Sally laughed: they had never seen Druze's wit silenced before.

While Druze explained she did not recall feeling any different, K'Pene and her entourage—now including several villagers—walked up. Druze shuddered.

"Are you certain you are okay, Druze?" Cynthia asked, reaching to touch her head.

"I'm fine, Grandmother. But I felt something. Something I distinctly do not like." She looked curiously at K'Pene. Like most highlanders, she had not seen anyone so dark-skinned. "Something grumpy," she added.

"That would be these," K'Pene said, placing a bundle on the ground in the shade by Cynthia's house. She untied and spread the fabric out. A dozen rough stones glowed an ugly yellow, albeit faintly in the daylight. "These encircled the village. They were all buried about a foot deep. The ground was still soft, so they must have been buried quite recently."

Those who had not been with K'Pene stared, horrified, as they realized what this implied.

"But who?" Sally demanded.

"Whoever is behind this must hate this village, or someone in it," K'Pene said. "There is great evil in these stones. Evil more ancient than I have dealt with before. This is not an evil that seeks only to kill. No, this is an evil that seeks to dominate and corrupt, an evil that delights in misery."

"Morgan le Fay. Again, le Fay!" Gerald spat. He rubbed his sword arm, which felt heavy and useless.

"The others agree with you."

"You do not?"

"I do not know anything of this person, but if it is she, she was no ordinary sorceress."

"The tales say she was far beyond all others."

"That would make sense."

Kenna spoke up. "K'Pene was able to sense and find the stones for us. She has dealt with such things back in her homeland."

"Not exactly," K'Pene noted. "Never have I found such this easily. I have met evil powers, but those were child's play compared to this." She knelt and began tying the bundle back up. "We must send these after the other relics. I would not call Selene back even if I could. The things she carries should be investigated as quickly as possible. As should these. Cuthbert and I will hasten to the clearing and send them. He has already sent Voices ahead so a dragon will be ready to descend when we approach."

Sally and Cynthia started to speak at the same time. Sally indicated Cynthia should go first.

Cynthia looked at K'Pene. "Would these stones be responsible for people here acting somewhat mad?"

"Quite likely. They were arranged in a perfect circle, equally spaced for maximum effect. You are fortunate they were not here longer than they were, or you would have had fights, thefts, and possibly murder."

Most of the others looked shocked. Sally simply said, "That was my question as well."

Kenna, K'Pene, and Cuthbert left as the group discussed the stones and speculated on how they had been buried without anyone noticing.

Murdoch explained, "All the burial sites were soft ground, a few minutes digging. Anyone could have done it by night, though they would have been busy."

But no one had any idea who had done it or why.

And that was even more troubling than the presence of the stones.

CHAPTER NINE

A SUDDEN DEPARTURE

"**S**antana!" Gerald cried.

Those who understood looked in vain to the sky. The rest stared at Gerald.

"Santana—the dragon. He was going to escort Folkvar and his troops. Did he come, Folkvar?"

"He did."

"Where was he when you arrived?"

"He went to the river to drink. Then he was going to join the guard in the sky."

Gerald looked around. He saw Voices on nearby roofs. "Voices! Is Santana near?"

The Voices all looked up and around. "Yes," they agreed.

Gerald could just make out tiny dragon shapes flying high nearby.

"Sally, do you want to meet Santana?"

"Of course!"

"If you will excuse us."

The others nodded.

Two minutes later as they passed their house, Sally slowed. "Gerald, I do not feel well. I can meet him later."

Disappointed, Gerald nevertheless saw Sally inside.

"Will you stay and rest with me, Gerald?"

"I need to see Santana."

"Please?" Sally asked piteously.

"Sally, no. If you need to rest, go ahead, but I should see Santana."

"I see. Go then!"

"Sally . . ."

But she had already stomped to her room and slammed the door.

Frustrated and hurt, Gerald hurried back outside and to the Broken Woods. There he found Nain and Santana speaking with K'Pene and the rest. K'Pene was tying a dragon hide bundle onto Santana's right front leg.

"Santana! Greetings!" Gerald called as he hurried up.

Santana bowed his head. "Greetings, Lord Gerald. Are you packed?"

Cuthbert shook his head. "He does not know, Santana. We three had only come to a decision just before you arrived." He held out his hands to indicate K'Pene and Kenna.

"Decided what?" Gerald asked.

"Gerald, King Donald only sent us to fight and guard against attack. There has been no hint of Argyll, and though Folkvar and his men—and you and Captain Murdoch—are excellent warriors, that is no use against magic. Kenna borrowed Voices to send to her father, and even now," he paused and glanced around to make sure no one else was nearby, "several faerie are gathering nearby to watch over Kiergenwald.

"Santana will carry you and Captain Murdoch back to Cair

Parn. The castle is along his route to deliver this package to Albania."

"You know where it is?" Gerald asked in surprised hope.

"Albania?" Santana asked in return, wisps of flame escaping playfully from the corners of his lips.

"The secret place there."

"If you mean where the stones go to be examined, no, but I have flown to the Teeth before."

"Oh." Gerald wasn't sure why he was disappointed.

Cuthbert continued. "At any rate, Santana will carry you to Cair Parn and continue on to the Teeth. Folkvar will pick four men to stay here. The rest will ride back tomorrow to Cair Parn, but in less haste than they came. The remaining four will come with K'Pene when she is ready to return. She wishes to investigate further here, and she wishes to trade healer knowledge with Cynthia and the other healers here."

"What of you and Kenna?"

"We will come soon by dragon."

"Very well. I will find Murdoch."

"We have sent Voices. He will come."

"Then I will get my gear," he said resignedly.

"K'Pene will accompany you."

"Very well. Are you ready?"

"I am, Lord Gerald."

They turned and started back to the village. K'Pene waited until they were a stone's throw from the others before asking, "What bothers you, Gerald?"

He glanced at her before answering. "Many things."

"Does something bother you especially at home?"

"Why do you ask?"

"I will explain after you answer."

He glared at nothing in particular. "I am . . . anxious. Even, at times, angry." This surprised him. He had not been thinking in these terms.

"Why?"

Gerald thought as they approached the short path through the trees. "I don't know. I want to blame Sally. She's certainly not herself. She acts moody, but at the moment I only feel concerned and frustrated. But at home," he fell silent again for a dozen steps, "at home I get angry at how she acts." Shame wafted over Gerald.

"I expected something like that."

Gerald stopped as they exited the trees and turned to K'Pene. "Why?"

She looked off to Kiergenwald, then into Gerald's eyes. He almost stepped back at the intensity she radiated.

"Gerald, whenever I pass or enter your home, I feel a subtle pressure to my ugly side—to anger, jealousy, pettiness, lust, and more. It's as if someone were probing my defenses, looking for a weak spot to set on fire. I cannot locate a source. It is very subtle, as if cloaked. This does not come from buried stones, or a gem about a neck, or something as blatant as a petrified stump with a sword in it. No, this is hidden and . . . personal."

"Personal?" Gerald resumed walking. "What do you mean?" He halted when he realized K'Pene had not budged from the tree line.

"Please wait, Gerald. Step back into the shadows with me. Let us finish discussing this before we go."

"But Santana is waiting."

"He knows we need to talk." Gerald returned to where she waited deep within shadow. "As for it being personal, I cannot easily explain, except that I believe it is mainly directed at you or Sally, or perhaps both."

"But how?"

"Again, I have no idea. I will say that were it my house, I would be tempted to burn it down! But there is no guarantee that would solve the problem.

"I can offer no more at this time. I would suggest Sally move, but as we have no idea what is involved, we have no way to know she would be safer anywhere else." She hesitated. "I would worry that she carries it with her somehow, but the effect is centered about the house, not her."

When Gerald could think of nothing to say, K'Pene held out her hand toward Kiergenwald and they began walking.

"I am sorry, Lord Gerald, that I have no better news."

"As am I, Your Majesty, but I do not blame you. How long do you plan to stay? And is it only for a healer's knowledge?"

"You are wise beyond your years, warrior. I do not know what I can do here, but I will be on my guard. Certainly if more of the same evil shows up, I will hunt it."

"Thank you, K'Pene. Use of mine whatever you have need of while you are here."

"Thank you, Gerald. Will you make sure others know that?"

"Of course, but we need a reason we can state publicly."

"Stick with the truth, as much as possible. I am staying to help guard against further attacks and to see if I can sense anything else related to your le Fay."

"Not my le Fay!"

K'Pene laughed, but quieted almost immediately. They were passing Cle's home, nearing Gerald's and Sally's.

"Where is Sally?"

Gerald sighed. "She grew tired as we passed the house, then angry when I would not stay with her." He lowered his voice still more. "She has been acting jealous of Kenna, and oddly friendly to Folkvar."

"Are you jealous of Folkvar?"

"No." A puzzled look crossed Gerald's face. "Except when I'm here." They had arrived at his doorstep.

"You see?"

He called Sally's name and opened the door. There was no

response. He entered. He called Sally again, to no avail. Her door was shut. He looked at K'Pene, shrugged, and went to his room to get his pack. K'Pene stayed on the path outside.

"Sally, I have to go back to Cair Parn. Are you there? Are you awake?" There was still no response. "I love you. I will send a Voice soon!"

He stared at her silent, closed door for several heartbeats. Hurt and angry, he turned and left.

They stopped to say farewell to Cle and Myrna. Gerald also explained to them K'Pene's decision to stay to help protect Kiergenwald and Sally, and that whatever he had was at her disposal. He took out a half ounce of gold and gave it to her despite her protests.

"Do not worry, lad," Cle said. "We'll make sure she has what she needs. At your expense, of course."

Myrna cuffed Cle's shoulder before embracing Gerald in a tight hug. She pulled away but grabbed his shoulders. "Gerald, I don't know what's happened to Sally, but try to be patient. She's really worried about Scythia."

"I know. And I think the evil in the air has touched her more than most."

K'Pene interjected, "Dark magic most easily influences those who are weakened—whether by fatigue, wounds, or fears. Sally was both tired and worried about Scythia when we arrived, was she not?"

The others nodded.

She continued. "People who use such sorcery often enjoy corrupting love and compassion."

Gerald said his thanks, hugged Myrna again, and then hugged Cle. He opened the door and preceded K'Pene out.

Neither of them spoke until they were stepping into the Broken Woods.

"I am sorry, Lord Gerald. If I find any clues as to what is happening, I will send word. Can you leave Voices here?"

"Half my Voices are always here, at Sally's disposal and watching for rogue dragons or Voices. Use them however you need to. Where will you stay, K'Pene?"

"I will discuss that with Cynthia. Normally I would ask to stay with Sally, but I'm not sure she would want me to. And I wish to spend no more time in that building than I must. I'm sorry if that sounds terrible."

"No, it sounds sensible. If you can think of a way to get Sally to stay away from it, I would be grateful."

"I don't know if that would help very long, because I don't know the source of the evil, but it might help now. I will see what I can do."

"Thank you, K'Pene. I cannot ask for more."

They ducked under a fallen tree trunk and approached the others. Nain was gone, presumably aloft. Murdoch had joined the small group—if any group including a full-grown dragon may be considered small.

"Where are Folkvar and his men?" Gerald asked.

Murdoch smiled. "Deployed about Kiergenwald, of course. The horses rest, but the men are rested enough and will do what they came to do, which is guard Kiergenwald. A few are scattered hereabout, keeping an eye on Cuthbert. The king is rather serious about protecting him."

Cuthbert laughed. "Mere dragons are not enough protection, it seems."

Gerald clasped Cuthbert's arm. "Thank you for everything. And please thank Folkvar and his men."

"I will. Take care, Gerald. I should see you within a day."

Gerald turned to Kenna. The faerie, having ascertained that no one watched their party, gave Gerald a fierce hug. "I am sorry a dead sorceress has somehow gotten to Sally. But we will do all we can to free her. Do not despair, and do not be angry with her!"

"Thank you, princess. I still love her. Will I see you in a day?"

"I cannot say. We will see."

Gerald froze as he noticed K'Pene and Murdoch were locked in an embrace, just finishing a kiss. He resisted the urge to clap. Realizing all eyes were upon them, the couple kissed again before breaking apart. K'Pene caught Gerald's eye and ran over to hug him. "Do you need a kiss as well, young dragon lord?"

"I do, Your Majesty, but Sally is apparently asleep."

She laughed and hugged him again.

Gerald grinned. "All right. Do we have blankets?"

Cuthbert produced a blanket for Gerald. K'Pene helped wrap Murdoch in one. Seconds later they were aloft, the dragon lore master and faerie dwindling rapidly as they waved farewell.

CHAPTER TEN

THE WISDOM
OF THE VOICES

Santana flew at a steady pace. It was almost sedate compared to what Gerald had become used to. He didn't have to shout, which he appreciated. Still, he spoke loudly. "Santana, will Selene still be near the Teeth when you arrive?"

"Gerald, you do realize that I have excellent hearing and can hear you even if you whisper?"

"Of course," Gerald said, though he had indeed not thought of this. "But Murdoch would not hear me then."

"True. I hope to see Selene there. She plans to eat and rest, as it has been weeks since she has done much of either. How is Sally?"

Gerald hesitated. "She is unhappy. We do not know what will become of Scythia, and Sally is exhausted. She was exposed in that state to the evil influences of the relics."

"And you left her thus?" Santana asked.

"I cannot help her now unless I take her far away, and even that might not help. But K'Pene remains, and she is a healer who has dealt with sorcerous maladies."

"She struck me as wise.

"Is that what attracts you to her, Murdoch? Her wisdom?"

"Oh, yes. That alone, wisest of dragons."

"I suspected as much. Even her kisses looked wise."

Gerald snickered as he imagined Murdoch's red face.

For the remainder of the brief flight, Gerald and Murdoch filled in the gaps of Santana's knowledge about recent events in Kiergenwald. When they finished, Cair Parn had just appeared, a mere black dot in a river valley. Santana altered course as if to go around it.

Murdoch cried, "Where are we going?"

"To Cair Parn, as promised, but we are taking the long way." He settled into a circular path several miles from the castle. "Describe the stump in more detail, please—its appearance, sound, feelings it caused, everything."

While Gerald gathered his thoughts, Murdoch described the stump's appearance, recapping its effects on people as he had heard them or the little he had felt.

Gerald told of his experiences: of Morticum and its singing and of the general malaise around the sword. He described what Kenna had said happened with his arm and his inability to walk unaided, and how Sally felt better not going near it.

Murdoch added, "The oddest thing was not even its appearance, or that it was streaked with light, or that it was hard as stone. Somehow it always made me think of dragons. And someone—I forget who—said something about there being more than one sort of magic involved, or something like that."

Gerald started. Someone had said that. Who? He rubbed his eyes with his fists. "Wait! Selene said something about dragon fire with the sorcery!"

Murdoch replied, "I think she meant Argyll's fire, Gerald."

"Perhaps she did," Santana acknowledged. "In fact, probably so." He seemed to think for a moment, changed course, and started down toward Cair Parn.

No one showed surprise at their arrival. Possibly Voices had come ahead, or perhaps one below had recognized them. There were always Voices about Cair Parn now, between Gerald's and Cuthbert's and those on the business of the Eldest, Younger, and other dragons.

As the two warriors dropped a foot to the roof of the keep, Drinn ran up to take Murdoch's pack. Murdoch bade him take Gerald's, too.

Together they thanked Santana, who bowed his head on his long neck. The dragon flew a short distance off to converse with several Voices before flying higher and toward the southeast.

The arrivals went straight to the throne room, where King Donald awaited them. "Welcome back! I have the gist of things from the Voices, but please give me a brief recap with anything you feel important."

Fifteen minutes later they had covered all the ground that seemed necessary. Donald stared at Gerald a moment. "You live quite the life, Gerald. I am not sure how best to make use of you. You have already been through more, and done more for me, than most with far more years behind them. No, there is nothing you need to say. These are mere facts. Allow, I pray, your king to speak."

Gerald showed no outward sign of his laughter within. *As if you need me to allow you anything!*

"Go now. Eat. Take care of your packs. Do what you will today and resume duties tomorrow."

Dismissed, they happily headed to the mess. Gerald glanced at Murdoch. "And what will you today, my captain?"

"The past few days have been nearly a holiday, Gerald. I think I will find out what has gone on in our absence and discuss training schedules with whoever is here. What of you?"

"It's been some time since I cleaned my clothes. And I will check on Dealanach. Shall I see to your horse as well?"

"She is well cared for, but thank you. And here is the mess!"

Cheese, bread, and pears had been set out for the watch, so

they helped themselves to these and to drink. When Murdoch left, Gerald stayed behind to see if he could talk someone out of bacon. As he wandered into the kitchen, a squeal assaulted his ears and he was nearly knocked down. He found himself in a tight embrace from Kari, half smothered in her hair. She pulled away, smiling as usual.

I'm glad Sally didn't see that. He hated himself for thinking that, because it was an innocent hug, but he didn't trust Sally to understand right now.

"Gerald, I'm so glad I got to see you one last time!"

"One last . . . oh, right! When are you leaving?"

"At first light."

"I've only ever heard you play and sing at a distance. I wish I could have heard you properly."

"I sang last night here in the mess. I'm sorry you missed it!"

"Me, too. How was it?"

"Fine until the end. At least three warriors around our age were sure I was singing just for them. One pledged his undying love for me. Dree and Peter almost had to drag him out."

"Oh, boy. Was one of them Drinn?" Drinn had been enamored of Kari a couple of months previously.

"No, he was quite helpful! He was acting silly a while back, but now he's really nice. He's one I will miss. Anyway, I have to get back to work, but I wanted to tell you goodbye. I'll miss you."

She hugged him again, kissed his cheek, and hurried off. "I'll miss you, too," he called after her.

Bacon forgotten, Gerald went to his barracks. It was midafternoon and no one was there. As he began pulling his clothes from the locker at the foot of his bed, a Voice settled on his pillow.

"Greetings, Lord Gerald."

"And to you, Voice of Gerald. Was this journey pleasant?"

The bird hopped about the pillow joyfully. "You recognize

me. Humans can seldom tell us apart."

"You have a certain glint in your eye. It reminds me of Goyim."

"I look dead?"

"I could mean nothing else. What brings you to my pillow?"

The Voice flew to the door, then to the window, looking out of each, before returning to the pillow. "Santana sent me."

"Santana should be far away by now."

"I have no doubt he is, but he spoke with me as soon as he left you. He said to wait until you were alone. Let us speak quickly, lest someone come."

Gerald nodded. "Go ahead."

"You know there are secrets among the dragons, things they seldom speak of, much less to men."

Again Gerald nodded.

"You have been dragon blessed. You know, I believe, that this is a great honor, seldom bestowed upon men. Has Cuthbert spoken much of this?"

"No. I have meant to ask more about this. I saw Selene bless Neakal, my brother."

"Santana feared Cuthbert might not have taught of this." The bird again flew to check that no one approached or skulked nearby. "In all of history, the dragons believe perhaps a hundred of you have been so blessed. Only once before were two blessed within a year, or even fifty years. That may change with the truce. We shall see.

"A dragon blesses someone who has done a great service for that dragon, or more often for multiple dragons. Gerald, never has an Eldest blessed anyone before you. And never has a dragon blessed one such as Neakal, who has done nothing for dragons, simply as a gift.

"But dragons have blessed those they wished to have help them. This has happened a dozen times. Three of those times the help desired bode ill for mankind, or at least for some."

A thrill of terror went down Gerald's back. "Morgan le Fay!"

"Yes, Morgan le Fay was one. Would you care to guess who blessed her?"

"I have no idea. Wait!" Gerald's hands clenched. "Argyll?"

"An Argyll, yes—the mother of the Argyll that laid waste to your family and the woods near your home."

"You have a way with words, Voice. Why did Argyll bless le Fay? No good purpose, I suspect."

"None know. Dragons know when a dragon blesses someone, but they know only who is involved. As far as we know, no other dragon heard why Argyll blessed le Fay, and those two unworthies took that information to their graves."

Gerald began to pace as the Voice checked the windows and doors again.

"Someone is passing but is not coming this way," the Voice said as she settled again upon the pillow.

Gerald opened his mouth to ask something, but the Voice continued. "There is more. First, Santana reminds you this is a great secret. We believe you and Cuthbert alone among men know this. The faerie know it. No others may know unless dragons tell them. Anyone else they would have first bound to secrecy, but the rules bend and warp when you are involved. They know they can trust you. As your Voice, I will add something in case you are tempted to tell someone for some unforeseen reason. Should you repeat this to another human without a dragon's permission, you would fall so deeply into their debt that you might die before you could take another breath.

"I exclude mad dragons, of course; their permission means nothing except as it involves them."

Gerald stopped pacing and sat on the nearest bunk. "Are you serious?"

"Yes. Did you plan on telling someone?"

"No! It's just a bit overwhelming, realizing the rules are . . . I thought they were immutable."

"They are. But our understanding of them is incomplete, and we like to think our understanding of the generalities extends to all cases. It does not. This belief is the one area in which dragons are as flawed as humans."

"Santana said that?"

"No, that is the wisdom of the Voices."

Gerald stared. *I had no idea you had your own wisdom.*

"Though we give ourselves to serve dragons and the occasional human, there is more to us than that."

"I once thought Santana was reading my mind. I could believe it of you as well."

"Thankfully, no. I have no doubt I would get lost in there or go mad, just as you would reading mine. Your expression told me what you were thinking."

Gerald thought on all he had heard as the bird checked again for interlopers.

"You said Voices served the occasional human. Was Morgan le Fay one?"

"She was. At Argyll's orders. Yesterday's Argyll, not today's."

Gerald grinned at this way of naming the generations. "Was that part of why the sorceress was so hard to kill?"

"It was. Her magic was almost unparalleled, but the dragon blessing made her nearly invincible. It took three dragons attacking at once to kill her, when she was already weakened from fighting the twelve strongest faerie warriors of that age.

"But there is more you need to know. Santana believes today's Argyll breathed blessing on the stump, then breathed fire on it, then blessed it again. That combined with one of le Fay's relics could well produce the crystallized effect and more.

"You know le Fay would at times pour part of herself into the sword when she was facing grave threats or planning perilous deeds. Many dragons—including the Eldest and his circle—believe le Fay probably did this when she realized the dragons were about to kill her. Or even if she suspected they might be capable of doing so.

"With the sword in the stump, today's Argyll's actions would have drawn into the crystallized stump part of whatever the witch left in the sword. Santana believes the rocks he is carrying to the Teeth were pieces knocked off the stump by Argyll. He has no idea who might have planted them about the village. Those small holes were hardly the work of a dragon."

The Voice paused. "Unless he poked them in with a claw!"

Gerald shook his head. "From what I heard, they were close to the village. I doubt he could have done that."

"We must at least have Cuthbert or Kenna see if it is possible. I will send word."

Gerald waited, but the Voice said no more. "Is that all?"

"Yes. No. Gerald, you know that as I am your Voice, I cannot keep secrets from you."

"I did not know that. Has anyone asked or ordered you to?"

"No. I just wanted to make sure you knew. Now you do. Perhaps King Donald should employ a Voice lore master. Cuthbert seems to be shirking his duty on that noble task."

"In his defense, I have been gone a great deal recently. Perhaps he has told the others."

"Perhaps. Please ask. If he has not, peck him on the knee as I would."

Gerald laughed. "We'll see. Thank you. Are you hungry? Thirsty? Would you like a pillow of your own?"

The Voice looked down. "Oh. I thought this was mine. My apologies for the holes in it. I will be nearby if you need me."

"Wait! The sword! How did it get into the tree stump?"

The Voice's eyes went unfocused for a moment. "Argyll must have put it there."

"But it's a dragon sword!"

"Did Santana not carry a sword and hide it in a tree?"

"Oh. Yes. I once meant to ask about that."

"Dragons hate those swords, and in some cases they will get burned just from touching them."

Gerald's eyes widened. "They can burn a dragon?"

"Yes, but if a sword has been used against a dragon without vanquishing it, the dragon is the master of the sword rather than the other way round. And if a sword has not been used against a given dragon, that dragon can safely touch it as well."

"But that would mean Argyll was after the sword, not after Scythia."

"Yes. Santana thinks so, as do his Voices—and yours. Argyll hates you, Lord Gerald. You know that. Since he cannot get at you directly, he is finding ways around the laws that would keep you safe from him. If he causes additional mayhem or hurts others in the process, so much the better. That is his nature, to sow pain. The items he left scattered about Kiergenwald and the fact that Scythia seems neither alive nor dead—all attest to this."

Gerald thanked her and dropped his gaze.

She flew out the window into the courtyard. Gerald was left with a great deal to think about and no one he could discuss it with.

CHAPTER ELEVEN

THE PERILS
OF ACTING NOBLE

Three days later, Tunstall led seven of Folkvar's warriors back to Cair Parn. Folkvar, Lauchlan the Dour, and Gerald's longtime friends Justin and Eoin remained with K'Pene. Gerald spent much of his free time with those a year older than him—Dree, Drinn, Peter, and Thomas. The latter had started talking so much, he was no longer known as The Usually Silent.

One lazy evening when none of them had duty, they lounged around the mess fireplace, trading stories. In the middle of Drinn's tale of confounding Gillian—one of the best tracking teachers—Gerald sat up straight. Drinn stopped and looked at Gerald. "What?"

Gerald rubbed his chin. "I'm sorry. It just suddenly hit me. Where are Aed, Shantaigh, and Afagdu?"

As no one else offered to explain, Drinn sighed and went on. "Afagdu had to return to Glasgow. His uncle Sinclair was robbed and murdered, so his kin needed Afagdu to help with the family business. He's also, from what we hear, working closely with the Glasgow guard to track down those responsible.

"On the plus side, his uncle had just recently sold Eoin's knife and the gold was put aside. It will be here soon."

While happy for Eoin, Gerald found himself responding to the theft and murder. "I wish I could go help Afagdu."

"He has family, and we hear the Glasgow guard are quite good at their jobs. As is Afagdu. He'll do well."

"I know. I would simply like to help him find justice."

"We all would, Gerald."

"Of course. And what of the others?"

Dree sighed. "Aed and Shantaigh just weren't doing that well. Captain Murdoch and the rest felt they were not going to get much better and might be weak links in battles. Aed and Shantaigh had expressed the same feelings to us. King Donald agreed to release them from their promise of service and sent them home."

Gerald felt a bit stunned. Neither of the two had been brilliant at anything, but he hadn't realized they were that weak. "Were they upset?"

"Embarrassed but relieved. And happy to be going home. Neither really got very close to any of us, did they?"

Gerald had to agree this was so.

Drinn declined to finish his story and they all decided to turn in.

Gerald lay awake a long time. *How would I feel if I had been released? I can't even imagine it! Of course, I couldn't have imagined not hating dragons, much less being friends with them, watching out for their interests, and fighting for their lives.* He fell asleep more contentedly than he had expected to.

At noon several days later, K'Pene and her escort returned. During lunch Gerald, Justin, and Eoin caught up on events. The big news for Gerald was that Nain had used fire and claws to dig a cave for Scythia three days before Folkvar's party started back. The human healers took turns spending a day or night there. The faerie healer had not left the cave since he arrived. No one had seen the faerie guards, but Kenna assured everyone that a half dozen were there.

"Why did you remain?" he asked.

Justin answered. "K'Pene and Cynthia were still swapping healer lore. Cynthia took K'Pene out to learn of local herbs and remedies. They had a few in common, but K'Pene surprised Cynthia by showing her uses for thistle she didn't know."

"Like what?"

Eoin laughed. "We weren't privy to details. We just heard bits and pieces."

Immediately after lunch, the three were summoned to the throne room. "Don't worry," Folkvar said with a smile. "It's not bad news!" He would say no more.

A guard waved them in through the open doors. They found King Donald upon his throne. Folkvar joined Murdoch, his fellow lieutenant Donald of Lochlorien, and Torquil the seer in flanking the throne.

"Greetings, warriors!" said the king.

The three young men glanced at each other briefly out of the corners of their eyes. They saluted with their right arms across their chests, then stood formally rigid.

"You may relax," the king continued. "Captain?"

Murdoch stepped forward. "Justin, Eoin, you should know Gerald was offered the title and belt of a warrior several months ago. He declined, wishing to wait until you achieved yours. I suspect he did not want you to know this. Since not long after, while Gerald was away, you were offered the same option, and you both declined until Gerald achieved his, we're telling you all anyway."

The captain's voice became formal. "If you are prepared to swear fealty to the king, present your weapons."

Three swords appeared. The king smiled at Eoin. "No axe this time?"

"All I have is at your service, my king, including both axe and sword."

The captain spoke again. "Repeat after me."

"I . . ." (each said his name) "do solemnly promise . . . to serve King Donald faithfully . . . to render him honor . . . to defend and protect the king and the realm . . . and its people . . . against all enemies . . . human, dragon, or beast."

As he had the day they swore fealty as young warriors, King Donald looked each of them in the eye before speaking again. "I accept your oath. In return for your fealty and two years' service, I will provide you a home here, shelter elsewhere, food, clothes, weaponry, a horse, and whatever else you need during that time. I will be fair, balancing justice and mercy, both to you and through you. Do you so agree?"

As he looked each of them in the eyes, they replied, "Aye, my lord!" When done, the captain spoke. "You are no longer young warriors, but full warriors, with the rights and duties that accompany the title. Remove your sword belts and take those Folkvar gives you."

The belts were identical, but instead of the blank buckle plate of a young warrior, the new belts bore plates with the Argyll coat of arms—a crimson gryphon facing a black dragon above a dark brown Viking longship.

As soon as all three had fastened their new belts, the king and his advisors congratulated them. The young men thanked the king and were dismissed.

Once the doors closed behind them, Justin snorted. "We're quite the set of fools."

"What do you mean?" Eoin asked.

Gerald smirked, sure he knew where this was heading.

Justin shook his head. "If we weren't so noble, we'd have all been warriors months ago."

"Does it really matter?" Gerald asked.

"Easy for you to say, Lord Envoy," Eoin laughed.

"They've had you two scrubbing the mess, have they?"

"Actually," Justin replied, "we were helping teach Aed and

Shantaigh until they left. There are no new young warriors, so there's no one for us to teach."

"Just become the best you can at what you're good at. Did you know Drinn has been giving lessons in tracking and evasion to his elders? Even Gillian?"

That stopped Justin and Eoin in their tracks.

"Are you serious?" Justin demanded.

Eoin nodded slowly. "I knew he had been going out with them a lot. I wondered why. I'd heard a couple of them ask him things like, 'How did you lose Gillian?' I couldn't understand what they meant. Now it makes sense."

Gerald continued. "Right. So do the things you're best at."

Eoin looked at Justin. "Just so. You teach them how to rescue princesses and I'll show them how to get a really ugly knife from a Druid."

"Eoin, you recall Afagdu's uncle Sinclair. Had you heard that he sold your knife?"

Eoin sobered. "Yes. I'll be happy to get the gold, but I was sorry to hear what happened to him."

"I know. What are you two doing this afternoon?"

"We have it off, but our clothes are really starting to stink. Laundry day."

"That's what I did when I got back. I will be on the wall this afternoon. I'll see you after supper."

It began to rain as dusk fell. Gerald was used to rain; it seemed as likely to rain as not most days. The afternoon had been windier than usual, reminding him of dragon rides. The rain hit him like a slap in the face. He thought long and hard about being in a dragon's claw in a rainstorm. When lightning struck one of the peaks nearby, he thought even harder about it.

He could barely wait for Cuthbert to return. They needed to talk.

CHAPTER TWELVE

HIDE & SEEK

It stormed through the night. Gerald fell asleep and woke to thunder. He was therefore surprised to find Cuthbert at breakfast with Murdoch and Folkvar. They were huddled together, speaking in low voices as they ate, so he left them alone. After eating he went to the stables, where he found Dealanach acting restless. "We'll go out soon, girl," he promised, patting her nose as he gave her a carrot.

Having no duties until the afternoon, Gerald went in search of Cuthbert. He had no luck, but noticed the throne room doors were closed. He decided to wait in Cuthbert's office.

There was a large scroll—a map—spread across Cuthbert's desk, with weights on the four corners: a block of glass with what appeared to be the heart of a dragon's eye in its center, an iridescent blue and green quill pen and ink set, a silver goblet with a beautiful bas-relief tree covering the entire exterior, and an intricately worked wire dragon nearly a foot long. The dragon had many bits of white—almost certainly dragon bone—worked into the design, including white eyes that might have been mother of pearl. It was clearly Kenna's work, but on a scale Gerald had not seen. He suspected, by the surfeit of white, that the dragon represented Younger.

He spent a half hour contemplating the map. It seemed

all peaks, forests, barren lands, and water. Gerald could read none of the words—they were in several alphabets, only one of which looked at all familiar. Finally he gave it up as a bad job and went to look out the window. As soon as he did, he heard his name.

He spun around. "Cuthbert! When did you arrive?"

"Late last night," the lore master said, as he came to look out the window. "We left during a break in the rain, but about halfway here it started raining again. Rain doesn't bother dragons, Gerald, but you don't want to be up high in the rain if you can help it when you're moving that fast."

"I know what it felt like last night atop the keep, and what it feels like on a horse running as fast as it can."

"Then you will understand why I plan to see what we can do to have dragon skin available for traveling." Cuthbert frowned. "Why are you laughing?"

"Because that's exactly what I wanted to talk with you about! And we need a way to get in and out easily without sacrificing protection from the elements." He paused. "Wait. If you came last night, what about lightning?"

"Ah, yes, lightning. Gerald, if ever you get the chance, you simply must ride with a dragon through a thunderstorm. It is one of the most marvelous—if terrifying—experiences there is. Rising and falling, banking left and right, sometimes dropping like a rock! Dragons can sense where lightning will be for a few heartbeats before it strikes. This enables them to fly safely through all but the worst thunderstorms. Dragons will not fly in those. When there are too many lightning strikes close together, they cannot see a safe path through. And while lightning will not kill a dragon, it may stun one enough that he may fall and break his wings, legs, or even neck.

"Dragons can tell well before things get that bad and turn back or aside, or go to ground. You are safer with a dragon in a thunderstorm than atop most castles."

"We'll see. And that answers my next question! You are

ahead of me as usual, Cuthbert. But how did you feel when you got here?"

"Be thankful I am not sick. It was certainly cold!"

"No doubt. Have you given any thought to how best we might use the dragon hide for travel? I dislike being tied inside. I was thinking of a frame."

"A frame?"

"Yes, a frame. Something that would give the hide a definite shape, like a very small cave. Ideally it would have a sort of door one could shut. It would probably need to open inward. For a short trip, a blanket would suffice, but for a long one, you would also want a pillow. An extra blanket if cold. And room for a pack."

"A dragon might feel you were making her a beast of burden."

"I would never do that, Cuthbert! The dragons have been offering to carry us. They have been carrying us! But in bad weather, what's the good if we arrive dead? Or too cold and wet to move? Or sick?"

"Those are all excellent points, Gerald. I will ponder this, discuss it with Younger and Nain, and tell you what they think. Meanwhile, what did you think of this map?"

"I can make neither head nor tail of it. What do you think of it?"

"I think it is an excellent map of thoroughly foreign parts, and I hope we get to make use of it soon. I will say no more for now. Did you have any other dragon-related questions?"

"Yes, I do. During our long ago first visit to the safe room beneath the castle, you said you would tell us in our second year of uses for dragon hide. I cannot recall ever hearing more on the subject."

Cuthbert smiled broadly but walked to the window and looked out for a long moment before turning around. He sat in his chair and waved Gerald to a chair across the desk from his.

"Gerald, you are one of the truest dragon lords at Cair Parn. I always put that topic off and wait to see who asks. You can perhaps guess who in the castle asked before, but I will say that no one from your year or Dree's has asked that question until now."

He paused again to collect his thoughts. "Dragon skin has been seldom used, as it is difficult to work. Only recently has it become possible for men to work with it, but with fresh skin being in short supply, we have had little chance to use it."

"What do you mean by fresh skin?"

"A recently deceased dragon. Even a month after a dragon's death, the skin is so hard that it is nearly impossible to work unless specially treated."

"How is it worked? How is it cut, tanned, fastened, and all the rest?"

"A dragon sword will cut it. If the sword vanquished that particular dragon, it will cut with ease. Dragons can rend skin with teeth and claws, but they seldom do so, and I would not like to ask one save in dire need. Only this year we found that a dragon sword heated by dragon fire cuts through dragon skin almost effortlessly."

"That's great! No. Wait. How would you not burn your hand?"

"You need to wrap the hilt in dragon hide. Which means you may need to cut a small piece first with an unheated sword.

"Dragon skin does not need tanning, per se. Instead, someone must beat on it continuously for a day with something very tough such as dragon bone or a dragon sword, until the color lightens. It won't change much, but if you keep a bit of the original for comparison, you can see the difference. Once the color has changed, it will be supple—at least for dragon skin."

Gerald interrupted. "Forgive me, but what does one do about the dragon's blood? Even a few drops could leave a gaping wound on human flesh."

"Very good! One must climb atop the dragon and work carefully. Someone should be nearby with water and salve to wash the blood away and treat burns. It is nigh impossible to get much hide off a dragon without getting burned, but waiting at least two days after death lets most of the blood pool in the lowest parts. Only dragons can safely remove large pieces of skin from a dead dragon.

"The easiest way to poke holes is with a sharpened shard of dragon bone or claw thrice heated by dragon fire. One can then use thin strips of dragon hide through the holes to bind pieces together. Nothing else will hold up. The sturdiest rope will quickly find itself destroyed against the edges of the holes. Chains will last longer but require much larger holes, and will still eventually fail."

Gerald pondered all of this. "How long will a sword remain hot?"

"Just as dragons can produce a fire that will burn indefinitely on wood, they can use that same fire to heat a sword so it stays heated if used continuously against relics. After about five minutes of disuse, the sword cools.

"While you did not ask, I would not recommend even considering the decoration of dragon hide."

"What an abominable thought!"

"Why do you say that, Gerald?"

"It would reduce a dragon's skin to mere commodity. I would no more do that than decorate your skin should you someday die."

"Death comes to us all, Gerald. You know that."

"Of course, but you seem timeless. Had you not assured me you have no faerie blood, I would assume you would outlive me by hundreds, if not thousands of years."

"You are most kind. And thank you for not planning to decorate my skin, although I assume I would no longer care. Have you other questions regarding the skin of dragons?"

"Will they be offended if we bring up the idea of cocoons with frames, and having several available?"

"That will very much depend on how it is put to them, and how we plan to keep men from then deciding on other uses for dragon skin, inviting a demand for yet more skin."

"That's an appalling idea! But now you've said it, I can see men like Urquhart doing just that. They would make shields, window coverings, and more."

Cuthbert checked outside his door and in the hidden stairway behind the wall hanging. He did not bother with the window given their height. He lowered his voice. "There was once a warrior who proposed using dragon hide to protect siege engines, and making fake, dead baby dragons for warriors to hide in to lure dragons to fight."

His voice returned to normal volume. "At the other end of the spectrum, some have proposed the most mundane uses, such as drumheads that never wear out."

Gerald nearly gagged. "What happened to that warrior?"

"Sadly—by which I mean thankfully—he died the next day. He attacked a dragon weakened by a fight with another dragon, but the warrior was less adept than he thought and died almost immediately. His companions decided it was a sign and the matter passed into obscurity."

"Then how do you know it?"

"He announced it to that last dragon he fought. 'Vile wyrm! I shall kill you and use your hide!' and went on to enumerate his plans. The dragon did not even let him finish. You might ask the dragon for the tale some time."

"Who was it?"

"Drachmaeius."

Gerald made no response. He wasn't sure how he felt about the dragon who had caused Samantha's death, but he had no desire to initiate unnecessary conversations with him. Then he realized such interactions might well have helped make

Drachmaeius cavalier about human life. He wasn't sure he wanted to think about this, but knew he must.

After a moment Gerald remembered something. "You said we recently discovered that dragon fire on a dragon sword works well for cutting dragon hide. How did that come about?"

"Do you recall Sterling MacLeod and Hamar?"

Gerald had to think for a moment. "The warrior/healer and the Viking warrior who were with the Eldest after Argyll's attack?"

"The same. When they and I were working with Wandap's hide, the Eldest and Selene were discussing the difficult time we were having and decided to try fire. We knew the sword would likely be too hot to touch, so we spent fifteen minutes cutting a small enough piece from a thin spot to make a wrap for the hilt. The result was quite gratifying."

There was a long pause as Gerald thought all of this over. Then he asked, "How does one get the scales off?"

"They come off easily a few hours after death, but even a little dragon fire will hasten the process."

Gerald could think of nothing else, so he took his leave. Glancing back as he exited the doorway, he saw Cuthbert engrossed in the map, applying some sort of measuring device and scribbling with the quill on another parchment.

CHAPTER THIRTEEN

FLYING CASKETS

The following Monday after breakfast, Lauchlan caught Gerald exiting the mess and informed him the king wished to see him. Gerald followed the warrior silently back to the throne room. As usual, Lauchlan said not a word more than necessary, and the dour expression never left his face. Lauchlan stopped at the open doors and moved into a guard position. The doors closed after Gerald entered.

Donald was in one of his favorite spots, sitting sideways on the windowsill like a carefree teenager, one leg inside and one leg dangling out the window. Cuthbert and Folkvar lounged on nearby stools.

Folkvar grinned. "Greetings, warrior! Murdoch was busy elsewhere, so they dragged me in."

Gerald caught himself and ignored the witty retort that leapt to mind. "Greetings." *Why did I hesitate?* Gerald wondered.

King Donald looked measuringly at Gerald. After a moment he spoke. "You wear the belt well, Lord Gerald, but then you did so long before you had the belt to wear."

Gerald was touched. "Thank you, my lord."

"No titles or honorifics here today, please."

"Very well, my . . . very well!"

The others laughed.

Gerald continued, "But no 'Lord Gerald,' either."

The king blinked. Cuthbert's eyes hinted at a smile while Folkvar snickered.

"Very well, indeed!" Donald relaxed against the window jamb. "Gerald, you have quite the penchant for stirring things up. I recognize in this case that Cuthbert was just as much an instigator. You may soon be on par with him! I leave it to you to determine whether congratulations are in order."

Gerald had learned that the king often spoke like this when marshaling his thoughts on a subject. There would be some truth in it, but it was just part of how Donald handled transitions. Since no reply was needed, Gerald made none.

Donald went on. "The last week has been interesting, to say the least. There have been constant streams of Voices between Cuthbert and a half-dozen dragons . . ."

Cuthbert surreptitiously held up ten fingers.

"Eventually the multiple streams of birds merged into two as dragons gathered together—one set on Mull and one somewhere toward Albania. Both sets of dragons were in on both conversations."

"And what were the conversations, my . . ." Gerald could think of no graceful way to continue the question. He saw a twinkle in the king's eye.

"The question of how to best use dragon hide for travel and the results of a dead sorceress's interference in all our lives."

"That makes sense." Gerald thought for a moment. "Except Mull. Why Mull? The dragons gave that back to clan MacKinnon."

Donald glanced at Cuthbert, who took over. "The Eldest wanted somewhere close to his home, where he happens to have the skin of three dragons. He and the other elder dragons had removed the skin from the deceased and personally seen to the skins' suppleness. None of them knew what the skins were for, but they had visions that such skins would one day be needed."

"They all had the same vision? Is that normal?"

"I do not know that they were identical, Gerald, but they all pointed to the same thing. Such shared visions are not common, but are known to happen every few hundred years."

Gerald sat down. "Why Mull? Why not Dunvegan?"

"First, they wanted somewhere without many humans. While Dunvegan has learned to accept dragons, increased activity would draw more scrutiny, possibly causing problems. The dragons needed humans who could work the skin, as well as smiths and craftsmen to build your flying caskets."

Gerald laughed. "Flying caskets?"

"That was Folkvar's name for them. They will, after all, be carrying precious cargo."

"But a casket is a small box. There would be no room to move, even in a huge casket. I have begun thinking of them as flying caves, albeit tiny caves." Gerald looked pointedly at Folkvar. "And I'm not sure we qualify as jewels."

Folkvar scowled. "Speak for yourself, varlet!"

Cuthbert nodded, conceding the point. "In return, they are providing Mull with additional resources and have offered the use of Voices to carry messages between Kyleakin and Mull. Queen Rhona and her people seem more pleased than not. At first they feared it would set back their preparations for winter, but dragons carried additional people to Mull and cleared the rocks from the entrance to a large cave. As the cave was only accessible from a rocky beach, the dragons laid down a black rock there which they melted with dragon fire, making a better path and a kind of seawall. Thus clan MacKinnon has a safe place to build winter shelters quickly.

"We went back and forth with several dragons on whether this was all a good idea to begin with, and how to work together on it. The most influential dragons are now in agreement.

"Everything we had to send has reached the faerie who are inquiring into the legacy of Morgan le Fay. Selene has replaced Andromeda as one of the dragons who knows the volcano's whereabouts. Santana was allowed to know as well, since he would almost certainly divine it whether he tried to or not. They and two others remain nearby. That information goes nowhere else." He looked around the room, awaiting nods of assent.

Donald resumed speaking. "The point of all this, Gerald, is that you are needed in two places at once. We should like you to go to Mull to work with the dragons and the craftsmen to design, build, and test the caskets—or caves if you like—that you and Cuthbert concocted. Not only did you help invent them, but you have traveled by dragon more than anyone here except Cuthbert, and even he has not traveled in a dragon's mouth, as far as I know."

Cuthbert shook his head sadly. "I fear Gerald has surpassed me there."

"You also know Rhona's commander, Kyla, and you have some sense of the Kyleakin nobles. Murdoch, of course, was with you in the Western Isles and in Kyleakin, but I do not wish to send my captain off again for God alone knows how long. I also do not plan to send Cuthbert. There is much going on in which I need his wisdom and knowledge. So I must again send Gerald off to gather fame, if not fortune."

Gerald gave an exaggerated bow. "I would be honored to be so sent, but the king—or rather the man in the window bereft of title—spoke of sending me to a second place at the same time as Mull."

"No, that poor soul did not! He spoke of the need for you to be in two places at once. The second need is not his, at least directly.

"The high king wishes to send an envoy to the faerie triad investigating le Fay. He sent word via Voice to the Eldest to see what he thought. The Eldest sent word to Kenna, who decided—we do not know whether on her own or not—that the faerie triad were most likely to accept you, but that she must accompany you. We assume that is because her father is one of the triad and because she knows you. King Dugald made it clear this is only a wish, not a command."

Gerald looked back and forth among the three men, thinking but getting nowhere. "Could Kenna not go as the envoy?"

Donald gave Gerald a wry smile. "She is a faerie, a mystery, even a possible danger in the minds of some, and the high king does not know her. Nor does she swear fealty to any mortal. King Dugald was very happy with your work to calm his council and to work things out between the dragons, Urquhart, and Kyleakin. At the present time, it appears to be you or no one, Gerald."

"And what of Mull? Is there anyone who could go there if I do not?"

"That's where I come in," Folkvar replied when Donald did not. "While I have not traveled by dragon as much as you or Murdoch—never mind Cuthbert—I have done it, and I can explain what things are like from a warrior's perspective. I'm not sure how he knows me well enough, but Younger apparently recommended me in the event you could not go."

"It's possible I slipped up and said some good things about you to Younger," Cuthbert said. "He trusts me."

Folkvar snorted. "We will see if he trusts you afterward, if I go!"

Gerald stood and began pacing. No one told him to stop; that seemed to be Murdoch's job. Without realizing it he slowed and walked taller and more formally. "Perhaps I should do both. It worked when we left Edinburgh. I can go to Mull to introduce Folkvar and give my perspective. It should help both dragons and the MacKinnon nobles accept Folkvar quicker. Kyla would accept him, anyway.

"I can go afterward to Albania as the high king's envoy. Where would I meet up with Kenna?"

Donald smiled and raised his eyes toward Gerald, who stopped pacing. "Are you sure you wish to do this, Gerald?"

"It needs to be done. I am willing to do it."

Cuthbert looked curiously at Gerald. "Since I have been back, I have not heard you mention Sally. Are things resolved between you two that leaving with Kenna would not bother her?"

Gerald collapsed back onto his seat. "I have sent a Voice every day. Most bring back at best terse replies. Eoin and Justin tell me she seldom left the house while they were there." Folkvar nodded agreement. "I don't know what to do."

The king looked at Gerald a long time before speaking. "Would you go back home for a time, Gerald, to try to soothe her?"

"I don't know that it would help. K'Pene seems to think it is related to whatever le Fay has done—or whatever someone has done using le Fay's magic. She had no solution. Cynthia, Selene, Druze, Eilidh . . . none of them have been able to help. Sally hasn't listened to me for some time. The best thing I can do is help get answers about the le Fay abominations. At least if the triad has questions, I can tell them what I know.

"So I have changed my mind." He looked intently at Donald. "I am not *willing* to go. I am *determined* to go, unless this council forbids it."

The king and his advisors looked at each other and nodded. Donald spoke. "Then go with our blessings. If my title were here, it might have ordered you to go, so it's as well it was not. I think it much better you chose to go on your own. Thank you, Gerald."

Gerald nodded. "Thank you."

Cuthbert spoke up. "The Eldest has asked Selwyn to take you. Gerald, you may recall him from Lochmaldie. He is the chief faerie lore master for Africa."

Folkvar stared at Cuthbert. "He's the what?"

"Very much the what. Just as we have dragon lore masters, the dragons have human and faerie lore masters. As our cultures and mores vary widely, they tend to limit themselves to regions. The dragons simply gave up on human lore in Europe for two centuries. They said each country would have needed three to five lore masters to even begin to understand the multitude of peoples, but the faerie vary far less.

"At any rate, Selwyn had business here. Albania is more or less on his way home, so the Eldest asked him to help."

"But Mull is the other direction, is it not?" Gerald asked, thinking of the three days or more it would take to ride that far on horseback.

Cuthbert nodded. "Yes, but it is hardly an hour's flight each way. Albania is a full day and night's flight, plus whatever privy and stretching stops you require. Selwyn's home is quite a bit farther than that, but at least he will not have to stop once he drops you and Kenna off.

"Have you further questions?"

"What was Selwyn's business here?"

"You will have to ask Selwyn that."

When neither Gerald nor Folkvar offered more questions, the king reached up and pulled a rope. A gong sounded and the doors swung open. "Titles and honorifics are restored. Lord Gerald, can you be ready to leave after breakfast?"

"I can, my king."

"I, as well," Folkvar added.

"Then make sure Gerald has no other duties today. After you have packed what you need, spend the rest of your time with Cuthbert making sure you all know as much of each situation as possible. And Godspeed."

The king and his counselors had already moved on to other matters before Gerald exited the room.

After breakfast the next morning, Gerald met Folkvar, Cuthbert, and a page Gerald didn't recognize at Cair Parn's main gate. A large, dark gray dragon waited just outside the arrow stones—alternating black and white stones used normally as a stopping point for unexpected visitors, and to let defenders know when attackers were within ideal bowshot. Cuthbert and a page carried thick blankets while Gerald and Folkvar carried their packs as they walked out to Selwyn.

"Cuthbert, why is he out there?"

"He's waiting for us."

Gerald laughed. "Thank you for that bit of enlightenment! Why is he out past the arrow stones?"

"It is a sign of respect, but in the future, that will not be necessary."

A moment later they were close to the dragon, who had deep, dark blue eyes. Cuthbert said, "Greetings, Selwyn. King Donald also greets you. He thanks you for your respect, but wishes you to know you are always welcome inside the arrow stones, whether you are expected or not. You may land out here or atop the keep, as you prefer."

Selwyn answered in a low, rumbling voice Gerald vaguely recalled from the dragons' moot at Lochmaldie. "Greetings, dragon lords, Folkvar. And my thanks to Lord Donald. Are you ready to go?"

"We are," Folkvar said.

Fiery laughter escaped the dragon's lips. "I expected the high king's envoy to reply."

"Alas, poor Gerald is for the nonce a mere warrior in my charge. He does not become envoy until he departs Mull. But unlike the hapless Murdoch, I will not travel with Gerald, but remain at Mull as King Donald's envoy. A lower position than Gerald's, but safely out of his reach."

Gerald snorted. "And a good thing, as I need someone to polish the Argyll coat of arms on my belt, lest the triad forget where I call home."

Cuthbert glared at Selwyn. "Do not encourage them or we shall be here all day and King Donald will have all of our heads on pikes outside the mess. Away with you!"

Folkvar laughed, slapped Cuthbert on the back, and took the blanket from him. Gerald gripped forearms with Cuthbert and accepted his blanket from the page. Wrapping themselves as securely as they could, they walked closer to Selwyn. Seconds later they were in the air.

"Keep those blankets tight," Selwyn called. "It's colder and wetter where we go."

CHAPTER FOURTEEN

DANCING ON AIR

Gerald soon noticed that Selwyn did not fly south to get the sun behind him on his way to Mull. He'd ask about that later; there were more pressing questions at the moment.

"Selwyn, what brings you so far from home?"

"So far? It is but two and a half day's flight."

Folkvar laughed. Gerald could see it but not hear it over the wind. Folkvar yelled, "Remember, Gerald, that when he says day, he means a day and a night. So he's talking about roughly sixty hours non-stop."

Gerald tried to imagine running even six hours non-stop. His legs ached thinking about it. He laughed to himself. "Fine! So what brings you next door?" Trails of dragon laughter threatened to set his blanket on fire. The men would have to watch diligently for that.

Selwyn's booming voice was even easier to hear in flight than the other dragons'. "I wished to speak with the Eldest of unrest among some dragons to the east because of the truce with men here and in Africa. It would have taken more than a week each way for Voices to carry words one direction. While here, I also met with K'Pene away from the castle to bring her news from home. She introduced me to Kenna, that I might add to my knowledge of the faerie."

"So you live near K'Pene's home?"

"Not as you would think of near. Africa is much bigger than what men call Europe. I live to the east in Abyssinia. K'Pene's people live on the other side of Africa, on the coast of the Kongo. That is a day and a half's travel for me."

Gerald gave up trying to fathom the distances involved. "And did you learn much of the faerie from your talks with Kenna?"

"I was only able to spend two hours with her, so we barely began to realize what we do and do not know. But understand this, Lord Gerald. There are at least a dozen distinct human cultures—with more cultures within cultures—in Africa, but that land has only three faerie cultures, and they are not as different as most human cultures are. While the faerie in Scotland are different from any I have known, they resemble what I have heard generally of European faeries, and I recognized major traits.

"The variety in humanity is both its beauty and, given the state of the world, its danger. You tend to see one another in terms of 'us' and 'them'. You draw lines and build walls around what you know and like. You label everything and everyone else 'other'. Some of you embrace the other, but far too many fear it, hate it, wish to stay separate, or even destroy it."

Folkvar yelled, "And dragons do not do this?"

"Clearly we do. If nothing else, the case of Argyll and his band of rebels would indicate this truth. But we seldom do so nearly to the extent humans do. The same is true for the faerie and the various myths and legends that avoid human contact."

"Myths and legends?"

"So you have deemed them and thus they refer to themselves

in relation to you. The Ghillie Dhu and the one Gerald calls the lady of the loch, for instance. These are real but have learned to avoid mankind after many battles, wounds, and deaths."

Neither of the men knew how to respond so they hung silently in the dragon's claws, occasionally trying to reposition themselves without falling. Selwyn recognized their problem. "Do not fear! Move about as you need to. I will not drop you; I have much practice with prey! But do not lose your blankets."

It was definitely getting windier. Selwyn was buffeted by gusts more frequently. Clouds hung in front of them, but the coast was in sight.

"We are not far. I believe we will beat the storm, but just barely. I am going to let the wind carry us out west a little to approach into the wind. It will make the landing easier and the flight more enjoyable." They flew in silence for a short time. "Can you see the small islands just in front of us?" Selwyn called over the wind.

"Yes!" Gerald called back. He could not hear whether Folkvar answered.

"That is Lunga, the isle where Goyim's murderers now live."

"But I see fire! They are not far from Mull, and there was supposed to be nothing light enough to float on that island!"

"When the final supplies were being left, their leader complained they would die without fire. The Eldest sent a large, rotting log. It was so fragile it broke into three pieces on the trip and part of it fell into the sea. Once on land, it was set ablaze with everlasting fire. It will not go out so long as any there live. If they try to use it in the ocean, it will come apart and be useless."

Selwyn veered left and right more than usual, leaving Gerald feeling somewhat queasy. Twice with particularly strong gusts, they flew in a large loop. They bounced up and down. Gerald saw a group of panic-stricken birds fly past. Selwyn's fiery laughter reached after them, causing them to scatter.

Gerald finally relaxed near the end of the flight. Selwyn

landed near a beach, well away from human activity. "I have not been here before so they will not recognize me. But the Eldest has Voices, some of whom should be here shortly. Lord Gerald, will you send word?"

"Yes, Selwyn. Thank you for the ride. Folkvar, where will you be staying?"

Selwyn moved a few steps and began drinking great gulps of saltwater. Folkvar made a face; he had not realized dragons did this. "Lord Gerald, we should use titles here. From what you have told me of the MacKinnon nobles, this likely matters. As for housing, I trust Kyla has made arrangements. Else I shall find space in this great cave I have heard about."

"Voices!" Gerald saw several flying their way. Selwyn moved back beside the warriors. Four Voices arrived. "Greetings, lore master, dragon lord, and warrior! The Eldest thanks you for coming so quickly. We have told Kyla of your arrival. She asks that you come quickly to the cave mouth. You may follow us, if Selwyn can fly that slowly."

"If necessary, I will walk."

"We are not *that* slow."

"Then we shall fly. Voices are slow, but only irritatingly, not impossibly."

A minute later they were landing on a beach again. A huge cave mouth gaped nearby. A small party stood waiting.

"Lord Gerald!" Kyla came to Gerald as soon as he was free of Selwyn's claw, before he was free of his blanket.

"Kyla!" They embraced. In but a few days, they had become fast friends in Kyleakin. Gerald felt a twinge of guilt and then irritation as he thought of Sally and how she might react. *What is wrong with her?* He caught himself. *Morgan le Fay's magic— not Sally—is the problem.*

Folkvar managed not to gape at Kyla, but Gerald could tell he was surprised the leader of the Mull hold was so young. She was twenty-two but looked eighteen. Gerald grinned but before he could introduce them, Selwyn spoke. "Lord Gerald, you must address the lady properly."

Gerald was confused. *Lady Kyla? Commander?* He thought furiously. "Wait! Which dragons have you dealt with here, Kyla?"

"Here? Nain, Younger, the Eldest, and now . . ." She raised an eyebrow.

"Selwyn, at your service."

Gerald bowed. "My apologies, Lord Kyla. I should have realized that you are a dragon lord."

Kyla grinned mischievously. "The Eldest started addressing me that way shortly after we met. Two of my nobles are convinced I must have killed at least three dragons. They refuse to be disabused of the notion. But the introductions are incomplete."

"My apologies, lord commander. This most noble dragon was so determined to correct my manners that he rode roughshod over my intentions. This is Folkvar, a fabled warrior descended from Vikings, perilously close to becoming a dragon lord himself, and envoy from King Donald of Argyll. He will be staying to work with the dragons, the smiths, and anyone else necessary to bring about the wee caves the dragons have graciously offered to carry us in.

"Folkvar, this is Lord Kyla, one of Queen Rhona of MacKinnon's most notable commanders, a warrior of renown and a noble lady in her own right. Like you, she has a quick wit. Unlike you, she can dance the legs off a nest of spiders. If I am correct, she speaks for the queen in all things here."

Kyla clasped forearms with Folkvar, impressing him with her grip. She gestured to the man and woman closest behind her. "These are William and Heather, two of Queen Rhona's most trusted advisors. You will meet the other nobles quite soon. Lord Gerald, you will recognize them, but I do not know if you spoke at length with any of them. Tavish did not come because he no longer craves adventure. Mirren, of course, preferred to stay at home and increase his power as other nobles came here, but Captain Ghillie's warriors overhear or ferret out Mirren's plans, and the man finds himself frustrated at every turn."

Gerald laughed, but then found himself shivering.

"My apologies," Kyla said. "Let's get you into the cave and to a fire. You have been through a gale, and a chilly gale at that."

"What of Selwyn?" Folkvar asked.

"He would fit, but I fear we have crowded the entrance more than we ought," Kyla said.

Selwyn replied, "Unless you need me, I will visit the Eldest until tomorrow. What time should I return, Lord Gerald?"

Gerald glanced at Kyla and Folkvar. Both shrugged. "Midmorning, I guess. I wish to see what they have done but we need to return quickly, and the work here is mainly Folkvar's."

Kyla and her crew watched with some gratification the expressions on Gerald's and Folkvar's faces as they approached the cave. The mouth was over forty feet high and the cave was enormous. Several dozen people were inside. Near the entrance, some were cooking and eating. Torches stood every two yards along the wall for fifty feet into the cavern's depths. Beyond that—on the edge of darkness—Gerald saw what looked like a wide curtain about ten feet high. Poles supported a rope every few feet so it didn't sag too much.

Kyla led them to the largest fire, where a dozen people ate. A few eyed them curiously.

"Beyond yon curtain are the sleeping quarters," Heather explained. "Right now only a few guards and some young children are asleep."

Folkvar looked around. "If people sleep here, where are the smiths and craftsmen?"

"They have set up near the cliffs atop the caves," William replied. "Thus the sound carries away and we hear nought in here. It's hike enough to the top the children won't get into things when no one is about."

Kyla directed someone to carry the visitors' packs to her quarters for the time being. "William will take you up the cliffs to see where the craftsmen are and discuss your work." Her face fell. "I must go to Dervaig to check on progress. It was our original settlement, and we only moved some people here because Dervaig will not be ready when winter hits. The dragons tell us it will be here within two weeks. At least it will not freeze here on Mull. Be that as it may, I will go to Dervaig and be back well before night fall."

Gerald glanced out of the cave's mouth toward the sea. "It's raining."

"As it oft does. I will still go, and have a better time of it on horseback than you will going up the cliffs!" Kyla took her leave and went to gather her party. Heather accompanied her. William beckoned Gerald and Folkvar toward Kyla's quarters. They changed into dry clothes and carried their wet ones to hang on lines and poles near one of the fires. Then William started toward the cave's mouth.

"Come along, Lord Gerald," Folkvar intoned. "It's a shame we aren't dragons. Rain wouldn't faze us and we'd have plenty of fire."

The climb turned out to be less tenuous and slippery than expected. Stonemasons had cut steps until the dragons stepped in to carve them far more quickly. Spikes protruded from the rock face at waist height with ropes strung along them. After strong gusts nearly knocked them down, Gerald and Folkvar held onto the ropes for the rest of the climb.

There was a tiny village above the caves. A group of large boulders, clearly placed by the dragons, protected it from the worst of the winds. While there were two small bunk houses, the dozen other crude buildings were all for work. William introduced the visiting warriors to the master craftsmen and smith. After a brief tour of the buildings, they all sat down to discuss the flying caves at a table in the crafts hall. They were met with parchment, piles of metal, pieces of dragon hide, and more. Gerald found he really had nothing new to share since

Cuthbert and the dragons had already explained things quite well. They got to work at once on what the craftsmen had tried and why these things might or might not work.

Lunch was delivered. There was a steady stream of craftsmen and craftswomen in and out with questions, ideas, reports, or simple curiosity and a few minutes to spare. They might have worked through dinner had not a messenger come to say that Kyla insisted they sup in the cave.

The rain had stopped but water still ran down the steps, and the descent was noticeably slicker. Niall, the head of the craftsmen, grumbled that dragons were quite useful, but far less so when dragon lords were scarcer. He mentioned several tasks he'd like to set the dragons to, starting with flaming the steps dry. When they reached the bottom of the steps, Folkvar turned to face Niall with a smile.

"Niall, would you mind restitching my pack?"

Niall blinked. "I suppose I could have someone . . ."

"And my boots need new soles. And my sword could use sharpening. And I'd like a chair by the fire. And one for Lord Gerald, while you're at it. And, let's see. . . . We'd like some silver bowls to eat from, preferably with six dragons worked around the outsides. Can you have that done today?"

The gray-haired master grew red in the face. "What are you playing at, man? We're not your servants, here for your every whim! Are all dragon lords this arrogant?"

Folkvar's smile grew. "But that is how you spoke of the dragons, as if you wished they were your slaves, or at least your apprentices. But they are not our servants. They are our friends and allies, as free and proud as any of us. Have a care what you say around them. They will not harm you if they feel insulted, but neither are they likely to be as helpful as they have been."

Niall stared. He clearly hadn't considered things that way. After a moment he nodded and averted his gaze.

Folkvar added, "And I am not a dragon lord."

"Yet!" Gerald added.

They were soon seated close together on benches at a long table. Kyla apologized for the crowding. "There will be another table ready in a day or two after more lumber arrives."

The table was piled with lamb as well as greens and tubers Gerald did not recognize. The food was blander than he was used to, but that didn't stop him.

Kyla did not discuss her day in Dervaig, saying only that it was a boring business. "But what of things at home, Gerald? You have spoken not one word of it."

Gerald thought for a minute, chewing a tough bit of meat. "Things overall are well. We had a visit from the rebel dragon's leader, which wreaked a bit of mayhem and put Sally's teacher out of action. There was some sickness and some mystery, but most things are back to normal."

Kyla searched Gerald's face and apparently heard his unspoken plea, for she asked no more. Instead she regaled them with tales of Tavish, the oldest nobleman among the MacKinnons. The youth loved playing tricks on him; he was just too easy a target. Still, he was well loved and the tricks were not malicious. Folkvar, in turn, told them stories his mother had told him of the Norse, including the Vikings. Gerald caught Kyla up on Urquhart. She had heard only that there had been a rebellion and that the king and his men had been banished.

"I wondered that I heard nothing of the rebels being punished," she said. "Although, having met King Urquhart and his top men, I was hardly surprised to hear something happened. But to attack the dragons who brought you, and who came to aid his people at his insistence? The man is insane!"

No one argued the point.

Kyla went on. "But you said they are on Lunga? That is not far, and there are smaller islands between there and here. The closest island is perhaps two miles from Mull, if that."

Folkvar replied, "The dragons assure us there is nothing on

that barren island but what they provided for the prisoners, and that none of it will float. So unless a man can swim that far, none will leave the island. I seriously doubt more than one or two would even attempt it. Though they lived by Loch Ness, they are land dwellers. Swimming in the ocean is daunting for those unused to it. The waves can be quite large and there are dangerous beasts. From what I saw in the air, there were treacherous shallows between some of those isles. A wave might drop you onto a reef and rip half your skin off."

"You sound as if you have experience, Folkvar."

He smiled. "My mother made sure I knew both boats and swimming as part of my heritage, but I am no seaman. Boats do not bother me but I would not want to try to go far in one, especially on a day like today. I have not swum more than a quarter mile on the open sea since I was a child. I might survive yon swim, but I would not try it unless I had no choice."

After supper, Kyla invited Gerald and Folkvar to a much smaller table near the farthest cave wall. "This is my office. There are obviously no walls, but none come here unbidden save my advisors. They will not be here this evening unless there is something urgent. Gerald, can you tell me now what you would not at the supper table?"

Gerald sat down, elbows on the table, chin cupped in his hands. Looking into the distance, he told Kyla of all that had happened. He made clear what he personally remembered and what he had been told. He noted what was known and what was guessed. He left out certain details—mainly where things were being taken and that the faerie were the investigators. Folkvar nodded approvingly.

Kyla asked but a few questions. "You do not tell me everything but I assume you have good reason. Gerald, I am sorry this has befallen you! I wish I could help, but given that the dragons have nothing to offer and your healers are helpless, I know not what I could do.

"Well. It is late and I have work. You may do as you will. William can show you your quarters." She beckoned the advisor. "William, please go to my quarters and have their packs brought out." She turned to her guests. "I did not expect anything to happen but had them put in my chamber, since it is always guarded."

"Thank you, lord commander," Folkvar said as he bowed his head. "You are most gracious."

"You are welcome, lord envoy. As are you, Lord Gerald."

"Thank you."

William laughed. "You two seem to have gotten it backwards."

Folkvar assumed a pained expression. "These youth live to mock us, William."

William looked pointedly at Kyla, then back at Folkvar. "You do not know the half of it, Folkvar."

Gerald and Folkvar ended up in a small, curtained room set a little apart from everything. They talked quietly for an hour about the day before going to sleep.

Gerald awoke in the middle of the night to the sound of snoring. Folkvar's loud, regular snores were supported by a dissonant symphony of snores, snorts, wheezes, and the occasional cough from around the cave. Gerald was used to the barracks, but this was noisier. Not only did the cave hold more people, but sounds echoed off the high ceilings and distant walls hidden in darkness. The surf pounded outside. Worse, Gerald was haunted by the feeling he had dreamed something important, but he could not recall one iota of his dreams.

He wandered to the cave mouth, where a guard directed him to a private place he could relieve himself. Once back in his bed, he expected the noises to keep him awake. He fell asleep almost immediately and his dreams were peaceful.

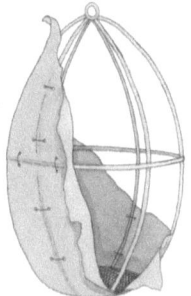

CHAPTER FIFTEEN

HATCHING AN EGG

S ince the cave's mouth faced west, its depths were only marginally lighter in the morning. Reflected light from the sea helped. Once the general noise level woke the envoys, Gerald stepped outside to look for Selwyn. After the cave's darkness, even the gentle morning light was overwhelming. When Gerald finished blinking, he found a Voice at eye level on a boulder a few feet away.

"Greetings, Lord Gerald. Selwyn and the Eldest hope you slept well."

"Thank you, I did. And I hope they, and you, slept well also."

"They talked throughout the night. The Eldest slept last week and Selwyn expects to sleep once he is home. I awoke to a new day, so I must have slept well."

"You do not dream?"

"Not as I understand you mean it, no. To sleep well means I was not eaten, mauled, crushed, or blown away in a storm."

"Those sound good to me! Where is Selwyn? Is the Eldest coming?"

"The Lord of the Western Isles has urgent business and cannot see you this trip, which he sorely regrets. He says that if you go to Albania, you must beware. He sees your time there like a series of dreams—some good, some bad, some that will make you question your sanity.

"Selwyn will have something to say on the matter when he sees you. He is eating and would like to know when he should arrive."

"I am hoping to spend some time with Lord Kyla. Midmorning should still work."

"The smiths also have some questions Lord Gerald." Folkvar had walked up quietly.

"Very well, call it noon. Are they ready now, Folkvar, or may we eat first?"

"They will have breakfast ready in the crafts hall any minute now."

Gerald bowed to the Voice. "Thank you."

The Voice bowed and spread his wings. The early morning breeze blew him toward the sea. He rode it a moment, looped and dove to get a fish, and then flew northeast, joined almost immediately by three more Voices.

"Folkvar, have you noticed that the Voices' behavior is changing, or is at least different here?"

"Yes, I have. I think the other three were keeping watch in the air, much as dragons would. If you watch closely, they only travel together for a moment, then spread out. I think they come together just long enough to hear the message being sent, then go their separate ways, as is their wont."

That made sense. Gerald followed Folkvar up the steps to the crafts hall.

Two hours later, they had a plan for what Niall had dubbed a traveling egg. It was more or less egg shaped with a flattened base. On the ground, the egg would rest on the flat end. For flight, the egg could stay upright or lie down, depending on the traveler's need. "Assuming the dragons can hold it upright. It might be too big for their claws," Niall added.

Gerald smiled. "If you made it large enough for a giant

of a man to stand upright with room to spare that might be a problem, but for the size we have chosen, the tallest men would not be able to fully stretch out. I don't think the height will be an issue for full-grown dragons."

Gerald looked the plans over one last time. The base was a steel rod bent into a circle two and a half feet across. This circle contained a wooden lattice covered by a straw pad inside a wool case. Six steel rods grew upward from this base. They spread out to four feet across halfway up, where another steel hoop was attached. They then curved inward, meeting at the peak like a simple bird cage. A small steel loop sprouted from the top to suspend it while being worked on, or to hoist out of the way when not in use.

A piece of dragon skin would be cut to fit inside, with pairs of holes every foot along each rod for hide strips to tie the hide shell to the frame. Along one side would be two larger holes, one at the top and one at the bottom, with flaps that could be tied shut. These were not only for getting in or out, but for looking out and communicating during flight. Folkvar wasn't sure they would be easy to manipulate in the air, but they could test that when the first egg was built.

Two large, thick blankets would be provided per egg. These were to protect passengers from bruising by the steel rods; dragon hide alone would not protect against that.

When Selwyn arrived heading for the beach, Gerald waved him up to the cliff tops. He landed near the crafts village, where Gerald introduced him to a nervous Niall. Between Niall, Gerald, and Folkvar, they described the traveling egg.

"That is not how I would build it," Selwyn said, "but it sounds worth trying, a good first effort."

Niall looked livid, but Gerald was curious. "How would you build it, Selwyn?"

"Much larger, Lord Gerald. I could never fit into the egg you describe."

Niall managed a laugh just before Gerald quit laughing. The

dragon lord continued, "I was not planning to leave just yet, Selwyn."

"I know, Lord Gerald, but I am through eating so I came. I would speak more with Folkvar and master Niall about the egg while you finish your business."

"Very well. If you will have one of your Voices nearby, I will send word when I am ready."

"There is no need for poaching!"

Gerald spun around to find three Voices staring up from the ground. "Poaching?"

"Yes, Lord Gerald. We are your Voices. We are here at your disposal."

Gerald reddened. "I still have not got used to that. Of course you are here and available. My sincerest apologies." He bowed, ignoring the laughter from Selwyn's lips.

Niall, not knowing what it was, jumped back with an alarmed look. Folkvar quietly explained dragon laughter.

"Very well," Gerald said. "I will send my Voices when I am ready."

Selwyn bowed. Gerald clasped forearms with Folkvar and Niall. "Unless you come down soon, I will not see you again. I look for a good report soon on the eggs!"

"As do I on numerous issues," Folkvar replied.

"Safe travels," said Niall.

Gerald descended the steps, stopping twice on landings to let men and women carrying heavy loads pass on their way up.

He found Kyla in her office poring over lists and a map with Heather. He caught Kyla's eye, then went to his room to get his pack. He wandered back to a table and sat on a bench to wait. Ten minutes later, Kyla came over. "Do you have time to talk?" he asked.

"Of course."

Gerald carried his pack to her office and dropped it against the wall. Heather barely glanced up from her lists. "Lord

Gerald," she murmured in greeting. "Heather," he responded quietly. He and Kyla walked out to the beach.

"It's a glorious day," she sighed happily.

Gerald looked around. Heavy clouds were rolling in, the wind was picking up, and the waves were crashing loudly against the rocks. His expression must have given him away.

"Do you not like the sea, Lord Gerald?"

"I've not seen it much, but I generally like it calmer and the skies less cloudy. That way I can see farther. And the waves are loud!"

"They are. The sea is powerful. He is neither friend nor foe but what you make of him. One who thinks the sea is tame will not last long. But if one respects his power, one can live at peace and enjoy the sea for what he is."

"You speak of him as a person."

"The sea has personality, so it is easier to think of him as alive." She laughed. "I cannot explain why. I do not think of the wind or the sun or the land that way, but I love the sea. Not as I love my people, but I love the sea."

They walked along the beach and eventually sat on a large piece of driftwood. Only then did Gerald notice warriors twenty yards away.

Kyla smiled. "Queen Rhona said to take no chances, whether with dragons or pirates. They are seldom much farther away than that. But you did not come to speak of my warriors or the sea. What is on your mind, Gerald?"

"I know not what to do about Sally." He went over recent events again. "Still she sends little by Voice or letter. I hear she leaves the house only when she must."

"And what have you been counseled?"

"To do whatever I can to destroy le Fay's magic. And that makes sense, but there should be more I can do."

"It seems that unless you go home and take her elsewhere— which might require force—there is nought you can do. From what I have heard, taking her away by force might harm her irrevocably."

"What have you heard?"

"Everything my healers and old women could tell me, all I could get from the Eldest by Voice."

"The Eldest?"

"He came here when the dragons were first bringing supplies. He left Voices and said I might ask him anything. So I asked him last night after I had heard your story. But I heard nothing else new."

Gerald spoke slowly, as if mesmerized by the waves. "I had a dream last night. I could not recall it after I woke, but I was troubled. I still recall none of it, but when I try, I feel lost and alone, as if Sally were gone."

"I would talk with your friend Kenna and with the healer who found the stones. And King Donald's seer. You should probably not mention to Sally that you spent time alone with me. At least until she is out from under whatever bewitchment has her in its grasp."

Gerald agreed. They sat and discussed Kyla's plans for Mull until a Voice landed in front of them. "It is time to depart."

Gerald raised an eyebrow. "Are you handling my appointments now?"

"Someone must, but this message came from Selwyn."

"If the two of you agree, then who am I to argue?"

"You are learning," the Voice replied.

"We will come now."

The Voice let the wind carry him a bit, then turned to head toward the cave.

"Do all the Voices do that here?"

"Do what, Gerald?"

"Let the wind knock them about as they get going."

"Some do and some do not. I have not decided if it is a game they play or if it serves some purpose. They're interesting, these Voices."

"Like the dragons they speak for."

"In different ways, but yes."

Soon they were at the cave entrance. William and Heather waited with Selwyn and a small crowd of curious onlookers. Gerald's pack was between Heather and William. Two guards held a large bundle Gerald recognized as dragon skin.

"Are you ready, Lord Gerald?" Selwyn rumbled.

"I am. Farewell, Lord Kyla." Before he could say more, she had embraced him strongly but briefly.

"Farewell, Lord Gerald. Go with the blessing of clan MacKinnon and know you will ever have a place here on Mull should you need it."

"Thank you, Lord Kyla." He grasped her forearm once more. "And blessings upon you and all your people, both here and back on Skye."

As he spoke the words, he felt a jolt in his arm. Kyla pulled away looking strangely at her arm, her face glowing faintly. A murmur went through the crowd. Gerald thought he caught the word "faerie" at least twice. His arm felt heavy, as if remembering the night it pulled sword from stump. Gerald turned, picked up his pack with his shield arm, and walked to Selwyn. Someone brought him a blanket. Guards helped wrap the dragon skin around him after he donned the blanket. Selwyn picked him up, rumbled a goodbye to the crowd, and they were off.

On the beach below, everyone watched dragon and envoy rise until they disappeared into a cloud. Kyla turned to watch the sea for a moment. As the others dispersed to their tasks, Heather joined Kyla.

Standing quietly for a minute, Heather looked around to be sure no one was near before speaking.

"Did I not know Lord Gerald was handfasted, I would think

my lady was considering him as a possible husband. And of course he is yet young."

Kyla gazed slowly around before responding. "Since he is handfasted, I do not let my mind go there. And I wish Lord Gerald and Sally nothing but good. If things stood otherwise, I would not be averse to such a course. Age is not everything, and Lord Gerald walks in wisdom and action well beyond his years. Yet things do not stand otherwise. I am not smitten, if that is your concern."

"I was not actually concerned, but I am even less inclined to be now."

Kyla laughed. "Good. Let us get back to work."

Heather looked closely at Kyla and nodded approval. "The glow is gone."

Kyla started. "The glow?"

"When he spoke his blessing, you glowed. You did not blush. You glowed. It was very strange."

"Heather, I think you must be seeing things."

"Perhaps, but William saw it as well, and from the reactions of those around us, we were not alone. The word 'faerie' was used."

"That's ridiculous. Gerald is no more faerie than you or I."

"There are those who have wondered about you, commander. You are rather extraordinary."

Kyla snorted. "So is Queen Rhona."

"Hmph. Such people have other words for her. But they still serve her, so no harm done."

Kyla glanced up before heading back to the cave. "I wish them well, in this weather especially. May they arrive home before any storm."

CHAPTER SIXTEEN

AN ELEGANT SOLUTION

Watching the MacKinnon settlement shrink behind them, Gerald asked, "Selwyn, what did you really think of the traveling egg?"

"I haven't seen one, so I don't know. It seems a good first try. There are likely flaws or things that could be improved, but the concepts seem sound. I have no doubt Folkvar and master Niall will work through any problems. Do you not have confidence in them?"

"I do. I simply wondered. I assumed you would have pointed out any glaring errors."

They flew on in silence a few minutes before Selwyn spoke again. "There is a storm coming. You will be safely at Cair Parn before it arrives, but you may not want to leave until tomorrow. And you will undoubtedly wish strongly for a traveling egg before we arrive at the Teeth."

"The flight will take a full day? As in noon to noon, or whenever we leave?"

"More or less. Longer, the more you need to alight to move about and deposit fewmets and such."

"Fewmets! I may have Voices, but I am not a dragon." Gerald thought for a long moment. "We can probably make do with three stops if I don't drink too much. And thank you for thinking of the skin. It's much more comfortable than flying in just a blanket in this weather."

"Thank the Eldest when you get a chance. He thought of it."

They flew on in silence. Gerald had no idea what Selwyn was thinking, but his mind wandered between what might lie ahead in Albania and what was happening in Kiergenwald. He desperately hoped he could do something that would help Sally and Scythia. *And keep others from ever having to deal with Morgan le Fay again. Those long dead should not be a problem!*

Gerald got to the nearly empty mess for a late lunch just before the storm hit. Justin and Eoin joined him at the table nearest the fireplace. As they sat down, Gerald laughed.

"What?" his friends asked at the same time.

"I was thinking, 'Poor Selwyn!' Which is blather of course. A dragon is no more bothered by wind, rain, or cold than we are here in the castle by this fire."

"True," Justin agreed. "They have staunch hide."

"And carry their own fire wherever they go," Eoin noted.

"And they are used to the wind," Gerald added. "Their usual flight is the speed of a light gale, and I understand they can fly much faster than that, especially in a dive."

"Can they outfly hawks?" Justin wondered.

"You should ask one," Gerald replied.

Eoin laughed, nearly spitting his drink on Gerald's food. "You can ask. You're the one who spends so much time among them!"

"I shall," was all Gerald said before diving back into his stew.

They sat and talked long after Gerald finished eating, until they were chased out by a girl insisting she needed to clean the mess. They went to their barracks and sharpened weapons until Peter appeared midafternoon. "The King wishes Gerald to come at once. His friends may accompany him."

They exchanged glances and stood. Gerald reached for his pack, but Peter said, "You can leave it for now." The four of them ran across the courtyard, getting fairly wet in the process.

With a storm raging, the king was not sitting in his window. In fact, the shutters were barred. He sat on the bench beneath the window, with Cuthbert, Murdoch, Torquil, and Kenna nearby. Justin and Eoin exchanged a look. This many advisors usually meant something big was happening.

"Welcome back, Lord Gerald," the king said. "What news from Mull? I was expecting Voices, but it appears a storm got in their way."

"Lord Kyla sends greetings and thanks."

"Thanks? Does she think Folkvar a gift?"

Gerald grinned at the thought of Folkvar wrapped in ribbon, a bow upon his brow. "No, my king, but the additional task of designing and building the traveling eggs brought them more people, and more help from the dragons, as well as more provisions. They are better off than before. And the dragons opening up the cave for them was a godsend."

"Traveling egg?"

"Because of the shape decided upon, that was what Niall—their master craftsman—called what we named a wee cave. Would you like me to explain the design?"

"You can explain it to Murdoch and Cuthbert later."

Gerald nodded. Then he looked to his right. "My king said the Voices had not arrived, yet I see three Voices sitting in this room and I do not believe any of them are mine." He nodded to the Voices, who bowed back.

Cuthbert now spoke. "The high king had sent word to the Eldest of his plan to send you to Albania. The Eldest sent word to Selene, who waited near the Teeth. Selene flew and spoke with the triad and with a local dragon named Constance. They sent introduction to the local ruler, who said you are welcome, but she can spare no help or guards at the moment as her neighbors are threatening her lands. Selene asked Constance—in the name of the Eldest and on behalf of the triad—to bring three Voices back to us with this information. Constance carried the Voices in his mouth the whole way here.

"There is an old barracks available that Selene says is only a short flight to the triad's lair. King Dugald proposes to send a small force of twelve men there to stay with the envoys. He asked if we wished to send warriors as part of this force. If we do, Murdoch suggested we offer Justin and Eoin the chance to go. Kenna was opposed to this plan until this morning." Cuthbert looked at her and waited for her to take up the thread.

"When I arrived this morning, Torquil met me at the gate. He had dreamed three times last night that Gerald and I were caught unawares by a small army and taken captive or killed. Then he dreamed he met me at the gate and told me this. When he awoke, even though it was barely daylight, he rushed to the gate and there I was. So it might be best if we do not go alone."

Now Murdoch spoke. "We were trying to decide how best to do this. It would take between three and four weeks on horseback. We could have dragons take everyone, but that would require a half dozen dragons if we purchased horses there—if we could. We could ask for more dragons to carry our horses, but I was not sure the horses would be worth anything upon arrival, even should they not die of fright.

"But Kenna assures us she can put the horses to sleep for the trip and wake them in a calm state upon arrival. Ivor says he has a sleeping draught that will let the men sleep most of the way, eliminating the need for stopping en route. King Donald has agreed to this plan."

King Donald resumed speaking. "King Dugald said we could send up to half the force. Murdoch would like to send six warriors from Argyll with you and Kenna. Do Justin and Eoin wish to go?"

The two warriors looked at each other. Justin nodded at

Eoin, who spoke up. "When would we leave? Do we know for how long? What will we do there?"

Murdoch replied, "You would leave the day after tomorrow. You would stay until Gerald's job as envoy is done. You would be there as part of King Dugald's garrison to protect his envoys. You would avoid joining in others' battles if at all possible, but as guests of the local ruler, you might be called upon to help repel invaders. That would be up to the garrison captain, who would be one of the high king's warriors. Argyll's warriors would report to Donald of Lochlorien as their captain, and he would report to the high king's captain."

The two looked at each other again before Justin spoke. "We would be honored to serve the king this way."

Donald smiled. "You will also be serving King Dugald and his envoy. In fact, the envoy would be in charge."

Gerald could tell by his friends' faces that this had not occurred to them. They looked at him with a bit of awe. Finally Justin said, "Well, he is our Eldest."

Everyone laughed. Gerald said, "I thought we were leaving today, or tomorrow at the latest."

King Donald replied, "You and Kenna leave tomorrow. Selwyn and an escort of three dragons will fly you to the Teeth, where Selene will take charge and carry you to the triad. Two dragons will follow the next day taking your horses to the barracks. The others will be flown with their horses to the barracks to get it in order and await your arrival. A dragon will take you to and from the triad's home. No one but Gerald and Kenna will be allowed there, or even to know where it is. There are quite a few dragons involved to make this happen quickly. Clearly they see this as important.

"Are there other questions? Have you any thoughts on the task?"

Gerald did. "How many dragons are involved?"

Cuthbert answered. "Apart from your flight, Gerald, there will be a dozen flying from Cair Parn—three carrying men, six carrying horses, and three as guards. The two dragons with your and Kenna's mounts will fly with them. Not counting those two, there will be an equal number flying from Edinburgh. You look a bit stunned, as well you might. It has been long since thirty dragons worked together this way for any purpose. Never has it happened in conjunction with mankind."

"It sounds as if dragons can only carry one horse apiece?"

"Yes. The larger dragons could carry two, but it would be burdensome. They would have to fly lower and more slowly, and they would have no speed in reserve for emergencies or fighting severe winds."

"Murdoch spoke of the high king's envoys, as if there were more than one."

Murdoch smirked. When no one replied, Gerald asked, "So who is or are the others?"

Kenna spoke. "I am. As my going was a condition of your going, there needed to be an explanation that did not involve the faerie. So King Dugald and I agreed I would go in the guise of a second envoy, much as Murdoch did on your last trip. It is an honor. Never before have man and faerie partnered in this way."

Gerald nodded. It was an elegant solution. "So none know the triad are of the faerie?"

"It is little known, especially near where we go. Over the centuries, Morgan le Fay and her disciples have sown much discord between human and faerie throughout that region. Yet many in Albania live in peace with dragons. And Albanians—both faerie and human—hate Morgan le Fay. Knowing the dragons have those they trust hidden away to investigate le Fay's relics and their mischief is good enough. Most people there have no interest in getting any closer to le Fay's legacy than they must."

Gerald was surprised. "So they have heard of le Fay? K'Pene had not."

"While le Fay primarily worked here and in England, she

traveled somewhat in Europe, and her influence went farther yet. Fortunately for K'Pene's people, le Fay was killed before she came near them."

After a moment the king asked if there were any further questions. Nobody offered any. "Then you are dismissed."

Murdoch added for Justin and Eoin, "Complete your duties today, but take tomorrow to prepare. Talk to Donald about anything you need—it will be better to have extra than miss something. But do not take more than you and your horse can readily carry."

Gerald asked, "Kenna, Cuthbert, may we talk?"

Kenna nodded. Cuthbert said, "Go to my office. I will be there shortly."

A few minutes later, Cuthbert entered his office to find Gerald and Kenna looking at one of his paperweights—the glass block with the heart of a dragon's eye in it. "Have a care. That is the oldest identifiable relic in the realm."

"Whose is it?" Kenna asked.

"Merlin's." He caught Gerald's look of confusion and added, "The heart of the eye is from the dragon Merlin. The wizard Merlin has nothing to do with this."

Kenna's eyes widened as she placed the block reverently back on the corner of a map. "And how, my dear lore master, did you get hold of *that*?"

"There is no time today to do that tale justice. Gerald, what did you wish of us?"

Gerald began to pace. "When we—Selwyn and I—were leaving Mull, I clasped forearms with Lord Kyla. I then said, 'Blessings on you and on all your people.' And something happened. I felt power go through my arm to hers and . . . her face glowed. And then my arm was heavy, as it was after handling le Fay's sword. But I had no sense of evil. Maybe it's silly, but there was nothing yellow about her glow. It passed quickly, whatever it was. Do either of you have any idea what happened?"

"How is your arm now?" Kenna asked.

Gerald swung it around in a circle. "It's fine. I don't feel anything odd. It was back to normal within a minute or two."

Kenna took Gerald's sword arm and held it gently. She closed her eyes and stood in silence for a half dozen heartbeats. "I do not feel anything unexpected, either good or evil. Could it be the Eldest's blessing?"

Cuthbert stroked his long, white beard. "I think it must be. Gerald, a dragon's blessing is a special sort of magic. The Eldest's blessing is the most powerful of its kind. Once bestowed, the recipient can impart a similar blessing to others. I do not know why your arm felt strange afterward. The flow of power is normal, but has no such after effect."

Kenna dropped Gerald's arm. "I think your arm, having been pummeled by the power in le Fay's sword, may simply react like that to power now, Gerald."

"Well, hopefully it won't get many chances to react."

"That's probably a good thing," Kenna agreed.

Gerald smacked his thigh. "I forgot to ask what time we leave!"

"As soon as we are ready after first light, assuming the worst of the storm has passed. Grooms will have our horses ready, but you should check on Dealanach and her gear. Make sure she has all you wish to take but no more.

"Gerald, there are two more things. The first is Sally. What have you told her of this trip?"

"Only that I have been given the task of supporting those looking at the sword and hoping to heal Scythia."

Kenna gazed seriously at Gerald. "You must tell her we are both going, along with a dozen men, and that I am going as an envoy as well. In her current state of mind, if she finds out later, it will be much worse."

Cuthbert added, "Kenna and I are in agreement on this, Gerald. I would just mention it in passing. To speak more of it would likely make things worse."

Gerald nodded. Everything else he could think of would be a worse option. "And what is the second thing?"

Kenna sat down. "You heard me say I could help the horses sleep on the trip. And Ivor has something that would help you sleep, if you wish. It would save an hour or two and lessen the chances of problems along the way. For the faerie, a day without food, drink, or a privy is of no consequence. But Ivor's draught is inexact. To assure you sleep most of a day, you might end up sleeping a day and a half. Or more.

"I would not mention this to others as it might feed their fear that the faerie practice magic on humans. But if you wish, I can put you into a sleep for most of the trip and wake you at any point you desire. The region is beautiful, and it would be a shame for you to miss it. Of course, you can see it when we return if you like. Hopefully we will not be in a hurry then."

Gerald thought for only a second. "My whole life the past few months has been one surprise twist and turn after another. For all we know, in a month Argyll will be crowned king of England and invade Scotland, and I will be urgently needed to distract him while Lord Cuthbert sneaks up and steals the crown. I should be awake before we land.

"Can you do this from the dragon's claw in flight, or do you need contact? I only ask that no one knows what happened. If nothing else, I would not want word to reach Sally that you had bewitched me."

"We will have Ivor appear to give you his sleeping draught. Cuthbert and I will be there to watch, but I will put you to sleep. I can easily wake you from a short distance—say, two hours from our goal?"

"Will I not be famished and thirsty?"

"You will not."

"I will trust your enchantment."

Cuthbert nodded. "I think this is a wise plan. I do not know the why of it, but your stopping on the way does not feel right. Nor does sleeping away your first day in Albania. Do you have more questions, Lord Gerald?"

"None, my lord. My lady. Have either of you more for me?"

Kenna looked sternly at Gerald. "Why are you still here?"

"I planned to have my assistant envoy take care of things for me while I lie up here in sloth."

"You will need another plan then, as your assistant envoy has plenty to do already."

"Then I am off to check on Dealanach and to send a message home. I will see you at supper, or in the morning, or in England, as we prepare to steal the crown from Argyll's head."

CHAPTER SEVENTEEN

THE MISSING
MOUSTACHE

After checking on Dealanach and finding nothing to complain about or change, Gerald returned to his barracks and pulled apart his pack. Then he repacked. He did this three more times and ended up with the same gear he'd started with. He finally admitted he was avoiding thinking about his message to Sally. A distant bell rang suppertime. Gerald glanced at his pack. *I'll compose and send a message immediately after supper.*

He sat with his garrison: Eoin, Justin, Donald of Lochlorien, Gillian, and two warriors Gerald barely knew—Ulf and Grant. He let them talk as much as possible, but first had to describe flying with a dragon for the edification of those who had never done so. Grant, at least, had never even considered it. "For most of my life I thought it unnatural and likely to end in death. Then I thought it reserved for a select few dragon lords. And here I am, about to fly in a dragon's claw like so much prey! It feels like a dream."

Ulf pinched him to prove it wasn't. Gerald was able to retreat into his meal. Once finished, he announced, "I must ask your leave. I have preparations to make."

Donald dismissed him and anyone else who wished to leave. Gerald went outside, signaled to his Voices, and asked them to take flight and watch for his signal from a window. He then went in search of quiet solitude. He finally sought out the tower roof. He explained his desire for privacy to the head of the watch and sat, cross-legged, as far from everyone as he could get. He waved for his Voices.

Three landed practically in his lap.

"That's cozy," Gerald said.

"You said you wanted privacy," a Voice replied.

"We have excellent hearing," another added.

"And yet you tend to speak loudly to us. We thought perhaps if we stayed close, you would not feel the need to shout," said the third.

Gerald smiled. "Just as well. It puts you all in reach of my sword, in case I decide to destroy the message and start over."

"Good. We understand one another," the first Voice replied.

"I want you take a message to Sally."

"We assumed as much. A warrior always does on the eve of a great campaign."

"Of course, it gets awkward when one sends a message to Sally, but his beloved's name is altogether different, such as Cleopatra," added another Voice.

"Then it's the warrior that loses his head rather than the messenger," the third added hopefully.

Gerald laughed. He thought for a long while before speaking again. He spoke deliberately but haltingly, choosing each word and phrase with care.

"Sally, I cannot say much. I am off as envoy again, this time to the triad looking into the things troubling Scythia and Kiergenwald. Kenna is going as a second envoy. We will have a garrison of a dozen warriors. Dragons will carry us and our horses. I may not be able to send word for some time. If there is real news, especially of hope or change in relation to Scythia, I shall endeavor to get word to you! I love you." He thought a minute more and added, "And I send you my blessing."

Gerald rubbed his forehead for a moment. "Voices, please repeat that so I'm sure what I am sending."

More or less in unison, the Voices did just that, including every pause Gerald had made.

"Hmm. Could you do it without the pauses?"

The birds looked at each other. Gerald wasn't sure whether they were surprised, amused, or something else entirely. If Voices wore expressions, Gerald could not read them. He laughed to himself. *I can't even tell them apart!*

Again, the Voices repeated the message as one, this time with no pauses at all. So Gerald repeated it as best he could, pausing naturally. After this was repeated back to him, he asked, "Is it always like that? The pauses or lack thereof?"

The middle Voice replied. "All speech is significant, or should be. When dragons communicate, they communicate in the pauses as well as the words. We see this in human communication as well. When given a message that requires precision, or that we dare not interpret, we repeat it verbatim in timing as well as words. While we have heard humans speak as you did tonight, we have never had to determine how to eliminate some pauses and keep others."

"Thank you." He reached out to touch each bird on the head in turn. "You have my blessings as well, Voices. Thank you for choosing me and serving so well."

Gerald felt nothing in his arm, but the Voices hopped up and down. They spoke over one another until two of them hushed.

"Never before have we felt a dragon's blessing, or a man's. Never have we heard that a Voice was given such. We have been nearby when one was given and felt the power flow near us. Tonight we felt its touch. You have done us great honor, Lord Gerald. This will not be forgotten."

The Voices bobbed at Gerald and took flight in various directions. Gerald smiled, recalling his confusion the first time he had seen that. It was a bit of dragon brilliance, having the birds fly away in such a manner as to confuse anyone trying to learn where they were headed. He sat and watched the stars a moment through breaks in the clouds, then got up and headed back to the barracks before the watch began to wonder at his continued presence.

Gerald and his fellow travelers could not say too much to the others, so the rest of the evening in the barracks included much speculation and guesswork. Dree eventually shut things down. "If the king or captain wanted us to know, we'd know. These warriors need their rest. Let them be."

To mollify his fellow warriors—most of whom he counted as friends—Gerald spent a half hour describing anew what flying with dragons was like and the idea of the traveling eggs. He felt a twinge of conscience when he realized he had not discussed those with Murdoch and Cuthbert, but it was too late for that now. Folkvar would surely send word.

Quiet descended upon the room like a blanket of snow, but eventually snoring bloomed like madness in the spring. Neither was prone to bother Gerald who, like all warriors, could normally sleep under any circumstances. This night it was well past midnight before he fell asleep. It felt like minutes later that a page woke him, but the hint of dawn slipping over the windowsill spoke of several hours sleep. With his fellow travelers and the morning watch, he threw on his overclothes, grabbed his gear, and headed to the mess. A half hour later Donald and his garrison escorted Gerald to the front gate. Donald and Gillian were in the lead and stopped suddenly at the portcullis as if it were down.

"Keep going!" Cuthbert ordered quietly.

Everyone automatically started moving again. Outside the gate, Gerald found King Donald, the rest of his advisors, and Kenna. Outside the arrow stones, six dragons sat or reclined, taking up a good portion of his field of vision. Gerald had not seen this many dragons together since the rebel attack on the Eldest. Of the others, only Cuthbert and Kenna might ever have seen such a sight. The awe on Donald's and Gillian's faces told Gerald why they had stopped suddenly.

Gerald laughed.

"What is it, Lord Gerald?" the king asked formally.

"Nothing worth telling, my king," Gerald replied. In truth it had struck him that the reality of the following day had just struck the garrison's warriors—the day they would all be letting dragons snatch them up and carry them aloft "like so much prey," as Grant had eloquently put it. But Gerald didn't want to offend anyone's pride. He knew all too well how overwhelming dragons could be.

Selwyn introduced the other dragons. A pair of yellow dragons, Archibald and Selah—both of whom had red eyes— would carry their horses the next day. The remaining three would be their guards. These were Jamie (sky blue with amber eyes), Frost (pale orange with black eyes), and Cheyenne (dark gray with light gray eyes). Cuthbert introduced the humans and Kenna, although only Cheyenne and Frost did not know her.

Farewells were said. Two pieces of dragon hide with blankets lay in front of Selwyn. Gerald lay down on one and was startled to find Cuthbert and the king preparing to wrap him with his pack. Ivor, K'Pene, and Kenna gathered around Gerald. Ivor explained in a loud voice about the draught and told Gerald to drink the contents of a small bottle. Gerald pretended to drain the empty bottle and lay back.

K'Pene smiled. "I would kiss your cheeks as my people do, Gerald, but I will honor Sally's fears and offer you my blessing instead."

Kenna, meanwhile, had laid her hand on his forehead. A deep peace came over Gerald. He was not yet asleep, but had no doubt he would be soon. King Donald and Cuthbert rolled him up in blanket and hide while others did the same for Kenna. A moment later they were aloft. Gerald saw their escort overhead. As they flew higher and eastward, the sun shone blindingly into Gerald's tired eyes. He tried to pull the skin closed about his face but instead fell fast asleep.

Gerald awoke to soft light, his bed swaying gently. As he tried to roll over, he realized he was wrapped heavily in his covers. Only when he tried to sit up and felt a warning squeeze from a dragon's claw did he recall where he was. He let himself wake fully, stretching his muscles repeatedly before thinking much. *It's hard enough waking from this. I'm really glad I didn't take Ivor's potion!* In a minute he had his head out of the blankets and hide. His hair whipped wildly and the icy wind felt like a slap in the face, but the view was worth it.

The moonlit landscape below ranged from snow-covered peaks to dark valleys. He could make out rivers, and far to the right he could see reflections off a huge lake . . . or possibly sea.

"You are right, Kenna. This is worth seeing," he called hoarsely. His voice was not quite working properly. "Can you hear me?"

"Yes, Gerald. A faerie's ears are not as good as a dragon's, but are on par with a Voice's. And we can project our voices quite well. I am not shouting as you would be."

It was a relief to know he did not have to shout. "Where are we?"

"We draw near to Albania. Off to the right, across the water, you can just see Italy, where lies Rome."

Gerald watched for a few minutes before pulling his head back out of the wind. "How far is where we go from . . . oh."

Selwyn answered anyway. "So you remembered we do not know? But if we did, it would not be wise to discuss such things even here, Lord Gerald."

"Yes, I recalled both of those points. Thank you, Selwyn."

Soon Gerald was watching the sun rise through clear skies. He was higher than he had ever been *(unless my unconscious trip in Drachmaeius' mouth had been higher!)* The sunrise across water from this height was glorious. Selwyn began singing a deep, rumbling song far different than Nain's. He sang for perhaps a minute.

"That was beautiful, Selwyn," Kenna offered.

"Thank you, Kenna. Do you hear many songs for sunrise?"

"I have heard dozens. I have yet to hear one that did not make me rejoice for the new day."

"And what of you, Lord Gerald?"

"I have now heard two. In fact, I just remembered what Nain said about dragons doing this. I have not heard such a song since he came to Cair Parn for a lesson. I wonder why."

"I do not know. But dragons seldom sing on the ground, and in the air we usually take to the heights for singing. Perhaps those are the reasons."

Gerald thought back over times he had dealt with dragons. "From what I recall, I believe that explains it."

Flames of laughter trailed close by. "The youngest dragon lord, once sworn to be the bane of all dragons, now knows enough dragons that he is not sure he can recall all his encounters!"

Gerald growled. "Do not anger the bane, varlet, lest he come upon you in your sleep and draw a great mustache upon your visage!"

"Kenna, can you not protect me from this monster?"

"I fear not, Selwyn, but perhaps you can convince Selene to drop him into the volcano."

"I will ask her to attend to that task. I am sure she would happily do so to preserve the dragons' honor."

Gerald laughed. "Selene said she would teach me to fly, and that it is simply a matter of controlling your fall. Then you would have a flying bane to contend with!"

"But one," said Selwyn, "who is incapable of breathing fire."

"I yield," Gerald said.

"Perfect timing," Selwyn said. "We descend now."

They landed near slender, towering peaks. "Those would be the Teeth?" Gerald asked as he shed his blanket and dragon skin cocoon.

"They would," Selwyn replied. "These are part of the Accursed Mountains, or Prokletije, as the Albanians call them."

"I'll stick with Accursed Mountains, simply because I can say that, but why are they cursed?"

"They are not, but perhaps Kenna can explain the name later. Selene approaches."

They looked up and saw Selene's deep purple form dropping from a great height. She slowed rapidly, landing so softly they hardly heard a sound.

"Thank you, Selwyn," Selene said.

"It was my pleasure," Selwyn replied. "Lord Gerald, Kenna."

"Thank you," they both replied. Without further ado, Selwyn took flight. He dwindled into the distance very quickly.

"You should not have bothered with removing your hides," Selene laughed.

Gerald realized he had not seen the other dragons since landing. He and Kenna rolled up in their blankets and hides as best they could. "Where are the dragons sent to guard us, Selene?"

"They remained high above." She scanned the sky. "They return to Scotland and Selwyn continues to Africa. Are you ready?"

She picked them up and launched skyward.

Selene was soon flying so fast that Gerald gave up trying to watch the scenery and hid in his cocoon from the cold wind. No one said anything until the dragon slowed and began to descend.

"We are here!" Selene cried. The ride became bumpier and the air at intervals warmer or cooler. Once Selene slowed to what Gerald thought of as a normal dragon pace, the young dragon lord looked out . . . and his questions died on his lips.

They were perhaps fifty feet above a curving rock wall. To his right, he looked down into an enormous bowl. It might have been a lake, but it was a lake of fire, as he had heard Father MacPherson mention from the Bible. It was red and yellow, almost too bright to look at. Vapors curled up, which Selene dodged whenever they drew near. "Gerald," she called, "avoid the smoke at all costs. It will eat you, starting at your nose and going deep down into your belly. You will die quickly but painfully."

"Right. I try to avoid painful deaths, however quick they might be."

Selene dropped farther, landing just above the trees a hundred yards below the top of the mount. Two large doors appeared to have been cut from the mountainside and then rehung in place, just below the treeline. Their outline was faint. Had Gerald not known to look, he would likely have never noticed them. A hint of a path wandered from the woods past the nearly invisible doorway toward the summit.

Selene spoke softly. "We are here. The triad is within. There is a dark spot in the shape of a hand on the rock beside the doors. Kenna must place her hand upon this to open the doors. It answers only to the faerie. You will spend the night here. I will come for you two hours before sunset tomorrow. It will be a bit later than you are used to, due to the height. Farewell."

She was gone before they could thank her. Packs and blankets on their shoulders, dragging the dragon skins, they approached the doors.

Gerald started to ask something but noticed Kenna looked pale. "Are you well, Kenna?"

"I will be, despite what awaits me."

Gerald could see no threat. "What do you mean?"

"I have not been back here since I was banished. And the one who banished me waits within."

CHAPTER EIGHTEEN

LIQENI I ZJARRTË

Gerald stopped in his tracks. "You were banished? Why have you not mentioned this?"

"It is of no consequence, or so I thought. It was lifted a century ago, but facing Darciere is proving more difficult than I thought."

"Who is Darciere?"

"The one who blames me for my mother's death."

Thrice Gerald opened his mouth to speak. Each time the words died on his lips.

Kenna laughed weakly. "Unintelligible silence does not become you, dragon lord. I will say no more for now. All will be well."

She moved forward. Gerald, having no real choice, followed. Looking herself again, Kenna calmly put her hand to the dark spot Selwyn had indicated. Seconds later the massive stones swung silently outward. An impossibly straight cavern loomed ahead. Torches hung from both walls every fifteen feet or so, staggered left and right to provide better coverage. The doors swung shut behind them, as silent in closing as in opening.

Gerald stared at the doors. "How do we get out?"

Kenna pointed to the wall on the doors' right. "See the

hand shape? It will open to anyone touching a hand there, but remember that only the faerie can open the doors from the outside. I doubt anyone could hear you from in here. I'm not sure we could hear a dragon through these doors." She turned and led the way deeper into the mountain.

One hundred feet in, the tunnel met several other passages in a large, well-lit chamber. The tunnel straight across presumably led to the lake of fire. Walking toward them from a passage to the right were what Gerald assumed to be the triad.

A slender man Gerald's height with long, red hair the color of Kenna's led the way. His features reminded Gerald of Kenna as well; surely this was her father. The man was not in a hurry yet seemed to close rapidly. To his right was a short, lithe woman who reminded him of an older Kyla—probably far older he reminded himself. She wore her dark hair short. On their left was a regal, tall, muscular woman with long, dark hair that seemed to move on its own, as Kenna's did. While the other two wore smiles, this one's expression gave away nothing.

"Can they hear me?" Gerald whispered as softly as he could.

"Not yet," she replied even more quietly. "The walls eat sound."

Gerald stared at the walls. *How can stone eat sound?* "I assume the tall one is Darciere?"

"A reasonable guess but no. Now hush and come."

She walked more quickly. When the two groups met, Kenna and her father held a long embrace. The taller woman's face held a ghost of a smile as she watched, but the shorter woman looked at Gerald. Her smile made him uncomfortable, but he relaxed and kept his features neutral.

Kenna pulled away from her father, bowed to Darciere, and hugged the taller woman briefly. Then she made introductions.

"This is Gerald of Argyll, currently of Cair Parn, bound to King Donald but serving as envoy for High King Dugald of Scotland. Gerald, this is Darciere, head of the triad. This is my father, Andreas, and this is Chloe. They are considered the most knowledgeable and skilled in dealing with the magic of others." Gerald bowed his head to each of the triad as they were introduced and they nodded in return. Kenna stepped back beside Gerald.

Darciere spoke. "Welcome to *Liqeni i Zjarrtë*, or Fiery Lake in your tongue, if you find the Albanian name difficult. You may leave the dragon hides and blankets against the wall in here. I assume you are spending the night?"

"If we may," Gerald replied. "No one has explained the accommodations to me, but as the garrison and our horses arrive tomorrow, it would be helpful—and an honor—to stay here."

"Then keep your packs and follow us." The faerie turned and started toward the passage on Gerald's left. Again, Andreas seemed to lead the way. Gerald found this confusing. He grinned; Kenna had confused him quite a few times. Perhaps that was just life among the faerie.

They came to a smaller antechamber with five doors spread around it. "These are the guest quarters," Chloe explained. "Pick any room you like, though they are essentially identical. You will find a small figurine just inside. If you leave it outside the door, other guests will know which rooms are taken."

"Are you expecting others?" Gerald asked.

"Not at the moment, but a few days ago we were not expecting either of you. Please leave your things in your rooms and we will go to discuss the business which brings you here."

Kenna chose the room on the left so to keep things simple, Gerald picked the room on the right. He found a basic, nearly square room carved out of the rock with what seemed to be living turf on the floor. The room contained a bed, a table, a small chest of drawers, two chairs, and a small couch. The bed covers were spotless white linen, the furniture a dark green. There were several torches on the walls. Curious at the lack of smoke, Gerald reached toward the flame. It was warm but did not burn. Remembering the dragon fire torch Santana had once given him, he did not let his clothes near the flame.

Gerald left his pack at the foot of his bed. He placed his sword belt on the table and his axes and knives in one of the drawers. He felt naked without them.

There was a two-foot statue of a pouncing weasel by the door. It turned out to be very light. Gerald moved it outside his door as he left the room. Kenna was already with the others, discussing something quietly with her father. A bat the size of a Voice stood near her door.

Gerald looked closely at the bat. "Is that modeled after a real bat?"

"Yes," Kenna and Andreas answered.

"It is not quite like any bat I have seen."

Kenna deferred to her father, who replied, "It is the greater mouse-eared bat, found throughout Albania and much of Europe, but not, I believe, on your islands."

"You are observant, young dragon lord," Darciere added.

"I have had to be to survive, and I have had good teachers."

Chloe nodded approvingly.

Darciere turned and they went up the hallway. At the large chamber they turned left and went toward the doorway that opened toward the volcano. They stopped a few feet from a waist-high rock wall. Andreas sniffed the air delicately, then waved them all forward. Gerald looked out at a beautiful, terrifying sight.

It was like watching a stew of living fire boiling in slow motion. It spanned four hundred yards. Though it was at least half that distance below them, Gerald could still sense its enormous power. The light was too bright in spots to look at.

"Why is there no heat?" he asked.

Chloe answered, "A great deal of effort has gone into building this place, including a great deal of what you would call magic—of the faerie, dragons, and others. There is a shield between us and the outside air, or the heat would kill us. Andreas tested the air as we approached. While we have never had a leak and never expect to have a leak, we will not take chances. The gasses released in the fiery maelstrom below would poison us even were they not hot. At the temperatures outside the shield, they would strip everything from our bones in seconds. The very rock we walk in is shielded lest the fortress become uninhabitable.

"The volcano was long dead when this fortress was built. Dragons melted a half mile of rock to get to the liquid fire that lurked beneath the surface. When it begins to cool every so many years, a hundred dragons come to reheat it. The result is that the molten rock contains more heat than the sum of the fire below and the fire of the dragons that assault it. It is a mystery, but one we use to our advantage."

Darciere turned and the group walked with her back to the central chamber and then off to their left, eventually angling back toward the inside of the volcano. They ended up in a large room with several tables, along with cabinets, shelves, and a variety of flasks, bins, tubes, and things Gerald did not recognize. A table in the room's center was covered with a polished chain mail tablecloth of tiny links. It was lumpy, clearly placed over a multitude of small objects. He stared around the room in fascination.

"Please have a seat," Andreas said, pointing to several cushions in a corner.

After they were seated, Andreas continued. "What does the word 'alchemy' mean to you, Gerald?"

Gerald thought for a few seconds. "I have heard it used for science—for studying how things work and making new things through natural laws; as a mixture of science and the occult for various purposes—especially for making gold from things of lesser value; and as a kind of mystical art hidden from all but a select few. I have no experience with any of these."

Gerald had not realized there was tension in the room until he felt it leave.

"Good. We shall have little to undo in your education. We use the term 'alchemy' interchangeably with the word 'science,' but we do not use these terms as humans do. Kenna assures me you do not fear the faerie, even though you have seen some of what you would call our magic. You have seen dragon magic as well. As you have not asked about the torches, I assume you recognize the cool fire of a dragon?"

"I did. I was amazed to see so much of it here. There are at least a hundred torches here. My only question is how many trips it took to get them inside."

"Very astute. For us, science—or alchemy—is not bound by the purely physical. We see far fewer barriers between the physical and what you might call the spiritual realm. When humans walk at all in more than the physical, you tend to see a fine line, or at best a thin ribbon, between the two, and think that is the only place they meet. In reality, they are both everywhere. Even we do not see all of that; rather, we sense a wide swath of overlap with no clearly defined edges. The faerie dwell upon that overlap.

"The dragons see it likewise, but their overlap is not our overlap. Our people have discussed this with the dragons over the centuries, and it is clear to us our swath is the larger of the two. The dragons are convinced theirs is the larger. Neither group truly cares about that. It is simply how we see things."

Darciere took over. "And that, Gerald, hints at the real reason you are here. Do you see it?"

"It sounds to me as if the faerie and dragons work together to understand this world, our lives, and everything around us. Neither group can see everything. And I would guess the ribbon—however narrow it may be—that humans can see may cover ground neither of your ribbons cover. So it behooves us to all work together."

Darciere's smile briefly reached her eyes. "I must admit that when I heard Kenna's proposition to have you here, I was not inclined to consent. I am now glad I listened. I will also note the Eldest spoke more highly of you than of any human in recent memory."

"Save Cuthbert," Andreas added.

"Save Cuthbert," Darciere agreed. "But Cuthbert is in a class by himself."

The others nodded.

"I don't suppose Cuthbert is coming," Gerald said.

"No, but we have been in touch. Now, Gerald, we have heard the story from Kenna, from Cuthbert, and from Santana, Selene, and Nain. We should like to hear it from you."

"Where do you wish me to start?"

"From the first you heard of anything to do with the affair involving le Fay's sorcery, or the dragon Argyll's association with it. Or anything that occurs to you that might pertain in the least. Please do not hold back for fear of judgement, or because you think something is inconsequential."

Before Gerald could reply, Kenna spoke. "We have not had food or drink since leaving Cair Parn. Have you breakfasted already?"

"We have," Chloe said as she jumped up. "But we will not allow any to faint for lack!" She walked quickly to a cabinet and returned with a large tray bearing five plain silver goblets, a flask, a loaf of bread, and a wedge of pale yellow cheese riddled with holes. She set the tray in the middle of the group, poured a nearly clear wine for everyone, and sat back down.

Suddenly hungry, Gerald nevertheless waited for Kenna to get her food before tearing off bread and slicing the unknown cheese for himself. As he did most of the talking the next two hours, it was some time before his hunger was sated.

During that time Kenna said nothing. The triad skillfully drew out details Gerald had not known he remembered, and facts he had not considered before. By the time he was through talking, he almost felt he had known Morgan le Fay for years.

It was a feeling he did not like at all.

CHAPTER NINETEEN

THREE SWORDS

Once the triad was content with Gerald's story ("for now," Andreas added), they stood and beckoned Gerald to the mesh-covered table.

"Stay back," Darciere said. Chloe and Andreas moved to opposite corners and began folding the mesh tablecloth up toward the middle of the table. When they reached it, they carried the mesh to a side table and left it there.

The room seemed to dim. Gerald glanced at Kenna, who stared grimly at the table. Gerald moved closer to see better. He found a forest of miniature trees, with those in the middle broken and burned. There were hints of yellow and steel.

"Is this the Broken Woods near Kiergenwald?" Even as he asked, he knew it was. "How would you know what it looks like if you haven't been there?"

Rather than answer, Darciere pulled a sheathed sword from underneath a table. She held the hilt toward Gerald. "This sword, ironically, is nearly a twin to the one Scythia carried. It has been worn and used by faerie leaders for millennia. It is thrice dragon blessed. I must swear you to secrecy on this, Gerald, before saying more. Take the hilt."

Gerald hesitated. "I am a man of my word, but I understand you may need more assurance. What am I agreeing to?"

Darciere's perpetual smile broadened. "The oath will explain that, but in short, as long as we hold the sword, anything we discuss that we call a binding secret can never be shared without permission of the secret's owners. And I mean quite literally that it cannot. We will not be able to speak it, write it, or otherwise communicate it.

"Once the oath starts, until all agree, none will be able to let go of the sword, so no trickery is possible. We will all take part. If you will remove the sword from the sheath, lay it on the table, and keep holding it, the rest of us will gather in and touch the blade."

Gerald found himself pressed up against Kenna, with Andreas, Chloe, and Darciere crowded together past Kenna along the sword.

The triad leader continued, "Everyone repeat after me: I vow to keep all that is called a binding secret here a secret, so long as I live."

The rest of them repeated the words together. Gerald felt as if thousands of ants were crawling along his arm up to his mind and around his mouth. It was not at all comfortable. The feeling passed after a few seconds. As a test, he tried to let go of the sword and could not. The others demonstrated they could not let go, either.

Darciere nodded to Andreas, who spoke. "This is a binding secret. It is given to a few of us to be able to speak mind to mind with certain dragons. It takes great effort and opens both to see things the other may wish hidden, so it is not used frivolously! Selene and Santana were willing to let us see what they saw, felt, tasted, heard, smelled, and sensed at the battle site. Thus it was as if we had been there.

"And Gerald, you must tell Selene and Santana in private that you know this at your earliest convenience. You may speak of this in private with any dragon who makes it clear they know this." He paused, eyes raised toward Gerald.

Seeing no reason not to and no easy way to avoid it, Gerald

agreed. He did wonder at the nature of this compulsion.

Darciere spoke again. "We have no other secrets to offer at this time, but the oath-binding shall remain in effect for twenty-four hours. During that time, should we need to share more secrets, we need only touch the sword together and note that we speak binding secrets. Do we all agree?"

They did and Gerald felt the ants again, only this time they raced down his arm to the sword.

He let go and flexed his hand as the others moved away.

Chloe held her hands over the scene and spread them rapidly. "Behold the stump!"

The miniature woods grew around them until they were standing beside the stump as if in the real Broken Woods. He looked around in wonder. Far overhead he could see the rock ceiling of the triad's workroom. Flames rose from torches high up and far away.

Kenna laughed lightly. "I believe you once lamented that you had seen no real faerie magic, Gerald?"

"That was long ago, in another world," Gerald said, awestruck.

Chloe actually smiled. "You are unafraid!"

"I do not know what I am. I knew there would be magic, but this is amazing! I feel as if I could reach out and take the sword!" As he spoke, his hand moved to grasp the sword. It felt real and slid easily from the stump, ringing mightily as it came forth. It seemed to Gerald that it glowed, though he could not be sure.

"That is Morticum," Andreas said. "We created the illusion of the place, but parts—such as the sword, are real. Does the stump look as you recall it?"

Gerald looked with distaste at the stump, which he now thought of as plague-ridden. "More or less. It's certainly close. I can't be sure. Wait. I don't recall that broken sword on top."

Chloe gripped an imaginary sword, drew it, and held it

aloft. A sword of crystallized wood rose from the stump and hung in the air as if Chloe were holding it, but five feet away from her. There was a chunk missing from the middle of the blade. "Strike it with Morticum, Gerald. Away from us, please."

"With a will!" Gerald smote the crystal sword. It shattered into roughly a dozen glittering shards. They flew and bounced malevolently across the clearing.

Chloe made grasping motions and the pieces moved into a pile atop the stump.

Kenna's eyes widened in recognition. "Gerald, do you recognize these?"

"Are these the stones K'Pene dug up and the jewel Neakal found?"

"Very good!" Darciere said. "Chloe, the sword."

Chloe moved as if sheathing a sword and the shards reformed into a sword, resting anew where they had been when Gerald first saw the stump. She turned to face Gerald. "Notice that there are thirteen pieces, not twelve. We believe when you find the extra piece and remove it from Sally's presence, whatever ails Sally will cease, or at least weaken drastically. As for the stump, we are working out what to do. The dragons refuse to touch it. I believe they are wise in this.

"Gerald, please replace Morticum."

He did so. The sword rang again, but did not protest as it had in the real Broken Woods. Gerald also noted Morticum did not bother his hand or arm this time. He suspected this was because the real stump was far away.

Chloe held her arms out and then brought them together quickly. "Behold the table!" Everything shrank back onto the table. "Gerald, please get the sword we swore the oath upon."

As soon as Gerald picked it up, Andreas and Chloe replaced the covering upon the table, hiding the scene.

"This mesh and table are specially constructed and blessed to contain the influence of the stones. They cannot affect us while covered," Darciere explained. "Shall we sit?"

Gerald happily collapsed onto a cushion. "How did you ever realize that was a sword?"

Andreas answered. "In part, we treated it as a children's puzzle. We manipulated the crystal pieces on the chance they were related. We saw patterns and fit things together based on those. But at first we only reduced it to four larger pieces, not seeing how the rest fit.

"We had already spent a great deal of energy and thought on things and had gotten nowhere before the puzzle approach. So we went to the edge of madness. We contacted one who can touch dragon minds, one who knows nothing of this place, or who is here. We told them only generally what we sought and which dragon should know something. We had her surreptitiously slide across the surface of Argyll's mind.

"She is one of only two who can do this. She spent hours hovering nearby—not literally, but mentally—skimming the surface of Argyll's thoughts as the faintest breeze touches someone concentrating on a task. Finally Argyll noticed and, like a flash, fought his way to her mind as well. But she was ready, pulling back even as he approached. He saw who she was but no more. While he cannot touch her, he will certainly go looking for someone to exact vengeance on."

It was a moment before Gerald could speak. "Did you get a warning out?"

"We did. Unfortunately, we have no idea where Argyll is. He is being far more careful than usual, but the faerie are vigilant and difficult to take unawares. Had Argyll not been thinking of his plans, we would not have learned anything of use. Because he was unprepared for this invasion, we learned three things related to the situation.

"First, his fire was involved in turning the stump into this evil crystal, as we suspected. Heating the stump after it was crystal made it soft so he could easily insert Morticum.

"Second, he somehow burned a claw. We do not know how

this happened, only that it did. It is incredibly difficult to harm a dragon with fire. Their claws are nearly impervious. Argyll could soak his claws in the Fiery Lake and not harm them. Our best guess is it was something to do with whatever ancient evil of le Fay's he released from the sword by breathing fire upon it. He likely cursed his own claw, but we do not believe it hurt him much."

"That's a pity," Gerald said.

"It is. The third thing was a sword made of crystal from the stump. The pieces your friend K'Pene dug up made the grip and blade. The gem Neakal wore was its pommel."

Gerald interrupted. "But Selene took that gem away! How could it return as the pommel to the sword?"

Andreas grimaced. "This was the most worrisome part. If you recall, the Voice who survived Argyll's attack after he vanquished Scythia and turned the stump to crystal spoke of a woman appearing and dropping something on the stump. We have delved into the Voice's memory—with permission, of course. The woman was almost certainly a ghostly remnant of Morgan le Fay—an echo of a memory of a powerful sorceress."

Gerald stared quietly at the table, envisioning it in his head. He balled his fists helplessly but said no more.

Andreas resumed his narrative. "The knowledge there was a sword gave us the key to the puzzle. A rock that is shattered will have many minute pieces missing. That is why we did not see how the pieces fit together before. But Argyll was thinking of the sword as whole just before he realized someone was watching his thoughts. We still do not know where the missing piece is, and we dare not attempt another look in his mind.

"We only learned of the sword last night. We will spend today attempting to divine the whereabouts of the missing piece, and of Argyll, and anything else of this mystery. But these inquiries are things of the mind and spirit, not hands and instruments. We must ask you to leave us for now. You are free to explore anywhere but this wing, although there is not much to see. Kenna knows where to find food and drink. You may enter and leave the fortress as you like, but Gerald will need Kenna to open the doors from outside, so we suggest you stay together if you go. Have you any questions?"

"I have many, but nothing pressing."

"Then go. Ask what you will of Kenna. She can likely answer many of your questions. We can consider the rest later."

Gerald raised Morticum's twin. "What of this?"

Chloe took it and returned it to its sheath under the table.

"Does it have a name?" Gerald wondered aloud.

Chloe paused, still squatting by the sword. She looked at Gerald curiously. "Yes. Her name is Vitae. It is Latin for 'Life.' Morticum is not a word, but has its roots in 'Death.'"

Gerald nodded. "You called the sword a her. Why is that? And who named her?"

Chloe stood and drew Vitae so quickly Gerald had no time to react. She held the sword out. "Binding secret. Everyone touch Vitae."

The ants scurried up Gerald's arm more quickly this time.

While Darciere had spoken little 'til now, she surprised Gerald by taking over. "We call Vitae 'her' because that is how she refers to herself. She told us her name. It was a different name as far back as the faerie have known of this sword, but a month ago she announced the name you have heard. She warned us Morticum was being sought by an unknown evil and that whatever le Fay had left in Morticum was only hiding, not abated.

"Lord Gerald, this sword was forged in service to Merlin. King Arthur wore it. It was blessed by Merlin, by priests, and by dragons. Merlin did not leave anything of himself in the sword as le Fay did; that is dark magic, indeed."

Gerald stared in wonder at the sword he could not release— or would not release him. "How, then, does it, or she, speak to you?"

Darciere frowned. "Have you not heard Morticum sing?"

Gerald looked up. "Is that what happened? I heard something when I drew it in the moonlight. Wait. Is Morticum a he or she?"

Darciere laughed mirthlessly. "Neither. Morticum is a powerful sword, but there is no life in it, only magic. You might call it a her for now because part of le Fay dwells—I will not say lives—within it. I will not deign to use such words for the thing."

Vitae hummed beneath their fingers. Chloe gasped.

Darciere scowled. "What?"

"Did you not hear?" When the others all shook their heads, Chloe explained. "She says Morticum is as much 'she' as is Vitae." She looked at the sword attached to their hands. "But she says no more on this."

Darciere glared at Gerald as if he had said something offensive. "Anything else?"

"Not for now."

"Then we are finished here."

Gerald wondered when the ants would go. The triad looked at one another briefly before Chloe said, "Agreed. We are finished with binding secrets for now."

The ants raced down Gerald's arm and the sword fell from beneath his hand. Chloe sheathed Vitae and returned her to the shelf.

CHAPTER TWENTY

FEWMETS & FISH

Kenna took Gerald on a brief tour of the fortress, ignoring the other doors near the room they left the triad in. Near the end, Gerald said, "We should probably go outside soon."

"Why is that?"

"Fewmets. I'd hate to just leave them on the floor somewhere."

Kenna laughed and kept walking. Near the shielded overlook, she opened a door to a small room with a hole in the floor. She explained, "The hole is the mouth of a small tunnel that descends to the fiery lake. There is a series of shields that cease to be when something falls toward them and exist again after it passes. Other magic forces air down the tube to prevent gasses passing upward. There are damp sponges for cleaning yourself in the green bucket. If you use one, leave it in the blue bucket afterward. I will wait outside."

When Gerald emerged, Kenna led the way to a smaller passage between the passage leading outside and that leading to their rooms. They came to a fairly large room with low couches, chairs, and shelves filled with books and scrolls. A table in the corner held fruit and cheese, dried meats, and wine. Beside these were two dragon bone mugs with detailed handles resembling dragon heads and necks.

The furniture here was unlike anything Gerald knew. Most of it seemed to be intricately patterned cloth in soft colors over plush cushions. Kenna chose a thickly padded chair that looked like a squashed bush. Gerald gingerly sat and leaned back on a huge fish leaping out of water.

His eyes lit up as he relaxed. "This feels great! I've never seen or felt furniture like this." He closed his eyes, wishing he had taken his boots off.

Kenna replied happily, "While we can sleep anywhere, including, if need be, in a patch of nettles, we prefer this. Only my people make such."

"This would be worth a fortune, save that someone would always be trying to steal it. Or enslave the faerie to make more."

"Even Morgan le Fay was unable to enslave the faerie. And she tried."

Gerald's eyes popped open. "But though dead, she has nearly enslaved people I love, such as Neakal and Sally."

"But Neakal is free, and I believe we are getting close to healing Sally."

Gerald lay back, pondering everything he had heard or seen. "Kenna, you once assured me you could not read my mind. And yet today I was told that the triad can speak mind to mind with dragons, and that at least two faerie can sneak into dragon minds."

Kenna hesitated before speaking carefully. "I cannot elaborate, but no one said 'two faerie.' Have a care in your assumptions."

Gerald stared in fascination at Kenna. "So these two are not faerie?"

"One is. I will not say more, as it is not my secret. Do not mention I said this, even to the triad, please."

"Of course. But there is a certain faerie, and another—let us say a myth or legend, who can sneak up on a dragon's mind.

Can any of them sneak into mine?"

Kenna shook her head. "No, Gerald. It is ancient magic from before men fell that lets us speak mind to mind with dragons, and precious few can still do it. Once dragons could all speak mind to mind, but today perhaps a dozen can still do so, and in limited fashion. We do not know why that is so. None can do this with men, as far as I know."

Gerald sat up and stared at Kenna. "Us. You said the magic 'lets us speak with dragons.' Can you do this?"

Kenna tensed, then relaxed. She wiggled more deeply into her bush and stared at the ceiling. "Yes. It takes great effort, and I have been able to communicate thusly with only two dragons."

"Who?"

"Younger and Wandap."

"But Wandap is dead!"

"Alas, she is. Fear not, Gerald, I cannot communicate with the dead! So now it is just Younger. I do it seldom because it drains me."

A long, peaceful silence stretched between them. Gerald found himself hovering over three low, flat couches, all a light brown hide of some sort. They were placed like spokes of a wheel. The triad lay upon these, their heads together where the spokes met. They lay still, reminding Gerald of Scythia. Even as he thought this, their eyes opened and found him. Chloe started to do something with her hands and Gerald was suddenly afraid.

He was back in the fish chair. Kenna was sitting up, staring at Gerald. "What did you do?"

"I think I nodded off and dreamed. Why?"

"You were here, but not here. Where did you go?"

"That makes no sense."

"Where did you go?"

Gerald described what he had seen.

Kenna stared wide-eyed at Gerald. "You have described the room the triad use when they seek answers beyond the merely material world. What was Chloe doing with her hands?"

Gerald thought briefly. "She looked as if she might be about to cast a net."

"That could have been to catch something they were seeking, or it could have been to catch their visitor. Gerald, I fear your presence is a distraction for them. There is more magic here in this fortress than anywhere you are likely to be in your lifetime. If we stay here, you will have visions and dreams. While some may be true, most will be mere possibilities, though they will feel like truth. You could go crazy trying to prepare for these futures. On top of that, you may cause the triad problems and they might inadvertently hurt you. I know we were going to wait for the garrison to arrive, but I think we should go."

"I wish I could take this chair, but otherwise, I agree. Can we leave now?"

"Almost. I will leave word."

"But where shall we go? We have no horses, and the barracks are neither ready nor manned."

She laughed, the fey laugh that always threatened to carry Gerald places he dared not think of. "Gerald, we are friends with dragons. Voices will be nearby. If nothing else, we can stay somewhere on a hillside with Selene." She sighed. "We shall miss our wonderful beds."

"Will they miss us?"

Kenna shook her head. "We no longer make living beds. It was cruel to leave them each day."

Gerald was half afraid she wasn't kidding, but he wasn't about to ask.

Kenna grinned at Gerald. "Once you would have asked whether we ever had such! You have grown in wisdom. Discretion is sometimes the better part of sanity."

They retrieved their packs and weapons and headed toward the exit.

Three Voices awaited them outside the doors.

"Greetings from Selene, man of many Voices! Greetings, Kenna!"

Gerald replied. "Greetings to you and Selene. What brings you here?"

"Your Voices are still on their way, or so we hope, so Selene asked us to await you here in case you had need of us."

"An excellent idea. We would like to stay somewhere besides Fiery Lake this evening. Where will Selene be? May we stay near her?"

"Selene will be where she is now, flying about the region watching for trouble. Unless you wish to spend the day and night in her claws, you should reconsider."

Kenna laughed. "I would offer Gerald sleep again, but if trouble should arise, Selene may need her claws and it could be a long way to the ground. This could test whether Gerald has learned to fly, which is even more difficult while asleep."

Gerald looked grave. "Yes, let's look for another site to while away the time, one less likely to require dropping us from on high."

The Voices were silent for a minute. They looked at Gerald, at Kenna, and at each other. Then one spoke. "There is a place not too far from here. Selene can come to take you there. It is safe." The Voices immediately scattered in different directions.

Kenna said, "I suppose you could stay awake in Selene's claw. Then you could practice flying if the situation arose."

"I think I'll wait for my wings to develop more."

The Voices reappeared. "Selene will be here soon."

"How did you get back before her?" Gerald asked.

"We did not fly to her; we simply went aloft and waited for her to notice us. Then we flew in the beckoning pattern."

Three minutes later Selene landed just above the treeline, about fifty feet away.

"Greetings, Kenna, Lord Gerald."

They both bowed their heads before Kenna spoke. "Those inside are busy and we would not disturb them. Where can we go until the garrison arrives? The Voices spoke of a safe place?"

Selene laughed, keeping the flames away from the trees. "Yes, there is a safe place, a cave. It is well known, and some suspected it of being the triad's fortress. It has been proven not to be, so it should be an excellent hole to hide in for a night. But where are your blankets and hides?"

"We will be right back," Kenna said. "Come, Gerald!"

They ran to the large chamber and grabbed their traveling cocoons. Back outside, they laid the skins down with the blankets atop, grabbed their packs, lay on the blankets, and rolled themselves up as best they could. Selene picked them up and took to the air.

Gerald could just see a bit of sky out the end of his tubular cocoon. He had no idea which way they were going, but he was glad the sun wasn't coming in. He found himself hollering. "Selene! Is there anyone nearby?"

"No, Gerald. Even the clouds are out of hearing distance."

"I know a few of the faerie can mind speak with dragons."

"I am not surprised you know this. Was it urgent I know this now?"

"The triad compelled me to tell you as soon as I could."

"Ah. Then you know it is limited and seldom used."

"Yes. Will you please tell Santana that I know?"

"If you like."

"Thank you."

"You're welcome," Selene replied. Then they dropped a few feet.

"What was that?" Gerald demanded when nothing else happened.

Selene replied, "I was bowing, of course."

Gerald did his best to bow in the cocoon, but succeeded

only in jerking around like a worm poked with a stick.

Five minutes later they were deposited gently on a level, rocky surface. Selene had them wait a moment while she rearranged them.

They unrolled from the cocoons and found themselves on a ten-foot rock ledge halfway up a mountain. In the rock behind them stood twins to the doors at Fiery Lake, complete with a hand-shaped dark spot on the right. Selene hung in the air close to the ledge, huge wings moving lazily.

"These open inward," said Selene, "or opening them would sweep you off the ledge."

Kenna's eyes snapped wide. "I have been here, but I was very little, very young. I had forgotten. I came here before ever I went to Fiery Lake. Thank you, Selene. Safe flying."

"Thank you. Safe resting." The flames came perilously close this time, but Gerald wasn't worried. He trusted Selene. He watched as she disappeared over the top of the mountain while Kenna opened the doors.

There were torches here as well. "Do these ever stop burning?" Gerald asked.

"Not unless we wish them to. Then we would need a dragon to light them anew." Kenna gazed into the distance a moment, shook herself, and said, "Let's go." This path led somewhat downward but came into a large chamber from which branched only three passages. They dropped their cocoons here. Kenna then turned left. Eventually they came to a small chamber with five doors.

"Are all your mountain fortresses the same?"

"Gerald, I have no idea. I don't even know if there are more than two. I have only been here and to *Liqeni i Zjarrtë*. I have not been here since I was a child. But it would make sense to have a common scheme. Put your things away and I will show you something."

"Wait," he replied. "You said you were going to leave word with the triad that we were going."

"I did."

"We spoke to no one."

"I told the bat outside my door." Her smile dared Gerald to ask, but he suspected the answer would be useless. He grinned knowingly, turned, and entered the rightmost room.

He put his pack at the foot of his new bed but kept his weapons this time. While he did not expect to need them, he did not want to have to get them if they wished to go outside.

This room had a bright red dragon sitting with its head cocked skeptically to one side. When he left the room and put the dragon outside the door, Kenna laughed. "I wondered if you would think to do this with no one here!"

"No one expected us, but here we are. Anyone might show up."

"You are right. Notice I have my dragon out here as well!" Hers was dark blue but otherwise identical. They looked in the other three rooms and found more identical carvings in lavender, pale green, and burnt orange.

Gerald shook his head morosely. "No Younger. What is the world coming to?"

They went to what Gerald called the library. The chairs were different here, but every bit as welcoming. Kenna sank deeply into a giant mushroom while Gerald leaned back into an impossibly open dragon's mouth. If anything, it felt even better than the fish had.

"Is it the same?"

"The same as what, Kenna?"

"As riding in Drachmaeius's mouth, of course."

"Not as warm, not as damp, not as nerve-wracking. Remember, at the time I had no idea whose mouth I was in, or what fate awaited me."

"You didn't think a dragon would just eat you rather than carry you?"

"It would not have surprised me if it was waiting for me to

wake, just to taunt me. Argyll might well do that."

"Truth. So we are here. Do you wish to read, talk of grand and glorious things, discuss the triad, or what?"

"Let us play the question game."

"Very well. You may go first since you suggested it."

They took turns answering whatever questions struck each other's fancy. Gerald learned the faerie had perfected the art of building rooms from living rock by combining the work of dwarves and dragons with their own magic. As a result of that he learned that dwarves were not fables, but that there were no more. Kenna would not discuss why.

Kenna learned more from Gerald than he realized. She had long been a student of human emotions, but seldom got such rich insights into how young men related.

Then Gerald caught Kenna off guard. "Why were you banished?"

She lay as if frozen for a long while. When she finally spoke, her voice wandered distantly, as if from a maze of twisty little passages deep in the mountain. "I was a child. My parents were both at *Liqeni i Zjarrtë*. Mother was part of the triad, and my father had come to teach them newly discovered methods of alchemy. Though I was young—I might have looked like an eight-year-old human—I had more experience and understanding than most humans get in a lifetime. And we do not rush our children's education.

"Anyway, I was helping. There was a relic—a woman's wire belt—infused with both magic and poison. Without the magic the poison would have been trapped in the belt. The triad wanted to remove the poison, leaving the belt its defensive power. My father asked me to bring him a beaker with a potion he had made. He carefully placed the belt in it and turned to look at his notes.

"Darciere had no idea I was supposed to help. She had not been around children since she was much younger than I was. She walked into the room and saw a child holding a beaker with acrid fumes coming from it. She screamed my name. Startled, I flung the beaker. Mother caught it, but a great deal of the potion hit her in the face. She was dead within seconds, much of her face and hair melted away.

"Darciere blamed me and banished me. Father was furious, but the triad answers to no one else regarding such things, so we left. The faerie tribes came together to pick a new triad member. They chose Father, but he would not agree to join until I was of age and on my own. Even then he would not join until Darciere revoked the ban. For many years the triad was no such thing.

"Today is the first time Darciere has spoken to me since she banished me. I do not recall seeing her smile before the accident, but since then she has rarely stopped smiling. I believe Mother's death—and Darciere's inability to cope with her part in it—drove her mad.

"I long ago forgave her. I do not know if she has forgiven herself."

There was another long silence. Gerald eventually broke it. "Kenna, I . . ."

"No, Gerald. Do not say you are sorry. I needed to say this. I have said nothing about it to anyone but Father, and that a long time ago. Thank you for asking and thank you for listening. And thank you for your friendship."

They sat in silence a moment before she asked, "Are you hungry?" Her voice was back to normal.

Gerald's stomach growled. "I was going to say no, but someone disagrees."

Kenna rose and walked to the table in the corner. That's when another question hit Gerald. "How is there food here?"

"It is not your turn to question, Lord Gerald."

"Fine. I shall eat instead."

"But I shall answer anyway. It is faerie magic, pure and simple."

Gerald froze, a bite of cheese in his open mouth.

"Pray continue eating. That look does not become you! It is real food—the magic simply has it ready when we need it. We cannot duplicate this today," she added sadly. "The faerie have learned much over the centuries, but some things we have lost. We can no longer build fortresses such as these, nor can we make food appear at need."

"I would ask another question, but it is not my turn."

"What is your question?"

"Oh, good! I can answer your question with a question! You once told me your father watched over me when I was wandering the Highlands after my first parents' deaths. How is that possible if he was part of the triad? Or is that a very recent thing?"

"No, he has been with the triad for many years. But the triad only comes together when there is need. Thankfully the world is not swarming with the sorts of inexplicable problems they pursue! And sometimes while one of the triad chases a hidden or tenuous lead, the others go about other business until there is need for them to meet. They spend far more time apart than together."

Several questions later Gerald recalled something else that had bothered him. "When you first spoke of Fiery Lake and the triad, you said they normally had three guards there, but might have up to a dozen for the things they now delve into. Where are the guards?"

"They are there, never fear. If they are needed, you will see them."

"Are they hiding, or in secret passages, or invisible, or what?"

Kenna smirked. "Only the triad may decide who knows that. Feel free to ask them."

They talked for several hours more. When Gerald yawned mid-sentence the third time, Kenna suggested they go to their rooms and sleep. "Your friends and the high king's men will arrive in the morning. We should be rested and ready to fly to the barracks then."

Though each trusted the other completely, Gerald and Kenna both barred their doors. Each would have said it was to honor Sally.

Just before falling asleep, it dawned on Gerald to wonder why doors in such a place would have bars. That thought kept him awake far longer than he expected, but nothing happened and the few hours of peaceful sleep he got worked like magic. He felt completely rested when he awoke at daybreak.

CHAPTER TWENTY-ONE

WAKING UP

A t breakfast Gerald realized something had been nagging at him. "Kenna, there is not that much light in here. How are these caverns so bright? Is it more faerie magic?"

"It is actually dwarf alchemy. The triad spent months trying to duplicate it after Father accepted the position. They failed. They were rather embarrassed."

"Why?"

"Pride, I suppose. The faerie and dwarves, though friends after a fashion, were always competing. The Eldest believes there are wonders that could have been but never were because the competition sometimes moved beyond the friendly. It is ineffably sad—things that should have been and are not, things that were but will not be again—all lost because of pride. It was nearly our downfall. It felled the dwarves."

Her forlorn look tempted Gerald to hold her. This made him feel guilty, partly because of Sally's jealousy and partly because . . . he simply wanted to hold Kenna. He shook his head to clear it. "What happened to the dwarves?"

Kenna sat for a minute as if she had not heard. "That is a tale for another day, and not in these halls. For now we must finish and go, or at least go out the door and see if Selene knows when the others may arrive."

Again there were Voices on their doorstep. This time there were five. One spoke. "We will get Selene." And then there were none.

"Rather rash of them to assume," Gerald said.

Kenna watched the sky as she replied, "I suspect they were under orders."

"Oh. Of course they were. If I were a dragon, those are the orders I would have given."

"You know this because you are a dragon lord?"

"I have Voices. By a dragon's own admission I make fewmets. Therefore I am a dragon. Therefore I know how dragons think."

"Your logic is faultless, dragon lord. Or dragon. Whatever you may be."

Gerald bowed. "Thank you, princess. My logic is honored to be so honored."

Just as the sun rose over the nearest peak, it was obscured by a rapidly approaching dragon. Then Selene was hovering so close they could almost touch her face.

"Good morning. Lord Gerald, the garrison draws near. They should be at the barracks in about an hour."

"How do you know this, Selene?" Gerald asked.

"I have been flying as high as I could. I saw them as dots far away. I know the distance at which I can first see them and how quickly they fly. Santana will meet them at the Teeth and take them to the barracks by a route that will avoid the triad's fortress. They should not be able to see it anyway, but we do not take chances."

"Why shouldn't they be able to see it?"

"It is shielded from sight unless you are practically in it. A hiker might stumble upon it, were it not constantly guarded. From a distance, there is nothing exciting or different about it.

We know where it is, so we come and go as we will."

Gerald shook his head, amazed. This was magic on a scale he had not imagined. "So when I first saw it, I could only do so because we were close?"

"Yes. And even then, had not the triad changed their magic with you in mind, you would have needed to be even closer to see it."

Gerald looked at Kenna, recalling a blazing sun in her hands that killed a dragon and wounded others. "Kenna, is the triad more powerful than you?"

"Individually, perhaps yes, perhaps no. But faerie together multiply their power. These three are skilled at working as one. As a group, they are many times more powerful than I."

Gerald shivered, something he rarely did unless he was cold. "That's a lot of power."

"True, Gerald, but there's a lot of power in Selene as well."

"True also. Selene, would you mind using that power to take us to the barracks?"

"That is why I am here rather than watching from the skies, dragon lord. Get your things and we shall go."

In a few minutes they were on their way. No one talked this trip. A half hour later they were on the ground in a small clearing near a two-story rock building with many small windows and a small tower in the middle of the roof. A smaller building with two wooden doors stood nearby. One of the doors had clearly lost a battle. As Gerald and Kenna folded their hides and blankets, Selene walked to the buildings and sniffed about for a moment.

"There have been no humans here for some time. There are small animals, however."

As she spoke, a red fox darted out of the smaller building into nearby tall grass.

"Wolves have been here recently, as well as jackals, but no bears." She sniffed again. "Definitely no bears."

"No bears is good," Gerald observed.

"Bears are no problem," Kenna said dismissively. "Wolves are more of one, because they travel in packs. I can easily handle one or two bears, but a pack of wolves is more difficult. I wish we had bows and arrows."

"The garrison will have them."

Gerald and Kenna had just finished examining the buildings when the first dragons arrived. These bore the high king's men and horses. While Gerald thought he recognized two dragons by sight from the moot at Lochmaldie, he did not know any of them. They all greeted him and bowed their heads, so he did the same. He was happy to see MacIntyre, one of King Dugald's most trusted captains.

Most of the high king's men were reasonably ready, but one was still woozy from a sleeping potion. They left him propped against a small tree, surrounded by hides, blankets and packs. The next wave of dragons hovered low in the clearing, gently lowering the slings that held their horses. Only after their mounts were all lying quietly and the dragons had left did Kenna begin to wake the horses.

"Wait," Gerald said as Kenna awoke the third horse. "You were going to put them to sleep but we came ahead. Who did that?"

"I do not know," she said, concentrating on the horse. The first two were already stumbling around drunkenly, being guided by their riders to a nearby cistern full of water.

MacIntyre knew. "He was both bard and alchemist, with a strange name . . . ."

"Hercule?" Kenna said as the third horse struggled to its feet.

"That was it, yes."

"I have not seen him in years."

MacIntyre called a guard over to get his horse before Kenna moved to the next one. "Have you been inside?" he asked Gerald.

"We have," Gerald replied. "We had a couple of ideas, but otherwise it's up to you."

"Do you want to show me now?"

"Let's wait until Kenna is through with the horses."

The faerie grimaced. "This horse is proving difficult. He is older than the others—not too old, but older, and they do not always take so well to the faerie sleep."

"Will he be okay?" MacIntyre asked.

"I think so. We will leave him alone for a few minutes." She moved to the next one. The remaining horses awoke easily. "So one man still woozy and one horse sleeping soundly. Wait!" She placed her hand on the horse's forehead for a few seconds before laughing. "Wake up, sleepyhead!" she shouted and slapped the horse on the neck. The stallion bolted awake and leapt to his feet. MacIntyre and Kenna grabbed him at the same time.

"Whoa, Mungo! Easy, boy!" MacIntyre called. The horse quickly calmed down, though he remained skittish until someone produced carrots.

Kenna explained. "Though I brought him out of the faerie sleep, he was asleep naturally as well. That happens so seldom I did not think of it at first."

MacIntyre nodded and grinned. "Ranald! Watch after Mungo for me!" He turned back to Kenna. "May we go to the buildings now?"

"Of course. The smaller one first, shall we?"

They walked around it before entering. It was about twelve feet long, six wide, and six high, with a slanted roof. Kenna explained, "The door obviously needs to be fixed. We originally thought of this as a storage shed, but we do not have that much to store, and there is plenty of room inside the barracks."

"It's a shame it's not bigger," MacIntyre mused, "or we might house the horses here."

"No need," Gerald said. MacIntyre raised an eyebrow but Gerald offered no more.

They entered the barracks through even larger doors, but these were in good shape. They were also thicker, with provisions for two bars to lock them from inside. MacIntyre nodded approvingly.

Then he looked around, nonplussed. There were columns and partial wooden walls everywhere, with a large, open area down the middle. Musty old hay was strewn heavily about the dirt floor except in the very middle.

"These aren't rooms! These are stalls!"

"Exactly!" Kenna laughed. "Gerald, I believe he caught on more quickly than we did."

Gerald nodded. "The actual barracks are upstairs." He pointed to stairs in the front two corners and ladders in the back two. "The ladders need some work, but the stairs are rock and as solid as the outside walls—which are quite solid."

Gerald led the way upstairs, where MacIntyre found what he had looked for downstairs—a large, open room with beds in neat rows. He counted twenty beds, most with trunks at their feet. There were two large fireplaces, one at each end of the room. At the far end were three small rooms on their right and a large room on their left. A small hallway just past the rooms led to the ladders at either corner of the building.

Each of the smaller rooms had a bed, a small desk, a block of wood for a seat, two trunks, and a shelf. The larger room had a long trestle table and benches.

"Kenna and I plan to use two of the smaller rooms," Gerald said. "We assume you would like the other."

MacIntyre shook his head. "I will stay with my men. We can use that room for storage, perhaps for the travel hides and such. Was there anything else?"

Gerald and Kenna shook their heads no.

"Very well!" MacIntyre looked out a narrow window and saw his men up and about. He glanced up and smiled. "More work. It looks as if the rest of the garrison is arriving. Let's go."

By the time they exited the barracks, the first dragons were placing their cocoons gently on the ground. In addition to Santana, Gerald recognized Drachmaeius. Only recently had he learned that the latter, who had once planned to eat Gerald's adoptive mother, Samantha, had been considering whether to release her when she had fallen to her death attempting to escape. Seeing Drachmaeius, he wanted to both greet him and smite him.

He settled for greeting him by name, as he did Santana.

"Gerald!" Santana called as Kenna began waking Donald, the warrior leading King Donald's men. "What do you think of my cave?"

"Your cave?" Gerald looked around to see what he had missed.

"My cave. You might have misconstrued it as a small building with a broken door."

Gerald stared at the building with a door hanging off. "Your cave? Why? How?"

Flames of laughter made the horses shy. Gerald winced. *I wonder if they will ever get used to dragons.*

Santana replied, "When I was young, I hid in it once. Argyll's mother Argyll was hunting me in anger, so I hid in there. After I was sure she was far away, I emerged just in time to thoroughly frighten a woman carrying laundry. Her young twins—furious at seeing their mother intimidated—came running at me waving sticks, screaming they were dragon swords. Having no desire to fight, I flew away. I could hear them behind me—one screaming her victory to the skies as the other told their mother not to worry because they were great dragon lords and would protect her."

Gerald and MacIntyre looked back and forth between Santana and the building, trying to imagine Santana small enough to fit inside.

"Are you sure it's the same one?" Gerald asked. "I can't believe it's as old as you."

Santana looked more closely. "You are right; that is new, maybe two hundred years old."

"New!" MacIntyre snorted.

"New," Santana agreed.

"New," added Kenna.

"New," Gerald said knowingly. "Definitely new. Not your cave after all, Santana."

"I will leave now lest you impugn my honor so far that I am compelled to eat you."

"I would merely carve my way out," Gerald responded.

"Farewell, dragon lord," Santana said with a bow. Drachmaeius and the other dragons on the ground bowed and took flight as well, making room for the dragons carrying horses. Gerald noticed three other dragons high above.

"No one should be looking for us, but if they are, they know where to find us." Gerald said with annoyance.

"Just as well," Kenna replied. "It's more likely to be friend than foe."

"I suppose," MacIntyre said, "but it's a warrior's job to prepare for the worst." He suddenly wished there were at least two dragon lords among the men at his command. Gerald was the only one here, and he might be gone about his business should an attack occur. He and Donald had some serious planning to do.

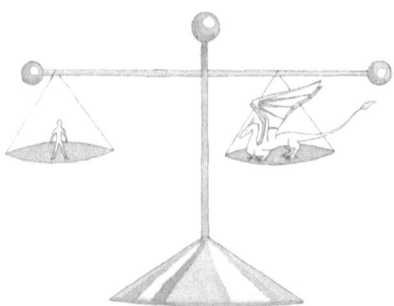

CHAPTER TWENTY-TWO

THE BALANCE POINT

By midafternoon they had done all they could for the barracks. It had been in reasonable shape but needed cleaning. A half-dozen, full water cisterns stood ready to help. Horses took turns hauling a cart with buckets to and from the nearby river, which Selene informed them was the Drin. The most onerous part was carrying the buckets upstairs to refill the cisterns.

Watching Justin and Eoin put the cart and buckets in the shed, Gerald remarked to MacIntyre, "It's too bad we can't get the horses to carry the water up the stairs."

Before the high king's man could reply, Selene spoke up. "If only someone thought to ask a dragon to help." She sighed, sounding eerily human.

MacIntyre looked wide-eyed at Gerald. "Dare we?"

Gerald kept his face straight. "It was her idea, after all."

MacIntyre straightened up, thought hard for a few seconds, and asked, "Oh mighty Selene, might you or another dragon hoist the water to the second floor for us?"

"No," Selene said, her eyes spinning mischievously.

MacIntyre stood rigidly, looking to Gerald for help.

Gerald shrugged.

"But . . ." MacIntyre sputtered at Selene, "it was your idea!"

"Indeed," the dragon replied.

Gerald burst out laughing. "Selene, clearly you have an idea. What is it?"

"Something I have seen on castles and other of your structures, though I have seen it used otherwise. Attach a strong arm of wood to the roof with a system of wheels and ropes to aid in raising and lowering the buckets, if not the casks."

MacIntyre smacked his head. "Of course. A pulley!" Red-faced, he addressed Selene. "Thank you, Selene. I don't know why we didn't think of that."

She shook her head woefully, again mimicking human behavior far more than Gerald was used to. "You are most welcome, captain, but I am disappointed in Gerald. Since he is a dragon, he should have thought of it."

Gerald hung his head in shame. MacIntyre refused the bait and smiled as if he understood.

Selene then made a suggestion. "Have you a list of what you need?"

Gerald and Kenna both said yes.

"Then you should go to see Lady Fjorela at *Kalaja e Rozafës*— Rozafa Castle—in Shkodër, and ask of her the nearest place to buy what you need. Much will undoubtedly be nearby, but you should visit the lady first. I know MacIntyre would prefer he or another warrior go, but I can only carry two of you easily. Gerald must go, of course. Kenna should be the second, both because she is an envoy and because Fjorela will feel less threatened with a woman there in a position of authority. Too many men here see her as a usurper."

"Is she?" Gerald asked.

"I do not know," Selene replied. "Her husband, the last of the Balsha line—arguably usurpers from their first day in the castle—disappeared three months ago. Some of the surrounding lords claim she has done nothing to seek him and imply she killed him so she might reign alone. As coincidence would have it, all of these lords wish to increase their lands and power. Rozafa is a large, strong fortress in the midst of much fertile land."

Gerald looked at Kenna. "Is there any reason we should not go? If the triad needs us, we can as easily go from Shkodër as here."

When Kenna nodded, Gerald continued. "MacIntyre, can you survive without us?"

"I do not know what we will do without your wit, Lord Gerald, but we will survive somehow. I would protest at your going without warriors, but I do not wish to insult Selene. And I seriously doubt there is anything she cannot handle that even all twelve of us could do much about."

"At last you have learned wisdom."

Ignoring this, MacIntyre turned to Kenna. "Do you recall everything we need?"

"I do, captain. I will not forget." She smiled.

MacIntyre blushed and excused himself. "I wish to check with the guard in the tower," he said as he left.

"What was that for?" Gerald asked, shaking off the giddiness her smile had invoked.

"I'm sorry. I didn't mean you to feel that. MacIntyre is a good man, but I think he is sometimes taken for granted. I simply wished him to know he was appreciated." When Gerald looked away, she winked at Selene. "I'm glad you had them use the smaller building to store the hides. Now we won't have to tote them up and down stairs. If we are leaving now, as I assume we are, we should get the blankets."

Gerald spread his arms wide. "Feel the air! Do we need them?"

"Perhaps not, so long as we do not fly back at night."

Kenna reminded Gerald to change into his nicer clothes

before they left. "It is especially important we show honor. And we represent the high king of Scotland!"

A half hour later they were on their way. Almost as soon as they were aloft, Gerald asked a question. "Selene, after your part in the rescue at Invercharnan, I asked about being further in your and Santana's debt. You said it was more complex than that, but I have heard no more since then."

"I am surprised, Lord Gerald. We assumed Cuthbert would explain things to you."

"We've all been a bit busy the last few weeks."

"I suppose you have." She paused for about a minute. "We speak of debt in terms of balance. I assume you are familiar with the scales traders use?"

"Of course. I have seen and used them throughout my life."

"Imagine, then, a scale where the arm on one side was longer than the arm on the other. How would the long arm affect things?"

"There are such things, though they are disguised. Afagdu said unscrupulous traders use them."

"Ah, so you know the principle. Imagine a much longer arm, say twice the length of the other arm. What would happen?"

"A weight in the pan on the long arm would have twice as much impact as the same weight on the short side. Or you could use a lesser weight by half to get the same impact as a weight on the short side."

"Afagdu taught you well," remarked Selene.

"I have used levers to move boulders."

"I did not think of that."

"I assume you have never needed to."

"True. Anything I would need a lever to move would be heavy enough that I would not know what to use for a lever! But back to the scales of debt. The arms are the same length, of course, and the scales are perfectly balanced under the laws of debt laid down at the dawn of creation.

"But imagine now that one of the pans can be moved at will along the beams. In this case, the weight of the debt upon that pan would have less impact as it was moved to the beam's center. If the pan were an individual, that individual's actions would cause them less debt, correct?"

"Would it not also lessen their debt relief?"

"In theory, yes, but such individuals seldom get far enough into debt that it matters."

"That would only be true near the balance point."

"I have never heard of anyone being anywhere except at the normal spot at the end of the beam, or in the middle, at the balance point."

"The balance point?" Gerald thought hard about this. "I do not see how they would any longer partake in the laws of debt. Nothing would impact them."

"Correct. The few we have known of who lived in the center tended to one day find themselves back at the end of the beam. At least two lived out the rest of their days in the center."

Kenna joined in. "You should explain that you speak only of men and dragons, Selene."

Dragon laughter trailed dangerously near Gerald's blanket. "I would have said so eventually, Kenna! But I suspect Lord Gerald knows that."

Gerald started. "I do, but I had forgotten the faerie are not under the same laws."

Kenna disagreed. "We are not and yet we are! There are laws of debt apart from those involving dragons. It is why Darciere is the head of the triad and likely will be her whole life. I cannot say more, but you may infer the rest."

"So what has this to do with us, Selene?" Gerald thought he was beginning to understand but was afraid to seriously consider it.

"This is why I said it was complex, Lord Gerald. One can move to the center, the very pivot point of justice, in one of several ways. It can be something they are born into—you would call it part of their destiny. It can be some deed or deeds they have done. It can be circumstances, such as something that happened to them.

"You, the youngest dragon lord in all of history, seem qualified in all three ways. You are your own triad, as it were. And you are part of several triads of enormous import: Gerald, the Eldest, and Younger; Gerald, Kenna, and Cuthbert; Gerald, Sally, and Scythia; Gerald, Argyll, and Morgan le Fay. There are other lesser but important triads as well."

Gerald started to pinch himself to make sure he wasn't dreaming, but recalled Cynthia telling him it proved nothing.

"Selene, I wish you had waited to tell me this until after I had gone as envoy to Rozafa."

"You asked me now, youngest lord envoy. Do you have more questions?"

"I am almost afraid to ask, but I must. Is there anything else we should know going to this castle?"

"Not that I know, but Kenna may know of something."

She did. "There is a legend, Gerald. It is absurd, but it has lasted through the ages. The legend claims three brothers originally built this castle. Or tried to. They would work on the walls all day, but every night the walls would collapse. Eventually they asked an old man, some sort of priest or wise man, what was wrong. He claimed a demon was destroying their work each night and they must sacrifice something of great value before they could build the castle. The brothers decided one of their wives must become a living sacrifice."

"What? Why?"

"Gerald, it is a legend. But think! Even today, women in many parts of Europe are not valued as much as among the Scots. If some local lord can conquer Fjorela, he will expect her to become his wife or mistress and meet his every whim or suffer punishment—possibly death. Legends often reflect cultures, and this one reflects the time and place that birthed it."

Kenna paused. When Gerald asked nothing further, she continued. "The brothers decided that whichever wife brought lunch the next day must be the sacrifice. They made each other vow not to tell their wives ahead of time. But the older brothers told their wives not to bring lunch the next day. The youngest brother's wife Rozafa, though it was not her turn, took lunch.

"When she was told of the bargain, she was of course sad but agreed to it. She did, however, request that she be walled up alive in the castle and holes be left: for her right eye—to see her baby, for her right breast—to suckle the child, for her right hand—to touch the child, and for her right foot—to rock its cradle. Her husband agreed but wept bitterly.

"There is a place in the entry passage with four holes lined up top to bottom, where a white liquid drips down. This is supposed to be Rozafa's milk, flowing miraculously to this day. Thus the castle bears her name, since she and the castle are one."

Before Gerald could think how to respond, Selene called out, "The castle is ahead."

Gerald had to squint to see the castle. He finally saw men and horses, which let him gauge the castle's size. He gawked. "Selene, that is a small town, not a castle!"

"There is a small town inside the walls, but the walls surround the hilltop. It is well fortified."

"It's huge. Edinburgh Castle would fit inside those walls with much room to spare!"

"Yes, it would. Room for dragons. And today they shall have one."

"Are they expecting one, Selene?" Gerald asked with some apprehension.

"Shortly after you two arrived at the Teeth, Voices were dispatched to inform Fjorela that they should expect the envoys of the high king of Scotland within the week. The envoys might arrive on horseback or by dragon after seeing the triad."

"What does she know of the triad?" Kenna asked.

"She knows only that they seek the end to problems caused by a powerful, long-dead sorceress, which is as much as anyone outside the faerie and a few people you are aware of know. They are unlikely to have heard the name le Fay. She went by another name here.

"We will not circle around to fly out of the sun; that may be seen as aggressive. Let us avoid that."

No one argued.

Just as Selene prepared to land, horns echoed off the walls. Dozens of warriors on horseback and another hundred on foot streamed from various buildings. As Selene dropped Gerald and Kenna gently, she said quietly, "It is but an honor guard. Still, be on your toes. The land has long been at war, and they are of necessity a suspicious people. They must be, or they would not have survived."

To Gerald's utter surprise, Selene took flight and was gone.

CHAPTER TWENTY-THREE

THE LADY OF ROZAFA

The envoys stood as if relaxed, Gerald drawing strength from whatever Kenna was doing. He could feel her radiating goodwill.

None of this was necessary. Everyone around them was calm. A few warriors watched Selene's retreat skyward. No hands neared weapons. A warrior on foot followed by two columns of six more approached.

Kenna spoke in a loud voice, but Gerald could make out nothing other than names. When she finished, she translated rapidly for Gerald.

"Greetings, warriors of Albania! The high king of Scotland, King Dugald, sends his thanks to you and your people for your hospitality, as do we. I am Kenna, and this is Lord Gerald. We would speak with Lady Fjorela."

The captain of the guard halted a few feet away and responded. Kenna continued translating. "They greet us in the name of their lady and lord. We are welcome, and he would take us now to Fjorela. We may leave our blankets here and they will see to them."

Gerald smiled at the captain, finally settling back into the role of envoy. "Then let us go."

The expectancy on his face was apparently all the guard captain needed. Before Kenna could translate, the captain gave an order and his men separated into two lines. The captain led the way between them. As Gerald and Kenna reached the middle, the group started forward around them.

"They're actually marching," Gerald noted. "Like the English."

"Gerald, the Scots and Irish are two of the few peoples whose armies do not put time into marching. Many societies—not just the English—have taken this as a sign of military weakness and lack of discipline. And once it was true, which takes away nothing from your people's spirit or fighting prowess. But until the dragons returned, you did not fight large forces well, except in rare cases where a few warriors had learned to do so. Many modern military leaders foolishly associate marching with the ability to fight effectively together.

"But I think these people simply take pride in it. And they are not alone. Do not judge an army by whether it marches. Wait and learn why they march."

"Very well. Why do you speak Albanian?"

"Later."

Gerald glanced at Kenna. Although she strode serenely with her face forward, her eyes darted about taking everything in. Gerald followed suit.

As they entered the castle proper, most of the honor guard fell back, leaving only the leader ahead of the envoys and two warriors behind. They walked in silence down long corridors and up a flight of stairs. Finally they entered a large office. A tall woman stood looking out a window. She wore a black cape with gold-highlighted black fur at the neck. Her hair was thick, black, and fell to her shoulder blades. The tip of a gold and black scabbard peeked underneath the left side of her cape. Her boots were black as well, with gold stitching.

The captain announced them. Gerald heard Dugald's name. Soon after, the captain indicated Kenna and said something that sounded like "ship."

"Ship?" Gerald asked quietly.

"S-h-q-i-p. The 'q' is silent. It's their language."

The lady turned around and took their measure. Gerald could read little from her expression, but was somewhat surprised at the makeup she wore on her tanned face. It reminded him of K'Pene and traders from exotic, distant lands. He realized he should not have been surprised. Albania was just such a land.

"Greetings, lady and lord. I am Fjorela. Welcome to Shkodër and to Rozafa." She said this in English and bowed her head.

"Greetings in the name of High King Dugald and the people of Scotland," Kenna replied. She and Gerald bowed their heads in return before Kenna continued, "Your English is very good."

The lady laughed. "I fear I speak little English and less Scots. I am told you speak *Shqip*."

"I do."

"Good," Fjorela replied in *Shqip*. "Let us have coffee and discuss the reason you came here. Or would you prefer wine?"

"Kafe, ju lutem." Kenna said softly to Gerald, "She offered wine and coffee. I replied, 'Coffee, thank you.'"

They were offered seats on supple leather cushions at a low table. A handmaid brought coffee, along with a platter of meats and breads. Kenna continued translating as they snacked.

"I apologize for not knowing your language," Gerald said in English. "I had little time to prepare for my visit to your beautiful country."

"I was surprised your king did not ask that you stay here at Rozafa."

"We will be coming and going by dragon, sometimes with no notice. He was not sure your people would be comfortable with that."

"Some would and some would not. We have few dragons nearby. We have made peace with three, but two others do not want peace. And some of my people do not want peace with dragons. This is true, even though a peace has been declared." She paused. "I admit to suspicion about this peace."

Kenna looked at Gerald, who wisely nodded and let her explain. She said in Shqip, "Lady Fjorela, Lord Gerald and I were there when the Lord of the Western Isles, the Eldest among dragons in all of Europe and Africa, brought the dragons together to propose peace. We, with Cuthbert, a wise master of dragon lore, witnessed over two hundred dragons discuss this. We saw with our own eyes and heard with our own ears the discussions and the results. Only a handful of dragons refused, and at least three of those are dead. The rest of the dragons have worked hard for peace, fighting mankind only when attacked in some dastardly manner."

When Kenna translated this part for Gerald, he had difficulty keeping a straight face. While they had, indeed, been at the moot, he had understood nothing of the dragon's discussion but what the Eldest said at the end. He glanced at his hands and repressed a smile. *A handful of dragons would be no dragons at all!*

Gerald felt he should add something. He spoke in Scots, pausing for Kenna to translate. "The leader of the rebels is my sworn nemesis. I will not relent until he is dead. The reason I am here is that he has found an ancient evil with which to attack my home. My betrothed lies under a spell because of this. We are here to help those looking to fight this magic invoked by Argyll against us."

Fjorela hissed. "You dare to say his name? Here, in someone else's home?"

"Please forgive me for not warning you! Argyll owes me a great debt and cannot harm me. He does not bother to come when I speak his name. I could stand on a mountaintop and chant his name for hours, and he would be unlikely to appear. If he did, it would be only to revile me. I have charged him through his fire and been unscathed, though it destroyed everything around me for perhaps one hundred feet."

When Kenna translated, Fjorela looked skeptical. The captain of the guard standing rigidly near the window looked ready to challenge Gerald.

Kenna interceded. "Lady Fjorela, have you heard of the youngest dragon lord?"

"I have heard a rumor through the dragons of a very young dragon lord who has befriended many dragons, and who was in part responsible for the peace. Is this then he?"

"It is."

The lady of Rozafa looked at Gerald and asked in English, "How old are you?"

"Nearly sixteen." Gerald suddenly wondered if he was the wrong man for this job, just as he had the first time Dugald asked him to be envoy.

Fjorela smiled at Gerald's expression. "Sixteen is a man, indeed. My captain had proven himself on the battlefield at thirteen. I asked only because I was curious, not because I doubted you." She looked at her captain and asked in Shqip, "Kreshnik, what do you think?"

"I judge a man by his actions, both on and off the battlefield. I have not seen the envoy do anything yet, so I must reserve judgment."

Fjorela smiled at Kenna. "Kreshnik is a warrior to the core." She drained her cup and her handmaid refilled it, as well as Kenna's and Gerald's. Fjorela switched back to English and addressed Gerald. "The day ends soon and your dragon circles above, so I assume you will leave soon. What can I do for you?"

"First, King Dugald thanks you for the use of the barracks. He asks that you accept this gift in return." Kreshnik tensed as Gerald reached into a pocket, but relaxed when a small bag of gold emerged. Gerald handed the bag across the table. Fjorela's eyes lit when she felt its weight. Gerald continued, "Kenna has a list of things we need. We are happy to bargain for them with those near the barracks but are not sure where to go."

"May I see the list?"

Kenna replied, "It is in my head. Shall I tell you?"

"It is no matter. While I am glad to have met you and honored you came, as soon as I heard a flight of dragons had been seen heading toward the old barracks, I sent one of my advisors who knows the area and can translate for you. She should arrive tomorrow by boat. Her name is Eviola. I ask only that if for some reason she is not there by noon, you send me word."

"How did you learn of our arrival so quickly?"

Fjorela smiled. "We have been invaded many times, especially by the Ottomans. We have many watchmen and many methods of communication. I will not say more."

"Of course."

The lady of Rozafa stood. "Please see me again if you have a chance. I would learn more of your country and your people, and of the peace with the dragons." She smiled warmly at Gerald. "And of the youngest dragon lord, whom your high king sends as envoy."

Both envoys stood as Gerald replied. "We will, and we would learn more of you and your country as well. Thank you again for your help."

"You are welcome. Anyone who comes against both ancient evil and fiendish dragons is a friend. Or at least an ally."

Kenna replied, "Let us be both friends and allies. We speak for Scotland in this."

Fjorela's response surprised them. She stepped forward and embraced Kenna, kissing her on both cheeks. Kenna reacted quickly, kissing back. Fjorela then did the same with Gerald. Prepared by Kenna's example, he did the same. Stepping back, Fjorela said, "Safe travels to you and your people, blessings to those you love, and destruction to your enemies."

After translating, Kenna spoke a blessing over Fjorela and

her people as well. Fjorela looked surprised and embraced Kenna again, thanking her (Gerald assumed) profusely. As Kreshnik led them out, Kenna said quietly to Gerald. "Do not ask. Part of the blessing was personal."

"How could you know . . . ?"

"Gerald, I will say no more about it." And she never did.

CHAPTER TWENTY-FOUR

TASTE OF A LEGEND

Kenna asked their guide, "Please take us through the front gate."

Kreshnik turned around, surprised. "You do not wish to leave from where you came?"

"We would see Rozafa's final home."

"Ah, of course. We can see that and then return to your blankets."

"Would not some of your people feel more comfortable if Selene—the dragon—landed outside the walls?"

He nodded. "Some might, but since we are at peace, they should get used to dragons."

"So you trust the dragon?"

"I trust no one, but I no longer trust dragons less than our kind."

Kenna glanced around casually and lowered her voice. "Surely you trust your lady?"

The captain dropped back closer and also glanced around. "I trust no one, including her. Including you. She knows and is content. In fact, it is why she entrusts me with the guard."

As they walked into a long manmade tunnel, he stopped

near a tiny grotto. To its left were a series of holes between floor and ceiling. The wall was white here and wet in spots. A pool of chalky liquid pooled at their feet. Two small, white stalactites hung from a protruding brick.

"This is it," Kreshnik said.

Gerald stared, unimpressed after all he had heard. "I would expect these," he pointed at the stalactites, "to be much larger, if the castle is anywhere near as old as I thought."

Kreshnik scowled. "People break them off. Vandals do it to prove they can. Worshippers think it a miracle, that Rozafa is an unknown saint, and they want a relic. Lady Fjorela says it is of no consequence and that we must not concern ourselves with it."

"You disagree," a woman's voice behind them said.

The envoys turned, surprised to find Lady Fjorela there.

Kreshnik said, "While it is a small matter, I still think it should be addressed. But my lady knows my opinion on this."

Kenna translated as quietly as she could during this discussion.

"So what do you think of Rozafa?" Fjorela asked in English, pointing to the damp, white wall.

"I think if she has survived all these years, there is some very great magic involved," Gerald said.

Kenna added, "And why should she stay, with her child long gone?"

Fjorela nodded and switched back to Shqip. "The legend changes over time. It is said that her lineage is unbroken, that some of her offspring have always lived here, and that she remains alive in the wall so the castle might stand. Some have even said the women in her line sneak their children here at night that she might feed them."

Kreshnik snorted at this. "Then she must bewitch my guards so they see nothing!"

Fjorela smiled fondly at her captain. "Did he tell you he

trusts no one? It is not true. He trusts his men. And he is jealous to protect their reputation."

Kreshnik did not reply, but his lady's praise clearly pleased him.

Fjorela continued. "I have challenged women I have heard say these things. I ask if they have tasted the milk. They have not, of course."

Gerald's eyes widened when Kenna translated this. "Have you?"

She leered at him. "Why should I not? It is the best way to prove whether it is milk! But it is only water tainted with minerals, a white mud. You can taste the lime in it. Any woman who fed her child this would be mad."

Kenna smiled. "Why are you here, since we said our farewells and had not mentioned coming this way when we left you?"

Fjorela laughed. "I knew you must come to see this for yourselves. I always learn something of who someone is by their reaction to Rozafa."

"May we ask what you have learned of us?" Gerald asked.

"You may," the lady replied. "I have learned you are who you seem to be, and I find no reason to revise my previous opinion or revoke my blessing. And what have you learned of me?"

"That you are bold, practical, and wiser than many who hold such positions."

"Have you met many such, Lord Gerald?"

As she interpreted, Kenna added, "Have care, envoy."

Gerald replied, "Lady Fjorela, I have thrice been called upon to act as High King Dugald's envoy. I have met with the kings and queens of Scotland. I have met with a self-styled inquisitor. There are good men and women, and there are fools, power seekers, and dangerous folk in such positions, just as there are anywhere. I have watched a king provoke his people to rebellion. His forces foolishly attacked dragons while waging that war. He lost his kingdom. I do not claim to know everything, but I know enough to see you are insightful and just."

"Thank you, Lord Gerald. I wish you could stay longer. May I walk with you to your dragon and meet him?"

"Her," Kenna corrected. "Selene is one of us."

Fjorela grinned wolfishly. "I have been called a dragon."

Kenna continued. "We would be honored to have you walk with us."

As they emerged from the tunnel back inside the grounds, Fjorela told Kreshnik to have his men give them more space. Kreshnik's expression betrayed disapproval and resignation. Gerald almost laughed. He had seen this expression on warriors' faces often enough when dealing with those they were sworn to protect.

Fjorela glanced at Gerald and back at Kenna. The faerie arched an eyebrow. Fjorela hesitated, then spoke quietly in broken English, using Shqip only where necessary. "You have not inquired about my missing husband. Why is that?"

Surprised, Kenna replied, "Selene said he is believed dead, but that some think you had a hand in that. She also said those complaining loudest were those wishing these lands—and in some cases yourself—were theirs. We saw no reason to ask further."

Fjorela relaxed a little. "That is true enough. My late husband was a pig. He came from a long line of pigs. His family took over this region mainly by trickery, thuggery, and possibly devilry. He chose me as soon as I began to look like a woman. I never chose him. It would have been foolish to deny him, though, because he was ten years older and already lord of this region. He asked me to marry him. When I asked for time to think, he raped me. He called it wooing me, but I knew there was no other choice but death. We married a month later. That was over fifteen years ago. Half of my life.

"Three months ago, he went hunting for Ottomans said to

be in the area. As soon as dragons spread news of the peace, our old enemies resumed their campaigns. I took steps to make sure Lord Hoxha would never return. It took many years longer than I first planned, but the land is free of his and his family's evil."

Gerald was amazed. "Why do you tell us this?"

She looked at him appraisingly. "I trust your fellow envoy and she clearly trusts you. I trust only a few more people than Kreshnik does, but I know dragons do not lie, and the one who told of your coming said she would trust you both with her life. When Kenna blessed me, she said that which spoke peace to the place in me that has died a thousand deaths since Enver first 'wooed' me."

They came to the blankets as Kenna finished translating. Gerald said in English, "Thank you for trusting us, Lady Fjorela. Is there anything else we can do for you?"

"Just rid the world of whatever evil you can."

"That is why we are here."

Fjorela looked at Gerald but spoke to Kenna. "*Nese ai tregon dikujt, preje ne fyt.*"

Without translating, Kenna replied in English, "What else would I do?" Both women laughed. They embraced again as Gerald waved Selene down.

Kenna introduced Selene and Fjorela. Selene said, "It is an honor to meet you, Lord Fjorela."

"Why do you call me lord?" Fjorela asked sharply.

"We call all those who have gained the trust of at least three dragons this. Man or woman, we use the title 'dragon lord' for such."

"Oh." Fjorela seemed taken aback.

Selene continued. "For some time now, Albania has taken the two-headed eagle as its symbol, and this is good for Albania. Yet there are times a single head is best. I wish you a long and healthy life, Lord Fjorela, and peace and prosperity for your people."

"Thank you. And our blessings upon you as well."

Selene bowed her head. As Gerald and Kenna had wrapped in their blankets and the sun was almost behind the taller buildings of the castle, Selene picked them up and departed.

Once they were well away from the castle, Selene asked, "How was the visit?"

"Productive," Kenna answered.

"Informative," Gerald added.

"Terse?" Selene added after a minute of silence.

The others laughed. Gerald said, "I learned that Kenna knows *Shqip*, the Albanian language. When did you learn that, Kenna?"

After a brief pause, she replied, "I didn't."

"What do you mean?"

"Darciere would want you to swear on the sword, but you already know more than she realizes and you have faithfully kept our secrets. The faerie can understand and speak any language. It is not so with writing. When we are near someone, we can understand their thoughts as they speak. Not all of their thoughts, only those they speak. When we speak to them, we can understand what they need to hear even before they hear it, and so we can speak in a language they know but we do not. Here, away from the castle, since neither of you speak *Shqip*, I could say no more than a half dozen words I remember, such as *kalaja* for castle."

Gerald whistled, or would have had not the wind made that impossible. "I wish you could impart that to me!"

"I wish I could impart it to many! But it is simply part of who we are, not something we can teach or give away."

"And what of your shopping list, Kenna?" Selene asked.

"One of Lady Fjorela's advisors was already dispatched by boat up the Drin to be envoy to King Dugald's envoys. Apparently she can speak either English or Scots as well as Albanian, and is familiar with the area."

"I saw Fjorela had recently been faerie blessed. Was that you, Kenna?"

"It was."

"That is good. She cares for her people and her life has been hard."

"We know. She told us some of her story."

"I do not know many details, but it was written all over her."

"What was?" Gerald asked in some confusion.

"Her pain, her freedom, her healing, her concern for others. She wears her soul close to her skin."

"If you say so."

Kenna laughed. "She was mostly kidding when she said to cut your throat if you told her secrets."

"She said that?"

"Oh, yes, near the end. I must have forgotten to mention it."

"I think I will invest in a mail collar."

"Then I would have to use a very large, powerful knife."

"I suppose I shall just have to keep quiet."

"Selene, what are the odds of that?" Kenna asked.

"I cannot count that low, Kenna."

A half hour later they were dropping through deep dusk toward the barracks.

"Good!" Gerald cried. "It's getting cold up here."

"I can warm you up," Selene said, shooting flames of laughter Gerald's way.

"Thank you, but let us assume the cold is my penance for my earlier brevity."

"And what of you, Kenna? You must do penance as well."

Gerald managed to reply before Kenna could. "Hers is having to live with knowing I thought of it first."

Gerald could feel her mock glare through the blankets. Then it was dark. Seconds later, just as Selene dropped them gently on the ground, a fire sprang up nearby and a guard shouted in alarm.

Recognizing the voice, Gerald called out. "Justin, you were not keeping an eye on the moon!"

Laughter greeted them, chasing away the cold of the last few minutes even before Gerald got to the fire.

CHAPTER TWENTY-FIVE

EVIOLA'S HUNCH

Two hours after dawn the next morning, Voices descended on the watchtower and the mess where Gerald, Kenna, MacIntyre, and Donald were discussing how best to utilize the garrison's time while waiting for word from the triad.

Two of the Voices landed on the table, nearly scoring a map with their talons.

"Greetings, lord dragon! Greetings, those of you who are neither dragon nor Voice! A sailboat approaches up the river."

Gerald smiled. "Greetings, Voices of Gerald. Do not give away my secret, that I am disguised as the youngest dragon lord. You seem giddier than usual. Is that exhaustion speaking, or have you been into some cranberry wine?"

The birds looked at each other. "Possibly both. We have certainly flown hard with insufficient rest, and the berries we ate recently may have been fermented. But the sailboat is real. We saw no threat, only a woman and five men. No cannons, siege engines, boiling oil, or obvious casks of cranberry wine."

"The latter is not usually considered a weapon."

"To the weary it may be so."

"True enough. Thank you and well done."

The birds looked around, snatched some meat from a platter, and flew off to eat elsewhere. MacIntyre seemed a bit stunned.

"You'll get used to it," Gerald assured him.

Kenna nodded agreement.

Donald caught MacIntyre's eye and shook his head morosely.

"I suspect we shall have plenty for your men to do now," Kenna said. They headed downstairs. By the time they got to the edge of the clearing, a slender, dark-haired woman with a four-man guard was exiting the woods on the path from the river.

Gerald and Kenna stepped forward and bowed. The woman stared at Kenna. From the corner of his eye, Gerald saw Kenna stare back. He decided to speak. "Greetings! I am Gerald and this is Kenna. We are envoys of King Dugald of Scotland. I trust we are meeting the envoy of Lady Fjorela of Shkodër?"

The woman composed herself the instant Gerald began to speak. She stood with the sort of healthy pride Kenna did. In fact, she reminded Gerald of Kenna—a bit shorter than Gerald, lean and lithe yet strong. Her eyes were deep, dark pools. Her black hair was straight and shoulder length, but did not move on its own. *Now why did I think that?* Gerald wondered.

She replied in perfect Scots with a highland accent. "Yes. I am Eviola, envoy and advisor to the Lady of Shkodër. How did you know?"

"We visited yesterday by the kindness of a dragon who carried us there and back." Without really thinking, Gerald added, "Lady Fjorela said you could translate. She did not mention you spoke Scots as if you had lived in Argyll all your life."

Eviola flushed the teeniest bit. "Does Kenna translate for you? Did she speak perfect Albanian?"

"Yes."

"Then you should understand."

It was Gerald's turn to redden. He should not have brought this up here. "Let us go inside."

"An excellent idea," Kenna agreed. "But first, this is MacIntyre, captain of our garrison, and Donald, his second in command."

The men nodded.

Eviola turned her head just slightly and the rightmost warrior moved up to her side. "This is Luan, the captain of my guard. Endrit is his second." She waved her left hand at the man behind her on her left.

The warriors eyed one another warily as they took each other's measure. Kenna and Eviola smiled and gently radiated peace.

Gerald glanced at MacIntyre, who nodded and spoke. "Eviola, would your captain like to send someone upstairs to look the building over before you go up?"

She spoke to Luan, who looked relieved. He spoke to the two warriors who had not been introduced. They stepped forward and Donald led them to the building.

While awaiting their return, Gerald said, "We were told there were five men with you."

"You were misled. There were six. Our pilot stayed with the boat and a messenger departed for Fierza and nearby towns." Eviola looked at Gerald a moment. "Are you the Gerald who was at Lochmaldie?"

"I am."

"I thought you must be, especially as Kenna is also here. It is an honor to meet you both."

Gerald blinked. Being King Dugald's envoy was proving to be stranger even than dealing with dragons. Although that was hardly a fair comparison, since the situations seemed inevitably to intertwine.

"What we have seen of your country is as fair as Scotland, Eviola."

"Thank you, Lord Gerald. I trust that is high praise. Most men love best that which is home."

Gerald almost said he had seen nothing but Scotland before now, but then realized that until a few months ago, he had never been outside Argyll and had seen little of that. Now he had seen the northern highlands, parts of the Western Isles, Urquhart, and Edinburgh. And now Albania. The world was proving to be far larger than he had imagined. He should probably ask the dragons just how big it was. His head hurt thinking about it.

Donald and Eviola's men returned. They shook their heads. MacIntyre and his men stared suspiciously at the newcomers. "Why are they saying no?" MacIntyre demanded.

Eviola answered. "But they are not! They shook their heads yes!"

"She speaks truth," Kenna said since some of the men clearly doubted. "I saw this in Shkodër. They shake their heads to mean yes where we would mean no, and nod their heads no where we would mean yes. I suggest we all try to not depend on such while we work together here."

Eviola quietly translated this for her guards.

Kenna continued. "Also, their words for yes and no sound similar to our no. They say *po* for yes and *jo* for no, so listen carefully."

"Listen for what?" Donald wondered aloud. "How would we be asking them anything? I haven't understood a word these two said."

Something about his tone must have bothered the Albanian warriors; they looked offended. Eviola spoke to them and they calmed. One even laughed. Eviola addressed Donald. "I told them you were confused by our odd language, that we probably sound as strange to you as you do to us. I suspect Ramiz finds that absurd. But they agree the barracks building is safe. Shall we go?"

Gerald hung back and let the women go first. At the stairs

he stopped to ask MacIntyre a question in case the two faerie wanted time alone. "MacIntyre, is there anything we need to add to the list?"

MacIntyre's eyes followed the women upstairs, uneasy at Kenna having no one with her. Then he smiled inwardly. She could probably handle everyone at the garrison. "No, Lord Gerald, I can think of nothing new. Donald?"

"Nothing." He shook his head, then nodded it, then tried to do both at the same time.

"Stop it, man. You make my eyes hurt. What are you trying to do?"

"Say no in two languages at once."

Gerald and MacIntyre burst out laughing. Gerald pointed his chin at Eviola's men, clustered by the doorway. "They seem to have orders to wait here. They appear on edge, probably because you two seem to be going upstairs. You should probably wait here."

"That makes no sense. We have to decide how best to use our men, and I would like to know more of the area."

"Then why don't you come, and wave Luan up? Bring Donald and Endrit if you like."

They explained this with hand gestures and names, but the Albanians refused. Eventually MacIntyre and Endrit went up with Gerald while the rest waited below. Gerald noticed Gillian and Ulf lounging against a tree outside, keeping an eye on things. He grinned. At least he wasn't alone in wondering what was intrigue and what was not.

An hour later, MacIntyre had plenty of notes on his map. He also had a stack of notes written in Shqip—lists of items needed, price ranges, and names or drawings of landmarks to seek out to find the items. He would send three groups of two of his men, each with one of Eviola's. Endrit was briefing the other two now. Luan would stay with Eviola at the barracks. Donald would lead one party, and two of MacIntyre's men— Stephen and Eric—would lead the other parties. MacIntyre took them aside, looked over the list, and gave them enough gold to get what they needed.

Soon after the parties left for supplies, those remaining sat down to lunch. Luan, MacIntyre, and the envoys sat on the ground with their backs against small fig trees clustered near the small building. Eventually MacIntyre expressed interest in the sailboat, never having been on one. When Eviola suggested Luan take MacIntyre to see the boat, Gerald started to get up. He had never been on a boat of any kind, but Kenna shook her head. He assumed this meant no, so he stayed. Kenna grinned as if she knew what he was thinking.

He snorted. *She often does.*

Once the warriors had left, Kenna looked at Eviola, who in turn looked at Gerald and spoke. "I thought your captain would never take the hint and go."

Gerald's eyes narrowed. "What are you two up to?"

They smirked so identically that Gerald wondered whether they were related.

Eviola continued. "I know why the triad meets. Many of us do. But Chloe I know well, and she recently sent word to me asking me to discuss with you a crystal sword, a missing piece, and your wife to be. There may be more, but she said I would need to find my way."

Kenna nodded. "She knows enough that she has certainly been in touch with the triad. I have told her a little in the limited time we had. We have perhaps an hour now. We should discuss these things."

Gerald looked at them. "When first you met, I thought you might be enemies. What was happening?"

"Normally the faerie can sense one another's proximity. We both knew the other as faerie at once, but neither had known a faerie was nearby. Thus we were suspicious. Once we got close, it was obvious, but neither of us has seen this before. We will have to ask our elders whether this is just the two of us, or perhaps if faerie in different regions might grow different enough that we cannot as readily perceive one another's presence. Either way, it was disconcerting."

Gerald and Kenna told the story as thoroughly and succinctly as possible. With Eviola's questions, that took half an hour. Then Eviola sat for a few minutes with her eyes closed. When she opened them, she wasted no time.

"The missing piece of this sword. What shape was it?"

Gerald and Kenna both thought back to the model at Fiery Lake. Kenna answered. "No particular shape. Just another piece of shattered rock." Gerald nodded, then added a yes for clarity.

Eviola smiled briefly. "Just do what comes naturally when it is the three of us. I am the interpreter, remember? In summary, the missing piece has not been seen despite searches by everyone available, whether human, dragon, or faerie. Now, someone said Argyll burned his claw?"

"Yes," Gerald replied. "I do not recall who mentioned it first, but apparently it was not bad. I have been wondering about that. At first I thought he might have burned it handling the sword, but we have no reason to believe the sword has ever vanquished him. So what did that?"

"We do not know whether that sword has ever been used to best Argyll or not, only that it did not do so this time. But we cannot make assumptions, so let us look further.

"Now, to human reactions for a moment. You say many in the village seemed to be going strange until your mystic healer from another land uncovered stones buried about the village, and those stones proved to come from the crystal sword of which Chloe spoke."

Gerald nodded self-consciously.

"Sally is—or was the last you knew—still angry, jealous, and lost within herself, staying home and doing none of the things she is accustomed to doing. You felt a strong reaction to the stump, and later you sensed its like near Sally. Where were you when you sensed that?"

"Always at our home."

"'Our?'"

"Sally's family adopted me after dragons killed my parents. Then Argyll killed our father, and another dragon . . . was involved in our mother's death. So we inherited the house of her parents. They had adopted me, so it is ours."

Eviola shook her head, then nodded. Gerald laughed. "I am not an interpreter, but if you just act naturally, I will understand."

Eviola grinned and relaxed for the first time since walking out of the woods.

"*Po.* But Argyll would have had no access to the house. He could not have buried the stone under the house. He could have thrown it through a window, but that leaves too much to chance. It would almost certainly be found. In any case, he would be observed. Any full-grown dragon would be seen, and from what Kenna tells me, Argyll is now larger than even the Eldest."

"That is true."

"So how . . . ?" Her eyes snapped wide open. She closed them, her mouth moving rapidly without sound. She opened her eyes again. "Kenna. We must go to the triad. We could send a Voice, but a dragon would be quicker. I think I know. I am nearly certain, but I don't want to get Gerald's hopes up."

"I don't . . . " Gerald began, but Kenna interrupted.

"Gerald and I have no secrets from one another, unless they belong to others. And I think he should know what you think."

"Very well, but I still wish to discuss this with the triad as soon as possible."

"Then tell Gerald and we will call Selene."

Eviola took a deep breath but Gerald spoke first. "No magic. No sending of peace. I want to be clearheaded. Just tell me, please."

Kenna nodded. "Fear not, Gerald. Eviola, I name him faerie

friend, and he is Eldest blessed. He will be well."

Eviola slumped against the tree. "Be it upon your heads. Gerald, putting the pieces we just discussed together, I can reach but one conclusion. A piece of crystallized evil has simply disappeared, but its effects are still noticeable, centered about the house Sally is in. We did not discuss the possibility it was on the roof, but of course a dragon would have spotted it at once. What kind of roof is it?"

"It is a form of thatch, but we use pitch to proof it against the weather and make the thatch last."

"Perfect for Argyll's purposes. Gerald, this is only a hunch, but my hunches are usually good. I believe Argyll burned his claw by destroying the stone. Yes, I see the question as to why forming in your face. He might have done this as he flew slowly over your home at night, crushing the stone in his claw and letting the dust fall to the roof. The dust's glow would probably be too dim to see unless you got very close to it on a dark night.

"And speaking of pitch, that is good news. Without it, the dust would more easily fall through the roof. It would be on everything in the house, including Sally. It might get on food or in water and thus into Sally. She might breathe it. In such cases, I do not know if we can help. With pitch, the dust would stick to the roof. This is also good news for the rest of the village, as the dust would not easily blow or wash off."

Gerald jumped up and ran the few steps into the clearing. He looked up, waved his arms, and bawled, "Voices!"

Within seconds, the first arriving Voice hurtled to the ground in front of Gerald. Six more came in as many seconds. "I need Selene," Gerald said urgently.

"She is coming," said one of the Voices.

"How?"

"When we fell like lightning, she naturally noticed and is coming to see what plight was upon us."

"Indeed I did," Selene said as she landed hard. She looked

around. "What is your need, Gerald?"

"I need you to take the faerie . . . Oh. This is Eviola, envoy of Lady Fjorela and a faerie. Sorry, you would know that part. Eviola, this is Selene. Selene, would you please take Eviola and Kenna to the triad as quickly as possible? Eviola may have the key to Sally's sickness."

"They have no blankets," Selene observed.

Gerald swore and ran to the shed. He was back within a minute with his and Kenna's blankets. In a few heartbeats, dragon and faerie were out of sight.

CHAPTER TWENTY-SIX

A GOLDEN GUIDE

Once Selene and the faerie were gone, Gerald was left standing alone with the Voices.

Their stares worried him. "What?" he demanded.

"We wondered what else you need," the largest one said.

Gerald stared back a moment but then relaxed. "Nothing, I suppose. Well, except for the triad to solve the mystery, Sally to be back to normal, Morgan le Fay and her relics to be history, and Argyll deceased. Can you take care of those for me?"

"Of a certainty. Or perhaps we will simply take turns watching from the sky since Selene is no longer here to watch over you." With a raucous noise the birds departed, half to the sky and half into the trees.

He looked around. Justin and Eoin were headed his way. He walked slowly to meet them, still mildly awed.

"Gerald, what's going on?" Justin asked.

"We may have the solution to what is wrong with Sally. Eviola and Kenna have gone to discuss it with the triad. If Eviola is right, it will answer several pieces of the mystery."

"So who exactly are these people, this triad?"

"That is their secret. But I can tell you they know a great deal. Imagine three people as clever and knowledgable as Cuthbert but in the realms of magic, history, and science. Together they are more potent than the three alone."

"Three Cuthberts? I would not want to go up against even one!" Eoin said.

"Thankfully we need not!"

"So what do you think has happened to Sally?"

"The triad has proven there is a missing stone. Eviola believes she knows how it was hidden." Gerald wasn't sure he ought to say more, but then recalled how Kenna had defended his right to know. Gerald looked around and lowered his voice. "Because of other evidence, it seems almost certain that Argyll crushed the missing stone in his claw, dropping the dust on our home. It would stick to the pitch on the roof, unlikely to blow or wash away. It would be difficult to detect."

"If that is the case, what will they do?"

"I don't know. Carry the roof away and drop it into a volcano, perhaps. But it seems the wind of a dragon's flight would pull the dust from the roof. They would need to wrap it in something. At first I was thinking they could just burn the house, but normal fire will not hurt these crystals, and sustained dragon fire would set the whole village ablaze. That seems excessive."

"A bit," Justin agreed.

"Cynthia and Druze would likely object," Eoin added.

"I suspect Cle would have something to say about it," Justin added seriously.

"And Myrna would have my head on a pike," Gerald laughed. His friends had a knack for cheering him up.

MacIntyre and Luan returned just then.

"The captain is walking oddly," Gerald observed. He called to MacIntyre, "What did you drink on that sailboat?"

MacIntyre scowled. "Boats move funny. Imagine if the land beneath your feet never stood still. It took the whole trip—an hour—to get used to it. And now the blasted earth beneath my feet feels as alive as the boat on the river felt! How a man can go between these two every day, I've no idea." He very carefully sat down on a rock, still a bit woozy. "That's better. Things still feel funny, but at least I won't fall. I think."

Luan was grinning from ear to ear. If he couldn't understand their words, he understood MacIntyre's tone and walk. He clapped the Scot on the back and said, *"Burre I mire!"* The others weren't sure what it meant, but decided it was an amused compliment.

Luan suddenly spun around, looking intently about. "Eviola!" he cried, then looked accusingly at Gerald.

Gerald said, "Eviola. Kenna. Dragon . . . *dragua*." *I hope I remember that word correctly!* He mimed flying, feeling a bit foolish but determined to calm the Albanian. Luan stared at Gerald as if debating whether to trust him.

The tension was interrupted a moment later when a Voice dropped into their midst. "Twelve mounted warriors come this way with great stealth from the west. They are half an hour away at their current speed."

"What do they look like?" MacIntyre demanded. "Gerald, draw in the dirt as you can."

As the Voice described an invader, Gerald sketched a crude figure with a stick. "Their skin is slightly darker. They wear cloth wrapped around their heads many times. They wear baggy shirts and baggy pants of varied colors. Their swords are curved."

As Gerald drew, Luan said something the others assumed was swearing by his tone and expression. *"Osman!"* He thought for a second and added, "Ottomans!"

"What?" MacIntyre demanded. Gerald held up a hand to stop Luan's useless attempts to explain.

"Lady Fjorela mentioned them. They are enemies of the Albanians. They have invaded many times in the past, and have resumed this since they heard of the peace the dragons made."

"And they head this way?"

The Voice spoke again. "They have been coming as straight this way as they can. They may be heading to the village just past this clearing, or they may have spies who told them someone is here."

"Told them we are here?" Gerald asked.

"Not necessarily you. Someone. Anyone. Foreign powers. The lady's envoy. A boat from Shkodër. Who knows? I do not."

Another Voice landed right on top of the drawing, accidentally cutting Gerald's crude Ottoman in half. That got a smile from Luan, if only for an instant. The new Voice spoke. "Half the visitors now race this way. We do not know where she came from, but they are pursuing a small child on a horse. Fortunately her horse runs like the wind, but they are close behind. They will be here very soon."

Gerald spoke. "Thank you both. Go. Watch. Wait! Can you send some Voices to Selene? Or get another dragon's attention?"

"There are none nearer than Selene. I will go," the first Voice to land said. They both fled, calling to those in the trees, who quickly joined them in flight.

MacIntyre said. "Get to your horses!"

Gerald said, "Luan has no horse."

"He must use Kenna's."

Gerald wasn't sure that was a good idea, but before he could respond, Luan was running down the path toward his boat. MacIntyre growled but could not blame the man; the boat and its captain were Luan's responsibility.

MacIntyre called to the two men on the tower to be ready with their bows. He and Gillian hid behind thick bushes near where the path opened from the woods. He spread out Justin, Eoin, and Gerald to confuse the enemy. Everyone had a bow and arrows but Gerald. He moved Dealanach beside the smaller building, thinking he might convince the invaders he had more men hiding there. He left his sword sheathed and pulled out the one-piece steel throwing axes King Dugald's chief armorer had made for him in Edinburgh.

The woods masked the noise of the approaching race. They had only a brief warning before a horse carrying a small girl burst into the clearing. Gerald stared. *The Voices did not exaggerate her speed!* She was across the clearing, heading down the path toward the village when the pursuers flew out of the woods behind her. They slowed for an instant to decide which way she had gone, then noticed the dust and started that way, when arrows hit one of the Ottoman and another's horse. The wounded man roared in anger. The horse reared and its rider dropped to the ground, then ran toward Eoin. Gerald threw his first axe at that attacker. The man dropped and rolled, then leapt up and kept running.

Gerald heard someone else yell but had no time to look. He called for Eoin and took off after the two riders who had made it through and were chasing the girl. As Gerald came out of the woods into Fierza, a Voice raced past him, yelling in what Gerald thought was Shqip. Several men stood with spears ready, but relaxed as they saw Gerald. He saw two horses down with spears in them and two dead invaders nearby. A villager lay bleeding as well. Gerald hardly slowed but kept after the dust trail, hoping to catch the girl.

Ten minutes later, a winded Dealanach slowed down. The path had run down to the rocky beach, along it a short way, and back into the woods when the beach—such as it was—disappeared. Dealanach was well up a steep hill when they came upon an open area and found their quarry.

The girl could not have been more than six years old. Her skin looked impossibly like pure gold. Her jet-black hair had an odd, golden sheen as well. She wore a simple dress of what appeared to be deer skin. She wore no weapons Gerald could see. She also wore no jewelry.

The latter relieved Gerald, but he had to think why. *Oh! Morgan le Fay would be wearing some gem of power. Or do we have all of those?* For some reason he was inclined to trust the girl, but then Neakal had trusted the version of le Fay he had seen. *I'll just have to wait and see.*

She waited patiently as Gerald approached. He stopped a few feet away. Her eyes were disconcertingly like her hair, deep black with hints of gold. She stared at him intently, her long, straight hair waving in the slight breeze. He realized it hung free, not at all tangled from the ride.

After a minute of waiting for her to speak, Gerald gave in. "Do you speak Scots?" Then he added in English, "Or do you speak English? I know a little of that."

She smiled—an odd smile that raised the hairs on the back of Gerald's neck. "I speak your language," she said softly in Scots, although he had never heard the accent.

Only then did Gerald realize he had not seen Eoin, or any of the garrison, since giving chase. They were alone here amidst an eerie quiet. No insects, no birds, just a light breeze rustling the flat top pines and the merest hint of the Drin's waters in the near distance.

A Voice soared just over the treetops and landed majestically upon the girl's shoulder. She glanced up at it, smiled, and looked again at Gerald. The Voice croaked, "Greetings, Lord Gerald."

"Greetings, Voice." Remembering his role as envoy, Gerald added, "Greetings, lady."

She giggled at this. It was a younger, more innocent version of Kenna's fey laugh. While it did not call Gerald into unknown worlds as Kenna's did, it offered gateways to them.

"So you are Gerald, the youngest dragon lord?"

"I am he." He bowed his head formally.

"I am no lady. I am Aurelia, the youngest guardian."

"And what do you guard, Aurelia? Or should I use a title?"

"No titles. I am Aurelia. You are Gerald."

She spoke with a quiet authority.

"Very well," he agreed. "But will you tell me what you guard?"

"I can show you. It is the otherness."

"The otherness?"

"It is extremely other. I believe the Eldest will not mind if you see, but only you can decide if you wish to see."

"But what is it?"

"I cannot describe or explain it. You can only see it for yourself, and what you see may not be what I see, or what the Eldest sees. I think many would call it a sacred place, but there is nothing especially sacred about it. And yet I can see why they would. Would you go? It is a place of much healing and much wisdom." After a moment she added, "And sometimes much madness."

"I need to think on this. Is there need for haste?"

"I should be there before sundown, but it is no great ride from here. We can leave within an hour and be there without pushing our horses."

"You rode like the wind. How did you learn to ride so well?"

"You mean for one so young! I have been on a horse as often as possible. This is Aphrodite, and she will not let me fall even in my sleep. I tell her the way to go when I know it, but she always seems to know. Today when the Ottomans attacked, she knew where to go."

"Did you, or she, know we were there?"

"I did not. I never know what Aphrodite knows. I cannot speak with her, of course." She smiled shyly. "Can you speak with your horse?"

Gerald smiled back. "I talk to Dealanach a great deal, but she seems to understand only my tone, and she tells me little except when she is pleased or annoyed."

"Maybe horses are all the same that way. I have not met many horses."

"Where are we?" Gerald asked.

"I do not know how to explain, except that we are up the Drin River from the place I first saw you. And thank you for your help. The villagers killed the two men closest, but you and your friends delayed the others."

"Are you sure they do not come?"

"Voice would have told us if they came."

Gerald glanced at the Voice. "Whose Voice are you?"

"I am the eldest Voice. I am no dragon's and every dragon's. The Eldest trusts me to be Voice where I am most needed. I have been the guardian's Voice since we found her."

"Found her?"

Aurelia replied. "I do not remember my family. I awoke one morning on the edge of otherness. I entered and thought I might go mad, but I did not. At least, I do not think I did! Are not the mad the last to know? A dragon found me there soon after and took me to the Eldest. No one can tell me who I am or where I came from." She looked sad. "I had no family. The dragons adopted me and said I should be safe here if I would guard the otherness."

"What does it mean, to guard it?"

"I wait. If more is called for, the Eldest said I would know. I am young, but apparently I am older than I seem."

"Are you of the faerie?"

"No."

"How do you know my language?"

She giggled again. "It is a mystery, like all of life! Voice, you are digging your talons into my shoulder. What are you thinking?"

"I am thinking we should go soon. Others will come looking, and none but Lord Gerald must know of you."

"Others have seen her."

"Thanks to Aphrodite's speed, they saw little and know less. But they will be looking, both for her and you. Lord Gerald, you must decide if you will come with us or not, and decide quickly."

"If I go with you, it will be easier to track us."

"There are ways that are difficult to track."

"My friends would worry."

"They will worry regardless, will they not? But you could send word."

"How?"

"If you two start toward the edge of otherness, I will get one of your Voices so she can vouch for the message. We will meet you farther on."

"I am intrigued but do not see how this fulfills my task for the high king."

"Nor do I, but I think it great wisdom if you go."

"I will ride fifteen minutes with Aurelia. If you return with my Voice by then and she agrees, I will continue on. Otherwise I will turn back."

"Very well!" said Voice. He flew off through the trees.

"Shall we go then?" Aurelia asked. She moved her horse a few steps to the east, then halted and looked over her shoulder at Gerald. Looking around the still quiet woods and second-guessing himself every step Dealanach took, Gerald rode toward otherness.

CHAPTER TWENTY-SEVEN

THE VALLEY OF THE
SHADOW OF DEATH

Two Voices arrived ten minutes later. Voice landed on the guardian's shoulder, while another landed on Dealanach's head. This rarely happened, and Gerald was always impressed Dealanach did not try to shake the Voices off.

"Greetings, lord envoy. I assume you recognize me."

"Greetings, Voice. Yes, even disguised as a butterfly, I recognize you."

"Moth, not butterfly."

"Of course, my apologies. Your colors are too boring for a butterfly."

"The eldest Voice said you doubt his word?"

"Let us rather say I do not recognize him, though he apparently recognized me."

"It is he. He is the most trusted of Voices."

"What if he said not to trust you?"

"Since I am trustworthy as well, that is beyond imagination."

"Very well. Thank you. Is there any other news?"

"Your friends at the garrison are perturbed that you have not returned. There are some injuries but nothing that threatens life.

The invaders are dead or fled. Those sent to trade are returning with their goods. Luan sent the sailboat to safety, then returned to fight, but he was too late. He borrowed a horse and went with Gillian and Eoin to hunt the invaders who fled. Others went to meet the six Ottomans who had not chased the girl.

"The Voices do not see any threats. Archibald and Selah, the dragons who carried your horses, saw our agitation from afar and came to investigate. They now watch over the garrison. Your friends will have nothing to worry about save you, and if you go, I will reassure them."

"What will you tell them, oh moth among Voices?"

"Voice suggested I tell them you go to accompany the girl safely home. Is that acceptable?"

"While I am not sure how much aid she needs, that is probably for the best. And I feel I must go, especially if the wisest and most trusted Voice suggests it. Although I have no idea what either King Dugald or King Donald will say. Or Kenna, for that matter."

"Kenna has met Voice and trusts him."

"How do you know?"

"She was speaking with Goyim at Lochmaldie when Voice joined them to talk. She greeted Voice as an old friend. As for the kings, your job here was not primarily as envoy to Albania, but to help solve the mysteries of le Fay's relics and remove that curse from the land. If there is wisdom wherever these two would take you, I suggest you go. Some wisdom would become you."

Gerald bowed his head, thinking and praying. He felt more peace about going with Aurelia than anything else he could do. He recalled his friend Sholto's gift for knowing what to do based on where he felt peace. Gerald wasn't sure if he had such a gift or not, but as he had no other guide, he would follow his peace.

He looked up at Aurelia and found her eyes boring into his. He had no idea he looked just as intense. "I will go."

His Voice bobbed at him. "This moth would applaud if this moth had hands. What should a moth do now?"

"Go tell the garrison. Watch over them for me. Thank you and good hunting, moth."

"And you, lord envoy to moths." Gerald's Voice took off. Immediately Dealanach shook her head vigorously and whinnied.

"You're awfully patient, Dealanach," Gerald noted. He looked up. "Let's go."

Aurelia wheeled around and let Aphrodite set the pace. The horse took off at a medium trot. Voice left to scout ahead.

Soon they left the trail and began threading their way through the pines. The earth was soft but covered deeply in pine needles. "Will this not be easy to track?"

"No. Within a few minutes the needles will have sprung back. Perhaps the faerie could track us, or wild animals, but nothing tracks me. I don't know why, but I don't mind."

Gerald laughed softly. "I'm sure you don't!" After a moment he added, "I tracked you."

"Because I wanted to be found. It felt right. Gerald, have you heard of the Valley of the Shadow of Death?"

"Father MacPherson has mentioned it."

"Your father?"

"No," Gerald laughed. "A Christian priest."

"Oh! I think I have heard of that valley. But I do not believe that is a real place, only a way to describe a situation and a feeling."

"This is a real place?"

"Yes."

A thrill ran down Gerald's spine. "What sort of place?"

"There is a mountain. Its name is Death. Nothing grows there. No one goes there. Even dragons avoid it. It looms over the river valley where lies our route. The valley is partially in shadow, and some who travel that route feel as if Death caresses them. I feel nothing but coolness in the shadow. I hope you will tell me what you feel."

"Of course." They rode on in silence. Gerald had many questions but he suspected Aurelia could not or would not answer them. She did not seem to have many questions of her own.

Shortly they started down a hill. Gerald could hear the river whispering below. The horses happily followed a gently descending dry, stony creek bed until they reached the river. There they turned left and followed the shore perhaps three hundred yards. As the river widened, Aurelia turned and rode through the sheer rock wall on her left. Gerald halted Dealanach. He stared at the wall. Then he urged his horse slowly forward. He reached out to touch the wall and his hand went into it. There was nothing there. Dealanach refused to move left. She began to lift her hooves nervously and snort.

Gerald dismounted and walked halfway through the wall. He held Dealanach's reins close to her head, patted her cheek, and patiently backed into the mountainside. Sniffing, she reluctantly gave in and followed.

Aurelia waited quietly. When Aphrodite whinnied, Dealanach perked up and came through. They were in what appeared to be a tunnel, but Gerald wasn't sure what was real right this moment. Aurelia's comment about madness danced through his mind. After glancing up to check the ceiling height, Gerald hopped onto his horse again. The walls were smooth and bore torches every twenty feet or thereabouts. It was very familiar, if not quite as well lit as the faerie fortresses. The tunnel turned immediately right and descended.

"Where does it go, Aurelia?"

"Down under the river and back up. Your horse seems uncertain, but you are at ease."

"She has never been in such a passage. I have."

Aurelia turned and led the way. Gerald's ears grew uncomfortable about the time the passage leveled and turned right. He held his nose, blew, and urged Dealanach on. She had to feel the pressure and he could not help her other than by hurrying. She snorted several times along the way. Roughly three hundred yards later, the passage turned left and began to ascend. Soon they emerged onto the north shore of the Drin. This side had a white, sandy beach and a path of crushed stone or shells. They followed this for well over a mile, pushing the horses to go quickly. As the path wound close to the low cliffs on their right, a soft voice called out, "Clear!" An instant later, Gerald noticed Voice flying lazily down the river past them.

Aurelia turned right and disappeared again. This time Aphrodite whinnied and Dealanach followed without hesitation. The passage turned left so that they continued downstream as they descended, turned under the river, turned right and ascended again. They emerged on the southern shore in shadow.

They were on a small ledge right beside the river. The barest hint of a path led onward. Looking carefully, Gerald recognized the odd black rocks used to build Fionn's bridge from mainland Scotland to the island of Skye.

"Aurelia, these rocks. Who made this path?" Before she could answer, he heard the crack of a whip. A shiver ran from his head to his toes. His right arm felt like a rock and hopelessness flooded his being. He heard Aurelia answer as if from far away. What did it matter?

But then he saw Sally in his mind, lying on the cushions in their house and weeping quietly. Whether a vision or his imagination, it spurred him on. He sat up straight, shook his head, and said, "I'm sorry. I couldn't hear for a moment. What did you say?"

She stopped and looked back. Dealanach had slowed and they were now twenty feet apart. Echoes of the whipcrack chased themselves randomly about the sky and mountainside like rolling thunder that had lost its way among the clouds. Gerald stroked the horse's neck and spoke of home, rest, and food. He remembered some carrots in a pocket and gave her one. She perked up and moved at her previous pace.

Aurelia said, "Keep your eyes and ears on me. Stay close so Dealanach may sense Aphrodite. Let us move quickly."

Gerald glanced around. Nothing grew on this side of the river and all was in shadow. He quickly focused on Aurelia. The whip sounds faded so long as he focused on the guardian. But now he felt hundreds of eyes watched him hungrily from just out of view, moving from cover to cover as they tracked his motion. He refused to look.

Aurelia started anew. "I do not know who made the path, but I know dragons were involved. I suspect faerie involvement as well. Whoever did it, it is the only safe place to be on this side of the river. Except . . . well, you will see soon."

Gerald noticed animal bones here and there to their left, never more than a few feet from the path. A thousand Ottomans with a three-headed Argyll would not get him off the path onto the mountain Aurelia named Death.

Nearly a mile from the tunnel under the river, she stopped and looked around, as if admiring the scenery. Finally she glanced up. Voice circled overhead, well out of arrow reach.

"Circling says we are alone. The only other safe place on this side of the river lies ahead of us under the mountain. But we must dismount. There will just be room for the horses. I will lead Aphrodite. You follow her and lead Dealanach." She pulled two sticks from her pack on Aphrodite's rump and handed one to Gerald. "Use this to feel where the sides of the doorway are. Go straight through and lead Dealanach straight through. Do not touch the doorway. The mountain is indeed deadly, but once inside, we are safe. Get your horse completely inside without touching the walls!"

They dismounted and walked a few feet forward. The path widened a little. Where it bulged out a few inches on their left, the guardian turned and began swinging her stick as she pushed it into a rock wall that wasn't there. She walked straight through, leading her horse by the same path. Her voice spoke softly from nowhere. "Gerald, you should see clearly once your head is inside."

Aphrodite whinnied. Dealanach tried to push past Gerald, but he held her back. She was shivering. Gerald smiled grimly. He wasn't sure he wasn't shivering, as well. He used the stick. Once he was certain where the sides were, he glanced up to see that Voice was still circling. He stepped through and immediately felt a thousand times better. The whip cracks ceased, as did the feeling of being stalked.

He carefully pulled at Dealanach. She tried to rush. As he worked to control her, she touched the side of the entrance! Gerald almost yelled before he realized only her saddle had touched. He moved a bit to one side to lead her better and got her safely through the doorway. He sat down on the passage floor, closed his eyes, and took deep breaths.

Aurelia asked gently, "Did you feel anything? Did Death caress you?"

He opened his eyes and stared at the girl. "I certainly felt something. Death's caress? If that hints at a lingering, maddening death, then yes."

Gerald stood and looked around, expecting something spectacular. It was just another passage with everlasting torches. He looked down at the guardian. If he got on his knees, they would be nearly at eye level. "Where are we?"

"Please do not ask any more questions here. I will tell you what I may. Anything else you learn will come to you on its own. Follow me."

They walked in silence for a moment before the guardian spoke again. "I can tell you where we are this one last time. It likely will not help. We are at the edge. We are inside Death, but we are not dead. We go where no man has gone since Merlin. Very few faerie come here. As far as I have been told, only one other race comes here, and how they come is a mystery. No dwarves, none of your other legends, not even those forgotten by men. Only you. And I, the guardian.

"The horses cannot go farther or they will go mad," she said as she stopped. She gestured to a passage on their right. It opened up a few feet in. There were stalls. There was hay. There was water. There were blankets and everything else a horse should have. "Since you have seen passages like these, you have seen the magic that provides food?"

"Yes."

"Such magic is at work here. The horses will be provided for. Farther on, the passage opens into a large cavern with room to run. No grass grows, but there is dirt covered with hay. Fresh plants appear for the horses to eat. There are many torches, so it is brighter there. Perhaps you shall see it later, but we must go."

Gerald expected Dealanach to protest, but she was standing nose to nose with Aphrodite, looking content. Gerald took all of the riding gear off so she could roam free, if but for a few hours. The guardian had ridden bareback. Dealanach suddenly lifted her head, spun around, sniffed the air, and trotted off down the passage. Aphrodite broke into a gallop and passed her. They raced toward the larger room.

"So, Aurelia," he began. He corrected himself by instinct. "I expect I should say guardian in here." She did not correct him but waited for him to finish. "Guardian, I am ready when you are."

She nodded solemnly, turned, and walked sedately back to the main passage. There she turned right.

Her voice took on a singsong quality. "And so we go into otherness. As the name—a name that is not a name for a place that is not a place where those who are, are not—implies, it will be different. I cannot say how. I am told only that the difference depends on who you are—both in general and in the instant.

"You will experience things. They may or may not be real. Who is to say? You must decide for yourself."

Gerald had noticed darkness ahead. Now they walked right up to it. It was a wall of night across the passage. Not just a mysterious blackness, but an actual nighttime there beneath the mountain. He could see stars. In fact, he could see the Milky Way, but it was in front of him, not overhead.

"Follow me, Gerald. I cannot guide you on this part of the path. Where your edge leads—over, under, sideways, or down—I cannot say. Just keep moving and you will come out. And then, the otherness."

Gerald gaped. All his training failed him. His muscles felt like jelly. "I thought this was the otherness."

"This is the edge of otherness. It is a gateway. Even if invaders should get through the outer defenses, they would get lost inside. But unless you prove very false—and that would mean you have deceived not only the Eldest and many dragons, but your own Voices, the faerie, and ultimately yourself—you will come through. And now we must go."

She sprang into the night and was gone. Gerald took a deep breath and stepped in after her.

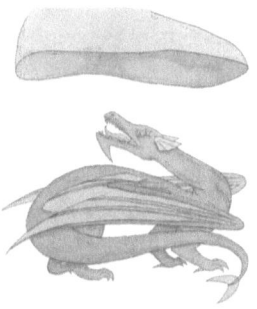

CHAPTER TWENTY-EIGHT

ON EDGE

As Gerald moved into the night, he fell. He landed immediately and began to slide down a very steep slope. The slope was unnaturally smooth; it did not grab at his flesh or clothes. Though his scabbard squealed softly against the stone, if stone it was, there were no sparks. The slope began to ease, but Gerald did not slow. Soon it flattened out. Gerald tried to sit up but could get no purchase. The slope started back up, steepened, and began to loop over the pitch-black abyss. He found there were no stars and no other lights. It went up and over and started back down again, as if he were circling the inside of a giant barrel on its side. He should have fallen—he felt the pull downward—but he didn't.

The third time around, he went only part way up, slowed, and slid back down. This time he barely passed the vertical before things reversed. Like the dying ringing of a cathedral bell he'd once heard in Edinburgh, he swung back and forth, slower and slower, traveling less distance with each swing. Finally he stopped. He wasn't sure which way to go. He managed to stand up. The ground had somehow regained its grip without snagging him. He turned left and started walking. After a minute he turned left just to see if he could go uphill, but there was no uphill. He tried several directions to no avail.

The giant barrel had become a perfectly flat plain. Everything was still pitch black.

Over the next hour he tried everything he could think of. He ran, hands in front, expecting at any second to hit something. He pulled out one of his hidden knives and threw it as hard as he could. It should have hit ground within a couple of seconds. He waited. And waited.

Ten seconds later, he heard a cry of pain and rage and a low thud. Mortified, he took off in that direction, calling out. No one answered. Some minutes later he gave up.

He prayed, both quietly and aloud. He felt more peaceful but got no answers. He swore at the darkness. He cried. He screamed. And he walked.

And he fell. He fell down a hole, slowly turning until he was falling head first, but then he was falling up. Balls of light in every color appeared, shot past, and disappeared in all directions. Some went through him. He went through larger ones. Some burned so that he felt his flesh melt away. Others froze his flesh until it cracked and fell off. Always there was more flesh, just as there were always more lights. He fell sideways, watching his hands morph into various animals' paws, claws, tentacles, fins, and more. At one point he was a herd of something like scrawny deer with long, thin spiral horns. Another time he was thousands of ants swarming one of those creatures. He was a nest of spiders dancing until their legs fell off. He was a dozen King Donalds, fighting one another for Morgan le Fay's throne. He was le Fay's throne, calling lustily for a queen or king. And then he was Gerald and on his feet again. He took a step and ran into a rock wall.

He fell, agony shooting through his nose. He saw stars. He felt blood streaming from his nose and suspected he had a black eye.

"I'm sorry. That had to hurt." He turned his head and saw— far away, down a faintly lit tube—the face of the guardian. He staggered to his feet, took a step that direction, and almost tripped over Aurelia. She darted aside as he fell to his hands and knees, retching.

She came over, squatted down, and began patting his back as if soothing a small child. With each pat, some of the fear, some of the madness, some of the pain, and some of the insane memories faded in intensity. After a few minutes she stopped.

He wished she hadn't. He was much better, but there were still things haunting the edges of his mind and eyesight. Voices and sounds played at the ragged edges of his hearing. He ached all over. Drops of blood fell gently from his face. He lay down and rolled onto his back. The cool floor helped.

"What . . . ? No, you said no questions." He took several deep breaths. "I will be honest. I do not want to move, but when you are ready, I will go."

"I am ready."

"I was afraid of that."

"Fear is not welcome here."

"It's just an expression."

"All humans have fears." She looked at Gerald a long moment, then closed her eyes. Gerald had the feeling she was still looking.

She opened them. "Yours do not master you, not much. Voice and Eldest chose well."

"You said Voice first."

Her smile brightened the air, chasing away the final, ghostly remnants of otherness. "I did. Come! There are no more edges such as you just went through. Even going back, and if you were to come again—which I doubt, as even Merlin came only once—all other edges will be mere transitions."

The torches grew farther apart as they walked. Ahead was more darkness, but this time it looked natural. There was no abrupt end to the light; it simply faded into a cavern without torches. As they reached the edge of the light, Aurelia stopped, turned, and put her hands over Gerald's eyes. She whispered something unintelligible, something that came from a wild place far away with waterfalls and waves crashing against rocks. It reminded Gerald of the sea by the cave at Mull.

When she removed her hands, Gerald could see after a fashion. There were rows of large hills nearby. They varied in hue and ranged from light to dark. There were things tapering from each side of each hill, wrapping around them. A few had spikes or sharp plates or . . .

"Dragons!" he hissed. "Here be dragons!"

"Yes and no. Remember, I told you this is a place where those who are, are not. You will notice I whisper. I do not have to, but I choose to. It seems right. These dragons both are and are not here. They are not asleep, so we cannot wake them. But we could disturb them, and that could have dire consequences for someone. I do not know who; that would depend on the dragon and the situation."

The question popped out without thinking. "How many are there?" He meant to ask it aloud, but no sound came out. Instead, his mouth caught fire. He managed not to scream, but pulled his waterskin up, splashed water on his lips, and took a long draught. His eyes brimmed with tears.

Aurelia shook her head sorrowfully. "There are no questions here. You may think them, of course, but you cannot seek the answers outside yourself. Answers will seek you instead. Some may even be the ones you wish for. Do not ignore any of them. They all come for a reason. Those that do not come do not come for a reason."

She looked up at him with pity. "I was about to say there are currently sixty dragons that seem to be here. I am told there have been over one hundred and there have been as few as three. The chamber could probably hold two hundred, with room for Eldest to walk between them."

He opened his mouth but caught himself as the heat built up. Ice water flowed over his lips, soothing them, as soon as he shut his mouth. When Aurelia said nothing more, he looked around. He found the Milky Way overhead, reminding him of his recent journey through seeming madness. He shuddered but did not panic.

Aurelia clapped her hands gently, squealed softly, and bounced on the balls of her feet, grinning like the child she was not. "Very good, Gerald! When you conquer fear, something insidious, something subtle and evil, something that lives under the surface in cold, dark waters breathing in life and breathing out death, dies. And that is a death we should willingly and joyfully celebrate!"

Gerald covered his mouth with one hand to be safe. He scratched his head with another. He felt pieces of something fall from his head. He turned around and found a small pile of tiny scales the same shade of green as Argyll's. He looked at his hands and arms, but they looked normal. His face felt normal. He forced himself to relax. "Scales. I just scratched scales off my head."

She nodded, once again solemn. "Argyll has long held your heart, dragon lord, or part of it. He has held it in a way Sally could not and would not. He has kept it close the way a dragon protects eggs from one who would take them. He kept it hidden. He breathed the fire of fear into it every chance he got, and thus he owned a part of you. When he owned enough of you, you wanted to become the greatest dragon lord and slay every dragon on the planet. You cared not if they died slowly. You might even have reveled in it."

Her voice kept getting softer, but Gerald's ears grew more sensitive with each word, so she seemed louder. "You regained much of your heart when you bound yourself to the quest with Santana and during that quest. And you have been freeing it ever since. Daily it grows stronger and beats harder.

"You believe you will only have your heart back when he is dead. But you must free your heart first, or he will take part of it with him into death, which is a far greater otherness than anything you have experienced—or will experience—here.

"I do not tell you to do this. I cannot tell you how to do this. I can only tell you that you must."

Lost in her words, lost without coherent thoughts but with dragons and Sallys and swords and balls of light swirling like mad around him, Gerald lowered his eyes to the floor.

He gasped. The green scales had formed a tiny Argyll, which was beginning to wriggle. Revolted, Gerald raised a foot.

"Have care, Gerald. Think what sort of dragon lord you wish to be. Everything we do has consequences, many hidden from us at the time, or perhaps always, but consequences nevertheless. If you choose freedom, do not lash out in fear. Let him go for now. Let him go until you can kill him without fear and when your hatred is perfect."

He dared not ask what she meant by perfect hatred, but he stayed his foot and let the tiny Argyll live. The dragon that had sprung from his scalp launched into the air, rose to chest height, and breathed flame. Gerald threw up his shield arm. Pain shot through it and he smelled burning flesh. He managed not to cry out but had drawn his sword before he knew it. Argyll laughed and faded out as he once had in Gerald's dreams, his revolting grin the last thing to go.

Gerald bit his finger as pain swelled in his arm. He forced himself to look. The skin was black with bright red cracks over half his forearm. A couple of spots oozed blood.

He managed to keep the question inside, but he was furious. *Argyll is not supposed to be able to hurt me! Is this a horrible side effect of being at the center of the balance?*

"No." "No!" "Nay." "*No!*" "No no no no no . . ." Dozens of voices, none of them familiar, all of them soothing, chimed in. The responses rolled through the countryside of his mind, sunlight glinting off them like polished steel and gems.

K'pene and Ivor appeared. As Ivor pulled a brush from a cup full of paste, K'Pene removed a mash of freshly chewed leaves from her mouth. She plastered them gently onto his burn, smiling sweetly as she did so. Ivor, frowning at the spot, brushed the paste on over the leaves. It dried almost instantly, tugging gently at his skin. Within seconds the pain was gone. Ivor held up three fingers. K'Pene mouthed, "Three minutes." They disappeared. He felt K'Pene's lips brush his cheeks.

He shook his head and looked in wonder at his arm and then at the guardian. She replied only with a faint smile. Gerald could think only in questions so he said nothing.

He did not exactly hear anything, but somehow Gerald's newly improved hearing told him something interesting was going on behind him. He turned around. Indeed, something had happened. A dragon was gone. It had been there before, a pale yellow mound between two others of tan and snot green. Those two remained, but the pale yellow dragon was gone.

He clamped his lips firmly shut.

"I told you they are not here. They are not here as much as they are here, and they are here as much as they are not here. So to see them or to not see them means nothing to you."

She began walking. "And I mean nothing. Do not follow me. Just watch." She walked up to the snot green dragon. She walked into it and disappeared. A few seconds later she emerged a few feet to the left of where she had entered. "Please do not try this. I am other, so I can do it without greatly bothering them. You cannot do so. You are also other, but you are the wrong sort of other to do this."

Gerald felt a headache approaching. It was a long way off and meandering like a drunkard, but it was coming. "No," he said. A dozen echoes in different voices raced through his head toward the headache. It looked at the approaching denials, shrugged, and wandered off in another direction. Gerald covered his eyes and sat down, wishing for wine. "But then I should be like the headache," he said.

The guardian giggled. "We should be moving." She held out a hand and helped Gerald up.

"You're strong," he said.

"I know. So are you." She turned and began walking.

The dragons did not seem to be breathing. Gerald walked up to the tan dragon and held his hand in front of a nostril. There was no breath at all. Gently he reached for it. He met skin. He had no idea how Aurelia had gone into one of these. The skin felt like dragon skin. It was warm to the touch—not really alive yet not dead. Gerald had no words for how this dragon felt. His fingers prickled. He could feel power in this dragon who was and was not here.

He suddenly felt the enormous power in the room. *How am I alive at all in the midst of this? It is as if the sun had come to visit. I should be ashes by now. Less than ashes.* His thoughts turned to lightning and raced off toward the Milky Way.

The feeling of power went with them. He could tell the power remained, but he no longer felt it, was not overwhelmed, was not . . . afraid?

A ring of tiny faeries danced atop his head, their joyful laughter brightening the room noticeably.

The guardian looked around, surprised. "Well done!"

They resumed walking, but as they passed the dragon whose nostrils Gerald had checked, the youngest dragon lord came to a halt. He had noticed the next dragon was rather large and light skinned, but now he could see it clearly.

"Younger!"

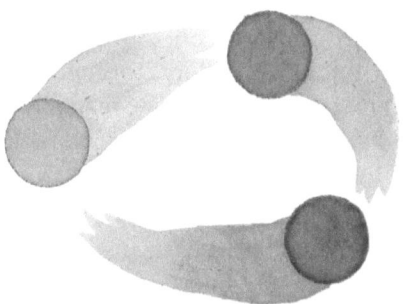

CHAPTER TWENTY-NINE

MARSHALING
THE FACTS

"He is here." It took a great effort of will, but Gerald made it almost wholly a statement rather than a question. His lips barely warmed.

"He is here," Aurelia said. Gerald dared not listen too closely.

"He is not here."

"He is not."

"I am marshaling the facts."

Three balls of light appeared, slowly revolving about Gerald's head, one each of purest red, green, and blue.

"Yes," said the red.

"True," said the blue.

The green just beamed at him.

The balls spun faster and faster, blurring into a ring of endless light whiter than Younger. The ring began to pulse, constricted itself, and dropped into Gerald's head. Words sprang unbidden to his lips, but as he spoke them, he saw how true they were.

"I want to see as clearly as you do."

The light swelled to fill Gerald. *I feel like I will explode!*

He exploded.

The pieces flew outward—out through the dragons and the mountains, through the floor, through the air, into the heavens, past the stars, out forever—eventually meeting again to form Gerald exactly as he had been before. Except now he could see only light.

Everything was made of light, and the light was fire and the fire was light. The cave walls and the torches were a very dim light, but light nevertheless. But the dragons! Oh, the dragons! They were more beautiful than ever, even though they were not there as much as they were. He could see them as they saw each other, as the light saw them. He could see how glorious they truly were, how different from mankind they were and yet how similar.

He turned to the guardian and was blinded. Not because she was brighter than anything else, but he simply could see nothing when he looked her way.

"No," said something red deep inside his head.

"Not yet," said something blue in his belly.

"Soon," agreed the green blood flowing through his veins.

His sight returned to normal. Almost normal. Everything still shone as if recently dragon blessed. He felt a deep, abiding love for the dragons, like nothing he had felt before. He felt the same way toward the guardian, even though he had not seen her in the light. And for Kenna and Cuthbert and Justin and Eoin and King Donald and King Dugald and Fjorela and Father Rodriguez and . . . Rodriguez?

Gerald stood lost in wonder. The former priest, the false inquisitor, the man who had murdered druids for not cooperating, who was willing to disembowel Gerald for consorting with dragons and druids and Voices. Gerald saw him as the broken, sad thing he had become and loved him as well.

And Sally. He nearly lost his breath. She was dying. He could feel it. Not today, not tomorrow, but if death were a vine, it had its tendrils around her ankles. His love reached for her but could not touch her. He wept.

He came back to the room. Three large balls of light hung in the air—red, blue, and green. If he looked straight at one, he saw its color, but if he looked elsewhere, he saw everything in a crystal clear daylight.

Its, he laughed inwardly. *They are not its. They are he and she! The red is she, the blue is he, and the green is both at once, and back and forth one at a time.*

Aurelia looked at Gerald in awe. "Almost I am jealous," she said.

"Be not!" cried the red.

"Nay," said the blue.

The green laughed with such pure joy that Gerald felt a week's dust fall from him.

The balls darted into and through Aurelia, spun briefly around her head, and resumed their former places. The room's light never wavered. Aurelia laughed as the green light laughed. She looked at Gerald. "You are still here!"

"Of course I am."

"I was gone so long I thought you might have left!"

"You didn't go anywhere."

"Oh, but I did. Not as you did when they entered you— yes, I saw—but I left. Anyway, I am here and you are here." She looked around. "And three more dragons have gone, but another has arrived."

Gerald saw it was so. He felt rather than saw a drunken headache meandering his way again. He laughed and it disappeared with a sad *pop!*

Aurelia looked down, concern on her face. "This dress is too tight!"

She strained. The deer skin stretched taut. Gerald thought the seams would burst, but instead it just grew. Not much, but enough. Gerald thought the guardian only slightly taller, but she seemed more muscular, as if she had been working hard and perhaps running a great deal. She pulled her hair back from her face and he saw a slight sheen of sweat. He also noticed a touch more gold in her hair.

Exhaustion slinked in and embraced Gerald. "I think I would like to sleep," he said with a long yawn.

"You must not sleep here."

The lights spun back and forth as if saying no as well.

Aurelia continued, "The only sleep in this chamber is for those who are and are not. You have seen such sleep is not natural. Dragons can do this safely. For you, it would be sleep until the end of time."

Appalled, Gerald stifled another yawn.

"Come, Gerald, I have said before that we must go. There is a place farther on where you can safely sleep. It is out of this chamber. Think of this place as Death's liver. It is deep within him. He does not know the odd things that happen here."

Gerald blinked. *Death's liver?*

"Of course," said one of the lights.

"It's certainly not his spleen," said another.

"Nor something as mundane as his bowel," said the last.

They all looked rather plaid at the moment, but he was beginning to recognize their voices despite constantly changing accents. As soon as he thought that, they smiled at him the way Kari smiled at everyone. And they disappeared.

The cave was again lit only by distant torchlight.

The guardian opened her mouth and shut it at once, a look of horror on her face. Gerald laughed. "You almost asked a question!"

"That has never happened to me before," she said. "I am chastened." Still full of love and wonder, Gerald stepped close and hugged her. The hug lasted a long time, with incredible thoughts flowing through Gerald at a maddening pace. When he eventually let go, he found she did not. She was sobbing. He held her.

Eventually she let go and he did as well.

She wiped her tears and looked up at Gerald. "Thank you. I never understood hugs before. Or maybe that was the first I have needed. But thank you."

She turned and walked in the direction they had been headed earlier. He rushed to catch up and walked silently beside her, looking fondly at the last few dragons and heading toward somewhere to sleep.

Sleep! How I have missed thee. How long have I been awake?

No answer was forthcoming, no voices echoing inside his skull, no balls of colored light. It felt as if he had been on a three-day campaign chasing and fighting raiders. Which was ludicrous. He hadn't seen a raider—the Ottomans counted, he thought—since earlier that day.

Somewhere a druid priestess laughed. He laughed with her, though he wasn't sure why.

They came to the edge of Death's liver. A short way down a small passage, they entered a familiar anteroom. Five doors stood before them. A miniature version of the guardian stood before the middle one. It beamed up at Aurelia and winked at Gerald. He rubbed his eyes and turned to stare at Aurelia. She held up a warning finger. "Don't ask!"

He bowed and chose the room to the right. As he shut the door, he realized three things.

His pack—most definitely his pack—sat on the floor at the foot of his bed.

The statue by the door was a perfect miniature of Gerald, complete with leaves and paste on its arm, a puffy nose with dried blood underneath it, and a black eye.

He'd forgotten about those last two, but was suddenly aware of them again.

He scraped the leaves and paste off his arm to find it as healthy as ever. The statue followed suit. Gerald pulled off his cape and tunic, along with his weapons, and lay down on the bed without bothering to pull his boots off. The statue kept its attire intact. It took only seconds to fall asleep. Just before his eyes shut, the miniature Gerald winked at him.

CHAPTER THIRTY

IN & OUT OF
OTHERNESS

Gerald awoke at what felt like midnight. He desperately needed to relieve himself. The torchlight in one corner brightened and he saw a hole in the floor similar to the one at Fiery Lake. There were two buckets beside it, one containing sponges. He had no idea where the hole led, since they were not sitting on the edge of a volcano, but neither did he care.

His business finished, he lay back on the bed but almost immediately bolted upright. The figure by the door was gone and the door was barred from the inside. He jumped up, lifted the bar, opened the door, and found the statue in front of his door. He closed and barred the door again before the statue could turn and wink.

He scanned the room, seeing a few differences between this and his room at Fiery Lake. Besides the privy, the color scheme here was different. There were three chairs—one red, one green, one blue. Wide awake, he decided to sit rather than lie back down. The green chair seemed the most inviting, so he carefully sat in it and looked at the strange floor.

It was not turf, but neither was it rock. He couldn't decide what it was, other than strong and soft at the same time. *Like Aurelia.*

"The guardian," came a mild rebuke in a voice like Death's.

He noticed the quill, inkwell, and parchment on a writing desk. *I wish I could write better,* he thought. *I should let Sally know I am well and that we may have a remedy for le Fay's curse.* Thinking back over everything that had happened, he decided to try. A half hour and three sheets of parchment later, Gerald sat back and stared at his hands in delight and astonishment. *I think that was as good as Cuthbert might do.*

The red chair tittered with delight. The blue chair snickered quietly. The green chair sat quietly—like any proper chair.

He read the letter slowly. The writing was perfectly legible and the thoughts coherent. "Now if only I had a way to send it," he mused. A black dot appeared on the wall right in front of him, growing quickly. He was reminded of a story Father MacPherson once told about a cloud the size of a man's hand rushing toward someone whose name he forgot. A few heartbeats later one of his Voices burst from the wall. It narrowly missed Gerald, frantically slowed, banked hard, grazed the wall, bounced off the next wall at the corner, and tumbled onto his desk.

It lay with a dazed look for a second, then staggered to its feet with assistance from Gerald. "Do not ask me about my flight, or I may peck you to death."

Gerald laughed. He felt the green chair laugh with him. "I ask no questions here. It is extremely unwise."

"Why do you say that?"

Gerald waited in horror for the bird to react, but nothing happened.

"Did . . ." he began and waited. Nothing happened. "Did you feel nothing?" he asked very quickly, looking to see where he had put his waterskin, but nothing continued to happen. "Forget I asked."

As the Voice looked around, Gerald recognized her. "How . . . how did you come here? And why?" He smiled as he realized how quickly it had become difficult to form questions aloud here.

"You called and I had no choice. Now I see why the dragons hate it so."

"And you came through a mountain, through rock, and very quickly." He shook his head. This was the strangest thing yet. *No, the otherest thing yet.*

"I found myself flying. Some of the journey was dark and thick, but I had to fly, so I did. And here I am. What do you want me for?"

"This is for Sally." Gerald began rolling up the parchment, which he now recognized as awfully large for a Voice to carry. He tied a string around it and knotted it carefully anyway. As he handed it to the Voice, the roll shrank to about an inch long. Gerald grabbed more string and tied it carefully to the bird's leg.

"How did you do that?" the bird demanded.

Gerald laughed and the chairs joined him. "You flew a great distance in a few seconds, you flew through solid rock, and you wonder how parchment shrinks? But to answer your question, I have no idea. This is otherness."

The Voice froze. "You jest."

"I do not. I was brought here by, by . . . ," the name refused to leave his lips, ". . . by someone with authority to bring me here."

"Does here have a name?"

"I have heard it called otherness, as I gather you have. There is a cavern called Death's liver. It is his only organ I have experienced, so far as I know." He looked around. "This could be someone's eyebrow, but I don't think it's Death's."

"True," the chair beneath him agreed.

The Voice did not appear to have heard it. Or perhaps she ignored it. "And how am I to get this to Sally?"

"Hopefully the same way you came here."

"And then what?" the Voice demanded, almost crossly.

"If there is an answer, bring it to the barracks or wherever

I am by then. Otherwise, do what seems right until I send for you or we meet somewhere."

The Voice closed her eyes for a moment. Gerald imagined her counting to ten, which was closer to the truth than he realized.

"Send me."

"Go."

The Voice just looked at him.

"What are you waiting for? Go! *Go!*"

With a startled squawk, the bird flew backward toward the wall. She turned and began flapping, shrank to a black dot, and vanished. Gerald realized he had been holding his breath from the moment she flew backward.

"You're still holding it," the chairs said in unison. He let it out and felt suddenly and inexplicably exhausted again. He stood, staggered to the bed, and collapsed onto it, asleep before he hit the mattress.

Gerald wished he were a dragon so he could travel as he needed to. A moment later, he was Gerald the dragon, flying lazily over Gerald the man, who lay asleep on his bed deep in the mountain. He turned his head to look at his body; it was a strange sensation on the end of that long neck. He was his normal color. *I ought to be something other than that.* And he was! Some of his scales were red, some green, and some blue. *And I should have spikes on my tail.*

"You're getting carried away," he heard the guardian say from somewhere, but he smiled in delight as a dozen spikes erupted from the tip of his tail.

"Go!" he said to himself. "Go to Fiery Lake!"

And then he knew what the Voice had meant. He could not have not flown. His wings beat frantically, stretching new muscles. He cringed as he came to the wall but flew straight through it. *Dark and thick, the Voice said. And so it is.* Seconds later he was outside the mountain, streaking across the night sky, the landscape below a blur. He glanced up at the Milky Way but wisely decided to watch where he was going. A few seconds later he missed Selene by perhaps two feet.

A mountain glowed faintly ahead. *That must be the volcano.* It grew rapidly and he found he couldn't stop. He flew straight through the side of the mountain. Terrified he would end up in the lava, he thought, *My room! Back to my room here!*

Gerald shot out of the wall like a cannon. He tried to bank and soar around the room to slow, but bounced off the far wall and fell onto the bed. Before he could check for injuries, someone screamed and jumped, tossing him across the room and into another wall. He managed to gain control of his wings and fly gently to the floor rather than fall.

Eviola glared at him from the bed, a tiny blaze of white light in her hand. Gerald recognized it as a miniature version of a magical weapon Kenna had used effectively against full-sized dragons and quailed. "It's me, Gerald!" he yelled in a tiny, squeaky voice.

"Gerald? What? How?" She stared at him a long moment before squeezing her hand so the miniature sun disappeared. "No. Don't worry about that now. Come with me." Wrapped in her blanket, she jumped from the bed and opened the door. Gerald flew after her. She went to Kenna's room and knocked quietly. The door soon opened and Kenna stared back and forth between the faerie and the minuscule dragon hovering near her head.

"Come in." As soon as they did, she closed the door and barred it. She looked at the tiny dragon hovering at head height. "Who are you?"

"I am Gerald."

"You feel like Gerald," she began as she sat. "But that is absurd."

"I *am* Gerald."

"Gerald is a man, not a dragon."

"I am *Gerald!*"

"Gerald is not a shape-shifter."

"*I am Gerald!*"

"I know. But it makes no sense."

Eviola finally sat. "He flew into the wall above my bed at great speed. I could not see where he came from."

Kenna patted the table. "Rest, Gerald, and explain."

Gerald settled onto the table. "You heard about the Ottomans, right?"

"Yes, but I do not believe they did this to you."

Gerald laughed and tiny flames flew silently from his mouth. It felt as if someone was tickling his lips. "Not directly, no, but they were chasing someone."

"Who?"

"I cannot tell you. I am under a geas—I think it something like the oath I took here, except I took no oath. But through this person I met Voice." Both faeries' eyes widened. "One of my Voices vouched for Voice, so I went with the unmentionable into otherness."

He stopped at his friends' expressions. They stared at him with a mix of wonder and disbelief. He continued. "Anything can happen there. And a great deal did." He looked at himself. "Like this. I have no idea if this is happening at Fiery Lake, or in my head, or even if I am framing correctly the question I am not asking. But I wished for a Voice and she came, so I wished I were a dragon and then wished I could come here."

"And you came," Kenna said.

"With a vengeance," Eviola agreed.

"Yes. I ache all over from the impacts."

"You had more than one?" Kenna asked.

"Eviola helped with the second," Gerald explained.

Eviola snorted. "He is fortunate I did not use the sunfire on him."

"I thought you were going to!"

"Gerald," Kenna said thoughtfully, "do you understand what happens in otherness?"

"No. Absolutely not. I do not believe I am meant to. Not yet, anyway. If ever," he added, with a lack of regret that surprised him.

"We shall see. Our people," she pointed at Eviola and herself, "have not gone there since Merlin."

"This person said no humans had been there since Merlin, so Merlin must have been part faerie and part human, as the legends state!"

Kenna nodded. "It fits. Anyway, whoever this person is, she or he told you precious few go there besides dragons?"

"Yes."

Kenna held a finger to her lips, traced something with her fingertip on the table, and arched an eyebrow at Gerald. He could not tell what she had drawn. He raised his front claws and shrugged, an awkward motion he suspected would interfere with flying.

Kenna kissed her finger and drew again. This time her finger left a faint, glowing line upon the table. She drew the letters "Au" and a stick figure of a girl. Gerald looked up and nodded. Eviola waved her hand and the drawing faded.

Kenna stood and Eviola followed suit. Gerald took to the air. Without a word, they passed silently out and through the passages to the outer doors. These swung open quietly onto the night, which had grown chillier while Gerald was inside, but he didn't care. As the doors closed, Kenna looked at the waiting Voices and pointed to the sky. The birds took flight.

Kenna spoke. "Eviola and I know of whom you speak, Gerald, but few of the faerie—or dragons for that matter—know of her. That must remain true. Thus we come outside to talk. Those inside do not know of her and must not. Darciere, in particular, would be tempted to try and coerce her to work with them. But that is not her job, and the results would be disastrous. Why ever you are here, otherness should no more be discussed."

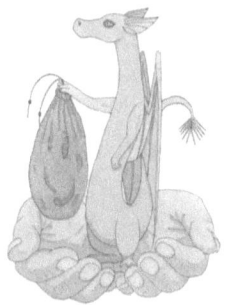

CHAPTER THIRTY-ONE

REVENGE OF THE SMALLEST DRAGON

Kenna thought a moment. "Why did you wish for a Voice?"

"To send a message to Sally."

Eviola's eyes narrowed. "Why did you not go, since you are like this?"

"I had not thought of being a dragon yet, only of needing a way to get a message to Sally."

Kenna replied. "Why did you wish to be a dragon, and why did you come here?"

"I don't know. It made sense at the time."

The faerie had no more questions at the moment, so Gerald asked one. "How is the alchemy going? Do they have a solution yet?" He read the no in their eyes.

"They argue," Eviola said. "Chloe is convinced we are correct. Andreas believes it true but wishes more evidence. Darciere believes it wishful thinking." Her frustration was evident. Gerald thought he detected a hint of anger.

Kenna added, "Father is trying to be cautious, but Darciere accuses him of recklessness. She cannot ignore Eviola, but she is back to not speaking to me."

Gerald could feel himself getting angry. It began as a heat

in his belly. He wanted to roast something. Or someone. And that made him feel ashamed. "I should not have come. I wish there was something I could do!"

"Beside roasting Darciere?" a rather quiet greenish voice asked with a gentle caress.

"There is!" added a blue one with a gentle hug.

"Go get proof," the inevitable red voice said as it tickled his belly.

Like lightning, both faerie held tiny suns in their sword hands. They looked around searchingly. "Who said that?" Kenna demanded.

Gerald said hesitantly, "My scales?"

"What?"

"That is absurd," Eviola replied.

"Tonight is absurd," Gerald agreed. "What color are my scales?"

They held the suns closer and stared in wonder.

Kenna started to move closer. Gerald flew as close to her hand as he could stand. The tiny sun's heat was intense, even to a dragon.

He laughed to himself. *If I am a dragon!*

A reddish voice said, "Well, someone is!"

The other voices snickered.

Kenna reflexively moved back. Gerald had never seen her this rattled and that rattled him. He tried to explain. "Yes, the scales speak—or something the colors of the scales speaks. The red voice is female. The blue is male. The green is both, or one or the other at different times."

"Exactly!" the green voice agreed.

"I first met them as balls of light. They joined and became white light. They taught me, became one with me, danced with me. When I became dragon, they indwelt my scales. They showed me the dragons as they truly are, and they are beautiful creatures, among the most beautiful on earth."

"Did you think that before you became one?" Eviola asked.

Gerald laughed without thinking. Kenna jerked her hand out of the way of the flame just in time.

"I'm sorry, Kenna! Yes, Eviola. I did."

Kenna rubbed her lips. "Gerald, I do not know if you saw dragons in all of their glory. I think that would have unmade you."

"I have no doubt it would have, had not the light been inside me. They were made of the same light, as was I. As was everything and everyone. I can see it in you, too, though far less clearly than in the heart of otherness." Joy danced across Gerald's hide as he spoke. "That feels even better than Sally's kisses!" He sighed happily.

Eviola's eyes snapped wide. Gerald's scales turned red for a second, which made both faerie laugh.

"What does?" Kenna asked.

"When the light dances for joy."

"Ah," Kenna said knowingly. Eviola nodded.

Gerald rolled his dragon eyes; the effect made him dizzy.

"The light suggested you go get proof," said Kenna. "Does that mean what I think it means?"

"I think so," Gerald agreed. He thought for a moment. "Do you have a small piece of the mail cloth, the mesh? And perhaps a tiny bag to put that in? One with a drawstring?"

"I can cut a piece of the mail cloth," Kenna said.

"And I have a drawstring pouch the size of a large gem," Eviola said.

"Perfect," said Gerald. "Let's get them."

"We will," Kenna said firmly. "You wait here. We will return shortly."

As they went inside, Gerald settled down on his rear haunches to watch the night sky. He was joined within moments by Voices.

"I have never been Voice to a dragon smaller than me," one said.

"I have never even seen one smaller than you," said another. "Gerald is the youngest dragon lord, you are the smallest Voice, and now Gerald is the smallest dragon."

Gerald remembered the ancient egg of the eldest, which had contained a perfectly preserved but dead baby dragon. It had been much larger than he was now.

"What news, Voices?"

"We have nothing new, other than seeing you."

"Did anyone else see me?"

"Santana saw *something*, but he wasn't sure what. He said it flew like lightning into the side of the mountain. He said it reflected moonlight oddly. He went to see what it was, but could find no trace of impact or creature. He is currently hiding, hoping whatever it was will reappear. I think he secretly hopes it is the ghost of Morgan le Fay, and he plans to cook and eat it."

"You can't cook or eat a ghost," Gerald said.

"We can't. If anyone can, it's Santana," a Voice replied.

A faint wind told them the doors were opening. They all launched into the night and hovered behind the doors, but it was just Kenna and Eviola.

"Caution is good," Eviola said.

Kenna offered Gerald a pouch of supple burgundy leather. "The cloth is inside this. I trust you will not touch any dust from the crystal, especially with your right . . . claw?"

"Your trust is not misplaced!"

"And how will you go?" Eviola asked.

"Like this. Gerald, go home. Go *home!*" and he took off as if shot from a cannon. He tumbled at first and feared his wings would be destroyed, but he gained control and began flying.

This makes no sense! I'm not really flying, and I would think

I should keep my wings folded tightly to me. And yet I must fly. Why?

"No questions here," the green voice laughed. "Only flight. Just because."

Gerald had no idea how fast they, or he—whichever it was—were going; he only knew it made normal dragon flight look like a doddering old man's pace. He could see the stars move against the sky.

He hit a wall of water. At first he thought he had somehow flown into the ocean, but he could feel thousands of needles hitting him. Not that they hurt. He was simply aware of them. The water was fresh. *I've flown into a storm.* He continued like this a moment more, angled down, and suddenly came out into clear moonlight. A faint yellow light flashed as he raced past a small devastation in the woods below. Then there were houses, and he suddenly slowed. He overshot his home by about twenty feet, as if sliding to a halt in the air. He tumbled twice, then flew back to hover above his house.

Water lay like a thin sheen of moonlight upon everything and gathered in moving pools on the ground. It ran down the roof and dripped from the edges. Clearly the storm had just passed Kiergenwald.

Gerald flew in a lazy circle around his house, looking to see that all was well and hoping for a glimpse of Sally. But then he remembered sunrise was still hours away, so she should be fast asleep. He avoided the windows to be safe.

He flew up over the roof, seeking the spot above the largest room where both he and Sally had felt the most hopeless. He began to drop, peering intently at the pitch, seeking a different color than the moonlight off the water, but the water did something with the light, throwing off tiny rainbows. *Dragon's eyes really are keen . . . .*

"Down!" something screamed in his ear. He dropped to the roof just as something huge and gray swung through the spot he had just occupied. As he turned near the ground, it encompassed him and jerked him skyward. A moment later it opened slightly, and a white orb that looked for all the world as if the moon were melting shone upon him.

A huge, deep voice tried to whisper. "You look and smell like Gerald. That is impossible."

The voice that replied must have been just as impossible in Nain's ears. "I am Gerald."

"How?"

"Otherness."

Nain's claw flew open and Gerald fell. His wings caught him almost immediately.

Nain hung in the moonlight, wings moving just enough to hold him aloft. "It is impossible, yet here you are. Why?" Nain spoke almost inaudibly, clearly not wanting to attract attention.

"I am here to seek evidence from the roof." Gerald looked around to be sure they were alone. He spoke as quietly as Nain. "We believe my nemesis crushed the final stone in his claw and dropped the dust upon the roof. But the triad requires proof. I will return with proof in this." He held out the claw dangling the pouch.

"I meant why are you a dragon, but I suspect you cannot tell me."

"I can in part, but there is no time. Say only I am a dragon because it was needful."

"At least I need not fear you wish to kill all dragons today."

"Only those who delay me!"

Nain laughed. The flames nearly touched Gerald, but he felt nothing.

Nain went on. "You said no name, only the word nemesis. Why?"

"I have no idea how I would face him like this should he decide to answer the call of a tiny dragon."

"An excellent point. Get on with it and with my blessing." Nain breathed on Gerald. His scales glowed and somehow breathed back at Nain. Nain's face glowed and he pulled back in shock.

"Don't ask," Gerald said. "Just be blessed." And he dove back toward his house.

Hovering an inch above the pitch-covered roof, Gerald located the problem by the despair it caused. Then he saw tiny bits of crystallized wood, like tiny yellow sparks. He thought for a moment, then went to the edge of the roof and broke off a three-inch wooden splinter. He transferred the pouch to his left claw, opened it, and put the mail on a spot where there was no dust. He breathed the barest hint of fire near the roof to soften the pitch, rolled the stick through it to get a blob of pitch on the end, and used that to pull bits of the softly glowing dust from the roof. When he had as much as he thought the pitch ball would hold, he broke the end of the stick off, put it on the mail, and repeated the steps. After three times, he thought he had enough to fill the pouch. Balling the mail cloth around the pieces of dust-covered pitch, he wrangled it into the pouch. He pulled the drawstring shut, looped it around a front leg, gripped the pouch tightly, and said quietly, "Go, Gerald, back to Fiery Lake! Go!"

This time he was ready and already flapping his wings, so his flight started much more smoothly. A second into it, something big and green nearly hit him. A wall of sound and flame knocked him earthward. He recovered quickly and looked back as he flew inexorably on. Two dragons were fighting fifty feet above the devastated part of the woods.

How did you know? His scales said nothing about this question. Angrily, relentlessly, helplessly, he flew on. The storm had either spent itself or moved out of his path. He encountered nothing more than wind, and as he was already moving much faster than a gale, the wind meant nothing. Soon he could see the glow from the volcano.

Where should I land? Where? "The room of inquisition,

of course!" he yelled at the night sky, diving toward the mountainside.

This time there was room to slow without smacking the wall. He circled the room twice and settled for a moment atop the mail cloth. He laughed quietly to himself. As he prepared to fly in search of Kenna, she walked in with Eviola. Their eyes lit up and they ran over. Kenna reached out and Gerald hopped into her hands.

He held up the pouch. "I got it. I got it! Despite Nain's and Argyll's attacks."

"You got what?"

It took a moment for Gerald to figure out who had spoken. As Kenna and Eviola turned around, he saw Darciere. Despite her smile, or perhaps because of it, she did not look happy that people were wandering her domain in the pre-dawn hours.

Eviola spoke formally despite her grin. "He has proof. He has dust from the roof of Sally's house, the dust from a cursed crystal crushed by Argyll's claw."

Gerald dropped the pouch in Kenna's hand. "It's in here, embedded in pitch from that roof, on bits of wood. I didn't want to touch it."

Darciere finally lost her smile. "Who and what is this?"

He drew himself up regally. "I am Gerald, the youngest dragon lord and the smallest dragon!"

Darciere screamed, turned, and ran.

CHAPTER THIRTY-TWO

DARCIERE'S MADNESS

E viola started to run after Darciere, but Kenna called, "Wait!" in a voice Gerald knew well, one impossible to refuse, but perhaps that was only so for humans. Eviola sped up.

Gerald darted between her and the passage she was heading for. "Eviola! Wait!"

She stopped. "Why?"

Gerald looked at Kenna. "Why?"

Kenna gestured toward the passage. "That's why."

Andreas came at a run, sunfire blazing in his left hand, a dragon sword shining in his right. He froze, looking suspiciously at Gerald.

"Father, wait!" Kenna said urgently. "There is no need for weapons."

"Then what happened to Darciere?" he demanded, still eyeing Gerald with suspicion.

"We do not know. We explained that this was Gerald and she fled screaming."

"Gerald?" He stared harder. "The young dragon lord?"

"At your service, Andreas," Gerald replied.

"At all of our service," Eviola said.

"He brought some of the dust, father! We have it in here." She held up the pouch.

As Andreas hurried over to examine what his daughter held, Eviola looked oddly at Gerald. She spoke softly. "How did you do that?"

"What? Get the dust?"

"Get to Scotland and back in under an hour? Nothing can fly that fast! It would rip your wings off."

Gerald blinked. "How did I become a dragon in the first place? It's all impossible. Yet here I am. Unless we are both dreaming the same dream."

Eviola frowned. "You said you came from otherness?"

"Yes," he replied warily.

She sighed. "I confess that I have always been skeptical. To my mind, such a place should not be. And yet, apparently it is. The legends are true."

"What legends?"

"Ha! You have your secrets and we have ours."

Chloe walked in. "Darciere is sleeping. Occasionally she whimpers, but she rests. What happened?"

Eviola pointed to Gerald.

Chloe glanced at him dubiously. "Did he attack her?"

"Of course not. This is Gerald. He brought us proof that the dust from a crushed piece of the crystallized stump is upon the roof of his home."

Chloe looked in wonder at Gerald. "Indeed, if he can take on the form of a dragon—even one so small—and accomplish such a feat, he is a dragon lord among dragon lords."

Gerald bowed his head. "But what of Darciere?"

"If you ask why she seemed terrified of this dust or the tiny dragon, I have no idea. And why so many colors? You surprise me."

"It surprised me, too, Chloe. Strange things have been happening. I wished to be a dragon and this is what I became. Even my Voices mock me. Then again, they always do."

"Chloe?" Andreas called.

She excused herself and joined him at a nearby table. He stared at some of the dust through a large magnifying glass on a stand. Eviola and Gerald followed her.

"Yes, I agree," Chloe said. "This is the same. The colors, the grain, the faint light and the feelings I sense when my finger is near it." She turned to Eviola and bowed. "Excellent work, Eviola." Then she bowed to Gerald. "And thank you as well."

"Yes," Andreas said, still staring through the glass. "Thank you, all."

"What will you do now?" Kenna asked.

"There really is no choice," Chloe said. "Eviola was right. We will need to have dragons gather the roof from the house, possibly with some of the soil around it, but we will check that first. We will need something to carry it all in. A dragon will bring it here and hurl it into the volcano while several of them flame it. The pieces on the table will suffer the same fate. That leaves only the sword." She looked at Andreas.

He sighed. "I believe the sword will lose much of its taint when the crystals are gone. I *hope* Scythia will begin to recover then, as well as Sally, though Sally should return to normal much more quickly. Once Scythia recovers, I believe we can help her remove the last vestiges of evil from the sword."

The others looked back and forth between the two members of the triad. Finally Kenna spoke. "But you are not sure? And you are not in agreement?"

Both shook their heads. Chloe said slowly, "Andreas is now the most sure of these things, and even he is not sure. I find myself less sure, for reasons I am also unsure of. Darciere, of course, was sure we were on the wrong track."

"Darciere is mad."

Everyone stared at Gerald, who seemed to have spoken in a clear, contralto voice.

"You're blushing," Andreas said with surprise.

Gerald glanced down at his body. "It's the red voice. She's speaking."

She was and she continued. "Many things have eaten at Darciere for years, most of which you do not know. Her pride would not let her admit fault in the death of Kenna's mother. This you know. But ever she felt your mother's shadow, Kenna. She was haunted. Further, as sometimes happens, the more she studied le Fay, the more she admired what the sorceress had accomplished. She did not admire most of her traits, of course, but part of le Fay's legacy is that those who admire her at all must beware or they will fall into the same trap that consumed her.

"Studying the crystals beneath the mail has warped her more. She hoped to eventually master the power therein, convinced she would use it for good, to undo darkness in the world. But evil can never drive out evil. It only causes more of itself. She had secretly hoped the final stone would be found, that she could convince the triad to let her study them alone. She would have made something to wear with the stones and—against every wish in her soul—become for all practical purposes Morgan le Fay."

Suddenly Gerald was blue and a man's voice spoke quietly from the scales. "Gerald should return now. You four can think of ways to verify your suspicions. When Darciere saw Gerald and realized he brought proof of the dust, and that the gems she thought would open her mind to all the knowledge of the universe would instead be destroyed, it pushed her over the edge. She has long stood on the cliff looking into the abyss and now she has fallen. Be gentle with her. She was never evil— only broken, hurt, and afraid. Now she is more so."

The scales turned green and spoke in a voice that sounded like Kari and Justin singing together. "Gerald, *go!*"

Gerald went. He wasn't thrilled. He really wanted to know what would happen next, but he had no choice. It was hard to flap his wings this time, but the order from whoever was in his scales carried authority he had hitherto only imagined. He was flying back to otherness even faster than he had so far flown.

"Do not pull your wings in. You will need the control," the green voice said.

They were already approaching Death. "Do not go back the way you came. Enter the cavern of those who are but are not. Slow there in Death's liver and fly to your room. The door will be open. And remember, no questions until you are in your room."

They hit the mountain going so fast that Gerald cringed. He couldn't breathe properly in the rock. He would have to remember to take a deep breath next time. *Next time? I don't want a next time!*

They flew out of the wall. Gerald immediately begin slowing, but it was a long process. They passed the first two dragons so fast, Gerald was sure the whistle of his flight would wake them. Then he remembered they weren't even breathing. Younger was back. He didn't see anyone else he knew. He wasn't going to quite stop by the far wall, but he had slowed drastically. Two loops around a group of dragons near that wall and he was flying sedately under his own power.

He flew down the passage to his room. As he hit the bed he bounced back up. When he hit it again, he was himself. The statue ran from the room and the door shut and barred itself. Gerald sat up, took a drink from his waterskin, and nearly spat it out. It was wine. He slowed down, drank more, lay back, and fell asleep for the second time that night.

When he awoke, he was sure he had dreamed, but could remember nothing. He laughed. *Whatever it was, it was nothing compared to the dreams I had earlier!*

CHAPTER THIRTY-THREE

DAYS OF
FUTURE PASSED

His belly rumbled. He was starving. Though he had food in his pack, there ought to be something fresh here somewhere. He looked around but none appeared in his room. He used the hole in the floor, put on his sword belt, and went in search of breakfast. The statue sidled out of his way. He winked at it and received a sly smile in return. Aurelia's door was open so he glanced inside, but she wasn't there.

He looked down at her statue. "I don't suppose you can tell me where she is." His lips grew warm, but that was all.

The statue covered her mouth with both hands and shook her head.

He turned and left the chamber. Halfway to the cavern he found a passage to the right. He followed it until it opened up into a room containing a table covered with food. He sat down and helped himself to bacon, cheese, and a fruit he didn't recognize. It was tart and delicious. He could find no water, so he drank a little wine from a clear crystal decanter. He might have to get water from the river.

Or maybe not. "I really need some water," he said aloud. He envisioned a slow-moving river. He reached into it and brought his hand to his face. His hand remained dry. He sighed and sipped the wine.

Satiated, he arose and followed the passage farther. It ended in a wall. He reached out and slapped it with his palm. It stung. The wall was real enough. He felt for a secret entrance. He imagined doors opening. It was to no avail. He headed back. Somewhere, someone snickered quietly.

Gerald smiled. "If I have learned anything here, it is to try. Nothing is impossible. It simply may happen or not happen when I least expect it."

The snicker changed to a delighted titter.

When he entered the cavern, he looked around. Daylight seemed to come from a passage farther to his right. He headed that way. Turning into the new passage, he was blinded by a light at the far end, reflecting off every nearby surface. Sitting in the archway was a dragon. No matter how much he squinted, the light was too bright and he could make out no details.

When Gerald was halfway to the arch, the dragon stretched, rose to its claws, and flew away. Gerald ran to the exit. He found himself on a ledge thousands of feet high. He had no idea where this could be; he had seen nothing this tall nearby. There was a river far below, but he had seen no river with a mountain this high, so he was unsure if it really was a river. He didn't trust anything about Death.

Well . . . other than the colors and the guardian. He looked around hopefully but saw nothing that could be the colors. Aurelia definitely wasn't present. He admired the view for a few minutes before going back inside.

He hiked to the antechamber by the bedrooms again. The only difference was that the figure of Gerald was slumped against the wall, reflecting how Gerald felt in the moment. He grimaced at it, shook himself, and headed toward the cavern again.

He was becoming aware of being sore in numerous places, but especially his back, around his shoulder blades. As he stepped into the cavern and saw the dragons, it dawned on him the soreness was where a dragon's wings would be.

"Was . . ." He shut his lips just in time. *Was that a dream? Or did it really happen?*

A deep blue voice responded from somewhere deep in his mind. "Are they always different?"

But I can't be in two places at one time, with one of me being a real dream the other is having!

"If you say so," the red voice replied.

The green voice said nothing, but Gerald was certain he heard another distant laugh. After a minute the green voice spoke. "There are times you have no words for something, so other words must do, however insufficient they may be."

Gerald thought a moment. "Like trying to speak another language when you don't know enough of it."

"Very much so," the blue voice said.

"You were expecting me to say something as well, so I am," the red voice added.

"Likewise," the green voice said, this time sounding like Cuthbert.

Gerald wandered through the cavern. Nothing happened this time, but his perspective had changed. The dragons belonged here, though he had no idea why they belonged, or even why they were there.

He came upon Younger. He looked different, brighter somehow.

"Less dust." The green voice had spoken first, this time sounding like Druze.

"Except there is no dust," blue added helpfully.

"Dust that is and is not," Gerald guessed.

"Precisely!" red applauded.

Gerald laughed. It was an incredibly imprecise precision. *Or precise imprecision?*

He heard, or perhaps sensed, something behind him. He wanted to spin around, but felt so solemn that he turned slowly.

Out of the corner of his eye, he watched a dragon soar by. It was in shadow, so he could not tell the color other than that it was not dark. It flew toward the edge of otherness—where they had come in yesterday—and was almost immediately obscured by the dragons arrayed about the floor.

Solemnity laughed, stuck out her tongue, and ran dancing off between the dragons. Gerald likewise ran to the open area to see this new dragon, but it was gone.

He checked on the horses. They were asleep on their feet. There was plenty for them to eat and there were pools of clear water in the floor. Without thinking, Gerald stooped, caught up some water and drank. To his relief, it did not turn to wine, or juice, or milk, or anything else. It was cool, clean water. Refreshed, he stood and looked around. The room was completely free of manure. And it was then he realized he had passed the edge of otherness without anything odd happening.

He checked the stables, which he found clean and in perfect order. He considered going to the entrance they had used yesterday but saw no point. With some trepidation, he headed to the edge of otherness again. He approached warily until he heard laughter both in his head and reflecting off the walls around him.

This time, no lights spoke. Instead, he heard Aurelia repeat something she had said yesterday. "When you conquer fear, something insidious, something subtle and evil, something that lives under the surface in cold, dark waters, breathing in life and breathing out death, dies. And that is a death we should willingly and joyfully celebrate!"

She was nowhere to be seen, but the words hung in the air awaiting his reply. Trying not to despair, Gerald asked without thinking, "How can I conquer this fear?" He clapped his hands over his lips, but nothing happened. Then he realized he was outside otherness and thus safe.

Unbidden laughter came to his lips. He snickered. He giggled like a child. He laughed. He laughed so hard he bent double. He laughed for a good five minutes, tears and snot running down his face. He laughed with the colors. He laughed with the water he had not drunk with breakfast. He laughed with the wine he had drunk. He laughed with the Milky Way and the ants that had crawled up and down his arm when he last held a sword.

When he could stop laughing, and when he had wiped the snot and tears from his face, he realized the fear was gone. He stepped over the edge, fell into a golden dragon's mouth, and was carried into otherness and deposited gently on the floor. The golden dragon winked and vanished. With nothing else to do, Gerald eventually walked back to Younger, sat down on the floor, and leaned against a massive white foreleg. He sat a long time. Many thoughts came and went. A few stayed; those seemed important. Some were big and some were small. He saw ways he could treat Sally better. He saw ways he could be a better warrior. He saw ways he could better honor King Donald, and Kenna, and his friends, and dragons, and spiders—even those without legs. He saw how people could better honor him, but he laughed and loved them anyway.

He grew hungry and wandered back to the table. It was still laden with food, but this time the cheese was yellow rather than white, the strange fruit was replaced by blaeberries, and the wine had become a dark ale.

It's a good thing I drank water while I could! I wonder if I can bring some in my waterskin, or if it changes in this part of otherness.

There was only one way to find out.

As he walked back into the cavern, Aurelia walked up. "There you are. I hope you are making good use of your time here."

He blinked and decided he would risk it. "Where have you been?" His lips grew warmer than he liked.

"Here, eat some cheese," she said, leading him back toward the dining room.

"I just ate," he replied as he reached for the ale.

"It will help with the burn. Eat and hold some to your lips."

"It's not that bad." But he tried and it helped far more than he had dared to hope.

"Sit," she ordered. He did so without thinking. "Last night you were a dragon."

It was a simple statement of fact, but it stirred mixed emotions for Gerald, from joy to anxiety to guilt. *Why guilt?*

In one of his biggest surprises of the past two days, no one answered. The guardian just looked at him. He realized he felt guilty for not following up on the dust, on Sally, on Darciere, on the garrison, on so many people.

"This is related to fear," she said with a happy smile. "You must not feel guilty over what you cannot change, or over what is not yours to do here and now."

He forced himself to relax and to let go of as much as he could.

"Good! You are not there, but you are closer. The dragon last night . . ."

"The dragon last night! Nain was fighting Argyll. Is Nain hurt?" He took a bite of cheese and pressed more to his lips for a second. "I thought perhaps he would be here if he needed to recover."

Somehow he knew he was on the wrong track. Perhaps it was Aurelia's expression. Perhaps not. But he was sure of something. "That's not why they are here."

"No, Gerald, it is not why they are here. Nor does it keep them away. It is unrelated. As for Nain, he was sorely hurt, but he lives. More dragons came. Argyll lost a claw, his right fore."

She reached across the table and grabbed Gerald's shield arm. "This is healed! Even here that should have taken longer."

Gerald had forgotten the burns. He thought back. "My arm quit hurting shortly after the leaves and paste were applied. My nose and eye quit hurting right after I became a dragon."

"And we are back to your being a dragon. That is . . . clearly not impossible, and yet it ought to be."

"The dragons are here and yet are not. I became a dragon and yet did not. This is indeed very other." He told her all that had transpired, occasionally helped or teased by colorful voices that spoke from a place more other than anything else Gerald had encountered. It was far away and yet right there with him.

When he finished, they sat long in silence. Finally Gerald broke it. "I wish to get some water."

"Oh, no need." She poured water from the pitcher full of ale. The pitcher was still full of ale, but now he had a goblet full of water. He drank deeply. It was almost as good as the horses' water. He laughed.

"I hope you did not drink water from the pools where the horses run!" She said severely.

"I did," he replied warily.

She laughed. "I jest. There is no danger in any drink for us inside this place."

He laughed, too. "You have said nothing of my adventures."

"I do not know what to say. Gerald, you know that few beyond the dragons come here. That is wisdom. Few could stand it. I would never have brought you had not Voice and Eldest encouraged it. And you have done well. But you break the laws that hold things in place as we know them. You have warped the laws of debt so that when debt thinks of you, it gnaws its tail in anguish. Were I the sort to fear, I would fear you, dragon lord who is and is not a dragon."

Gerald laughed. Not as he had earlier, but still hard. At least until he realized the guardian was not jesting. He froze. "You're serious." His lips tingled but he hardly noticed.

"Completely serious. It is a good thing you have come here. I know this. But where I have learned new things every minute I have spent here, now I learn that part of what I learned is not as true as I thought. Some things are still true, but whereas I thought they were truth, they were not. They are only true.

"Gerald, were I you, I would not seek to become a dragon again. I do not know why, but it does not feel like a good thing."

"The lights were with me."

"This time, yes. Perhaps even again. That does not mean it is a good idea. You have always had the lights, but you did not know them until you went over the edge."

Something in Gerald rose up in defiance. "There is no other way to see if I can help. There is no other way to know whether they have gone for the dust, or how any of them are."

She leaned over the table. "Gerald, look into my eyes. Tell me what you see."

"In your eyes."

"Yes."

He looked. He had to admit they were glorious eyes. They were as black as the darkest night, but with gold streaks so thin they were almost invisible. As he looked more closely he realized the gold strands glowed with a faint light. He started to shudder, but sensed these were as unlike le Fay's crystals as could be. They were very like the green, blue, and red lights, or the ring of endless white light. He fell off the edge into the otherness of her eyes.

He was a dragon again. This time he was larger, roughly his normal size. He was a deep purple like Selene. He saw himself in a pool of water, his eyes bright gold with thin strands of pure black—the inverse of the guardian's. He was flying around the indoor pasture the horses were in. They watched him nervously.

There must be a purpose to this, he thought. *Of course! I can go check on the faerie and see their progress. Go to Fiery Lake! Now!*

He was across the open space and into the dark, thick rock of the mountain. He burst into the sunlight. Looking up to find the sun, he saw a rapidly growing shadow. Flame erupted from it just as he realized it had no right foreclaw.

The pasture! To the pasture! Go! He tumbled twice before he found himself flying back to Death, flames around him warm but unable to harm him. Immediately after entering the rock, he felt and heard a thud and a scream of pain and rage. The scream dwindled rapidly in the rock and he was flying around the pasture. It shrank and grew dark. Dealanach and Aphrodite shrank to fine gold threads. Gerald found himself tumbling out of the guardian's eyes. He fell in a heap on the floor.

He lay for a moment, stunned, before pulling himself back onto a chair. He stared at Aurelia in shock. "I brought him. I brought him here. He knows. I am so sorry."

She smiled gently. "You did not. That was only one possibility, but it *is* a possibility, and a somewhat probable one. None of the probable possibilities are good if you take that route. I cannot tell you how I know, because I do not know the how. But I know.

"I cannot say you never will or should be a dragon again, though I know not how that might happen. None expected it to happen this time! But anything can happen once you go into otherness, and some of it does. I am glad it went well.

"Gerald, I cannot command you, and I would not, although part of me would!" This last part was spoken in wonder, as if making a great discovery. "But I will not! Yet I would advise you to stay three more days. I know it will be difficult at times, but please consider it."

Tricolor lights flashed behind Gerald's eyes. Somehow they were urging the same thing. A Voice flew from the wall on his left, nodded and winked at Gerald, and flew into the wall on his right.

"It seems I am the only one with doubts. I will stay."

The next three days were not nearly as exciting as the first had been. The guardian came and went. Gerald rode both Dealanach and Andromeda. Wherever the guardian disappeared to, she usually left her horse.

Gerald had grown up riding bareback. He had traded some of his hard-earned gold for a saddle before going to the castle and used one since. But he remembered now how much he enjoyed riding without one. It was clear Andromeda was comfortable this way and, to his surprise, Dealanach quickly adapted as well.

Twice more he saw a dragon fly through the cavern, although he never saw it very well. *Perhaps it is also both there and not there. At least these horses are completely here! But why does it always fly the same direction? Where does it go? Where does it come from? Why does it never stop?*

Gerald spent some time in exercise; he ran with the horses and he moved rocks around. He could not chance growing slothful. He surprised himself by looking and feeling better and stronger each day.

Apart from these activities, meals, and sleeping, he spent most of his time in otherness leaning against Younger and learning. Some of what he saw, or thought he saw, made no sense. At first he tried to understand everything, but the red voice warned against this. "You will drive yourself mad." So the things he could not understand, he set aside in his mind until he could one day see them in the right light. The voices commended him.

Midafternoon of the third day, he grew restless. He realized it was time to leave. He had not seen Aurelia since morning, but he felt the need to see her before leaving. As he walked toward the center of the cavern, the mysterious dragon flew in from the tunnel that led to the precipice in the light. It flew high overhead near the roof but dropped past Gerald. It slowed and flew in a circle, looking straight at him. Even in the dim light it shone gold. It seemed to be waiting. Gerald walked toward it. It turned and flew slowly toward the edge of otherness. Gerald broke into a loping stride to keep up. The dragon led him all the way to the exit, went through the magical curtain, and was gone. *How did it fit through that narrow opening?* Gerald stepped outside and gasped.

It was cold. There was snow on the ground. A bitter wind hit him like a dragon's tail. He staggered back. Aurelia ran up holding a stick. Seeing his footprints in the snow, she dropped the stick, grabbed his hand, and pulled him through the curtain that looked like plain rock.

Inside, the cold fell away into nothingness. He heard no wind. There was no snow on the floor. He rubbed his forearms and was warm again. "What? It's . . ."

"Yes, I know. Winter has come. Now you come and have a last meal and we will talk." She said nothing more as they walked. When they arrived at the edge of otherness, Gerald found himself floating on a river of yellow and brown sand that reminded him of the crystal dust he had taken the triad. It radiated confidence and lavender. A herd of rampaging slugs erupted from the river and carried him to the far shore, where Aurelia floated down from the heights holding a giant dandelion seed head. As she touched the ground, it shrank to the size of Gerald's fist. She blew on it and the seeds floated away, laughing merrily and speaking to one other in burbling tones. Guardian and dragon lord walked in silence through the cavern. When they arrived at the table, Gerald saw it was piled with bacon, carrots, and steaming hot green peas. His mouth watered.

"Interesting," Aurelia said as they sat down. "Eat."

Gerald obeyed with joy.

"I am unsure where to begin, Gerald. I suppose I will start with otherness. A great deal of your life has been spent in one form of otherness or another. Many spend their whole lives trying to destroy otherness, to make everything the same, whichever same they happen to prefer. This leads to painful things, from bickering among friends to divorce to murder to war.

"Sometimes you have embraced otherness, such as when you allowed Santana to change your heart. Other times you have tolerated it, such as when you listened to Drachmaeius.

Other times you have resisted, such as when you wanted to become a dragon again. Oh, yes, by attempting to tame it, to make it normal, you deny the other.

"Do not fear it. Do not assume all is good simply because it is other, but do not assume the other is bad, either.

"There are two secrets I can, and must, tell you now. Only twelve people of any sort—human, faerie, or anyone else besides dragons or guardians, have come here. Only four left alive and sane. I may not speak of those four except to say one managed to come unbidden. The other three were told what I am about to tell you. One of the guardian's functions is to explain this.

"First, time is not the same here as outside. You noticed the extreme cold and the snow. It is winter out there, Gerald. When you arrived, it was late October. Now Christmas has passed and it is almost the new year. No, I assure you it is true. Argyll is far away and no longer hunts for you. And he cannot hear his name here; no dragon can.

"Next, when we met, I told you truthfully that I did not know who I was. I have never been sure exactly what I am. I seem to be other. Have you seen skin like mine? I have heard of nobody who has, and I have inquired. But when here, there is a way I can become like a dragon. Not as you were. Not as a normal dragon is. It is a gift, I think, for being the guardian.

"You know the ledge high above the world where you first saw me as a dragon? The instant I leave by the arch there, I take on dragon form. Outside I am bound to a small area about the cliff; I cannot fly far. When I enter again, I remain in dragon form until I exit by the gate to the Valley of the Shadow of Death. I was the dragon you saw flying in Death's liver. You were not allowed to know this until now.

"I cannot tell you the why of all of this, Gerald, for I do not know it. When I need or want to know something of the history here, it comes to me. Much comes to me, anyway. I looked into my own eye in a mirror and walked with the one who came unbidden, that I would understand how and why and the dangers.

"And I know it is now time for you to leave. Get your things. You will find a warm coat with them and pants of inside-out skin so the fur keeps you warm and the hide keeps water out. There are fur boots and mitts and something to wrap round your head.

"Your garrison awaits you. They have grown restless and irked, but they know you are safe and well—at least if they still believe what dragons have told them.

"Here, have some cheese and ask what questions you will, but hurry. You need to go soon to arrive back before nightfall."

He had at least a hundred questions, but most of them she had already said she would not or could not answer. Beyond that, while he had taken it all in as best he could, he'd actually gotten stuck as she discussed time. Four days was somehow over two months? Of all that had occurred, this bothered him more than anything. It seemed the most impossible and the most unfair.

But he had no reason not to believe her.

"I may think of dozens of questions later, probably as soon as I leave. But I can think of few that you will answer." He closed his eyes and thought for a few heartbeats. "I wondered for a day, or perhaps a month, who was guardian before you."

Aurelia's eyes sparkled even more. "I told the lights you would ask! I think they know, but at times pretend they do not—to play with me. But you must add that to the list of questions I cannot answer right now."

Gerald sighed. "And yet you know all my secrets."

"What gave you that idea? I know of you what I need to know and what you tell me. No more. For instance, I have no idea how many times you have kissed Sally."

Gerald laughed. "I have no idea how many times Sally and I have kissed!"

Aurelia arched an eyebrow. "Well, you should. I am certain Sally knows."

Gerald stared at the guardian, unsure whether she was serious. After a moment he decided to just ask Sally later.

"Guardian, if you are not going with me, and it sounded as if you are not, how will I know the way?"

"I will speak with Dealanach and she will know. Aphrodite has been telling her, too. Have no fear on that part. If you become concerned, listen hard. You will hear."

Since he was finished, he got up. She went with him to his room. He picked up his pack and coat, but he could not carry everything and did not want to wear it all in the cavern. Aurelia smiled. "We will help."

She picked up the pants and boots. The statue of Gerald ran over and grabbed the mitts and head covering, as well as his waterskin.

Gerald looked around, smacked his head, and put everything down. Most of his weaponry was still on the table or in a drawer. He put the throwing knives in his pack, keeping only his belt knife and axes out. Those went to their places on his sword belt. He picked up the rest and they left. His statue winked at Aurelia's as they left the antechamber.

The walk across the cavern, to and over the edge, and to the horses was both painfully slow and painfully quick. Soon he had Dealanach outfitted again. They went to what Gerald thought of as the front door, where he tied his pack onto Dealanach while Aurelia laid a hand on each side of the horse's lowered head and whispered to her. Gerald took off his sword belt and put on the pants, boots, coat, and head cover. He just managed to fasten his sword belt around his increased girth and donned the mitts. Aurelia bowed to Gerald and he bowed back. His statue winked at Gerald and took Aurelia's hand, looking a bit forlorn. Gerald wondered what would happen to it now he was gone.

He walked through the door with Dealanach in tow. There

was no wind for the moment, but the bitter cold attacked through the cracks between his outer layers. Sunlight glistened blindingly from the snow. Gerald mounted Dealanach and she took off to his right. She seemed to know the way. A faint red ghost of something patted him on the shoulder reassuringly. He almost heard green and blue laughter. It was the laughter of good friends around a warm fire. He sighed contentedly and urged Dealanach to a faster walk. He really wanted to be back before nightfall.

There was little color in the sunset, but as always, the sun on the horizon thrilled Gerald with beauty and promise— magnified now by the snow. He watched for a moment with Fierza at his back, then started into the woods. He had pushed Dealanach and she had not resisted. They would be home and warm before dark. Voices greeted him as he approached the clearing. Two flew ahead to announce the envoy's return. Four riders waited in the clearing as an escort. Two flags flew above the barracks—the white saltire on a celestial blue background of Scotland next to Albania's two headed black eagle on a red background.

The flags brought a fresh smile to Gerald's face as he imagined a third—a plain black flag with almost invisible gold threads. If otherness had a flag, it ought to look like its guardian's eyes. Large doors opened as Gerald and the guard dismounted. He led Dealanach in. He could smell chicken cooking. Or perhaps it was goose. Given the inevitable interrogation, that would be fitting.

CHAPTER THIRTY-FOUR

NEWS ALL AROUND

When his escort removed their head coverings as well, Gerald found Justin and Gillian with Ulf and Grant.

"Welcome home!" Justin said, wrapping Gerald in a bear hug.

"*Miresevjen ne shtepi,*" Gillian agreed as he and Gerald clasped forearms. Ulf and Grant followed suit.

"It's good to be back," Gerald said. He paused, not sure what to say. "I'm sorry it's taken so long. I guess it gave you time to learn *Shqip!*"

Once the horses were in their stalls, Gillian led the way to an empty stall with many pegs driven into the wall. More winter gear hung on these. As they peeled off their outer layers, Gillian asked, "Where did you get that, Gerald? It's a bit different than what we were provided."

Gerald opened his mouth but no words came out. Somewhere a male voice suggested vagueness. "It was provided by my host. Where did you get yours?"

"The lady of Shkodër sent them by boat at the end of November. The first storm hit a day or so later. I've no idea what we gave in trade."

"The king sent far more than was necessary to pay for the barracks and supplies, even if we have been here longer than expected," Gerald replied.

Exchanging a meaningful look, Ulf and Grant excused themselves and went upstairs. Justin asked, "Are you hungry? We were just about to eat when a Voice said you were nearby."

"No, thank you. I ate not long ago."

They eyed him curiously, clearly expecting more.

Twice he opened his mouth but could not form words. *All right, I get the point.* He thought a moment, then tried again. "I met someone the day of the attack here. I cannot say much, but the Eldest and others urged me to go with this person. I have been in a fortress much of the time, although I also spent time with the triad and went to gather evidence for a theory Eviola had. It proved to be true and should help Sally, and possibly Kiergenwald as a whole. That is all I am permitted to say for now."

Justin and Gillian glanced at each other before Justin spoke. "We guessed you might not be able to say much. The Voices and dragons have been vague, other than assuring us you were safe and doing your job. Kenna said the same."

"You have seen her? Did she bring news?"

"Yes, but let us go upstairs. I'm starving!"

"Aye," Gillian agreed. "I haven't heard half what you said. My stomach was louder."

Laughing, they went up.

Each warrior got a large bowl of stew and some bread. Gerald insisted on a small serving. He tasted the stew. "Oh! That's spicy! And hot!" He blew on the next spoonful to cool it. "What is it?"

Ulf spoke up. "It's called *paçe*, a local dish that's very popular, especially in the winter."

"Who makes it?"

"We pay Valmira, a woman from Fierza, to bring us dinner.

This is made by boiling a sheep's head. Tomorrow night we will have *gjiri gic*, a roasted pig."

"I like the bread here, too," Justin said.

Gerald paused between bites. "Where are the rest?"

Gillian sighed. "MacIntyre and his men have returned to Edinburgh. Eoin has gone back to Cair Parn so the healers can mend his leg. Donald is up on the watchtower with Rezart, an Albanian guard sent by Lady Fjorela. There is another, Taulant, who is out hunting. He prefers to hunt alone, no matter the weather. He brings in about half our meat."

"Donald takes a watch?"

"Yes. He says since there are so few, it would be ridiculous if he did not. And Rezart is teaching him *Shqip* and some of their ways."

"What happened to Eoin?"

"The day of the first Ottoman attack . . ."

"The first? There were more?"

"Oh, yes. Eoin and Luan and I set out to track down those who fled. They ambushed us. We prevailed, but Eoin was wounded in the leg. It did not seem bad, so we set balm upon it and wrapped it. It was slow to heal.

"Twice more we came under Ottoman attack. Each time we prevailed. The third time we took several prisoners. Luan found they were seeking the 'golden one.' They said it in awe. We told them she had gone home and was well guarded. Your Voice suggested her guard included dragons. When Selwyn came to visit, he told them she was something sacred and that if they laid hands on her, they might very well die. They begged to go home and promised never to return. Selwyn made their chief swear he would warn his superiors. We set them free and whatever happened, we have seen no more of the Ottomans."

Justin spoke up. "You never finished Eoin's tale! Gerald, Eoin was wounded in the same spot again. It swelled and his whole leg was turning green. He could barely walk. Selwyn took him to Cair Parn so Ivor or K'Pene could help."

Gerald put his spoon down. "Has there been word?"

"He will keep the leg, but it's game. He refuses to ask to be released from service, but it is clear he would be at a disadvantage in a foot battle." He grinned. "Horseback, he is better than ever."

"Aye," Grant chimed in. "The English have been making noises about how we fear to joust with them. Of course we just think it's stupid, but King Donald is considering having some give it a go, including Eoin."

"Jousting! That means armor. We have no armor," Gerald scoffed.

"Edinburgh has a bit, as do some of the kings down south. They took it off the English dead after battles many years ago."

Gerald shook his head. He had no interest in armor. "So two Albanians and five Scots."

"Six, as you're back," Ulf pointed out. "Assuming you're still a Scot."

"As much as you are," Gerald quipped.

Ulf grinned. "There's those who would argue I'm not!"

"Anyway, why did you stay?"

Gillian looked at Gerald as if he was daft. "We're here as long as you are, of course. Even when your idea of here is elsewhere. Frankly we were surprised when MacIntyre and his men left. You are the high king's envoy in this."

"Am I still? What has happened with the stones? What of Sally and Scythia?"

Gillian rubbed his face. "I think Donald wanted to discuss these things with you."

"Then I hope he's down here soon."

"I am, as it turns out. Or will be." Donald and another warrior traipsed through on their way downstairs, unwinding scarves from their faces as they went. They were back quickly without the winter gear, sitting with their backs close to one of the blazing fireplaces.

Donald sighed happily as he rubbed his shins. "There's clouds and little enough light to begin with, and a fog has moved in. We don't keep a night watch in this weather, but tonight a man would freeze to death and someone five feet away not know it. Assuming he hadn't frozen, too. So, Gerald, where have you been?"

Gerald repeated the brief story he had told the others.

Donald eyed Gerald oddly. "Dragons, Voices, and faerie all told us not to inquire too much. Lady Fjorela sent a message saying the same thing. So I'll not ask for more, but you've left us a queer task, Gerald."

Gerald grinned. "I promise you my task was queerer. Did you say Lady Fjorela sent word?"

"I did. We've no idea what she knows or why she said it. Luan and his crew took Eviola back to Shkodër about ten days after you left. Which was funny, because she was gone most of that time. She also told us you had helped the triad with the mystery, and even hinted you had briefly gone back to Scotland surreptitiously."

"I was," Gerald agreed, "but I have heard no news since. Did the dragons get the roof from Sally's and my house? Was it replaced? Were the stones destroyed? Are Sally and Scythia better? Is there any news of the triad? Where is Kenna?"

Donald shook his head. "King Donald never asks more than one or two questions at a time. He says it helps clarify the thoughts. He drums that into the captain's head, and the captain drums it into Folkvar's and mine. I thought we had drummed it into those of our pupils, but apparently not."

Justin bristled. "I don't do that!"

"True, but this one certainly does."

"It comes from spending so much time with dragons, I think. They approach things differently," Gerald mused.

"Except you've been that way as long as I've known you," Justin pointed out.

Gerald hung his head. "Stabbed in the back by a friend."

Donald continued. "I'll do my best. Ask again about whatever I forget, though I may not know the answer!

"Dragons and two members of the triad went with Kenna and Eviola to your village. I hear Cuthbert and others met them there. They spoke at length with Cle and his wife, as your Sally did not seem to care. They called the village together and explained a little of the situation. The roof was poisoned by something left of Morgan le Fay. They would take the roof and the stump away and destroy them, along with the stones. They hoped this would free Sally and Scythia from whatever curses were upon them. At the least, it would remove the source of distress Sally and others felt.

"One of the triad brought silver to pay to have the roof replaced. A bargain was struck. Men were hired to help your brother disconnect the roof. Dragons brought blankets to put the pieces on, and pulled the roof apart to fit the blankets. Then they rolled those up, crushed them together, put them inside some kind of mail and carried them off. Ah, and they wrapped all *that* in dragon hide. The stump also went as promised. Kenna reported that Cle said they could feel the difference immediately, and where things had been dying near the stump, now they are growing again.

"Sally refused to make any decisions so Cle oversaw the roof. By all counts it's thicker and sturdier than what you had. The triad did some sort of blessing over it.

"But the house is empty. Druze has Sally with her. Sally no longer grows more listless with each day, but neither has she improved as they hoped. Voices tell us Scythia has not changed a whit.

"As to the roof and the stones and stump, I have not heard whether they are destroyed or not. Gerald, I'm sorry I've no better news. But I'm glad it's not worse."

Gerald sat quietly for a long moment. He considered moving closer to the fire until he realized the cold he felt blew from a wind somewhere inside him. "Thank you. What of Kenna?"

"We haven't heard from her for a month. The last we knew, she was with the triad."

"Did they leave any word for me?"

Donald started to shake his head and stopped. He grinned at Rezart. "No word for you, only about you. They took pains to assure us that you were alive and well, that you were about the business you were sent on, and that you would be back soon. We had the impression soon meant a lot sooner than it turned out to be."

"It surprised me as well."

There was a tapping on one of the shutters. Ulf groaned. "I hate when they do that."

Gerald was sure it was a Voice. "Why?"

Ulf lurched to a window, unlatched a shutter, and cracked it open. A Voice rushed in, accompanied by an icy wind and snow. Ulf closed the shutter and fought the latch until the shutter would not move. "That's why. Brrr!" He hurried over to the fire, rubbing his hands.

"Greetings, Lord Gerald, and most worthy warriors," the Voice cried. They all returned the greeting, even the wary Albanian.

"Lord Gerald, the triad would like you to come at noon tomorrow. A dragon will arrive by then to take you." A gleam came into the Voice's eye. "Unless you would prefer to turn into a Voice and fly there yourself."

Gerald laughed. "Could I become a bird, I would become an eagle or hawk to get there quicker. But thank you, I shall await the dragon."

The Voice looked around. "Cozy. If I may, I will stay the night here."

Gerald looked at Donald, who shrugged. Gerald said, "We would be honored."

The garrison, having had a long day, was ready to retire.

Gerald thought he was tired as well, but he could not sleep. It was just as well, for soon the Voice was knocking softly at his door. He got up and let her in. Then he lit two more candles from the one beside his bed. He stared at the walls a moment in confusion, then laughed. *I've gotten used to lights that never go out.* "What brings you to my room, Voice? And did you have a good flight?"

"Brrr, as one of your guards is wont to say. I come to bring you word of Sally. She sent few messages while you were gone and they were all terse, but she seemed to feel neglected at first and later rejected. Those whose advice Gerald values urge him to send a message to Sally."

Gerald glared at the candle, then looked up at the bird. "Will you take a message to Sally?"

"I will take the message to other Voices and we will take it, as Voices do. Or you can send word by dragon."

"A dragon would be quicker, certainly, but I have Voices for that. I have no dragons at my beck and call."

"You do at the moment. Ask tomorrow as you fly to Fiery Lake what the state of things is in that regard. A dragon will know best."

"Thank you. I will. Is there anything else?"

"No, except that I would like to not spend the night in the barracks. Some of them snore."

"I am told I do, for that matter. Perhaps downstairs?"

"An excellent idea. Thank you, Lord Gerald. May your dreams be enlightening."

"I want no dreams tonight, thank you. Rest well, Voice." He let the Voice out and lay back down. If he dreamed, he didn't recall it, but surely if he did, the dreams were far quieter than what he had become used to of late.

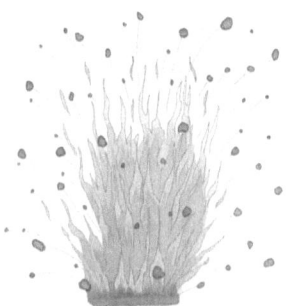

CHAPTER THIRTY-FIVE

ANOTHER DAY, ANOTHER ABYSS

When Gerald woke the next morning, the barracks was empty. Cheese and bread awaited him on the table. He found hot water by the fire for coffee. After eating he cracked a shutter to gaze out and saw it was still early—perhaps an hour after sunrise.

As envoy, Gerald had no assigned duties, but he couldn't sit around idly. When he went to check on Dealanach, he realized the stalls needed mucking. While he worked, Donald wandered in. "Ah, at last young master is up. Did you sleep well?"

"Well enough. Why did no one wake me?"

"Well, we weren't quiet about things and you slept through. You looked tired last night, so we left you to wake when you would."

"What do you do here?"

"That, for one thing," Donald glanced at the shovel full of manure Gerald was carrying to a nearby wheelbarrow. "We do much the same as at Cair Parn, plus cooking and cleaning. Though we have dinner cooked in Fierza! We keep watch, but the dragons will warn us if they see trouble coming. They are watching all routes. They would also tell the lady Fjorela and her magician friend, and invaders would likely never make it this far.

"This week has been the only really cold week; it's mostly like back home. We do some hunting, though Taulant mainly does that now. The man has taught us some things, but it's his home and he knows it well."

"Who is this magician you speak of?"

"Ah, yes. Not long after you took off after the invaders and the child—and did not return, much to our concern despite all we were told—refugees came through from south of here. They told tales of an evil wizard who demanded money and a wife. When they gave him neither, he cursed their food and water and people began to die. Fjorela's men hunted him for a month to no avail. Several of them died as well.

"A man from Fierza—we thought him the sort of court magician who does tricks to amuse people—donned a simple cloak and went south hunting the wizard. He would allow no one to go with him. A week later he returned and told us where to find the wizard. He suggested we send a dragon.

"Our court magician had somehow found the man and erected a sort of dragon skin and mail house around him, which the evil wizard could not escape! We sent Voices to Shkodër. A dragon was dispatched to retrieve the man and he has been carried off somewhere the triad can look into him. Eviola and Luan returned by boat and asked the local magician, whose name is Leotrim, to go to Shkodër. Leotrim had already disposed of most of his property and was packed and ready to go. The lady has asked him to stay there as advisor and mage and he has agreed. Selene thinks there may be more to it than that, but we shall see."

Gerald pondered all of this. "I heard little news while in the fortress unless it pertained to why I came. But dragon skin is resistant to magic, and the faerie have a kind of fine mail cloth that withstood even Morgan le Fay's magic, so I have no doubt it will handle local wizardry. But two wizards this close together!"

Donald interrupted. "Magician, not wizard. He is adamant about that. I've no idea why."

Gerald shrugged. "Regardless of the words used, how long has it been since we have heard of even one true mage being alive? Eoin found a druid who dealt in magical items on his quest the first year, but he was no wizard—only one who understood relics and such. Have you heard of others?"

Donald rubbed his chin for a moment. "Other than the faerie, who seem to eat and breathe magic though they seldom show it, no."

"Were either of these wizards faerie?"

"How would we know? No one has said so. Leotrim seemed like a man, but all thought Kenna a woman like any we know. Her hair was always a bit odd. Come to think of it, this man has hair like a porcupine. It stands in three-inch spikes. None know if he does something to it or it simply grows that way. But he has a kind face and a good reputation. He has a ready smile, is generous with what he has, and would as soon show you a trick as discuss the weather.

"Which we can do just a bit of now. Taulant is gone too much to help with that, but Rezart is a wonder at teaching us his language, and at learning ours. I dare say he understood at least half of what was said last night, though had it been in *Shqip*, I'd have understood at best a tenth."

Gerald had finished cleaning the stalls. He rolled the barrow to the door and outside. Donald pointed toward the outbuilding. Gerald hurried across the yard to a snow-covered mound with a shovel beside it. He unloaded the barrow, scrubbed it as best he could with frozen grass and snow, and raced back to the barracks. Donald slammed the door behind him.

"I should have at least worn my coat!" Gerald said with annoyance.

"And by the time you'd put it on, you'd have complained it wasn't worth it."

"True enough," Gerald said with a laugh. He looked around and saw nothing else amiss. He patted Dealanach and asked,

"What else needs doing?"

Donald looked around. "Nought. Let's go upstairs and talk of plans."

Back in the mess, Gerald put more wood on the fire and sat near it, rubbing his hands. "Plans. Do you have plans, then?"

"I was hoping to know the envoy's."

"The envoy has no plans yet save to go to the triad. Perhaps he will have plans, or plans for plans, after that."

"Then let us go back downstairs, get dressed, and patrol the area. If we are to remain here, you might as well know where you are."

Gerald glanced ruefully at the fire as they started back to the stairs.

The next two hours were long, cold, and unexciting, though Gerald felt more at home afterward. As they peeled off their outer layers, Gerald again explained that his were a gift from his host at the fortress.

Donald looked up. "Rezart was surprised to hear of this fortress. He and Taulant are from nearby, and he insists there is no fortress within a day's ride."

"It is well hidden."

"It must be. While you were gone, the people of Fierza grew concerned and offered to help us search for you. When we told them we had been assured you were safe, they looked askance. They said no one lived anywhere nearby. One of them took it upon herself to visit two hermits and found no trace of you."

"I wish I could say more, Donald, but I cannot."

"I understand. Or at least, I believe you. Gerald, you live in a strange world. I am content to live solely in this one."

Gerald smiled wryly. "I was, too. But I am content in this as well." He thought back over the past few days. "Most of the time, anyway."

A beak knocked rapidly on the shutter. Donald grinned. "It's a good thing Ulf isn't here." He opened it but no Voice flew in. He opened it farther and laughed. "Gerald, someone is here to see you." Gerald jumped up and looked out. Santana lay on bare ground with several Voices perched on his head. Snow had melted for several feet around him and steam rose from his nostrils.

Santana's eyes spun with joy. "Your chariot awaits, dragon lord."

"I will be out soon. I need my heavy clothes for this flight!"

"You do not. Bring them in case you need them, but tie them in a bundle and bring them along with your pack."

Gerald stared for a few seconds until Donald closed the shutter, saying, "It's getting a bit cold in here."

"Of course. My apologies, captain."

"If you wish to start on your clothes downstairs, I will bring your pack."

"You don't need . . ."

"Please do not tell me my duties! At Cair Parn, you may well carry mine, but I am here to aid the envoy, and aid him I shall. Now go."

Once ready, Donald opened a door and they ran to Santana. The dragon stood and Gerald saw something dark blue between his forelegs. "A travel egg!"

"Yes, Lord Gerald. Folkvar is quite proud of it. And you will be the first to ride in one after those on Mull who worked on it."

Gerald walked over. The muddy ground under Santana was starting to freeze again. "Could you move it here out of the mud?"

Flames of laughter came close, and Gerald wished they were warmer. Santana nudged the egg onto the snow. Gerald found the lower flap already open. He didn't see a frame, but the cold urged him not to spend time on questions. His pack and bundle went in first. Gerald clasped Donald's forearm briefly, thanked him, and clambered into the egg. As he tried in vain to find straps to tie it shut, Santana laid the egg on its side and lifted off. Falling as the egg turned sideways, Gerald decided to hold the flap shut. As he pushed the stiff edges together, they shut suddenly and tightly with a dull clank. He found he could pull them apart only with great effort.

The egg was warmer than he had expected. The barest hint of freezing wind snuck in. Some kind of padding lay under the hide. *There must be two layers of hide!* Gerald could feel metal rods under the padding. The whole thing was much more complex—and wonderful—than he had hoped for.

Recalling the lesson on a dragon's hearing in flight, he spoke in a normal tone. "Santana? What is this magic that holds the flap closed?"

There was no reply. *Too much padding and too many layers of skin!* He repeated his question, bawling it loudly.

This time Santana replied. "It is the magic of rocks and metals, Gerald. Have you heard of lodestone?"

"Yes, but what I have seen is weak. This is strong!"

"There are strips of refined steel in the egg's shell which attract lodestone. The faerie have found a way of distilling and forming lodestone to make it stronger. There are strips of that in the flaps."

Gerald marveled at what Folkvar and the craftsmen had wrought. "And it's warm!"

"Yes. There is a way to take it apart to remove the straw and blanket padding, so that summer travel will not be too hot. I think you will want the flaps open in warmer weather, too."

Gerald lay down. It was cozy with both his pack and the winter clothing bundle, but he wouldn't mind a long trip in this. *Like the day-long trip home. Home!* He sat up suddenly.

"Santana! How are things going? How are you and Selene? How are things back home?"

"That depends on which things, Gerald. Selene and I are well. And which home?"

"All of them, dragon!"

He could hear the smile in Santana's reply. "Today we dispose of le Fay's legacy. Things in Scotland are little different than when you were last there, save that your house has a new roof and Nain is injured. Folkvar thinks they can make an egg every two or three days, and they have enough skin to make a dozen more, though the last one may be different colors inside and out."

"What of Nain?"

"He was sorely injured in his battle with Argyll. He has wounds that will not heal. The Eldest believes Argyll's claw may have held traces of le Fay's stones and that this is the problem. That was the claw Argyll lost in the battle. Nain bit it off. Nain's mouth has not been right since, either. The falling claw damaged a corner of a house, but no one was hurt. Harem retrieved the claw and took it to the Teeth. Selene carried it to Fiery Lake. It awaits the same fate as the le Fay stones and dust."

"Harem?"

"He is from Africa. He had destroyed many villages there after humans killed his mate. Since the truce, he has been attempting to reconcile with humankind. Several of the groups he found told him they would not talk with him unless he made peace with their queen, but she had gone they knew not where. She had left her title and land behind. He came to seek advice from the Eldest, who told him of K'Pene, and it was she. She has not completely forgiven him, but they are talking. Their talk reminds me of you and Drachmaeius, but writ large, as there were far more people involved."

When Santana said no more, Gerald asked, "And should K'Pene and her people forgive him?" Another question sprang from his lips unbidden. "Should I forgive Drachmaeius?"

"Harem forgave humans. I know the argument that he killed far more people than those who killed his mate, but as you know, the origins of the enmity between our kind lies millennia back. None of us were involved, but all of us were harmed. All but a few dragons chose at Lochmaldie to forgive the atrocities perpetrated against us, but the peace will work only if humans do the same."

"Including me."

"Including you, my friend. You have forgiven much, but this still weighs you down."

"And must I forgive Argyll as well?"

Santana waited a moment to answer. "I do not know whether you *must*, but if you do, you will be far stronger and happier. Forgiveness does not mean condoning his actions. Nor does it mean he should not be stopped. The eldest dragons agree nothing short of death will stop Argyll.

"Eldest will send for you soon. He has something to discuss with you, Cuthbert, and Kenna. Did your Voice mention you should send word to Sally? You have said nothing of this, which surprises me."

Gerald sat quietly for a while. Why had he forgotten? He seemed to have forgotten Sally quite a bit lately. *Perhaps it is because she does not seem to care. Or she is not Sally anymore.* But he knew that wasn't it. Not really. Something urged him to go deeper. He grinned. The something felt red. He never felt alone now, and he suspected it was because he wasn't. *Have I ever been?*

As he cast about for answers, a wave of fear hit him. That was it! Fear. He was afraid he had failed Sally, that he had lost her, that because of his war with Argyll, some irrevocable doom had come upon her. How could he counter this? The memory of laughter in otherness killing his fear came, but he could find nothing to laugh at now. That left him feeling guilty.

And then, as if she stood there in the flesh, he saw Aurelia. "Your guilt is related to fear," she said again with a happy smile. "You must not feel guilty over what you cannot change, or over what is not yours to do here and now."

That helped with the guilt but not the fear. As he sat trying to get past the fear enough to think about how to deal with it, he felt dizzy. Colored lights swam before his eyes. Images formed. He saw Sally as they were handfasted. He saw K'Pene and himself working frantically on Cuthbert. He saw Wandap, who had given her life fighting to save the eldest. He saw Samantha adopting him. He saw Father MacPherson, speaking of love casting out fear.

Gerald thought on these images, of those he loved and who had exemplified love to him. And the fear left.

He was lying on something soft, looking up at dragon skin. He recalled where he was and the discussion he and Santana had been having.

"My Voice said I had dragons at my disposal. What did she mean by that?"

"Very good! While you sit at the pivot point, as I know was explained to you, you have far more authority and right to call upon us than at any other time. We will serve you willingly, up to a point. I cannot describe that point, but it will vary from dragon to dragon and we will not know it until it arrives. I fully expect that you will see it and avoid it. We would not, for instance, carry Sally a poem a day simply because you felt like writing one. Yet Sally is important enough that we would do it if we believed it would help her recover."

Gerald could not absorb this, so he set it aside for later. "Who would I send the message with?"

"Selwyn or Harem will be at the Teeth. You can tell me. I will take the message to the Teeth while you are at Fiery Lake. They will carry it to near Kiergenwald. Voices will deliver it to Sally. Any return message will come the same way."

Gerald thought only a moment. He gave a brief explanation of his adventures, wishing desperately he could tell Sally everything. He promised to come see her as soon as possible, expecting it would indeed be soon. He asked how she was and for news of home in general. He sent his love.

They flew on in silence a moment before Santana responded.

"That is good, Gerald. Your voice sounds a bit rough. You should be quiet now. We will have to think on building the eggs so shouting is not necessary. They eat sound."

A few minutes later Santana began to drop. "We approach our destination." Two minutes later he laid the egg on a flat spot. As Gerald worked his way out, the doors opened. Kenna and Andreas stepped out to help Gerald from the egg. It was warm here, but there was snow just past where the doors swept—presumably faerie magic at work.

They helped Gerald drag the egg inside the passage. He turned to wave, but Santana was already gone. The doors closed. Andreas beckoned. "We go now to watch the destruction of that which has wreaked much havoc and promised more."

They walked solemnly to the room where alchemy was performed. The table was now devoid of trees and sheet. Only a mail drawstring bag sat in the middle. Something large wrapped in mail sat off to one side. As he looked at it, Kenna said, "That is the stump. Whatever Argyll and le Fay's memory had wrought extended about a foot underground and about a foot into the roots. Dragon fire burned away everything around it that was not transformed by magic."

Andreas spoke again. "Gerald, please take the pouch. It contains both the stones and Eviola's small pouch with the dust you gathered. And carry this." He pointed beneath the table. Kenna pulled Scythia's sheathed sword out and handed it to Gerald.

Chloe walked in and bowed to Gerald. He returned the honor, wondering why she had bowed. Darciere was nowhere to be seen. Kenna reached toward the stump and raised her hands; the mail-covered lump rose an inch from the floor. Andreas and Chloe led the way. Kenna followed, propelling the stump. Gerald brought up the rear.

They stopped at the overlook. Andreas and Chloe waved their hands slowly in front of them, concentrating so their foreheads broke out in sweat. A wave of intense heat hit briefly, but a strong wind blew from behind them to drive the heat back. Andreas looked up and Gerald followed his gaze. Dragons flew overhead, circling the volcano. As one would disappear from sight, another would appear. Gerald saw Selene, Santana, and . . . was that the Eldest? Selene reappeared.

"There are three dragons here?" Gerald asked.

"Yes," Andreas said, "unless you count the one who watches from afar. But he cannot interfere."

Chloe held out her arms and moved them as if raising a heavy object. Kenna gestured Gerald closer to the low wall. Looking down, they watched something rise from the fires below. A stone ramp—white like the walls in which they stood—pulled itself from the burning mayhem. One end rose to the top of the wall before them, blocking some of the heat. The far end rose to about half their height. It formed a ramp whose lower end curved up.

Chloe joined Kenna in focusing on the stump. Slowly they moved it atop the wall, over the edge, and onto the ramp. Chloe reached out with a hook and caught the edge of the mail. Kenna made a shoving motion and the mass beneath the mail broke free and began sliding, faster and faster, down the ramp. As the stump reached the end and arced back up, it was hit by three streams of dragon fire. The dragons dropped with the stump as it fell, flaming the whole way. As they reached the fiery mess below, there was an explosion. Molten rock and fire washed over the dragons but they arose, unhurt, bugling victory cries.

Chloe flung the mail off the hook. It slid down and met the same fate.

The dragons returned to the heights and resumed circling.

"Empty the pouch onto the ramp, dragon lord," Andreas commanded. Gerald loosed the strings and did just that. As he watched the stones and dust tumble onto the ramp and begin their slide downward, Chloe added, "And now the pouch. We will not chance residue." Gerald threw the pouch after the stones.

Chloe and Andreas waved their arms and restored the shield. The dragons dropped, repeating the scene with the stump. Though this time the rocks were far smaller, the explosion was bigger, rocking the dragons backward. Again they were unscathed and sang victoriously.

The dragons slowly flew up the ramp, bathing it in fire. Chloe explained, "Some of the dust undoubtedly did not make it to the bottom. We take no chances. But dust is more easily destroyed." Gerald jumped as flame washed over the invisible shield that divided them from the furnace outside. When the flame was finally gone, so was any vestige of the mail. Chloe made a motion as if dropping something, and the ramp slid away. A moment later, a fountain of fire and burning rock leapt up.

They waited. Soon a large bundle fell from the sky. Again the dragons chased it into the fiery lake, burning it as it descended. This time there was barely a splash.

"Was that my roof?" Gerald asked.

"That was your roof," Andreas replied.

"Good."

Andreas and Chloe worked to remove the shield again.

"We must deal with the sword, Gerald," Kenna explained.

With the shield again gone and wind pushing the heat back, Andreas turned to Gerald. "Hand Kenna the scabbard and pull the sword. Hurl the sword as far out as you can. And be ready to do your part."

Puzzled, Gerald obeyed. The sword resisted until Gerald ordered, "Come out!" It unsheathed so fast he nearly fell over. He swung his arm back and threw the sword as hard as he could. It left a trail of yellow sparks. Gerald's arm went numb. Within twenty feet, the sword was clearly falling. The Eldest was falling, too, and caught the sword by the hilt between two claw tips. But both continued to fall quickly toward the fiery lake.

"Now, dragon lord!" Andreas called. "Reach for the sword and pull as you never have!"

Gerald had no time to think. The command seemed to have taken over his body. He reached out as if to grab the sword. To his surprise, he could feel the hilt under his fingers. A familiar ache went up his right arm. He grabbed with his left hand as well, cutting a finger in the process on a sword that was far below. As he started to pull, the sword pulled back and he nearly flew out the window. The three faerie caught him.

He pulled with all his might, his arms feeling as if they would rip from his body. Was the sword bent on suicide? Was he feeling the dragon's weight as well as the sword's? As Morticum touched the molten lake, fire shot up Gerald's hands and into his arms. He watched the skin on his hands blister and crack. A knuckle bone showed on one finger.

The sword slid into the fire. It stopped at the guard leaving the Eldest hovering over what Gerald thought the face of hell must look like. He held on and kept pulling; slowly the sword pulled back out of the lake. Gerald's fingers were mere bone now but miraculously he held on and kept pulling. When at last the sword left the fire below, the Eldest shot into the sky while the sword flew in an arc back toward the window, trailing red sparks. Morticum came to Gerald. Its fiery hilt slammed into his right palm. He screamed in pain and the world went dark.

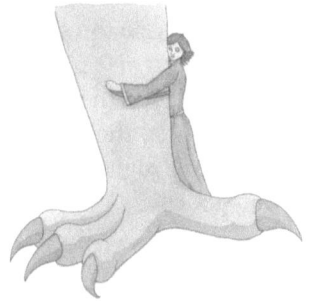

CHAPTER THIRTY-SIX

UNEXPECTED VISITOR

Gerald lay on a hard surface in the dark watching hundreds of tiny green, red, and blue birds dart about overhead. Their soothing song made him forget something. He suspected the something was pain. Then a face like pure gold in sunlight appeared over him—a face wearing both compassion and confusion.

"Gerald! What are you doing here? No one comes into otherness twice, not even Merlin!"

"I don't know. I was with the triad and . . . my hands!" Now he remembered the pain, although it was far less. He held up his hands, which looked horrible. The palms were blackened and ravaged, the fingers and thumbs skeletal. He held a tiny sword in his right hand, reminding him of the miniature scene on the table at Fiery Lake.

The guardian took his hands. "This is easy, Gerald. Give me the sword." She had to pry it off his fingertip. A final bit of burnt flesh came away with the sword. She helped him up. "We must go to the edge."

She turned into a giant golden bat, picked Gerald up, and flew through otherness back to the edge. As they approached the wall of darkness, she resumed her human form and they both tumbled into whatever awaited behind the veil. Gerald fell atop a pool of fire like the one the sword had dipped into, but this was cool and refreshing. He held his hands under for a moment and when he removed them, they were whole. He laughed and swam for a while, then looked for Aurelia. He saw something golden flying high above. He reached for it, it reached for him, they touched, and he was back on a hard surface . . . .

He was back on the floor at Fiery Lake beneath the window overlooking the volcano. The faerie were looking around frantically. Just as Kenna backed into him, screamed, and nearly fell, the sword—full sized once more—reappeared in his hand.

The others froze, staring at him with stunned expressions.

"Where did you come from?" Andreas demanded.

"Where did you *go*?" Chloe insisted.

"Your hands. They are whole!" Kenna squealed.

And they were. He looked at them in wonder. Only the barest memory of their pain remained. He groaned; his back and head hurt from the fall. *Really? It couldn't all be fixed?*

He heard distant laughter of an uncertain color. A ghost of a whisper said, "What was broken is fixed. The rest is mere inconvenience." Gerald laughed at himself even as he winced.

He worked his way up onto one elbow. The others helped him up. "Well?" Andreas demanded.

Gerald opened his mouth. As expected, nothing came out. He tried again. "I was somewhere dark. Someone came and helped me. They turned into a bat at one point. Then I was back and Kenna nearly tripped and impaled herself on this." He held out the sword. Whereas before it had felt like power desperate to be used, now it was simply a finely crafted sword. The faerie each examined it before Kenna put it back in its scabbard.

"It is clean now," Andreas pronounced. He reached for Gerald's hands and examined them. "Were they not burned as you fought the death of le Fay's magic?"

"They were. Or seemed to be."

Kenna grimaced. "Gerald, they were. I could smell the burning flesh. I am sorry. None of us foresaw that!"

"And yet they are well now," Chloe grimaced. "You will not tell us where you went?"

"I cannot. When first I went to speak and no words came, I could not speak of it. Thus has it been so each time I have tried."

Kenna's eyes widened but motion outside the window distracted them—flaming dragons were dropping toward the lake. They flew upward screaming a joyful song as a small explosion rocked the fires below.

Andreas smiled. "That would be Argyll's claw and whatever cursed dust it carried."

Kenna returned to the previous subject. "You returned?"

Gerald nodded. "I think so. I thought I had dreamed it, but if I was gone, there I was."

Andreas hissed. "Otherness."

Gerald arched an eyebrow, but the ruse fooled no one. Chloe's eyes widened while Kenna shut hers briefly. Gerald shrugged but grew increasingly uncomfortable under their stares. Finally he broke the silence. "What of Darciere?"

Chloe grimaced. "She lies as one dead, though she clearly lives. We have all told her she is forgiven. It has made no difference. We have done all our people know to do. We sent word to the council. They fear she is dying of guilt and have suggested we ask a dragon to bless her."

Kenna's face lit up. "Gerald, you could bless her."

"What?"

"Remember what happened on Mull? You blessed Kyla and the Eldest's blessing flowed from you to her."

Andreas started. "You were Eldest blessed?"

"Yes."

"By all means, let us try."

They escorted him to Darciere's room. It was large but sparsely furnished. A chest sat in the corner with three locks—gold, silver, and black—on heavy clasps. Darciere's bed lay empty, covered by a pale-yellow blanket that glowed softly and soothingly. The faerie stopped just outside the doorway. Andreas indicated with his hand that Gerald should proceed.

Gerald stepped inside, looked around, and said, "But where is she?"

The others rushed in. They stared at the empty bed and at each other. They hurried back outside the room, Kenna pulling Gerald with them. "Wait here," she said. "If you see her, or anything unusual, yell."

There was a gentle breeze. "The front doors!" Chloe said. They all ran up the passage, through the chamber, and up the long passage to the doors. Andreas put his hand to the wall. As soon as the doors cracked open, they squeezed through.

There was no sign of Darciere. They looked up, down, left, and right. The mountainside was empty and undisturbed. While the others peered out over the edge, Gerald scanned the sky more thoroughly. A pair of Voices was descending. They soon arrived.

"Greetings, Lord Gerald." They glanced at the faerie. "Did they lose something?"

"We did—a faerie we all thought injured in spirit. Did a dragon come just now?"

"Yes, one did."

"Did the dragon catch up a short faerie dressed like two of these on the ledge and carry her over the mountain behind us?"

"Yes. How did the dragon lord know?"

"It made the most sense. Going that way gets them immediately out of our sight. What dragon was it?"

"It is not our place to say, but Lord Gerald will know soon."

"How do you know this?"

"The Eldest has requested your presence, and that of Kenna's, atop Bienn Mhor. He hopes you can wrap up your business here and leave tomorrow by noon."

Gerald gaped at the Voices. *My time is not my own! I am the high king's envoy, here to . . . but Morgan le Fay's works are destroyed. So perhaps I can go!* "I must speak with Kenna and the triad. Or what's left of it."

The Voices remained. Gerald walked over to where the faerie were whispering together. Kenna spoke up. "Gerald, is it possible a dragon came and took Darciere away over the volcano?"

"That's exactly what happened."

Chloe gasped. "Who took her?"

"The Voices say it is not for them to tell us. But the Eldest has requested that Kenna and I leave for his home atop Bienn Mhor on South Uist. It sounds as if we will learn there who fled with Darciere. He asks that we leave by noon tomorrow."

Kenna looked at her father and Chloe. "My work here is finished, is it not?"

"Yes," her father replied with a wistful smile, "though I had hoped for a few days to visit afterward."

"As did I. But the Eldest does not call anyone lightly, much less to his home."

Andreas looked at Gerald. "You speak as if you know this place."

"Not well, but I was there with Kenna after Lochmaldie, when the rebel dragons attacked. Kenna saved our lives and we thought her dead after."

The other two stared at Kenna, who rolled her eyes. "It wasn't that bad. I was going to tell you about it. In fact, we needn't leave until tomorrow, so I can still tell you."

"The Eldest has called. You should go."

Gerald smiled. "He said he 'hopes we can wrap up our

business here by noon tomorrow.' It sounds as if that is what Kenna is trying to do."

"Let us finish this discussion indoors," Chloe suggested.

Gerald nodded and spoke to the Voices. "We will be ready at noon tomorrow. We have but one traveling egg, though."

"It is enough," Kenna said. "I will be fine in a blanket and skin. Or if there is room, I might share the egg with you."

Gerald thought a moment and shook his head. "For a short flight, perhaps, but I'm not sure it would work for a long flight."

"We can check. If not, I will be warm enough on my own."

Once inside, they walked to the egg. Gerald showed them how lodestone sealed the flaps. "Santana said the faerie developed this."

Chloe smiled. "We did."

"Perhaps you can thank whoever . . . wait. When you say 'we,' do you mean you?"

"Yes. The triad. We were looking into the properties of lodestone and wondered whether we might be able to refine it. It became far stronger than we had hoped." Her face sagged. "The triad must be whole. If Darciere is no longer one of us, we must tell the council."

Andreas bowed and said, "Meet me at the dinner table in ten minutes. We can continue the conversation there."

Gerald and Kenna got into the egg. He realized that so long as they both sat, it did not feel too intimate. Were they to lie down, it would be different.

"If you put me to sleep, will I fall over? Or will I be able to sit up?"

"You should be able to sit up," Kenna said. "But if you get a good night's rest, you will not need that much."

"I do not see any of us getting a good night's rest; there is too much to discuss! But I will want to be fresh when we arrive on South Uist. Whatever the Eldest wants, I will want to be fully alert."

She agreed and added as they crawled out, "It is a marvel what they have wrought."

Chloe led them to the dining room. Andreas arrived shortly. "I have sent word to the council. Chloe, let us leave tomorrow when Kenna and Lord Gerald go. Is that acceptable?"

"Of course, Andreas."

When no one explained how Andreas was able to contact the council, Gerald put the question aside.

They talked long into the night, slept a few hours, and were up early to talk more as they made preparations to leave. Gerald had little to do.

"What of Scythia's sword?" he asked.

"It should go to Scythia, of course," Chloe said. "You will undoubtedly have an escort. Fasten the belt about a dragon's leg and . . . why are you laughing?"

Tears were indeed streaming down Gerald's face as he bit his hand to keep quiet.

Kenna managed not to laugh. "Gerald, behave yourself. Chloe does not consort with dragons in all her spare time as you do. Chloe, a dragon's leg is much too large for any normal sword belt. Even were Skanderbeg as huge as legends say, his sword belt would not fit about the leg of any grown dragon I know."

"Then attach it with something else."

"I guess you mean for one of the escorts to separate as we near Kiergenwald and deliver the sword? That makes sense. But what if Santana tells us when we are over the clearing? We then throw the scabbard from the egg and the escort catches it and delivers it. The Voices there will see us coming, meet the escort in the air or on the ground, and find someone to get the sword. Then the escort can rejoin the flight."

"That would work," Gerald said as he wiped his face dry. "Chloe, I am sorry. I was envisioning you trying to get your arms around a dragon's leg to fasten the belt, and it struck me as funny."

She sat a moment and chuckled. "I can see that."

"Who is Sanderburg?"

Kenna replied. "Skanderbeg, the hero of Albania. He helped unite the princes of the region to fight the Ottomans and then the dragons. The dragons were the only reason the Ottomans ceased trying to take over Albania. Like the English, they devoted their time and resources to survival rather than conquest. Skanderbeg became a dragon lord of renown. He is rumored to have been twelve feet tall, a giant of a man. Truly larger than life. Be glad no Albanian heard you butcher the name, Gerald!"

"Glad I am. I should hate to be a pariah, unable to rejoin the garrison." He jumped up. "The garrison! I'm a fool. What of the garrison?"

Andreas smiled. "You are no fool, Lord Gerald! The garrison is not your responsibility. You are theirs! You should let them know of your plans and send word to King Donald. He will decide what they should do, and he or they will notify Fjorela."

"I had hoped to visit Shkodër again. And I had hoped to meet Leotrim, the magician with porcupine hair. Perhaps another time. And speaking of time, I believe it is."

"You are correct. We will see you off and leave ourselves not long after," Chloe said.

At the front door, as Kenna embraced her father, Gerald turned uncertainly to Chloe. She pulled him close and kissed his forehead. "The blessings of the triad, Gerald."

Before he could think, Gerald had kissed her forehead as well. "And the blessings of Argyll, Chloe."

Then he was hugged by Andreas. They too blessed each other. The door was opened. They stepped out, Gerald and Kenna dragging the egg. As soon as they put it down, Santana descended. Gerald noticed three more dragons aloft. "Our escort?"

Santana nodded.

As usual, some of his Voices were there as well. Gerald asked them to send word to the garrison of his change in plans and then to get word to King Donald. They immediately left to do so.

Gerald turned to ask Kenna what she wanted to do, but she was disappearing into the egg. Their packs and his bundle of cold weather gear were already inside. He bowed once more to the faerie, climbed in, and they were quickly aloft. He watched for a second the dwindling faerie below, but snapped the flap shut as he realized how cold the air was away from the fortress doorstep.

"The sword!" he shouted.

"It's here," Kenna said with a smirk. "One of us remembered."

They talked until two hours after nightfall, when Gerald began yawning. Kenna told him to lean back and relax. She put her hand upon his and he knew no more until she woke him an hour from Kiergenwald.

CHAPTER THIRTY-SEVEN

A LAST HURRAH

Gerald found it far more difficult than he had expected to throw the sword out as they neared Kiergenwald—not because he was throwing the sword out, but because he wanted to deliver it in person. He wanted to see Sally, hold her in his arms, take her away, hear what she was thinking, talk her back to her old self.

He knew that even if they landed, he might not be able to do any of that, but he desperately wanted to try. Instead, he threw the sword out and watched it tumble, scabbard and belt glistening in the midday sun, until Cheyenne caught it and leveled out, heading toward Kiergenwald.

Santana called out, "We will slow and perhaps circle until she returns." That took only a few minutes, as Voices had met her and gone straight to the village to get someone to come to the Broken Woods. Or what had been the Broken Woods.... Gerald had seen a true clearing as they had flown over. He wondered how much more had changed during his absence, and what else he might not recognize.

Nearly two hours later, Santana dropped their egg lightly atop Bienn Mhor. Kenna sniffed. "Gerald, you will likely want your clothes on," she said as she shoved the bundle his way.

Gerald soon had the extra clothes on. Had the egg been any

smaller, or had Gerald been larger (Folkvar and MacIntyre leaped to mind), the task would have been nearly impossible with an extra person in the egg. They opened the flaps and exited. Kenna's exit was far more graceful than Gerald's; he got stuck. When he eventually got out, his fur pants had been pulled halfway off and his nether regions were frigid. He pulled the pants up as quickly as possible. "We need a bigger flap!" he said.

The nearby air rapidly filled with dragon laughter. Gerald hoped they were extra careful; the winter clothes looked unusually combustible. The air was not quite as cold as in the Albanian mountains but wind and moisture made it feel worse. Squinting against the wind, he saw several dragons.

"Greetings, Lord Gerald," the Eldest began. He paused. "Gerald, would you do better with shelter?"

"Yes!" he shouted over the wind.

"Get back in your egg, young dragon," the Eldest replied. Kenna scrambled in as well, and they were soon in the air again as Gerald pulled up his over-pants, laughing at the situation. A short time later, they were back on land. Even before he could begin to get out of the egg, Gerald heard booming noises and the ground shook. "What's going on?"

"All is well. Just stay put a moment," Santana called. When the noise stopped, he added, "Come out."

Wriggling through the hole, Gerald found himself in a large, haphazardly built room of large rocks and stonework. Then he saw a familiar dragon's skull and human skeletons scattered about. "Lochmaldie?"

"Lochmaldie," the Eldest agreed. The room was thirty feet wide and at least that deep. The open side faced a nearby hillside. The Eldest, Santana, and Younger all lay on the ground with their heads inside the room, blocking most of the wind and much of the light.

Younger smiled. "We warmed the ground and walls."

Gerald bowed in gratitude. "Thank you."

A moment later, much of the remaining light was blocked. Nain dropped heavily to the ground and his head snaked in between Santana and the Eldest. He leaned against the Eldest and sighed. "Greetings, Lord Gerald."

"Nain, are you okay? Why are you here?"

Nain closed his eyes a long moment, then opened them. "To say farewell. I am spent, Gerald. Whatever poison was in the wounds I received from Argyll, I will not recover. I have lived a good life, but it is time to go."

"Go where?"

"Go on." Nain closed his eyes again and sighed, nearly blowing Gerald off his feet.

The Eldest explained. "Dragons are allowed to choose the time we leave this world, Gerald. Not all get the choice. Wandap died as humans and faerie do. If we do not die in battle, we may choose our time within reason.

"It is rare, but it happens that occasionally those of other races may choose as well. Perhaps once in a few hundred years, a dragon and faerie choose to go together."

Gerald interrupted. "Nain, it was you! You took Darciere!"

"Yes, and it nearly killed me to fly this far back. I told her we might not make it. She was determined to come with me, even if we fell to our deaths. She is as weary and sick in her soul as I am in body."

Younger took up the thread. "Gerald, you already know many of our secrets. This is another, that we may choose when we go. The how is not an issue. Once we decide to go, we fly from this world to the next. We do not let people see this. Seldom even do other dragons watch. You and Kenna may watch Nain and Darciere go if you like."

They both nodded mutely.

"Darciere, if you are ready," Nain called quietly.

Darciere stepped out from behind the dragon skull. "I am."

She did not look at anyone but Nain. She appeared ready to collapse and burst into tears.

Nain got to his feet with a nudge from the Eldest. Darciere walked over. Nain dropped his head to the ground and opened his mouth. Darciere climbed in, turned around, and sat down on his tongue. She sat up against one of his smallest teeth, legs splayed to either side of it, arms wrapped around it. "Let's go, Nain."

He backed out and waited for the others. The dragons stayed close beside him, Santana and Eldest steadying Nain at times as he walked slowly up a small hill of rubble and bones.

Dragon lord and faerie followed solemnly. When they crested the hill, Nain ran down the other side. At the bottom he spread his wings and took flight, soaring majestically out over the sea as if nothing were wrong. Perhaps a hundred yards out, he looked back briefly. Gerald thought Darciere nodded. Nain turned back to face forward. There was a flash of green light where a hole ripped the sky apart. Nain was through it and the sky was whole. Dragon and faerie were gone.

Gerald blinked as things got blurry, realizing he had teared up. Out of the corner of his eye, he saw Kenna wiping hers. He reached over to put an arm around her shoulder and an instant later she was holding him tightly and crying. It had never occurred to him the faerie might cry like humans. As he held her, he wondered whether she cried for Darciere, Nain, or both. Gerald cried mainly for Nain.

Kenna pulled away a minute later but gripped his hand so his arm remained on her shoulder. "Thank you, brother," she whispered. "And don't let the tears freeze your eyes shut."

He wiped his eyes and realized he was nearly too late. He laughed. They pulled apart and ran back to the shelter. The dragons were already nearly there.

Once back inside, the Lord of the Western Isles said, "You should both sit down."

Glancing at one another, they found a large rock and sat side by side. "I thought Cuthbert was to be here," Gerald said.

"That was the plan, but he had urgent business. You will

hear about it soon enough. We have told Cuthbert already what I am about to say. Lord Gerald. Kenna. I am no longer the Eldest. I have stepped down, as it were. Of our group of twelve, only Santana, Younger, and I remain now that Nain has gone. And we are also tired. It is time. No, do not worry! None of us are following Nain anytime soon. I mean only that it is time the next group of eldest, those young usurpers, should take over.

"Choosing a new Eldest is seldom quick, though it has twice happened in less than a day. Because the times are strange and troubled, it was deemed best to hurry. The youngsters happily picked their Eldest at once. The new Eldest will take over the name 'Lord of the Western Isles'; it seemed best to let humanity think nothing has changed. As very few have met me, few need know this. I will stay on Bienn Mhor. The new Eldest will live somewhere nearby, though she will probably be gone far more than I have been of late. She is young and accustomed to being in the thick of things. Every flight of eldest has to work things out for themselves."

"She? Who is the new Eldest?"

Santana said with pride, "Selene. They chose Selene."

"That's wonderful!" Kenna exclaimed.

Gerald sported a huge grin. "I have no idea who else they might have picked, but I'm really happy for her. What a great honor for a magnificent dragon."

"Thank you, Kenna. Thank you, Gerald," Selene's voice said from outside. "Ferdinand, may I speak with you a moment?"

"Of course, Eldest," the dragon Gerald had known as Eldest said. "Kenna and Gerald, I was about to say you may call me Ferdinand from now on." He pulled out and flew over the hill alongside Selene.

"Ferdinand! His name is Ferdinand?"

"It is now," Younger said.

"Do you mean it's a new name? That it wasn't before?"

"I mean it is now." Younger did something that made Gerald think of someone cocking an eyebrow, except Younger had none.

"Younger, I think you have spent too much time studying humans."

"I agree, though it's not nearly enough to actually understand you."

Kenna sat quietly through the banter. Finally Gerald asked what she was thinking.

"I have heard of such things, but I have never known a time when Eld . . . , when Ferdinand was not Eldest, when Younger, Santana, Nain, Wandap, and others you never knew were not his council." Then she laughed. "I suppose you haven't, either! But it's been far longer for me."

As her voice trailed off, Gerald shivered as he felt the weight of the years behind her voice—and yet she was young. She looked twenty-five as she had the day they met. Gerald did not know how old she was, and that did not bother him at all. Old and new Eldest walked purposefully back over the hill. The former waited outside while the latter stuck her head into the dragon-made cave.

"Gerald, I would guess if you had your way, you would go to Kiergenwald."

He nodded somberly. "There is nowhere I would rather go."

"Good. Because it seems best to us that you do just that. You should see how things are there and whether you can help bring Sally and Scythia back, if they are not back already. This would seem to be the final part of the task set you by King Dugald, would it not?"

He smiled. "I have thought just that."

Selene now addressed Kenna. "Will you go with him? We know Sally has been jealous of you, but she has also admired you and wanted to be friends. Gerald can use faerie wisdom, and there is none better suited for this task. Will you go?"

She stared at Selene. "I hope you don't think I would refuse."

"No, but I want to be sure you go willingly and joyously."

Kenna smiled in spite of herself. "Why joyously?"

"Because it is possible you step into a place where some lack joy. If so, they will need yours, for you have much to offer."

The cavern lit up and Gerald felt springtime blooming. "I will go as a fountain of joy!"

"Then go, and go with our blessings." All four dragons breathed on them. Gerald staggered as a wall of power washed over him. There was something far more than peace this time. He felt fierce joy and steely eyed determination. He also felt something he could not define but knew he would be happy to have someday. Whatever it was, he recognized he would once have seen it as weakness.

He bowed, as did Kenna. The faerie took Gerald's hand and raised it. "And you have our blessings. We rejoice this day with those who step down and with those who step up. Long may your reign be, Eldest, and wise, full of light and life." Their hands glowed. Gerald could have sworn light radiated from them to gently touch each dragon's eyes. Kenna held their hands aloft a second more before letting go.

"Shall we go now?" she asked.

"Yes," Selene replied. "Santana, will you carry them?"

"It would be my extreme pleasure, Eldest."

Selene continued, "You should both know Ferdinand asked for that honor, but I have much to discuss with him. I have need of both his knowledge and wisdom."

"As did I of the Eldest before me," Ferdinand said.

"As do all the wise," Kenna laughed.

She and Gerald pushed the egg back out of the shelter. They said their farewells and climbed in, and were soon off. Gerald had his outerwear off as quickly as possible.

They landed in the clearing. Gerald laughed as he realized

Santana had dropped the egg in the hole once occupied by the defiled stump. They took their packs. Santana would move the egg for them once they decided where to put it. Meanwhile he would wait beside it.

"Like a mother dragon!" Gerald chortled.

A small flame came perilously close. "Beware, varlet! You may live at the balance point, but you may combust there as well!"

Laughing, Gerald ran toward the village. Kenna tripped lightly behind him. He went first to his and Sally's house, but it was empty. He stopped at Cle's but no one was there, either. He then went to Druze's home. He knocked and a moment later heard Druze call, "Who is it?"

"Gerald and Kenna!"

The door rattled and after a moment opened. "Come in quickly!"

They did and the door shut. Druze took a moment to tie it thoroughly.

Gerald looked around. "Why are you tying the door shut? Are there vandals about?"

"No, just the wind. It blows open, puts the fire out, and freezes us."

"How are Sally and Scythia?"

To his surprise, Druze left the room. Gerald stared at Kenna, who looked at him sadly.

Cynthia came from somewhere in the house, with Druze right behind her. "Welcome back. Have a seat." She pointed at cushions around her table.

Gerald groaned. "This sounds familiar."

"I doubt that," Cynthia snorted. "Druze—coffee, please. My bones are cold."

Druze pulled the kettle from the fire and made four mugs of coffee as Cynthia stared at Gerald.

"I know you want to hear of Sally first, but I must first speak of Scythia. Two days before her sword arrived, she sat up in bed and screamed, the first noise she had made since the night you found her in the tree. She fought us like a madwoman. Her whole face took on the yellow of her eyes and she grew almost too hot to hold onto, as if she would burst into flame. And then! Her hands began to smoke! I know it's impossible, but it's true. She screamed so loudly the whole village showed up outside the cave, yelling to ask if we needed help. Scythia's hands blackened and bled, and Druze and I will swear under oath her fingers were but bones.

"Then she fell back with a gasp and the room went dark for a few seconds. When the light returned, her hands were fine and she seemed her old self. The yellow was gone from her eyes. She croaked out words, begging for food and drink. Within the hour she was whole. She should not have been able to move; her muscles had been unused for nearly three months. They ought to have wasted away, but within minutes she was up and about. Her memory of the night she fought that dragon was fuzzy, but she was glad to have her sword. She said it steadied her." She looked long at Kenna and Gerald. "She also said that while it was her old sword, it felt as if it had been born anew." She took a long drink of coffee.

Gerald stared into the fire. "I believe you. We saw something similar as the sword was being cleansed."

"I doubt you saw anything like this," she retorted. Kenna and Gerald smirked.

"And now, what of Sally?" Gerald insisted.

Cynthia took another long, slow drink of coffee and put the mug back on the table.

"We could do nothing for Sally. She seemed lost. I mean in her thinking—often she did not seem to know where she was or who she was. She began to get a little better the day Scythia returned to us. She perked up and decided to go for a walk.

"She did not come back, but someone came for her things."

"What? Who?" Gerald began, but Cynthia glared at him.

"Did you happen to come from the north?"

"More or less," Kenna said.

"Were you looking at Kiergenwald as you came?"

"We were inside a dragon egg and could not see out," Gerald said.

Cynthia plowed on determinedly. "You know the mount where the dragons dug the cave for Scythia—Craneshead. There is a house being built atop it, a small fortress. A merchant from Glasgow moved here shortly after you left, showed a deed for the peak, and began building atop it. He also claimed right of way for much of the mount, but the dragons would not let him have property close to the cave.

"I've no idea, and nor has anyone hereabouts as I can find, how he got so much stone up there that fast, but the whole top of the hill is now inside a stone wall and he's got half a very large stone house built. He lives in the part that's finished. Wagons come and go. None are sure what he's trading, but we guess that's how the rock arrives, though most of the traffic there clearly is not in stone.

"Anyway, one of the merchant's men brought me a letter from Sally telling me to send her things with him. She sent one letter to Cle and one to you. She asked Cle to take care of her affairs until you arrive. Here is your letter." She pulled a letter from a skirt pocket and handed it across the table.

Gerald broke the seal and unrolled it slowly. He stared at it but could not seem to focus. Kenna took it gently from his hand, moved closer to the fire, and read it in a soft voice.

"Gerald. Since you seem to have forgotten me, have abandoned me, have left me in a desolate place with no light, no joy, no love, I must assume our engagement is off." Gerald gasped as Kenna paused for a breath.

"The merchant Tiberius has asked for my hand. I have said yes. We cannot marry yet, but he has graciously given me my own quarters in the home he is building. He is very jealous of you, though I don't know why. I would not suggest you attempt to come here; he has threatened to have his archers kill you if you come up the hill. I wish you no ill, though you have given me plenty. Sally." Kenna looked up at Gerald, the horror plain in her eyes.

Druze cleared her throat. "She also sent this." She pulled something off the mantle and held it out. It was Sally's and Gerald's handfasting tartan.

CHAPTER THIRTY-EIGHT

TO WEEP, PERCHANCE
TO DREAM

Gerald was in a daze for some time afterward. He could not face his empty house so he stayed with his cousins. Cle told him those who had gone more than halfway up Craneshead unbidden had an arrow shot into the dirt at their feet. None had climbed farther until Cle and three others had gone up on horseback with full weaponry under King Donald's flag. They had been met at the fortress gate by Tiberius. The man had been cordial but firm; he wanted no visitors. He claimed no quarrel with anyone, but it was his property and he expected everyone not on his business to stay away.

When Cle had asked to see Sally, she had come to the gate, said she was content, turned, and left. This brought Gerald out of his daze for a short time.

"Was she? Content?"

Cle rubbed his face. "Something is very wrong, Gerald. It's . . . different and yet the same. I cannot describe it. Sally has been acting half dead for months. Now she is up and moving, but there is still something wrong—more extreme and less at the same time. As if half the spell was broken but the other half grew stronger. Does that make sense?"

Gerald suspected it ought to make sense, but he felt dull

and listless again. The next morning, which had warmed considerably, he went to see Kenna at Cynthia's home. "Am I under a spell? I feel like a walking dead man, like Sally."

Kenna shook her head. She grinned. "We're back in Scotland, so that means no." Gerald tried to grin back but didn't quite make it. "Gerald, if you were under a spell, you would not think to ask that question, or likely be capable of it even if someone suggested it to you. I think you are just hurting. This hit hard at a time you were already worn out."

She looked toward the door, where slivers of sunlight came through cracks. "Let us go for a walk. The sun will do you good." They ended up in the new clearing, sitting on a log near the trees. Gerald leaned over against Kenna and fought tears.

Kenna looked around. "They call this Scythia's Glade now. Dragons blessed it. It should be beautiful in the spring."

The sounds of horse hooves and wagons creaking made them look up. "Those must be Tiberius's," Kenna remarked. Several riders followed the fourth wagon. One was a young woman in a fine dress such as Kiergenwald had not seen, and wearing a complicated hat. She glanced around the clearing. Her face became like stone when her gaze got to Gerald and Kenna. It was Sally. She gave them a hard look, then turned her eyes forward. The man beside her saw this and turned to look at them.

The man was tall and powerfully built with short arms and legs. He stared at Gerald with pure loathing. He gave Sally a calculating look, then leered back at Gerald. Infuriated, Gerald jumped up, but immediately the other two riders raised bows with arrows nocked. They did not lower their weapons until the party re-entered the woods on the far side of the clearing.

Gerald stared after them with his fists clinched. Eventually he realized he was straining forward but held in place.

"You can stop the magic, Kenna," he said through clenched teeth.

"It's not magic. I'm holding your belt."

"Well let *go!*"

"Are you sure?"

"*Yes!*"

Kenna let go and Gerald exploded forward, barely breaking his fall without getting a face full of dirt.

"What did you do that for?" he demanded.

"You insisted."

Somewhere someone said, "You did, you know."

Embarrassed, Gerald mumbled, "Then thanks, I guess."

The haze fell over Gerald's vision again. Gerald and Kenna retrieved their packs from the village, returned to the clearing, and called for Voices. Santana arrived in short order. "Gerald, are you leaving already? What of Sally?"

"I am the high king's envoy. I must report. Please bring the egg." He would say no more. Once they were underway, Kenna told Santana the story. Gerald glared at her at first, but that took too much energy.

Santana stopped and hovered out of bowshot near Edinburgh Castle, away from any cannon's line of fire. When Voices arrived, he told them who he carried and awaited an invitation to the castle. It came quickly. Santana landed in the main courtyard. He dropped the egg, sent his greetings to King Dugald, and retreated with several Voices across the river.

After waiting an hour until the king was free, Gerald and Kenna spent two hours with him. They told as much of the story as they could, leaving out the various secrets they were entrusted with. When they finished, the king sat quietly for several minutes.

"Lord Gerald, Kenna, you have my thanks. For Morgan le Fay to come back in any form—much less allied with the likes of the rebel dragon leader—was a most revolting thought, especially now. Invasions are on the rise since we no longer have dragons as a common enemy. Scotland owes you both a large debt. How can we repay you?"

Kenna grinned mischievously. "I'll let you know. Does interest accrue?"

The king roared with laughter. "So few dare jest with me! Just for that, yes. What of you, Gerald?"

"Who are these invaders?"

"Everyone from riffraff and pirate scum to English nobles plotting on our southern border. It's as if the last two hundred years of common ground washed away in a squall. Why do you ask?"

Gerald had risen from his stupor. *Why? Because I want to fight. I need to hurt someone, so I will go after those who hurt others. Every face I see will be that of Tiberius.*

The shock his thoughts brought him must have shown on his face. The king asked, "Gerald, what's wrong?"

Gerald didn't want to answer, but the king insisted. "I find I am bitter and I like the taste."

"That should scare you."

"It does and does not."

"I have no bitterness to pay you with."

"I would go back and serve King Donald. If the high king needs me again, I would serve him as well."

"Hmmm." Dugald searched Gerald's face carefully. "Send word when your bitterness is satiated and we will see then, dragon lord."

They were dismissed.

Three hours later they had a similar conversation in King Donald's throne room at Cair Parn. This time all of the king's advisors except Cuthbert were present. Gerald bristled under the pity and love he felt from his friends, but he kept his face neutral. When Kenna and Gerald had answered what questions they could (leaving no one quite satisfied), King Donald asked Kenna the same question King Dugald had. She gave the same answer. After consulting with his advisors, he said something rather different to Gerald.

"Gerald, during your time here—most of which we called training—you have done more for Argyll and Scotland than most men do in a lifetime. If you wish, I will release you from your duty. We will provide you whatever is reasonable to do what you wish to do. What would that be?"

Gerald stared dumbly at Donald. Most of his life he had just wanted to kill dragons. A few hours ago he had wanted to kill Tiberius. Now he had no idea. As someone who had let too much of his life be defined by pain and hatred, he was completely lost. "My king, I do not know. May I have time to think about it?"

"How much time?"

"A week at the most. I hope far less."

The king looked at each advisor in turn. No one argued. A couple nodded. "Very well. Send word when you have decided. Now go. Thank you both again."

Kenna left slowly. Gerald hung back with her. As Murdoch passed, Kenna sped up. "Murdoch, where is Cuthbert?"

Murdoch shrugged. "No one seems to know other than the king, and I'm not sure if he does. It's all very secretive." He looked around. "But I can tell you this. He was very excited when he left. And a bit smug."

"When Cuthbert feels smug, something interesting is about to happen. Something big," Kenna suggested.

"It seems that way, doesn't it?"

Gerald thought of something. "Murdoch, how are things between you and K'Pene?"

Murdoch shrugged again. "They were going well, but after Harem arrived, she decided she needed to go home to her people. Harem took her back. He returned later with Selwyn. K'Pene stayed at home to—as she put it—help her people on their journey to healing. I hope to hear from her through Selwyn's Voices, but their journey takes many days. When they are ready, Harem will go back. I plan to go with him."

"How long would you be gone?"

"An excellent question, Lord Gerald. Perhaps a month. Perhaps a lifetime."

Kenna smiled. "It sounds as if things still go well."

A ghost of a smile touched the captain's face. "I suppose they do."

The former envoys had naturally followed Murdoch as he talked. He stopped in front of a doorway. "This is Gerald's room until he decides what to do. Kenna, your room is the third on the left in the next wing."

"Statues," Gerald said.

"What?"

"We need statues in each room to show who's there."

Kenna looked away. "He gets like this at times, Captain. He makes no sense."

Murdoch looked alarmed. Gerald said nothing but walked into his room and shut the door. Outside he heard Kenna say, "I was just teasing. He is referring to a practice of my people . . ." The voices faded down the hall. Gerald hung his weapons on pegs, took off his cloak, and sat in a chair by the window, looking vaguely at the horizon.

He was still staring out when dusk came. Gerald realized his hands and face had grown numb from cold. He closed the shutters, threw more wood on the dying fire, and sat by the fireplace.

He thought back over the past year. He had enjoyed traveling but foresaw little more of that soon. He thought of places he had visited. He did not want such a bleak landscape as Mull. Kyleakin was nice, but he did not want to face their intrigue without Kyla nearby. Urquhart was interesting, but only in theory—he couldn't say why. Albania, on the other hand, called to him on several levels. He could see going back as envoy to maintain relations with Albania, or at least Shkodër. He could see binding himself to service to Lady Fjorela for a time. He could easily see himself returning to otherness for a few months. By then everyone he knew would be dead, save the faerie.

"And what would that solve?"

Gerald looked around, startled. That had been a clear voice, not the distant echo of a ball of color, but there was no one there. Still, he thought about it and answered. "Nothing."

"Exactly. If you take your fears in with you, they will define your time there. And that's if you are allowed to return."

He sighed. He had already defied the odds and returned once, but he had no control that time. It simply happened and he had no idea how.

"Then what am I to do?" he asked in frustration. After a second, he laughed that he had actually expected an answer.

"Go to Cuthbert's office."

Gerald froze for an instant, then spun around. He carefully opened a shutter. A Voice hopped in. Gerald closed the shutter.

"That's what you should do," the Voice continued. "Go to Cuthbert's office."

"Why?"

"Ask him when you get there," the bird said in an exasperated voice.

Gerald stared for a minute, then rushed out like an excited child. He ran to the tower steps and up to Cuthbert's office.

"Cuthbert! You're back! Where have you been?"

"Cleaning up messes. Looking into problems. And perhaps, finding solutions. Please sit down. Dinner will be along in a minute."

Gerald sat. "Have I made a mess?"

"I believe you were about to. But I have news and a proposal as to what you might do next."

"What?"

"Pirates."

"Pirates!"

"And a mystery."

"There's plenty of that at the moment," Gerald growled.

"And you're going to be a father."

"*What?*"

"There is no need to shout, Lord Gerald."

"But that's impossible!"

"Very few things are impossible. As for the pirates—no, please, let us take them in order—you no doubt recall Ferdinand had a dispute with pirates somewhere near North Uist. I believe I know roughly where they are. Their nest needs to be cleaned out.

"As for the mystery, a solution to that of Cair Nonesuch is overdue. I have some clues about that as well. I do not know if Kenna would agree to go, but if she is available, the two of you make a good team.

"And finally, since you were adopted, you should not be so shocked at the idea of adoption."

"But I am only fifteen!"

"That will be no problem where you will be going to adopt."

"And where am I supposed to be going to adopt?"

"A quick trip to Albania. There is a girl named Aurelia . . ."

END OF BOOK THREE

The story continues in

GOLDEN
DAWN

Volume IV of the Dragon Lord Chronicles

PRONUNCIATION GUIDE

NAME	PRONUNCIATION
Aed	Eyd (between aid and I'd)
Afagdu	Uh-făg-due'
Argyll	Arr-gile'
Chloe	Clō'-ee
Craneshead	Crane's head
Darciere	Dar-see-ehr'
Dealanach	Jyal'-awn-akh
Drachmaeius	Drakh-may'-us
Druze	Drooz
Eilidh	Ay'-lee
Eoin	Ee'-ahn (similar to Ian)
Fionn	Finn
Hercule	Err-kyūhl'
Invercharnan	Inn'-věr-chärn
K'Pene	Kəh-pehn'-nee
Morag	(closer to Mor'-ak than Mor'-ag)
Urquhart	Ürk'-hart
Vitae	Vee'-tahy

SHQIP GLOSSARY

TERM	DEFINITION
Burre I mire.	Good man.
Liqeni i Zjarrtë	Fiery Lake
dragua	dragon
Eviola	woman's name: courageous, determined, independent
Fjorela	woman's name: little flower
gjiri gic	roast pig
jo	no
ju lutem	thank you
kafe	coffee
kala	castle
Kalaja e Rozafës	the Rozafa Castle
Kreshnik	man's name: warrior or knight
Leotrim	man's name: courageous
Luan	man's name: lion
Nese ai tregon dikujt, preje ne fyt!	If he tells anyone, cut his throat!
paçe	A soup made from animal innards. The soup here is actually paçe koke, or sheep's head soup. A traditional breakfast food, Gerald's companion preferred it for supper. The Albanians found this amusing.
po	yes
Shqip	(the Albanian language, pronounced "Ship")

WORD

This book felt like a roller-coaster! There are a variety of inspirations for otherness, only a few of which I will mention here. Did you catch a whiff of *Doctor Strange?* Otherness was much on my mind when that movie came out. I remember watching the scene where Strange keeps not dying as he faces down Dormammu and thinking *This reeks of otherness.* We keep a lot of random toys around the house; some of these inspired bits and bobs of otherness as well. I've been known to get lost in daydreams; they become my reality for a while. When that happens, I occasionally realize my body is elsewhere and wonder where that is. The last influence I will mention now is my college days; you can salvage good from anything, even the dumb things. My dumb things included a lot of hallucinogens.

My college days (as well as before and after) also influenced some of the dialogue, particularly the banter. I have always had brilliant and witty friends. Some of our dialogue was verbal, some took place on the walls of the Third Street tunnel under I-75 by Georgia Tech before we met and became friends, and some took place on a computer forum at Tech long before most people knew what a network was.

I was thrilled to get to use my experiences in Albania in this book. The characters there are people I know in real life and are pretty true to life (okay, the magician I know doesn't do actual magic, but he has exposed a charlatan who fleeced people while claiming to do real magic). And look up Rozafa Castle. I didn't invent Rozafa or her legend.

They say to write what you know, and I do. And now you have a little more insight into my world.

ACKNOWLEDGEMENTS

This book is much better thanks to the early readers who gave me invaluable feedback and encouragement: Abi Penner, Chelsea Boyd, Jeremy Miller, Josiah O'Neal, and Lyndsay Bila. Thanks to Esther Dale for encouragement and suggestions.

My wife, Sharon O'Neal, again played the roles of early reader, early editor, sounding board, and motivator. Without her, these books might well never have seen the light of day.

Thanks to Alli Walker for the great artwork prefacing each chapter, and for lots of other great art. She works in a variety of mediums; you should check her out.

Thanks to Allison Metcalfe for the design, cover, and production. You turned a manuscript into a beautiful book. Again!

Thanks to Sally Hanan for her editing, patience, and general brilliance throughout the journey of turning my stories into books.

Thanks to Chris, Fjorela, and Eviola for keeping me on track with Albanian issues and translations.

A special shout-out to Cari Q, whose music, again, often provided a soundtrack to work over, and for swapping tales of Scotland.

Thanks to all my Albanian friends and the other beautiful people there who both drew me into their lives and culture, and helped me shed cultural baggage.

Thanks to Skanderbeg for Albania.

Finally, thanks to all of you who read my writing. I'd love to hear from you!

ABOUT THE AUTHOR

Miles O'Neal has written throughout his life—short stories, songs, poems, software, documentation, government computer system contract proposals, you name it. He wrote his first novel entirely in his head, only to discover he could not manage to get it onto paper afterward. He has not made that mistake again. This is his third published novel, with many more planned.

Miles is a husband, lover, father, grandpa, friend, storyteller, author, musician, and former youth pastor who believes passionately in young people. He lives just outside Round Rock, Texas, with his wife, Sharon, whoever else is living with them at the time, and all manner of people and creatures that wander in and out of his imagination.

"People ask where my ideas come from. I don't know. How is that even a question? I've had this imagination as long as I can remember. I've never lived completely in this place we call the real world. I was constantly in trouble in school for daydreaming. It doesn't feel like I'm having ideas or inventing things; it feels like I'm just sharing a little bit of the worlds I live in."

ABOUT THE ILLUSTRATOR

Alli Walker graduated from Texas State University with a BFA in Studio Art with an "all level teacher's certification" in 2009. She loved teaching art, but realized she wasn't ready to manage classes of her own. Alli currently works as an accountant at a local dealership by day and a freelance artist and crafter by night.

She uses a wide variety of media, including unconventional combinations such as coffee and salt with India ink. Alli has had a number of successful shows in the Austin area.

Follow Alli: https://www.facebook.com/alli.gray.96

ABOUT THE DESIGNER

Allison Metcalfe is a graphic designer, typesetter, and photographer. She has a deep love for the beauty in people and good design. Her goal in producing any work is to capture the client's voice and design with innovation, style, and longevity. Best-selling author Ted Dekker is one of her recent clients of note.

Allison's skills include publishing, book cover design, typesetting, logo design, and working with Adobe CS: Illustrator, Photoshop, and InDesign.

Follow Allison: https://www.facebook.com/
allisonmetcalfephotography

ABOUT THE EDITOR

Sally is a copywriter, editor, and author of four books. She has been writing and editing for over ten years, and is passionate about excellence in everything she does. Best-selling author Shawn Bolz is one of her recent clients of note.

Sally and Allison often work together to produce books authors can be proud of, and Sally's skills include Word and a smattering of Adobe CS's Photoshop and InDesign. You can see more of their projects at www.inksnatcher.com

Follow Sally: https://www.facebook.com/inksnatcher

COMMUNITY, NEWS, & MORE

Blogs, news, short stories, books, merchandise, and more about the author, upcoming works, back stories, etc.:

http://www.milesoneal.com/

Facebook:

https://www.facebook.com/milesonealauthor

Twitter:

https://twitter.com/miles_oneal